Lander glimpsed a dark figure rising out of the sand. It was about the size of a man, but its legs and arms seemed to stick from its body at peculiar angles, like a reptile's.

The Harper needed to see no more to know that Musalim, and probably Bhadla, too, had ridden into an ambush. He slapped the flat of his sword against his camel's shoulder, but the sluggish beast refused to charge. The shadow raised a crossbow, and a pair of yellow, egg-shaped eyes flashed in the dark night.

The bolt took Lander below the right collarbone, nearly knocking him from his saddle. His arm went numb, and the sword dropped from his hand. Two more shadows rose out of the blowing sand.

THE HARPERS

A semi-secret organization for Good, the Harpers fight for freedom and justice in a world populated by tyrants, evil mages, and dread creatures beyond imagination.

Each novel in the Harpers Series is a complete story in itself, detailing some of the most unusual and compelling tales in the magical world known as the Forgotten Realms.

Also by Troy Denning

WATERDEEP
(As Richard Awlinson)

DRAGONWALL

THE PARCHED SEA

Troy Denning

THE PARCHED SEA

Random House and its affiliate companies have worldwide distribution rights in the book trade for English language products of TSR, Inc.

Distributed to the book and hobby trade in the United Kingdom by TSR Ltd.

Distributed to the toy and hobby trade by regional distributors.

Cover Art by Fred Fields

FORGOTTEN REALMS is a registered trademark owned by TSR, Inc. The TSR logo is a trademark owned by TSR, Inc.

First Printing: July, 1991
Printed in the United States of America.
Library of Congress Catalog Card Number: 90-71500

9 8 7 6
ISBN: 1-56076-067-2

TSR, Inc.
201 Sheridan Springs Rd.
Lake Geneva,
WI 53147 U.S.A.

TSR Ltd.
120 Church End, Cherry Hinton
Cambridge CB1 3LB
United Kingdom

For Barry,
who's always been a great brother.

Acknowledgements

I would like to thank Jon Pickens for burying me beneath a mountain of research material, all of which proved crucial; Jim Lowder for being so courteous with his scalpel; Lloyd Holden of AKF Martial Arts in Janesville, WI for recognizing the techniques in the fight scenes; and most especially Andria Hayday, for not killing me in my sleep when the words wouldn't come.

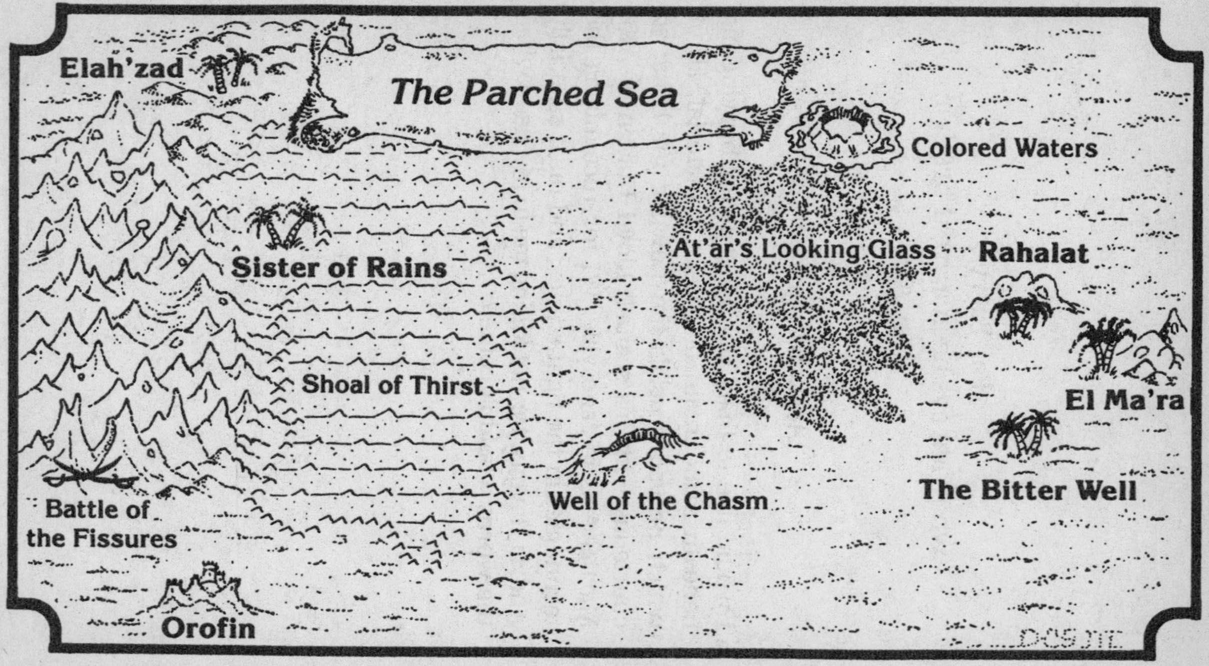
Elah'zad
The Parched Sea
Colored Waters
At'ar's Looking Glass
Rahalat
Sister of Rains
Shoal of Thirst
El Ma'ra
Well of the Chasm
The Bitter Well
Battle of
the Fissures
Orofin

One

Ruha woke abruptly, unsure of what had disturbed her languorous nap. The young woman lay next to her sleeping husband, their bodies touching at the hip and shoulder. She turned to look at his weathered face. Ajaman had the rough skin and thick mustache of a mature man, but his hairless chest was young, lean, and muscular. He was the only man Ruha had ever seen undressed.

As the young wife gazed at her husband, her vision suddenly blurred. An instant later, it cleared and the face of another man appeared in place of Ajaman's. She gasped in astonishment, but did not cry out.

The stranger's visage was unlike any she had ever known. His skin was red and sun-blistered, with a creamy white underlayer showing through where he had peeled. A black patch covered his right eye, and his left eye was as blue as the desert sky. Though his features were drawn and haggard, they were not so care-worn that he could have been more than twenty-five.

1

Any other bride would have run screaming from her new home, concluding that her father had married her to a djinn—but not Ruha. She had been suffering visions since before she could walk, so she recognized the image for what it was: a mirage from tomorrow. Sometime soon, the stranger would appear. What would happen then, Ruha could not say, though she knew it would be some mishap or catastrophe. She lacked the talent to interpret the mirages, but nothing good had ever followed one.

Her first vision had been of thousands of butterflies. The butterflies had turned out to be moths, and within two months every yard of cloth in the tribe was full of holes. Another time, during a terrible drought, she had seen a vast green meadow to the south of the tribe. Her father, the sheikh, had taken the herds in search of the fresh pasturage. After a week of thirsty riding, they had finally found the meadow. It was on the edge of a contaminated pool, and half of their camels had died from drinking poisoned water.

Not surprisingly, Ruha had come to regard her premonitions as more of an affliction than a gift. Without giving the vision further thought, the young wife shut her eyes tightly and hoped it would pass.

Ajaman stirred beside her. "Is something troubling you, my wife?"

The heat rose to Ruha's cheeks, for being addressed as "wife" gave her a capricious feeling that she found embarrassing.

Opening her eyes, she was relieved to see Ajaman instead of the one-eyed man. The young bride smiled and answered, "Nothing we should worry about."

She said nothing of her vision, for she did not want Ajaman to blame her for whatever misfortune the one-eyed stranger was bringing. Besides, the desert tribes were wary of magic, and if her new husband suspected her of being a witch, he would cast her from his tent.

Abruptly Ajaman glanced at his nude body, then blushed. He reached for his *aba*, the loose-fitting robe of the Bedine tribes, and pulled it over his head. The couple had only been married for two days, and the bride knew it would be many weeks before they felt completely comfortable together.

Ruha sat up and pulled her own *aba* over her nakedness, then studied her new *khreima* with a warm feeling of satisfaction. The dimly lit tent was nearly empty, for she and her husband had not yet acquired many possessions. A dozen cushions lay scattered over the ground carpet, her loom and cooking pots rested in one corner, and Ajaman's weapons dangled from hooks on the wooden tentpoles.

The afternoon breeze drummed gently at the *khreima*, and Ruha heard feet scuffling outside. Several men began whispering to each other in jocular tones, probably speculating as to why the tent was closed on such a hot day. Irritated by the men's presence, Ruha lifted her chin toward the entrance.

"We have visitors," she said. By the custom of her people, only her husband could welcome guests to their *khreima*.

Ajaman nodded. "I hear them." Turning to the entrance, he called the host's traditional greeting, "Has somebody come to my *khreima* in need of help?"

"Time for the watch," came the reply. Ruha didn't recognize the deep voice, but that was to be expected. She had not been a member of the Qahtan tribe until her marriage.

Ajaman scowled. "It can't be dusk so soon."

"You have the night watch?" Ruha asked, frowning at the memory of her premonition. "We've only been married two days. Let someone else take the duty."

"And shame our family so soon?" Ajaman replied, rising

from the carpet.

Given her husband's reply, Ruha knew arguing the point would do no good. If Ajaman considered the watch a matter of family integrity, even the certain knowledge of impending death would not have stopped him from going. Like all Bedine, he considered honor more important than his life.

"Besides," Ajaman added, "there is danger of raiding tonight. The Mtair Dhafir is not the only *khowwan* within riding distance, you know."

The Mtair Dhafir was the tribe of Ruha's father. Her marriage to Ajaman had sealed an alliance between their tribes. There would be no raiding between the two *khowwans* while both Ajaman and Ruha lived. Unfortunately, there were many other tribes with whom the Qahtan had no such ties.

It was not raiding that worried Ruha, however. By his pale skin, she knew that the one-eyed foreigner did not belong to any Bedine tribe. Whatever his reason for coming to the camp of the Qahtan, it was not intertribal raiding.

"Come, Ajaman," grumbled the deep voice outside. "We're due at our posts."

Ajaman took his *keffiyeh* off its hook and slipped the white head-cloth over his hair. Ruha stood and straightened it so the long apron hung square across his shoulders. "Stay alert, Ajaman," she said. "I would be disappointed if you let some boy cut your throat."

Ajaman grinned. "Have no fear of that, Ruha," he replied, reaching for his scimitar. "I watch from El Ma'ra's crown. I'll see our enemies from miles away."

Ruha knew the place to which her husband referred. A mile outside the oasis, a lonely spire of yellow sandstone towered more than one hundred feet over the desert. That pinnacle was El Ma'ra Dat-ur Ojhogo, the tall god who lets men sit upon his head.

Keeping her voice low so she would not be overheard,

she said, "After dark, I'll bring you apricots and milk."

Ajaman nearly dropped his scabbard belt. "You can't do that!"

"Why not?" the young bride demanded. "Is there any shame in a wife bringing food to her husband?"

Ajaman scowled at the challenge to his authority. "There is enough shame in violating your *purdah*," he countered.

"The *purdah* is to keep frightened young brides from returning to their father's *khowwan*," Ruha said. "I am hardly frightened, and I have no desire to go back to the Mtair Dhafir. You have no need to isolate me."

"I know," Ajaman whispered, his tone losing its earlier sternness. "But if someone should see you—"

"I'll say you told me to bring you supper," Ruha responded slyly.

Seeing that his wife would not be denied, Ajaman sighed. "If all women of the Mtair Dhafir are this willful, perhaps they are the ones who should pay camels the next time they send us a bride."

Ruha smiled, pleased that her new husband was not the type to bully his wife. The young bride had no idea how she could safeguard Ajaman from whatever the vision presaged, but at least she would be with him to watch for ominous signs.

As Ajaman fastened his scabbard belt, Ruha kissed him. "How much supper should I bring?"

"What you can carry easily," Ajaman answered, still whispering.

Outside the tent, the deep-voiced man called, "Ajaman, quit your bed games and come to the watch!" The exhortation brought laughter from a dozen throats.

"How many men does it require to fetch you, my husband?" the bride asked, irritated by the intrusive gathering outside the *khreima*. Though Ruha had addressed Ajaman, she had intentionally spoken loud enough for the men to hear. They tried to pretend they had not heard her complaint, as it was forbidden for a bride in *purdah* to speak directly to any man except her husband. Despite their efforts, several men could not stifle snickers.

Ajaman raised an eyebrow, but did not seem upset by Ruha's audacity. He covered the appearance of impropriety by repeating her question, "My wife wishes to know how many men are required to summon me."

"More than we have brought, apparently," the deep-voiced man returned. "To keep you from your duty, she must truly be as beautiful as her father promised."

Ruha smiled at the man's comment. Her father had also promised her that she would be pleased with Ajaman. So far, it appeared that her sire was as skilled at matchmaking as at camel herding.

Picking up his quiver and bow, Ajaman beamed at his new bride. "Indeed, my wife's father comes from an honorable family," he called. "It is a pity you cannot see how well he keeps his promises, Dawasir. My words cannot describe her."

Ruha's smile vanished with her husband's words. The comment made her feel as if she were on display. Like all Bedine women, Ruha reserved her beauty for her husband's eyes alone. Outside her home, the curves of her firm body would always remain concealed beneath her baggy *aba*. A shawl and veil would hide her sable hair, her proud nose, and the strong features of her statuesque face. All Dawasir or his comrades would ever see of Ruha were her sultry eyes and, perhaps, the crossed hash marks tattooed on her regal cheeks. She could not help feeling betrayed by Ajaman's boasting.

Ruha caught her spouse by his sleeve and pulled his ear close to her mouth. "If you don't watch your tongue, my husband," she whispered, "your friend Dawasir is not the only one who won't see how well my father keeps his promises." Her tone was serious enough to make Ajaman heed her words, but also light enough not to sound like an insult or challenge.

Ajaman clutched at his breast, feigning a wound. "Your words have pierced me deeper than a raider's arrow," he responded, his mouth upturned in a roguish smile. "I shall die with your name upon my lips."

Laughing, the bride pressed her mouth to her husband's. "I'd rather you die with my kiss on your lips than my name."

Ruha retrieved Ajaman's *amarat* from its hook. Before giving it to him, she stopped to run her hand along its hand-carved curves. The horn was already the source of her fondest memory, for when Ajaman had come to claim her as his bride, he had announced his arrival by sounding the *amarat* a mile outside the Mtair Dhafir's camp. Its brazen tones had been Ruha's first hint that she would like her new husband, for she had not even met him before he came to take her away.

Their marriage had been arranged by fate, or so her father claimed. A waterless summer in the north had driven Ajaman's tribe, the Qahtan, into the sands traveled by the Mtair Dhafir. Instead of chasing the strangers away, Ruha's father had proposed an alliance. In return for the Qahtan's promise to return north at summer's end, the Mtair Dhafir would share their territory for a few months. The bargain had been sealed by Ruha's marriage to Ajaman, the son of the Qahtan's sheikh by his second wife.

What the Qahtan had not realized was that they were solving another problem for their new allies. Witches were no more welcome in the Mtair Dhafir than any other Bedine *khowwan*, and Ruha had always been a problem for her father. When the strangers wandered into Mtair territory, the sheikh seized the opportunity to marry his daughter into a tribe that had no way of knowing about the visions she suffered. Of course, her father was risking a blood feud if the Qahtan ever found out that she was a witch. Since it was in the best interest of everyone involved in the deception to keep the matter hidden, he was willing to make the gamble. It was a risk that Ruha intended to see that he never regretted.

As she hung her husband's horn around his neck, Ruha pushed him toward the *khreima* exit. "You'd better go before Dawasir comes in to get you," she whispered. "I'll join you after dark."

"Don't let anyone see you," Ajaman said, turning to leave. "It might not dishonor our family, but it would embarrass me."

Ruha shook her head at his unnecessary concern. Ajaman had no need to worry, but could not be blamed for his apprehension. He did not realize that his wife could shroud herself in the shadow of a dune, or that an owl would envy the silence with which she slipped through the desert night. The young husband could not have known these things, for he did not know of the magic that made them possible or of the old woman who had taught Ruha how to use the spells.

Ruha's marriage to Ajaman was not the first time her father had tried to find another place for her to live. Her mother had died when she was only five. Because of her premonitions, none of the sheikh's other wives would agree to raise her. Her father was left with no choice but to give up the young girl. He led the tribe to a remote watering hole where an old witch lived in exile.

Like most "shunned women," the witch was lonely, so she gladly agreed to take the child as her own. With a peculiar blend of love and forgetful indifference, Qoha'dar set about teaching Ruha how to survive alone in the desert—a talent that relied heavily on the use of magic. By the time Ruha reached the age between childhood and womanhood, she could conjure sand lions, summon wind dragons, and scorch her enemies with the heat of the desert.

In Ruha's sixteenth year, Qoha'dar passed away. For several months, the lonely girl pored over Qoha'dar's books. Without the old woman to explain the runes and act as a guide, however, most of the effort was wasted. In all that time, Ruha learned only how to make a wall from wind and dust.

After accidentally enlarging a scorpion to the size of a camel and spending twenty-four hours hiding from it in a rock crevice, Ruha realized that sand magic was no substitute for companionship. She decided to return to the Mtair Dhafir, pretending that her premonitions had stopped.

Ruha made copies of her favorite spells by sewing them inside her *aba*, then hid her mentor's books in the foundation of an ancient ruin. As much as she hated to abandon tomes of such value, there was no other choice. If she brought the books along, her tribe would never believe her curse was gone.

Unfortunately, after spending a year locating her father's *khowwan*, she discovered that the memories of her tribesmen were long. Less than a week after Ruha had entered camp, half the families threatened to leave if she remained. Although the sheikh had no desire to abandon his child, he was forced to consider the wishes of the malcontents. If he allowed the *khowwan* to split, both halves would become easy prey for raiders from other tribes.

He had called Ruha to his side, no doubt to ask her to leave. Before he could force himself to bring up the painful subject, a pair of herdboys burst into the tent to report the presence of an unfamiliar tribe at El Ma'ra oasis. Because El Ma'ra was one of two other oases located within a two-day ride of the Mtair Dhafir, the news would normally have been received with alarm. Unallied Bedine tribes seldom camped so close together, for their camels would compete for pasturage and the close proximity would make raiding a virtual certainty.

Instead of receiving the news with a frown, however, Ruha's father had smiled broadly. He sent a messenger to arrange a meeting with the strange tribe, then told Ruha to prepare herself for a new life. Seven days later, Ajaman's *amarat* had sounded outside camp as he came to fetch his bride.

Remembering the short ride back to the Qahtani camp, Ruha smiled. Ajaman had led her camel, while a dozen friends surrounded them with drawn scimitars to discourage anybody from stealing the new bride. Ajaman had dared to speak to her only a half-dozen times, to reassure her that she had no reason to be frightened. When she had finally told him she was not at all scared, he had blushed and looked away. He had hardly looked at her until twilight the next day, when his father had filled their marriage cup with honeyed camel milk.

Now, as twilight set on her marriage for only the third time, Ruha sat inside her new tent and listened to noises as comforting in the Qahtani camp as they had been in that of the Mtair Dhafir. Loudest was the petulant braying of the camels when they returned from grazing and went to drink at the water hole. With the camels came the sound Ruha found most pleasing, the joyful cries of the children who had been tending the herds. From the rocky outcroppings east of camp came the eerie calls of raptors taking wing for their nightly hunt. More haunting still was the incessant tittering of the desert bats as they swooped low over the oasis pond to scoop up tiny mouthfuls of water.

Finally dusk faded to night. The camels were tied up, the children called to their parents' tents, the noisy birds drawn to the hunt, and the bats lured away to distant clouds of insects. The desert again grew as quiet as it had been during the day. In camp, the men plucked their *reba-*

bas and sang stories to amuse each other. The women, as always, were more silent than gazelles, but Ruha did not need to hear to know they were serving hot salted coffee to the men.

After allowing the camp to settle into the comfort of darkness, the young wife tied her belt around her waist, slipping her *jambiya* into an empty scabbard. The curved, double-edged dagger was Ruha's prized possession, for Qoha'dar had given it to her on her twelfth birthday. Next, she wrapped herself in a billowing, black robe that would camouflage her in the darkness. It would also keep her warm, for the desert was as cold at night as it was hot during the day.

Ruha started to leave the *khreima*, then realized she had forgotten Ajaman's meal. She returned and put a skin of camel's milk into a *kuerabiche*, then filled the rest of the shoulder sack with wild apricots. Carrying supper to her husband would hardly have seemed a valid reason for visiting his post if she forgot the food.

The young wife returned to the door and paused to study the camp. A hundred feet ahead, the full moon glistened off the oasis pond. As a steady breeze rippled the water, the tiny waves sparkled like white diamonds. The tangled branches of wild apricot trees ringed the pool, perfuming the air with the scent of ripe fruit. Above the apricot trees towered thirty majestic palms, their fernlike fronds splayed like open fingers against the starry sky.

Scattered amongst the trees were the silhouettes of nearly one-hundred *khreimas*. Robe-clad figures moved among the tents like specters. Outside the doors, men sat in small groups, singing and drinking salted coffee, yet simultaneously listening for the distant blare of an alarm horn.

With a bright moon overhead, there were precious few shadows in which to hide. Fortunately, there was wind

enough to cast an illusion if need be, so Ruha felt confident
of reaching Ajaman undetected. She slipped out of the
doorway, then cast a sand-whisper spell that allowed her to
move across the desert in complete silence. She circled to
the back of her *khreima*, careful to stay downwind of camp
lest a camel or dog catch her scent.

A few moments later, she left the oasis. The trees gave
way to spindly chenopods spaced at such even intervals it
almost looked as if men had planted them. Beyond the low-
lying bushes, the terrain became completely desolate.
Without tree or chenopod roots to hold the soil in place, the
wind shaped the sand into an endless sea of towering crescent dunes that stretched to the horizon and beyond.

Ruha knew that the sand sea spanned more than twenty-
five thousand square miles. When the dunes finally waned,
they abdicated only to a land of baked earth and wind-
scoured bedrock, even more desolate and lifeless than the
sands themselves. This bleak expanse stretched, as far as
Ruha knew, to the ends of the world itself.

Of course, she had heard stories of a kingdom beyond
the desert, but she had also heard tales of lands beneath
the sands and beyond the clouds. To Ruha, who had met
only three tribes in a year of riding across the most heavily
populated part of Anauroch, tales of ten-thousand people
living in a camp that never moved were unthinkable. She
could not envision a pasture that would support all of their
camels month after month.

As Ruha stalked toward the dunes, the biting odor of the
chenopods stung her nose more sharply, drawing her
thoughts back to the desert. She returned her attention to
the sand sea.

The moon shone brightly on the gentle slopes of the
dunes' convex sides, but the steep slip-faces on the con-
cave sides were plunged into darkness as black as Ruha's
robe. Between the crescent-shaped hills ran a gloomy

labyrinth of barren and rocky troughs.

A mile away, El Ma'ra rose a hundred feet over the sands. Ruha knew that Ajaman lay on top of the one-hundred foot pillar, his eyes scouring the shadowy desert for raiders from rival tribes. Several hundred yards to either side of the high rock, more sentries would be crouching on the dark sides of the highest dune crests. Ruha paused to cast a sand-shadow spell on herself. The spell would render her invisible as long as she was in any shadow. To avoid Ajaman's fellow sentries, all she would have to do was stay on the unlit sides of the dunes. She only hoped that her husband had left the rope dangling on the dark side of the pillar.

As Ruha studied the desolate scene ahead, a cold sense of dread settled over her. It might have been the night's cooling air that sent a shiver down her spine, or it might have been the steady drone of the desert wind. The young wife did not know the reason. She only knew that she wanted to be with her husband.

Ruha slipped into the trough at the base of the first dune. Even taking care to stay in the shadows, the young woman made good progress. Before long, she had traveled half a mile into the barren labyrinth between the hills of sand.

A distant boom sounded to the south. In the desert, such noises were not uncommon. Sometimes they were caused by faraway thunder, sometimes by a thousand tons of sand sloughing down the slip-face of a high dune. The superstitious Bedine even attributed the roars to the knelling alarms of long-buried fortresses. All those sounds were rumbles, though. Ruha had heard something more like a sharp crack. It had not been a natural noise, and the young wife's anxiety gave way to panic.

The shrill whine of an *amarat* horn rang from the post south of Ajaman's. Ruha glanced at the top of the sandstone pillar. Her husband's silhouette rose, then faced south.

Discarding her shoulder bag, Ruha slipped her *jambiya* from its scabbard. She started for El Ma'ra at the best pace her heavy robe allowed. The bride felt certain the *amarat* alarm was related to her vision. No raiding party would have made the sharp sound that had preceded the siren. Even if a Bedine raider could have created such a noise, he would not have given his enemy time to prepare by announcing his arrival.

Ruha was within one hundred yards of the high rock when she heard the sonorous tones of Ajaman's *amarat*. She looked up in time to see him drop his horn, then nock an arrow and loose it at something near the base of the pillar.

As she watched her husband attack, Ruha felt guilty for her panic. Ajaman was a Bedine warrior who had grown to manhood in the desert. He had honed his prowess by raiding other tribes and by defending his own camels against those who came to steal from his herds. Doubting his ability to defend himself almost seemed a violation of wifely duty.

Ajaman nocked a second arrow and fired again. Ruha stopped running, realizing that her presence would only disturb her husband. From the sands just beyond El Ma'ra, a brilliant flash erupted and shot toward the top of the pillar, momentarily blinding the young wife. A thunderous clap crashed over the dunes, nearly sweeping her off her feet.

Ruha's vision cleared just as Ajaman's limp body tumbled off El Ma'ra. It landed in the sand at the base of the pillar, then lay motionless in the moonlight.

"Ajaman!" Ruha gasped. For a long moment she stood motionless, knowing she had been right to fear for her husband. Ajaman had fallen, not to a raider's arrow, but to something no Bedine could shoot from his bow—a bolt of light.

Ruha shook her head and rushed toward her husband, her mind functioning on two tracks at once. Ruha longed to take Ajaman in her arms, to hear him speak her name. Rationally, she knew this would do no good, for if the flash had not killed him, the hundred-foot fall certainly had. Still, she could not—would not—believe it until she kissed his lifeless lips.

At the same time, Ruha realized the Qahtan were under attack, and not by another *khowwan*. She felt sure that the blinding flash that had killed Ajaman was magical, for she had once seen Qoha'dar destroy a mad jackal with a similar bolt. Even if he felt compelled to assault another tribe so openly, a Bedine tribesman would never have cast such a magic bolt. His fear of sorcery would not allow it.

It was this line of thought that made Ruha pause before stepping out of the last trough. The hesitation saved her life. She stopped just in time to see a gruesome creature scramble up the dune upon which Ajaman lay.

Ruha had never seen anything like it. Though the thing could obviously walk on two legs, it scurried up the moonlit slope on all four, moving as swiftly as a snake. The beast was shaped like a lizard, with sinewy arms and legs that protruded from its body at right angles and moved with quick, ungainly gestures. Its narrow skull had a sloping forehead that ended in a protruding brow, and sat atop a thin, awkward neck that swung from side to side as it clawed at the sand. Despite its brutish appearance, the thing was clearly intelligent. It carried a sword, had a crude crossbow slung across its back, and wore a faded leather corselet.

When it reached Ajaman, the creature extended a long, forked tongue and touched the body in several places. After inspecting the dead man in this manner for several moments, the thing glanced toward the far side of the high rock, then waved a clawed hand. A moment later, several more of the beasts scurried into view.

After seeing the ugly creature touch her dead husband, a weighty sorrow settled over Ruha. Realizing that she could do nothing more for Ajaman, the young widow retreated the way she had come. She had spent enough time in the desert to know that, even with her sand-shadow spell, she would be easy to spy if she ran. Ruha did not even consider fleeing ahead of the creatures. Instead, she took shelter in the shadows of the nearest sand dune's slip-face. She leaned back against the steep slope and pulled a layer of sand over her body, leaving only her dark eyes exposed. The sand could do nothing more than her sand-shadow spell to hide her visually, but she hoped that it would help to mask her scent.

Clutching her *jambiya* tightly, Ruha focused her thoughts on calming her pulse and breathing evenly. She did not even consider trying to return to the Qahtani camp, for she knew she would eventually be discovered if she started moving. Besides, she had no doubt that the warriors had heard the *amarat* warnings and were even now preparing for combat.

A moment later, the first creature stepped into the trough in front of Ruha, crossbow cocked and ready to fire. It paused to study the terrain, looking directly at Ruha's hiding place. The young widow summoned a wind-lion spell to mind, hoping she would not have to give away her presence by using it.

After several seconds of indecisive scrutiny, the lizard-thing finally flicked its tongue and moved on. Ruha let a silent sigh of relief escape, then remained absolutely motionless as a river of similar creatures flowed past. They poured through the trough ahead of her without any pretension of organization. Several times, the beasts passed so close that Ruha could see their yellow, egg-shaped eyes. One even stopped to flick its tongue at the sand next to her. The thing had slit pupils that sat horizontally in the iris. Its skin was rough and pebbly, with narrow gashes where its ears and nose should have been.

The ugly creature left, then a long line of baggage camels followed. Black-robed men with turban-swathed heads led the caravan. At their belts hung long thin swords with curved blades. The weary procession seemed to continue forever, but the last camel finally passed out of the trough. A handful of humans scattered ten to twenty yards apart came next. This rearguard was composed of fatigued stragglers who could do little more than stare at their own feet as they shuffled through the dark labyrinth, and Ruha dared to hope she would survive the strange group's passing.

Then, as one of the last men shuffled within a foot of Ruha's hiding place, he stumbled. He reached out to catch himself against the steep slope, pressing his hand against Ruha's sand-covered body. He gasped and jerked himself upright, then peered into the black shadows.

Ruha did not hesitate. She clamped her free hand over the straggler's mouth, then thrust her *jambiya* into his stomach. He uttered an astonished and pained groan, but Ruha's hand muffled the sound. The young widow drove the blade of her weapon toward his heart, simultaneously pulling him onto the slip-face beside her. She quickly dragged several armfuls of sand over his head and body. In an instant the man was dead and buried.

Her heart beating madly, Ruha turned her attention back to the trough, fearing that one of the dead man's compatriots might have witnessed the struggle. The last stragglers were more than fifteen yards away, and they were all as lethargic as ever. Relieved at the carelessness of the strange procession, Ruha again leaned against the dune and covered herself with a thin layer of sand.

She stayed in hiding for what seemed an eternity, even

after the last straggler had gone. She could hardly control her breathing, and found herself alternately struggling to stifle mournful sobs for Ajaman's death and joyful chortles celebrating her own survival. At the same time, Ruha remained terrified that the dead straggler would be missed or that one last group of attackers would shuffle into view just as she left the shadows.

Finally Ruha conquered the indecision born by these fears and dared to leave her hiding place. In the same instant, she heard the patter of sand sloughing down the steep slip-face above her. The young woman spun around and looked toward the crest, *jambiya* poised to strike.

Fifty feet above her, kneeling atop the dune and silhouetted against the moon, was one last man. His face was turned toward the oasis, and he seemed oblivious to Ruha's presence. Unlike the men who had passed ahead of him, he wore only a yellowish *aba* that matched the desert sand. Even in the pale moonlight, it was clear that his face was red, sun-blistered, and peeling. And though he presented only his profile to her, enough of his face was visible that Ruha could see his eyepatch and the pale, golden hair that protruded from beneath his *keffiyeh*. His features were drawn and haggard, though there was still a certain boyish softness to them.

Ruha's heart began to pound like the hooves of a racing camel, and her knees grew as weak as those of a suckling calf. The man atop the dune was the one she had seen in her premonition.

Two

At'ar the Merciless hung in a deep blue sky, bathing the desert in the fiery radiance of her insufferable passion. Though At'ar's orb had risen less than three hours ago, the heat already shimmered from the golden sands in skin-blistering waves. To Ruha, crouched atop a dune ninety yards from the oasis, it seemed nothing dared to stir beneath the yellow goddess's gaze. The wind lay heavy and listless upon the barren ground, and the green fronds of the palm trees dangled motionless and lethargic. Even N'asr's children, those great white-bearded vultures that ferried spirits to the camp of the dead, hovered overhead without so much as flapping a wing or twitching a tail-feather.

Ruha envied the vultures their patience, for her own thirst was making her grow desperate. Three hours beneath the morning sun had made her tongue so swollen it occasionally gagged her, her throat so dry she could not swallow, and her mind so muddled she could not keep the events of the previous night separated from what was happening at the moment.

Ruha recalled that her last drink had come from Ajaman's waterskin, after she had left her hiding place last night and gone to him. She remembered the despair washing over her as she had taken her dead husband's head in her lap and, in her mind, she returned to where she had sat in the sand at El Ma'ra's base.

In Ajaman's chest was a charred hole as big as her head, but his face betrayed no fear or sorrow. He held his dark brow furrowed in astonished fury, more angry at being soiled by magic than at being killed. The widow touched her mouth to her dead husband's, then slipped his *jambiya* and its sheath off his belt and took the crushed *amarat* from beneath his body. These would be her only keepsakes.

Though Ruha had come to like Ajaman during the two days of their marriage, she could not say that she loved him. It was a surprise to her, then, that tears were streaming down her cheeks. It was proper for a widow to grieve her dead husband, but for Ruha to claim that she wept on Ajaman's account seemed out of place and insincere. The tears, she realized, were for herself. With Ajaman gone, she was likely to spend the rest of her life as Qoha'dar had spent hers—a shunned woman.

In similar circumstances, any other woman might have returned to her own *khowwan*, assured that her tribe would have received her with open arms. For Ruha, that possibility did not exist. Even if she returned to the Mtair Dhafir, the old women would blame her for the Qahtan's disaster and, with a grim air of reluctance, the elder warriors would persuade her father to banish her.

With her magic, Ruha knew she could survive alone in the desert, but the thought of being forced into hermitage made her stomach queasy, and it horrified her. The young woman had not asked for her premonitions, and she had never done anything to deserve banishment. Still, she did not blame her father or the Mtair Dhafir for ostracizing her. To them, her presence seemed dangerous, and they were just doing what they thought necessary to survive. Given similar circumstances, any Bedine would have done the same.

"You do what you must to survive, and I will do the same," Ruha said, speaking to the distant tribe of her birth. "I'll ride with any *khowwan* that will take me, though it be the blood enemy of the Mtair Dhafir."

As she spoke, Ruha found her throat so dry that the words came out in a series of croaking gasps. Realizing that she was desperately thirsty, the widow reached for Ajaman's waterskin. The fall had burst the neck open, leaving only a few last swallows in the corners. Ruha placed her lips over the neck to prevent the loss of even a drop, then tilted her head back to drain the precious water into her parched throat.

Nothing.

Ruha tried to swallow again. Still nothing.

With a start, Ruha snapped back to the present, and she realized that she was a half-mile from her dead husband. He was still at El Ma'ra, buried in the cool, shallow grave she had dug for him earlier. Now, she was sitting atop a dune, exposed to At'ar's full glory and so sun-sick that she was hallucinating.

The young widow angrily pulled Ajaman's crushed *amarat* horn from around her neck, then threw it down the dune's slip-face. It slid clear to the desert's rocky floor.

"Why did you fall on your waterskin, husband?" she croaked, looking toward El Ma'ra's tawny pinnacle. "An honorable man would not leave his wife without water!"

Of course, Ajaman did not answer, but Ruha did not doubt that he heard her.

"Ajaman, if you do not send me some water, there will

be nobody to wash your body before the journey west," Ruha threatened, still staring in the direction of her husband's body. "Tonight, when the vultures come to take you to N'asr's tent, the odor of life will cling to you like blood on a newborn calf. Surely, the Pitiless One will give you to his djinns, and it won't be my fault."

Bartering with the dead was dangerous, the widow realized dimly. Even those who had been friends often repaid their debts with plague and pestilence, but Ruha thought she had done everything she could to find water on her own. She remembered checking the canteen of the straggler she had killed last night. It had been empty. She had even found the milk skin she had been carrying when the attack started, but it had been trampled into the sand by the caravan. Ruha was desperate.

At the oasis there was plenty of water, but she did not dare approach it. In the entire *khowwan*, not a Qahtani remained alive. The men had fallen in contorted, inert poses at the camp perimeter. In the oasis itself, dog and camel corpses lay scattered among the tents and trees. The women and children were gathered beneath shredded and charred *khreimas*, their locations marked by lumps and dark stains in the cloth.

But it was not corpses that prevented Ruha from going to the oasis pool and drinking the water she needed so badly. The pale-skinned stranger who had appeared last night in the caravan's wake was searching the entire camp tent by tent. He had been since dawn. Methodically he furled back each *khreima*, then kneeled amongst the corpses. After a few moments, he covered the bodies again and went to the next tent. Never, as far as Ruha could tell, did he take anything from the dead or their households.

His behavior was a stark contrast to that of his companions, two creatures who stood about four feet tall. Ruha could tell little about the pair, for they were swaddled head to foot in white burnooses. The short bipeds were robbing the Qahtani warriors, pulling rings off dead fingers and prying jewels from scimitar scabbards.

Watching the strangers continue their desecrations, Ruha wondered who they could be and what they were doing at El Ma'ra's oasis. Her muddled mind could not even guess at an answer, any more than she could imagine the origin of last night's murderous caravan. She had never seen anything like either group in the desert, and her ignorance of the lands beyond Anauroch was complete. Both the caravan and the three strangers remained an utter mystery to her.

For the next hour, the widow pondered her ignorance and waited for the strangers to leave. A gray haze appeared on the southern horizon, and Ruha knew that a sandstorm was ravaging some distant part of the desert. She paid it no further attention, for it would not arrive soon enough for her to sneak to the oasis pond beneath its cover.

As At'ar grew brighter and hotter, Ruha's skin became pale and clammy. She felt sick to her stomach. Her head ached. Spots appeared in her vision, and she could not make them go away.

Ruha turned her gaze toward the vultures, barely able to distinguish the birds from the dots before her eyes. "Surely, N'asr will punish these defilers of the dead. Ask him to do it now, so that I may live and prepare my husband for the journey to your father's camp."

If the vultures heard her plea, they gave no sign. The bulky birds continued hanging in the sky, steady as clouds.

The widow waited. She did not exert herself by searching for non-existent shade. In the summer, At'ar rode proud in the sky, and it would have been futile to attempt escaping her heat. Only a tent or a palm tree's gaunt fronds could offer shelter from the sun, and the only sign Ruha saw of either was in the oasis. Everywhere else, on the gentle slopes and steep slip-faces of the dunes, and in the rocky valleys between them, At'ar blazed down on the parched sands in all her fiery radiance. The yellow goddess could not be avoided.

Ruha could feel herself growing perilously weak, but she resisted the dry voice whispering to her to sneak back to the oasis. Whoever the strangers were, their desecrations made it clear that they were no friend of the Bedine, and from what she had seen last night, the instincts of the one-eyed stranger were too sharp to challenge.

As she thought about the stranger, Ruha's mind wandered and she once again found herself standing in last night's shadows, the dead straggler lying in the sand beside her. The stranger was crouched atop the dune, where he had appeared so suddenly in the wake of the caravan. As the screams of dying Qahtanis began to drift over the sands, he continued to watch the battle, his attention fixed impassively on the oasis.

Ruha wondered if he was the man who killed Ajaman. Confident of the magic that kept her hidden and unheard, she gripped her *jambiya* and prepared to take vengeance.

As she picked up the handful of sand she needed to create her magical lion, the one-eyed man whirled about and drew a straight-bladed dagger. He stared into the quiet darkness protecting the young woman, seeming to sense her presence in spite of the spells hiding her. The stranger shook his head once, then sheathed his dagger.

Was he warning Ruha not to attack, or did he doubt the instincts that had alerted him to her presence? Before Ruha could decide, the stranger slipped down the other side of the dune and disappeared. The widow's knees were ready to buckle and her stomach felt as though her heart had dropped into it. She did not follow.

With a start, Ruha realized that the ache in her stomach

was more than fear, and that her confused mind had again lost track of reality. Heat cramps were causing the pain she felt, and the reason it seemed like night was because her eyes were closed. She had lost track of reality again, drifting into a dream of last night.

Ruha held her head with both hands, vainly trying to stop the fierce pounding inside. The young widow realized she had to risk going to the pond, even without any spells to conceal her. With his acute instincts, the stranger would probably see her as she drank, but to wait was to die.

Ruha slid a few feet down from the dune crest, then turned toward the rocky labyrinth behind her.

To her surprise, a string of ten white camels stood two hundred feet away. Believing that her mind was playing tricks on her, she closed her eyes and whispered, "Husband, by the last drop of water in my mouth, if this is a mirage, I will be slave to N'asr himself before I wash your filthy corpse."

When she opened her eyes again, the beasts were still there. Though clearly mature riding camels, they had no halters or saddles. Instead, their driver had looped long ropes around their lanky necks and run lines from one beast to the next. The sight puzzled Ruha, for any man who owned ten matched camels could certainly saddle them properly.

Only the lead camel, an indistinctive brown gelding, carried a proper saddle or halter. Upon this beast sat a lone tribesman, his bow strung and his lance resting across his thighs. He wore a tawny *aba* similar to Ajaman's, and a white *keffiyeh* covered his hair. Though Ruha could not see his face at this distance, his head seemed turned toward her. Ruha guessed by his dress that the driver belonged to the Qahtan tribe, perhaps even her dead husband's clan.

Continuing her slide down the dune, she croaked, "Worthy Ajaman, I should have known better than to doubt you, but I am a frail woman and thirst affects my judgment. Please forgive my nagging and don't send any blights to punish me."

When her feet touched the rocky desert floor, she checked to see that her veil was still in place, then staggered toward the man.

Upon seeing her condition, the rider unfastened his waterskin and slid off his saddle. He thrust his lance into the closest dune, then wrapped his lead camel's reins around the shaft. Without actually running, for a wise man never ran in the heat of the day, he rushed toward Ruha.

The widow's first impression was that he was a herdboy, for his face lacked even the hint of whiskers. His features were proud and strong, like Ajaman's, but his skin looked as soft as a pup's fur, and he did not stand even as tall as she did. He could have been no more than thirteen or fourteen. Still, Ruha stopped short of asking him to fetch his master. If the Qahtani customs bore any similarity to those of most Bedine, a herdboy would not carry a lance. That privilege belonged only to a warrior.

Instead, as the boy approached, she managed to gasp a question. "Whose fine camels are those?"

The youth showed a smile of pearly teeth. "They once belonged to a sheikh of the Bordjias," he answered, straightening his shoulders as if donning an *aba*.

The answer explained the lack of saddles and halters. What the youth had left unspoken was that now the camels belonged to him. He had stolen them on a raid. If, as he claimed, the animals had belonged to a sheikh, the pasture had undoubtedly been a well-guarded one. Ruha was glad she had not insulted the young man by asking after his master.

The youth stopped a pace away from Ruha and passed the waterskin to her. Observing that he self-consciously kept one hand close to the hilt of his *jambiya*, Ruha said, "A careful warrior will make a wise elder."

The boy nodded, then answered, "My father says it is honorable to help a stranger, but to remember that no friend is ever a stranger."

"Your father is right," Ruha answered, lifting the skin to her mouth.

Though the water was hot and tasted of several days in the skin, to her it seemed as if it had just come from a cool spring. Still, she stopped herself after three swallows, for drinking too much too quickly would make her feel worse than she did now. Besides, when a stranger shared his water, one never knew how much he had to spare. She offered the skin back to the youth.

The boy shook his head. "Drink. I have another." He spoke with an exaggerated tone of authority.

Ruha allowed herself two more swallows. "Your water is sweeter than honeyed milk," she said. Though she meant what she said, the words were weighted with exhaustion. They sounded insincere even to the young widow.

The youth smiled and shook his head. "That water's been in the skin for five days. You've been out here watching my *khowwan* too long."

"It's my *khowwan*, too," Ruha answered. "Or at least it was."

The boy's smile faded. "What do you mean?"

Ruha pointed at the vultures hanging over the oasis. "Surely you've seen N'asr's children?"

The young warrior nodded. "That's why I hid my approach behind the dunes, but I meant to ask why you claim to be Qahtani. If you were a member of the tribe, I would know you. There aren't that many of us."

"I'm Ruha, Ajaman's wife," she answered.

The youth's hand drifted back toward his dagger. "Ajaman has no wife," he said suspiciously.

Shrugging aside his skeptical tone, Ruha lifted the waterskin to her lips again. She still felt weak and dizzy, but with an ample supply of water at hand, she would soon be better. After a few swallows, she lowered the skin and said, "I came to the Qahtan three days ago."

"Forgive me," the boy said, flustered. As an after-thought, the boy offered, "I was on *el a'sarad*."

Ah, Ruha thought, that explains the warrior's age. The *el a'sarad* was a solitary camel raid undertaken as a rite of passage—after a boy killed his first man.

The youth continued, "I had not heard that my brother had taken a wife."

"Brother!" Ruha gasped.

The youth nodded. "Sons of the same mother."

In her weakened state, the shock was too much for Ruha. She began to wail uncontrollably, half sobbing and half laughing at her fate. A man was obligated to care for a dead brother's wife for two years, after which time he had the choice of sending her away or marrying her himself. Ruha found it pathetically ironic that her new protector and po-tential husband was a thirteen-year-old boy. Dropping the skin, the widow collapsed to her knees and buried her face in her palms.

The youth quickly picked up the waterskin, then took Ruha's arm and helped her to his camels. He sat her in the shade beneath one of the beast's musky udders, then said, "I am called Kadumi."

As the camel stamped its fleshy feet on the ground, he poured water on the only exposed parts of Ruha's face, her cheeks and her brow. The water evaporated as soon as it touched her skin, without cooling her at all.

Regaining control of her spent emotions, Ruha put her hand over the spout. "Save the water. I'll be fine."

Kadumi closed the skin and placed it beside her. Turning in the direction of the unseen oasis, he asked, "Where are the other women? How badly is the tribe hurt?"

The young widow touched the ground in front of her. "Sit."

Kadumi shook his head. "I'll stand," he declared, as if hearing the report on his feet made him more of a man.

"Kadumi, this was no camel raid," Ruha began.

"Tell me what happened," he replied, still refusing the seat she offered.

Ruha shrugged, then began. "It was after dark. Ajaman had the night watch, and he wanted me to bring him some apricots and milk."

"Ajaman wouldn't ask his wife to leave their tent during the *purdah*," Kadumi interrupted, frowning.

"He *did* ask it," Ruha snapped, irritated that the youth had noticed her misrepresentation. "Do you question the honor of your brother's wife?"

Startled at the terse reply, Kadumi turned his gaze aside. "Let's say he asked you to come to him. Then what?"

Trying not to sound defensive, she continued, "Before I reached him, a caravan of men and fork-tongued monsters came out of the sands."

"Fork-tongued monsters?"

"Yes," Ruha replied. "With a lizard's skin and a snake's eyes. Where there should have been nose and ears, the beasts had only gashes. There were hundreds, maybe thousands. Behind them came caravan drivers in black burnooses."

Ruha paused, smelling once again the scent of singed camel-hair and scorched flesh as the strange caravan attacked. Over the dunes rolled the mournful howls of anguished mothers, the terrified screams of dying children. Peering over a dune crest, Ruha saw a thousand silhouettes marching through the oasis, setting fire to anything that stood, cutting down anything that walked.

"What do they want?" she asked. "How can I stop them?"

Water trickled down her face, and then she was no longer
watching the battle.

"Drink," Kadumi said, offering her the open waterskin
as his face replaced the dark images from the previous
night. "You're seeing mirages."

Ruha pushed the skin aside. "There were too many
strangers," she replied. "I couldn't save anyone."

"I understand," Kadumi answered, sealing the skin.
"What of the others who escaped? Where are they?"

"Others?" Ruha yelled. The camel beneath which she
sat brayed and stepped forward, brushing Ruha's head
with its udders. She ignored the beast. "Haven't you been
listening? There are no others!"

Kadumi's face went pale and the waterskin slipped from
his hand. An expression of disbelief and bewilderment
overcame the boy, and Ruha immediately regretted her
sharp tone.

Before she could comfort the boy, he set his smooth-
skinned jaw. "Who did this to my tribe?" he hissed. "Who
were these men and fork-tongued monsters?"

Ruha shook her head. "I don't know," she whispered.

"What color were their *keffiyehs?*" Kadumi pressed.
"Did they ride the long-wooled camels of a northern tribe?
If they are a Qahtani enemy, I will know them from your
description."

Ruha looked straight into Kadumi's eyes. "They weren't
Bedine," she said. "I don't even think they were from
Anauroch."

The youth sneered doubtfully and declared, "That cannot be." He studied her for a moment with accusatory
eyes, then demanded, "If everybody else is dead, how did
you survive?"

Ruha pushed herself from beneath the camel. "What do
you suggest?" she snapped, standing. "Do you insult the
woman whom you are duty-bound to honor?"

Cowed by her sharp tone, the boy retreated two full steps, shaking his head. At the same time, the camels echoed Ruha's indignation and roared with impatience. They could no doubt smell the oasis and were anxious to quench their thirst in its pool.

Remembering the one-eyed man and his two guides, Ruha quickly turned to calm the camels. Until now, she had not worried about being overheard by the three strangers, for she and Kadumi were far enough away from the oasis that their voices would be muffled by sand dunes. A camel's bellow was a different matter. A roar like the ones the creatures had just voiced could be heard miles away.

"We've got to keep the camels quiet," she said, urgently grabbing the nose of the nearest one. "There are three strangers in the oasis."

Kadumi did not move to help her. "Just three?" he scoffed, stepping toward his brown riding camel. "I have my bow and plenty of arrows. They shall pay the blood price."

Ruha moved to the boy's side and caught his arm. "No," she said. "They weren't with the fork-tongues." She told him about how the one-eyed stranger had appeared in the caravan's wake last night, then of spending the morning watching the man and his short companions in camp.

"It does not matter whether their hands bear the blood of battle or the blood of desecration," Kadumi insisted. "They deserve to die." He pulled his arm free of her grasp.

From his stubborn tone, Ruha realized that the boy was looking not so much for vengeance as an excuse to vent his anger. Unfortunately, remembering the sharp instincts of the one-eyed man, Ruha knew that allowing Kadumi to attack would mean his death. As the youth reached for his arrow quiver, the widow slipped between him and his camel. "They are three and you are one."

Kadumi side-stepped her and snatched his quiver off the saddle.

Wondering if her husband had been as stubborn and foolish in his youth, Ruha grasped the boy by both shoulders. "It is foolish to attack," she said. "Even Ajaman would not have tried such a thing."

Kadumi ignored her and tried to pull free. When she did not release him, he drew his *jambiya*. The boy's anger took Ruha by surprise, and she found the curve of his knife blade pressed against her throat.

His lower lip quivering in anger, Kadumi yelled, "Ajaman is not here!"

"But you are, and you are dishonoring your brother by threatening his wife," Ruha countered. "You must protect your brother's widow for two years. If you get killed, who will take care of me?"

Tears of despair welled in the boy's eyes. After a moment of self-conscious consideration, he rubbed the tears away and sheathed his *jambiya*. He turned from her and stared at his camels for several minutes. Finally he said, "I will take you to your father and return to kill the defilers later. Anyway, from what you have said, it appears that the fork-tongues are moving toward the Mtair Dhafir's oasis, so we should try to warn them." The youth looked westward. "I have extra camels, and they are all strong. We can ride hard, and perhaps we will reach the Mtair Dhafir ahead of the fork-tongues."

The widow shook her head. "I've made certain promises to Ajaman. We must wait here until we can take his body to the oasis," she said. "Then we can warn the Mtair Dhafir."

Ruha was not anxious to return to her father's tribe, but Kadumi was right to alert them to the danger traveling in their direction. Besides, even though she knew it would be impossible for her to stay with the Mtair Dhafir, there was no reason for them to turn out the young warrior, and the widow suspected that it would be easier to find a new tribe for herself if she left her young brother-in-law with the

Mtair.

Accepting Ruha's plan with a respectful nod, Kadumi cast a wary eye toward the southern sky. "Let us hope the strangers leave soon," he said. "If that storm catches us in its path, we will have to wait it out."

Three

From beneath a fallen tent, Lander heard his guides approaching. Pitched on the southern end of the oasis pond, about a hundred feet from the camp, this tent was the first in which he had found no bodies. It was also a stark contrast to the clutter of the other tents, for there was nothing inside except a ground-loom, three cooking pots, a dozen shoulder bags of woven camel hair, and a few other household items. Apparently the inhabitants of this household had escaped the massacre. Lander wondered how.

"Lord, there are camels out in the sands!" called Bhadla, the elder of his two guides.

"I'm not a lord," Lander responded wearily, correcting the solicitous servant for the thousandth time. He found a twelve-inch tube made of a dried lizard skin and sniffed the greasy substance inside. It was foul-smelling butter.

"Whatever it is you wish to be called," Bhadla said, "I

hope you have finished whatever you are doing with those dead people. We must go."

"Go?" Lander asked, crawling toward the voice. "What for?"

Like his guides, he had heard the camels roaring outside the oasis, but he had no intention of leaving. He had come to this wretched desert to find the Bedine, not flee from them.

Lander reached the edge of the tent and pushed his head and shoulders out from beneath it. The blazing sunlight reflected off the golden sands and stabbed painfully at his one good eye. "What's this about going?"

"Someone is coming," the short guide repeated. "We shouldn't be here when they arrive."

"They'll think we did this," offered Musalim, Bhadla's scrawny assistant.

Like all D'tarig, Bhadla and Musalim stood barely four feet tall. Each kept himself swaddled in a white burnoose and turban from head to foot. Lander wondered what they looked like beneath their cloaks and masks, but knew he would probably never find out. He had met dozens of the diminutive humanoids over the last few months, and he had yet to glimpse anything more than a leathery brow set over a pair of dark eyes and a black, puggish nose.

"I doubt anyone will think the three of us murdered an entire tribe," Lander said.

"The Bedine might," Bhadla said. He brushed the back of his fingers against his forehead in a disparaging gesture Lander did not understand. "They have very bad tempers."

"When I hired you, you assured me you were very popular with the people of the desert," Lander said, crawling the rest of the way from beneath the tent.

As he stood, he noticed that a gray haze was spreading northward from the southern horizon. In Sembia, his home, such a cloud signaled the approach of a storm. He hoped it meant the same thing in the desert, for a little rain might break the oppressive heat.

Turning his attention back to his guide, he said, "Are you telling me you lied, Bhadla?"

Bhadla shrugged and looked away. "No one can say what the Bedine will do."

"I can," Lander countered.

Musalim scoffed. "How could you? Bhadla cannot even tell which tribe this—"

Bhadla cuffed his assistant for this indiscrete admission. In the language of his people, the D'tarig said, "Watch your tongue, fool!"

Though he wore a magical amulet that allowed him to comprehend and speak D'tarig, Lander feigned ignorance. Since both of his guides spoke Common, the universal trade language of Toril, he had seen no reason to let them know he could understand their private conversations.

"I do not need to know the name of this tribe to know they will kill those who loot their dead," Lander said, looking pointedly from one D'tarig to the other.

The hands of both guides unconsciously brushed the pockets hidden deep within their burnooses. "What do you mean, Lord?" Musalim asked suspiciously.

Lander smiled grimly. "Nothing, of course," he replied. "But if *I* had taken anything off the bodies of the dead—rings off their fingers or jewels from their scabbards, for example—I would also be anxious to leave."

Musalim furrowed his barely visible brow, but Bhadla seemed unimpressed. "Bah!" the older D'tarig said. "The survivors will think the raiders took these things."

Lander looked toward the sand dunes. "I don't think so," he said. The figure that had been watching them all morning was gone—but not far, he suspected. "They've seen with their own eyes who looted the dead."

Musalim's eyes opened wide. "No, Lord!"

"I'm no lord," Lander snapped. "Don't address me as if I were."

Bhadla's eyes narrowed. "You're lying."

"Not at all," Lander replied. "My father was a wealthy but untitled merchant of Archenbridge, and my mother was . . . well, there's no need to discuss her. Let's just say I'm no lord."

Bhadla shook his turbaned head angrily. "I don't care if your mother was a goat who gave milk of silver and urine of gold!" he yelled. "Were the Bedine watching or not?"

Lander flashed a conciliatory smile. "I never lie."

The D'tarig uttered a curse in his own throaty language, then began pulling jewels and rings out of his pockets. Laying the booty on the camel-wool tent at Lander's side, he hissed, "You should have told us!"

"You shouldn't have taken it," Lander replied.

"It's not our fault," Musalim complained, also emptying his pockets. "Those who attack should take the plunder, not leave it to tempt us. Who razes an entire camp and steals nothing but camels?"

Studying the devastated oasis with a grim expression, Lander answered, "The Zhentarim."

"Black Robes?" Bhadla echoed. "They couldn't have done this. They're just traders."

Lander could understand Bhadla's misconception. The D'tarig lived on the fringes of Anauroch. They survived by goat herding, but the most adventurous and greedy ventured into the Great Desert. These "desert walkers" collected resin from cassia, myrrh, and frankincense trees, then sold it to merchants sponsored by Zhentil Keep. The Zhentarim resold it to temples all over the realms for use as incense. As far as the D'tarig knew, the Black Robes were nothing more than good merchants.

"The Zhentarim are much more than traders," Lander

explained, turning to face Bhadla. "They're an evil network of thieves, slave-takers, and murderers motivated by power, lust, and greed. They rule hundreds of towns and villages, control the governments of a dozen cities, and have placed spies in the elite circle of practically every nation in Faerun."

Musalim shrugged. "So?"

"The Zhentarim want to monopolize trade and control politics over all of Faerun," Lander said. "They want to make slaves of an entire continent."

Dumping his last ring onto the collapsed tent, Bhadla said doubtfully, "I don't believe that. Wealth is one thing, but who would want the trouble of so many slaves?"

The Sembian shook his head. "I don't know why the Zhentarim want what they want, Bhadla," he said. "Maybe they're working on Cyric's behalf."

"What is this *Cyric*?" interrupted Musalim, still searching the hidden pockets of his robe.

"He was once a man, but now he's a god—the god of death, murder, and tyranny," Lander answered.

"In the desert, he is called N'asr," Bhadla explained.

Musalim nodded thoughtfully, as if the god's involvement explained everything.

"The Bedine claim N'asr is the sun's lover," Bhadla continued. "The sun, At'ar, forsakes her lawful husband every night to sleep in N'asr's tent."

Lander ran his fingers over the blisters on his sunburned face. "I don't doubt it," he said, squinting up at the sky. "She certainly seems brutal enough to be Cyric's lover."

"Perhaps N'asr, er, Cyric has sent the Zhentarim into the desert to kill At'ar's husband," Musalim suggested. "Jealously has caused many murders."

Lander chuckled. "I don't think so, Musalim. In this case, I think they're after gold."

"Gold?" Bhadla queried, perking up. "There's none of

that in Anauroch, is there?"

"They're not looking for gold *in* the desert," Lander explained. "They're going to carry it *across* the desert." He pointed westward. "Over there, two thousand miles beyond the horizon, lies Waterdeep, one of many cities of great riches." Next, he pointed eastward. "Over there, five hundred miles from the edge of the desert, are Zhentil Keep, Mulmaster, and the other ports of the Moonsea. They serve as the gateways to the ancient nations of the Heartlands and to the slave-hungry lands of the South."

The two D'tarig frowned skeptically, and Lander guessed that the desert-walkers were having trouble imagining a world of such scope. "In the center of all these cities are six-hundred miles of parched, burning sands that fewer than a dozen civilized men have ever crossed."

Musalim picked up a handful of sand and let it slip through his fingers. "You mean these sands?"

"Yes," Lander confirmed. "And whoever forges a trail through this desert controls the trade routes linking the eastern and western sides of Faerun."

"There you are mistaken," Bhadla said, his eyes sparkling with faintly kindled avarice. "The land surrounding the desert belongs to the D'tarig, so we will control this trade."

"If you think the Zhentarim will honor your territorial rights, you are the one who is mistaken," Lander said. "When the time comes, they will find a way to steal your land."

"You underestimate us, Lord," Bhadla said. "The Zhentarim may have cheated many in your land, but they cannot beguile the D'tarig." As if he had said all that needed to be said on the matter, the guide turned to Musalim. In D'tarig, he asked, "Have you returned all you took from the Bedine?"

"Yes," Musalim answered, a note of melancholy in his

voice.

Bhadla turned back to Lander, then took the Sembian's arm and tugged him toward their camels. "Come, it is time for us to ride."

Lander refused to budge. "I'm waiting for the Bedine."

"If they have not come by now, they are not going to," Musalim said. "They are a shy people, and the survivors of what happened here are certain to be more so."

"There are two more oases within two days' ride," Bhadla added. "Perhaps another tribe will be camped at one of them."

Lander's stomach tightened in alarm. "Where are these oases?"

Bhadla pointed in the direction the Zhentarim had taken after destroying the camp last night.

Without speaking a word, Lander started toward the oasis pond, where the camels were tethered. Previously he had been puzzled by the Zhentarim's quick departure last night. Now he realized they were trying to reach the next tribe before it learned of the slaughter at this oasis.

When Bhadla and Musalim caught up to him, Lander glared at the guides. "Why didn't you tell me about the other oases earlier?"

Bhadla shrugged. "I would have, if you had told me we were being watched."

Irritated by the D'tarig's reply, Lander quickened his pace. "Don't fill more than three waterskins," he snapped. "We'll have to ride hard to beat the Zhentarim to the next oasis, and the extra weight will only slow us down."

Musalim pointed at the haze on the southern horizon. "But, Lord, we may need a lot of water. That storm could force us to stop for several days!"

"We're not going to stop because of a little rain."

Bhadla snickered. "Rain? In Anauroch?"

"That's a sandstorm!" added Musalim.

The trio reached the camels a moment later, and the beasts lowered their heads to the water for one last drink. Lander undid the tethers of his mount, then paused to look southward. The haze was creeping steadily forward, streaking the sapphire sky with gray, fingerlike tendrils.

"I don't care if it's a firestorm," the Sembian said. "It's not going to stop us."

In the end, the D'tarig insisted upon filling six waterskins, but at Lander's direction, they agreed to push their camels along at a trot. The trio covered more than a dozen miles by early afternoon, and the sands paled to the color of bleached bones. The dunes changed orientation so that they ran east-west and towered as high as five hundred feet. Lander was glad their path ran parallel to the great dunes rather than across them. The Sembian felt sure that scaling one of the steep, shifting slopes would have been as hard on the camels as trotting for an entire day.

The dunes' great size did not make them any less barren. The only sign of vegetation was an occasional parched bush that had been reduced to a bundle of sticks by an untold number of drought years. Even the camels, which usually tried to eat every stray plant they happened upon, showed no interest in the desiccated shrubs.

The storm crept closer, obscuring the sky with a haze that did nothing to lessen the day's heat. The blistering wind, blowing harder with each passing hour, felt as though it had been born in a swordsmith's forge. On its breath, it carried a fine silt that coated the trio's robes with gray dust and filled Lander's mouth with a gritty thirst that he found unbearable. Soon he was glad his guides had insisted upon filling extra skins, for he found himself sipping water nearly constantly.

Bhadla slowed his camel and guided it to Lander's side, leaving Musalim fifty yards ahead in the lead position. The

D'tarig always insisted upon riding a short distance ahead to scout. Lander did not argue, for it spared him their constant, inane chatter.

"This is going to be a very bad storm, Lord," Bhadla said. "I fear that, when it grows dark, we will have to stop or lose our way. There will be no stars to guide us."

"Don't worry. I will always know which direction we are traveling." He purposely did not tell his guide about the compass he carried, for he suspected the D'tarig would steal such a useful device at the first opportunity.

Bhadla shook his head at his employer's stubbornness. "It may not be as important to beat the Zhentarim to the next oasis as you think," he said. "Bedine scouts range far. They probably know of the Black Robes already."

"If what you say is true," Lander countered, "why did the tribe at the last oasis perish?"

The D'tarig frowned, then shrugged. "Who can say? But we will do no one any good if we lose our way and die."

"You really don't understand what's at stake here, do you?"

"What is there to understand?" Bhadla asked. "The Zhentarim are trying to cross the desert, and the Bedine are in their way."

"There's more to it than that," Lander replied. "The Zhentarim need the Bedine to open their trade route. Merchants can't survive in the desert alone, and the Black Robes know that. They need the Bedine for guides and caravan drivers. What the Zhentarim want is to enslave the Bedine."

Bhadla laughed. "Enslave the Bedine? They would find it easier to cage the wind."

"The Zhentarim have caged things more powerful than the wind," Lander noted flatly, then took a sip of water. "If they approach the desert tribes in the same way they have approached villages all over Faerun, this is how the Bedine will fall: The Black Robes will approach the sheikh in the guise of friendship and offer him a treaty. Once he agrees, they'll find a pretext to invite his family or other important tribe members into their camp. The Zhentarim will not permit these guests to leave and will use them as hostages to guarantee the tribe's submission. They will send agents, whose job it is to report murmurs of rebellion, to watch over the tribe. Before they know it, the Bedine will be subdued."

"If the Black Robes want slaves, why did they massacre the Bedine at El Ma'ra?"

"I'm not sure," Lander said, shaking his head. "Perhaps the sheikh wouldn't cooperate, or perhaps they wanted an example to use in intimidating other tribes." He closed his waterskin. "The Zhentarim are usually more subtle than they've been in Anauroch—probably because it's so empty that they think brazen actions won't be noticed. In any case, the change of style makes it more difficult for me to guess their reasoning."

Bhadla furrowed his brow, then shrugged. "If you say so," he sighed. "But what concern of yours is it? What does it matter to you if the Black Robes conquer the Bedine?"

"I've come here to help the Bedine retain their freedom," Lander answered, looking at his saddle and pretending to adjust a strap. Even though he wasn't lying, he was intentionally dodging the D'tarig's question; he had often been told that his face was too honest when he was trying to hide something.

"So I have gathered," the D'tarig replied. "What I want to know is why?"

Lander opened his waterskin again and lifted it to his lips, more to hide his face than to wash the grime from his mouth. Between sips, he said, "Someone had to."

The little guide shook his head. "Not so. Only a fool

strays from his path to search out another man's trouble. You may be gullible, but you do not strike me as a fool. What is your reason for coming to the desert?"

Realizing it was useless to dodge Bhadla's inquiries, Lander tried an honest reply. "I can't tell you why I'm here."

The D'tarig's eyes sparkled, and Lander guessed that Bhadla was smiling beneath his mask of white cloth. "I think I know the reason for your discretion," the guide said.

"Oh?" Lander asked, confident that the D'tarig could not guess his secret.

Black eyes locked on Lander's, Bhadla said, "The Harpers sent you."

Lander's jaw dropped.

Bhadla's eyes shone with triumph. "You see, nothing escapes my notice."

From the guide's manner, Lander realized there was no use in denial. "How do you know?"

Bhadla pointed at Lander's left breast. "The harp and the moon."

Lander looked down and saw what had given him away. Beneath his burnoose, he wore a light tunic of cotton. On the left breast of that tunic was pinned the emblem of the Harpers, a silver harp sitting within the crescent of a silver moon. On the exterior of his burnoose, there was a vague, dirty outline of the symbol he wore over his heart.

"Very observant," Lander noted. "I'm surprised you recognized it."

"The Black Robes have told us how to identify a Harper. If I had seen your symbol before we entered the desert, it would have meant five hundred gold pieces."

"I'm glad my robe was not as dirty in your village," Lander answered, rubbing his palm over the patch of cloth that had given him away. "What else have the Zhentarim told you about the Harpers?"

"That you are a tribe of meddling fools who stand in the path of free commerce and the growth of kingdoms."

"That's wrong," Lander objected, shaking his head sternly. "We're a confederation of individuals dedicated to preserving the tales of those who have passed before us, to maintaining the balance between the wild and the civilized, and to protecting peaceful and free people everywhere in Faerun.

"The Harpers oppose the Zhentarim because they trade in slaves and because they hope to subvert the free nations of Faerun. We have nothing against peaceful commerce—as long as it doesn't involve treachery and slavery."

"Meddlers," Bhadla concluded gruffly, studying the sky with a manner of preoccupation.

"Perhaps," Lander conceded, also glancing heavenward. He was glad to see that the dusty haze had disappeared overhead, though the sky was but a turquoise imitation of its usual sapphire blue. "But we are meddlers with a purpose. Without us, all of Faerun would be slaves to the Zhentarim."

"So you say," Bhadla replied, returning his gaze to Lander's face. After a pause, he asked, "If the Harpers truly oppose the Black Robes, why didn't they send an army?"

"The Harpers don't have armies. We prefer more subtle methods."

"You mean you get others to do your work for you," Bhadla laughed.

Lander frowned. "We use our influence to guide events along the best course."

"The best course for the Harpers," the D'tarig insisted, pointing at the pin beneath the Sembian's robes with a leathery finger. "If you ask me, this time they've made a mistake. Sending one man to oppose an army is madness. No one would blame you if you deserted. They've ordered you to your death."

"I wasn't ordered to come here," Lander replied, adjusting his robe in a vain effort to cover the emblem's outline.

Looking confused, Bhadla withdrew his gaunt hand. "Did they send you or not?"

"I volunteered," Lander replied, remembering the informal meeting in which he had decided he would spy on the Zhentarim in Anauroch. It had been in Shadowdale, a wooded hamlet as different from this dismal wasteland as he could imagine. He had been sitting on the fringes of a comfortable gathering in the Old Skull Inn, staring at a roaring blaze lit to ward off the chill of an icy drizzle falling outside. Little had he known how he would come, in the months ahead, to long for just a few drops of that cold rain.

The company had been impressive. Next to the fire sat the beautiful Storm Silverhand, she of the silvery hair and the steely eyes. Beside her stood the tall man who had suggested Lander join the Harpers, Florin Falconhand. Across from Storm and Florin sat a burly, bearded man called only by his nickname, Urso, and the radiant High Lady of Silverymoon, Alustriel. There were others also— Lord Mourngrym and the ancient sage Elminster—not exactly members of the Harpers, but close enough that they felt more at ease in the distinguished company than Lander.

Over mugs of cool ale and goblets of hot spiced wine, they discussed the most recent item of concern to the Harpers. Zhentarim agents had been seen buying camels and skulking about the edges of the Anauroch, asking too many questions of D'tarig desert-walkers. There was a general consensus that the Zhentarim were making preparations for an expedition into the Great Desert and that someone should go see what they were doing. Whenever one of the elder Harpers said he would take the task upon himself, however, the others had grimly vetoed the suggestion, citing a hundred more important duties that he or she could not neglect.

It was Lander himself, sitting quietly on the edges of the crowd, who proposed the solution. He would go to Anauroch as the Harper's spy. The others protested that he did not have enough experience with the Zhentarim and that he was too young for such a dangerous assignment. Lander, tenacious and unyielding in his determination to prove his worth, insisted that he was capable of the task and pointed out that no one else could go. In the end, it was Florin's support that decided the issue. The lanky ranger simply place a hand on Lander's shoulder and nodded his head. As if at a signal, the others stopped arguing. The matter was decided.

What happened next surprised Lander. Lord Mourn-grym gave him the names and locations of a half-dozen men through whom he could send messages, and Storm Silverhand gave him a sack containing a hundred gold pieces and a half-dozen vials filled with magical healing potions. Observing that the hour had grown late, the ancient Elmin-ster rose, placed a surprisingly firm hand on Lander's shoulder, and assured him he would do well in Anauroch. The gathering broke up with as little formality as it had convened, each Harper pausing to wish their young comrade the best of luck.

The next morning, Florin saw him off, and Lander under-took his first important assignment as a Harper. Considering the formidable reputation of the secret society, the whole thing seemed incredibly casual and spontaneous, but he could not deny that its operations were efficient and quiet. Lander understood that things were a bit more organized and formal in Berdusk, where the Harpers maintained a secret base at Twilight Hall, but he preferred the less pretentious way of operating practiced in Shadowdale.

The fact that, other than Storm Silverhand's gift, Lander was expected to pay his own expenses while on assignment had not troubled him at all. One did not become a Harper in order to seek wealth or glory. Of course, Lander told none of this to Bhadla. Considering what the D'tarig had said about earning five hundred gold pieces by informing the Black Robes of a Harper's presence, the Sembian thought it would be better if Bhadla did not know that there was not much to be gained from his present master.

"Six months ago, the Harpers sent me to spy on the Zhentarim," Lander offered after a time. "I crossed the Desertsmouth Mountains, then traveled Anauroch's edge for four months posing as an incense trader. During this time, I saw little that would be of interest to the Harpers."

"So why didn't you go home?" Bhadla demanded, casting a watchful eye ahead to make sure that Musalim was not neglecting his duties as scout.

"I was about to," Lander continued, "but as I was leaving I learned of a group of Zhentarim who were buying whole herds of camels."

"Naturally, you went to investigate," Bhadla surmised.

"Yes, and what I found astounded me. The Zhentarim had gathered enough supplies at Tel Badir to equip a small army. At first, I couldn't imagine why, but I soon learned the reason through a few bribes," Lander explained.

"So you hired Musalim and me to help you find the Bedine," Bhadla concluded.

Lander nodded. "There you have it. That's what I'm doing in Anauroch."

Bhadla shook his head. "This is foolish business," he said. "It will probably get you killed."

"Perhaps," Lander agreed. "I'll try not to take you and Musalim with me."

"Good. For that, we would charge extra," Bhadla said, urging his camel forward. "I'd better check on Musalim.

He will lose the way if I leave him alone too long."

As the afternoon passed, the wind grew stronger, roaring with a menacing ferocity and carrying with it a pale cloud of blowing sand. This cloud streamed along only a few feet above the dunes, shooting off the crests in great plumes that rolled down the leeward slopes in magnificent, roiling billows.

The trio moved along the troughs between the great dunes, where the sand swept along the desert floor like a flood pouring across a dry creekbed. The heads of the riders and camels protruded above the white stream, but the sand rasped across the robes of the riders and scoured their exposed hands into a state of raw insensitivity.

Lander discretely checked his compass every few miles to make sure they were traveling in the right direction. Bhadla's knowledge of the desert proved unerring. He never varied more than a few degrees off-course, save when he led the small party around one of the mammoth dunes that periodically blocked their path.

At'ar sank steadily toward the horizon ahead, a great disk of blinding yellow light that turned the sea of dunes ahead into a foreboding labyrinth of silhouettes and dazzling yellow reflections. Finally the sun disappeared behind the dunes, curtaining the western horizon with a stark light of ruby and amber hues. A rosy blanket of ethereal light bloomed on the crests of the sand hills, while velvety shades of ebony and indigo spread through the troughs below.

Lander did not remember witnessing a more spectacular sunset, but he could not honestly call it beautiful. The sight left the Sembian in a bleak and lonely mood, for it only reminded him that he was a stranger in a dangerous and alien place.

Bhadla and Musalim stopped their camels and waited for Lander to catch up. The Harper quickly checked their heading on his compass, then, as his camel came abreast of theirs, he said, "There's no need to stop. Your course is the same as it has been all day."

Bhadla furrowed his leathery brow. "Of course," he said, pointing in the direction they were traveling. "I have been watching El Rahalat for the last hour."

Directly ahead, a gray triangular cloud the size of Lander's fingertip rose above the sands and stood silhouetted against the scarlet light of the setting sun.

"At the base of that mountain is a large oasis," Bhadla said, then he pointed northward. "Over there is a well, but the water is bitter and you must work hard to draw it. If there are any Bedine in the area, they will be at the mountain."

"That makes sense," Lander replied. "What are we waiting for?"

Bhadla glanced at the sky. "Not many stars tonight," he said. "I will lose my way after dark."

"I'll let you know if we're straying," Lander answered.

"A mistake will cost us our lives," Musalim warned. "I don't trust your instincts."

"I'll be using something better than instincts," Lander replied, "but I won't make a mistake. You just keep your eyes open. If we're going to beat the Zhentarim to the oasis, we'll start overtaking stragglers."

"Yes," Bhadla agreed, nodding. "We have made good time and could catch them at any moment."

"It's too dangerous," Musalim said, an air of resignation in his voice. "We should wait." Despite his protests, he urged his camel forward and once more assumed the lead position.

Bhadla watched his assistant for a few moments, then asked, "How will you be certain of your directions? Magic?"

"Yes," Lander replied, justifying the lie by telling himself that a compass would seem like magic to the D'tarig.

Bhadla nodded, then finally urged his camel forward. "If I sense that we are straying," he called over his shoulder, "Musalim and I will stop."

Lander followed twenty yards behind Bhadla, checking his compass every few minutes. At'ar disappeared, and the faint glow of the full moon appeared above the eastern horizon. Overhead, a few stars penetrated the dust cloud, but they were too dim and too few to identify. It became more difficult for Lander to read his compass, but the milky light of the moon was just bright enough to illuminate the needle.

As the night darkened, Lander worried more about the Zhentarim. Trusting his camel to find its own footing, he spent the minutes between compass checks anxiously peering into the torrent of blowing sand, searching for the faintest silhouette or the barest hint of motion. He saw nothing but an endless cataract of sand sweeping over the dunes and across the path ahead.

The wind picked up speed and raised the height of the sandstream, stinging Lander's one good eye and rubbing his face raw. Unable to see anyway, the Harper covered his face with his hands, placing his complete faith in his camel to follow Bhadla and Musalim. Every now and then, he would pass close to the lee side of a great dune. Sheltered from the wind and blowing sand, he would quickly read the compass and check to make sure that the dark silhouettes of his guides were still ahead. A few minutes later, he would pass the dune and the driving sand would force him to close his eye again.

The trio followed the troughs northward for what seemed an endless time, and the sandstorm grew worse. Lander finished the last of his water, and then waged a constant battle with himself not to think about drinking. Grit and silt clogged his throat and nose. He could not keep his mind off the oasis ahead.

The storm grew worse. Even when sheltered by a great dune's leeward side, the sand blew so hard that Lander could only keep his eye open for periods of five and ten seconds. He began to worry about losing sight of his companions and wondered if, even with its protective eyelids, his camel could see well enough to follow its fellows. He urged his mount to move faster, but no matter how hard he prodded the beast, it would do no better than the steady stride into which it had fallen.

Sensing that his mount was too frightened of losing its footing to trot, Lander tried yelling to his companions. "Bhadla! Musalim!" No reply followed. He tried again, but the wind drowned out his screams. He finally gave up when his voice grew hoarse, hoping that the D'tarig would wait for him. Bhadla's probably noticed how much visibility had decreased already, Lander decided. He's probably just ahead, trying to catch Musalim.

The hope that his companions were nearby was short-lived. Lander entered the shelter of a dune and peered into the night. In the darkness ahead, there was no sign of Bhadla or Musalim. Turning his back to the blowing sand, he quickly checked his compass and saw that he was still on course.

Lander cursed his guides for leaving their charge behind, then urged his camel forward. As he passed out of the little shelter that the great dune had afforded, he tried to shield his face with his hand and forced himself to keep his eye open.

Blowing sand and darkness was all he saw.

At last Lander closed his eye and stopped to consider his options. At the most, he knew, his companions could only be a hundred yards away. In the dark and the storm, the distance might as well have been a hundred miles. Trying to track them would be as useless as trying to out-scream the blustering wind.

With his compass, he could easily continue toward the oasis, but that would not help him locate his companions. They might have lost their bearings and be riding in a completely different direction. In that case, his own movement would simply put more distance between them.

The best thing I can do, Lander realized, is wait as close as possible to the point where we separated. Perhaps Bhadla will be able to retrace his steps when he realizes that I've disappeared.

As the Harper turned his camel toward the shelter of the great dune behind him, he heard a camel's bellow to his right. Though the roar was faint and muted by the wind, Lander cringed. There was a note of urgency and terror to the bray that no storm could muffle.

He started forward in what he guessed to be the general direction of the sound. In the howling wind, one roar alone would hardly be enough to lead him to his companions, but it was all Lander had to follow. Besides, it occurred to him that his guides might be tormenting the beast so that its cries would lead him to them.

Lander rode a hundred steps forward and stopped. No bellows sounded. He turned his head to and fro, trying catch a glimpse of a silhouette or the hint of some sound other than the interminable wind. There was nothing.

Finally the Sembian glimpsed a bulky shadow stumbling toward him. He urged his mount forward when he saw that it was a limping camel. When he came closer still, Lander recognized the beast as Musalim's and went forward to grasp its reins. The saddle was empty, and the camel seemed dazed and weak.

Lander inspected the beast from his own camel. There were no wounds, but a dark blotch stained the saddle. He touched the stain and found it warm and sticky. Musalim's blood, he guessed. Lander dropped the dazed beast's reins and drew his sword.

When he turned back toward the place from which Musalim's camel had come, the Harper glimpsed a shadow rising out of the sand. It was about the size of a man, but the legs and arms seemed to stick from the body at peculiar angles, like a reptile's.

Lander needed to see no more to know that Musalim, and probably Bhadla too, had ridden into an ambush. The Sembian slapped the flat of his sword against his camel's shoulder, but the sluggish beast refused to charge. The shadow raised a crossbow and a pair of yellow, egg-shaped eyes flashed in the dark night.

The bolt took Lander below the right collarbone, nearly knocking him from his saddle. His arm went numb, and the sword dropped from his hand. Grasping the reins with his left hand, the Sembian jerked his camel around. The beast reacted slowly, resentful of Lander's harsh manipulations. Two more shadows rose out of the blowing sand.

"Turn, you stubborn scion of Malar!"

A bolt struck the camel's flank, and Lander felt the beast quiver. It decided to obey and sprang away with the proper sense of urgency.

The wounded Harper dropped the reins and slumped forward, sprawling face-down over the beast's hump. Agony assaulted him in crashing waves, but Lander hardly realized it. He was only dimly aware of his knees squeezing his mount's hump and the fingers of his good hand clutching its coat. Lander could not tell how long the camel continued to gallop. He knew only the agony in his chest, the warm wetness trickling down his arm, and the black waves assaulting his mind.

Eventually, the camel slowed to a trot. It could have been hours after the ambush or just minutes. Lander could not tell. He tried to sit upright and realized the effort would leave him unconscious. He settled for holding on.

At last the camel collapsed. It did not lie down or even

stop moving. The beast just belched forth a plaintive moan, stumbled once on its buckling legs, then, in midstride, it pitched Lander face-first into the sand.

They lay together in a twisted heap, the camel wheezing in shallow gasps and Lander moaning in disjointed pain. The sand worked its way into their wounds and welled up against their windward sides, but neither the man nor the beast showed any sign of caring. Soon, the camel stopped panting, and Lander was alone in the storm.

Four

By dawn the god of tempests, Kozah, had vented his wrath. The storm died, leaving a hot, dreary calm in its place. The heavy, windborne sand dropped back to the ground, but a pall of silt lingered high in the heavens, diffusing At'ar's morning radiance and setting the eastern horizon ablaze with crimson light. Ruha knew it would be many more days before the dust returned to the ground and Kozah's mark disappeared from the morning sky.

The widow went to the oasis pond and knelt at its edge, then rinsed the night's grit from her mouth. She and Kadumi had spent the night huddled under the remnants of her *khreima*, but the wind had worked its way under the heavy camel-hair tarp, covering her *aba* with sand and coating her nose and mouth with dust. More than once during the night, she had awakened with the feeling of being suffocated and found herself spitting out a mouthful of powdery silt.

Kadumi came and stood behind Ruha until she put her

veil back in place, then kneeled beside her and splashed water over his grimy face. "Kozah must be angry with At'ar again," the boy said. "Maybe he saw the faithless harlot entering N'asr's tent. I have not seen such a storm in a year." He looked toward the camp.

The boy's camels were couched near where he and Ruha had slept, though so much sand had gathered against their windward sides that they looked more like a string of miniature dunes than a line of dromedaries. Beyond the half-buried beasts, the fallen tents of the Qahtani were covered by small knolls of sand. The only clue to what lay beneath the drifts were protruding bits of dyed cloth. Mounds of yellow sand buried even the stone-covered graves Ruha and Kadumi had dug for Ajaman and his father's family.

"I don't think Kozah is angry with At'ar," Ruha said, astounded by how tranquil the oasis looked compared to the gruesome scene she and Kadumi had found yesterday. "I think he is offended by the sight of the massacre."

Kadumi's mouth tightened, and he surveyed the oasis with narrowed eyes. "Then let us hope we can reach your father's tribe before this caravan of fork-tongued monsters," he said. "It would not be good if they made Kozah angry again."

The boy glanced at the sky for several moments, then looked back to Ruha and said, "With the dust from yesterday's storm still hanging in the sky, at least it will be a cool day. We'll trot our mounts. With luck, we won't lose them."

Ruha caught his arm, concerned. Pushing camels hard over long distances dehydrated them, which could be fatal for both animal and rider if they happened to collapse too far from water.

"Do you think it's wise to take such a risk?" she asked. "Even with favorable weather and extra mounts, we're a day and a half behind the caravan. If the drivers know where they're going and want to get there fast, we can ride all your camels to death only to find more corpses at Rahalat."

"The Mtair Dhafir are allies of the Qahtan. It would be dishonorable not to alert them to the danger," Kadumi said, freeing his arm. "Besides, I thought you'd want to warn your father's tribe."

"I do, but I don't want to die trying—especially since the strangers could already be there.".

"The caravan might have reached Rahalat already," Kadumi conceded, "but I don't think so. Whoever they are, they're not from Anauroch, so I don't think it'll be easy for them to find the shunned mountain."

"They found El Ma'ra easily enough," Ruha pointed out.

Kadumi scowled. "Is there some reason you don't want to go to the Mtair Dhafir?"

Behind her veil, Ruha bit her lip. Her brother-in-law was right, she realized. She was not anxious to return to the Mtair Dhafir because of the reception she would receive. Forcing herself to put aside her anxiety, the widow shook her head. "No, we must warn my father's tribe. I just don't want to risk our lives for no reason."

"The caravan might be slower than you think," he said, "or it might not know about Rahalat. We can't tell about these things. The only thing we can do is get there as fast as we can."

Kadumi turned toward his camels again. This time Ruha followed, feeling a little foolish at being lectured by a thirteen-year-old boy.

They wasted little time preparing to leave. While Kadumi watered his animals and filled half-a-dozen waterskins, Ruha packed some food and their belongings into a pair of *kuerabiches*. After tying the sacks onto a saddle, the pair mounted and, ignoring the bellowed protests of the camels, started westward at a trot.

The storm had spread a deep layer of shifting sand over the ground, but the unsteady footing did not bother their mounts. With the broad, fleshy pads of their feet, the camels sank less than two inches with each step and barely slowed their pace. Ruha and Kadumi rode all day, changing mounts every hour to avoid exhausting them. Other than these brief pauses, they did not stop. By midday, they had reached the region of the great white dunes, and by dusk Rahalat was poking its gray crown above the horizon.

They stopped long enough to eat a meal of camel's milk and sun-dried fruits in weary silence, then continued their bone-jarring ride in the dark. They circled a few miles north, just to be sure that they did not overtake either the caravan or the one-eyed stranger. The pair did not stop or allow themselves any rest until the moon's milky light began to fade and their sore backs felt like they would crack with the next step. When they did lie down, covering themselves only with their night cloaks, they did not even notice the bone-chilling cold.

They rose with At'ar and continued westward in the dawn's ruddy light. Rahalat now loomed directly ahead, its gray crags obscuring the largest part of the western horizon. Ruha could even see the shunned mountain's familiar slopes of loose rock and the boulders strewn about its base. Remembering that they had been nearly seventy miles away at this time the previous morning, the widow found it difficult to believe they had come so far so quickly.

Ruha and Kadumi rode for several more hours, and the sand gave way to stony ridges. As they started up the first rise at the base of the mountain, an *amarat* sounded. The pair stopped their camels side-by-side and waited for someone to challenge them.

"We made it," Kadumi announced. "If guards are posted, there's still a tribe."

As he spoke, a short, gaunt sentry appeared from the

other side of the ridge. He waved Ruha and Kadumi the last hundred yards up the hill, then awaited them with his hands on his hips.

As the widow and her brother-in-law reached the summit, Ruha recognized the sentry as Al'Aif, a ferocious warrior who had killed more men than anyone else in the tribe. The left side of his face was marred by four red scars where a lion had mauled him, and a sentry's dagger had left his right eyelid folded over at the corner. Al'Aif was also one of the men who had insisted that Ruha be banished from the tribe.

For the moment, Al'Aif seemed content to ignore Ruha. He eyed Kadumi's string of white camels appreciatively. "A fine string of *goouds*," he commented to the boy, using the special term that applied to mature camels. "I have heard that the sheikh of the Bordjias lost ten white camels."

Kadumi smiled proudly. "He did not lose them. Kadumi of the Qahtan took them," the boy bragged.

The frank admission elicited an appreciative smile. "The Bordjias are our allies," Al'Aif said. "I hope you did not kill many men when you stole them."

Kadumi shrugged. "No, not many."

Al'Aif chuckled at the boy's swagger, then eyed Ruha. "I thought the Mtair Dhafir rid of you."

"And I of them," she answered, lifting her chin. "But I return out of duty, not desire, Al'Aif."

Kadumi frowned at the apparent enmity between the two. "We are all that remains of the Qahtan. We have come to warn your sheikh of the danger that destroyed our tribe."

Al'Aif raised an eyebrow. "Does this danger have to do with black-robed men and a caravan larger than ten tribes?"

"How did you know?" Ruha and Kadumi asked together.

Al'Aif pointed to the south. "They are camped at the Bitter Well. They have sent two jackals with tongues of sugared water to speak of alliances." The Mtair gestured at one of Kadumi's camels, then said, "If you'll lend me a ride, I'll take you to camp. I want the sheikh to speak with you as soon as possible."

Al'Aif led the party to a gulch filled with the drooping, twiggy branches of *ghaf* trees and lined with tasseled sedges of *qassis* bushes. The tinkle of a tiny stream rang from the bottom of the draw, and the camels, thirsty from yesterday's hard ride, bellowed angrily at not being allowed to stop and drink.

As the trio rode into camp, the old women and the children gathered outside their tents. When Ruha passed, many of them hissed and trilled disapprovingly. One little boy even yelled at her to go away.

Kadumi's outrage showed on his scowling face. "This is a disgrace," he uttered, addressing Al'Aif. "Do the Mtair Dhafir treat all their guests so wretchedly?"

"They do not mean to offend you," Ruha said. "Their disdain is for me alone. There is something you should—"

Al'Aif lifted a hand to silence her. "They believe Ruha has shamed the tribe by violating her *purdah*," said the gaunt Mtair. "To them, it looks as if she is returning to her father."

The older warrior's words satisfied Kadumi. "Of course," the boy said, smiling and nodding to the angry women. "I should have realized how her return would look to such an honorable tribe."

Behind the boy's back, Ruha raised an eyebrow to Al'Aif. The last thing she had expected him to do was lie on her behalf. The Mtair responded with a quick shrug, then nodded toward her father's tent and continued forward. Ruha could not guess the meaning of the gaunt warrior's gesture.

Outside the sheikh's *khreima*, they left their camels with a herdboy. Al'Aif entered the tent without announcement, as was the right of any warrior in the Mtair Dhafir. He motioned for Ruha and Kadumi to follow.

Inside, Ruha's father sat upon a gaily colored ground carpet at the far end of the tent. He was a bony old man with cloudy eyes and a wispy gray beard. Across from him sat a man wearing a black burnoose. Though his face was swaddled in a turban, the cloth had been pulled down to reveal a silky mustache and sharp features. In front of each man sat a small silver cup filled with hot salted coffee.

Behind the stranger stood a second man, this one with skin and hair as pale as white sand. A hooded robe of deep purple hung off his shoulders, and a pair of silver bracers encircled his wrists. He held himself in the humble posture of a servant, but when his flashing blue eyes inspected Ruha and her companions, the widow immediately suspected that this man was more than he wished to seem.

The sheikh and the seated stranger continued speaking in low, muted tones, neither appearing to notice the trio's presence.

Al'Aif stepped forward. "Sheikh Sabkhat," he called.

Ruha's father scowled. Addressing the seated man, he said, "Excuse me, El Zarud." As the sheikh looked in the trio's direction, his eyes seemed glazed and vacant. "What?"

Al'Aif pointed at Kadumi and Ruha. "I bring visitors from the Qahtan," he said. "They have come to warn you about the strangers."

"Warn me?" the sheikh frowned. "Of what? The Zhentarim are our friends." He waved a hand to dismiss the trio, then looked back to Zarud with a smile.

Kadumi's jaw dropped, and he seemed too surprised at the sheikh's rudeness to speak.

The gaunt Mtair turned to Ruha. "I have never seen him

like this." Al'Aif put his mouth close to the widow's ear so that Kadumi would not hear his question, then whispered, "Is it magic?"

Ruha now understood why the gaunt warrior had lied to Kadumi. He believed the strangers were using magic to influence the sheikh and wanted her to confirm his suspicions. The widow placed her veiled lips next to the scarred man's ear, then whispered, "I had never thought to see the day when the mighty Al'Aif asked a witch for help."

The Mtair shrugged sheepishly. "The enemy of my enemy is my friend," he said, repeating an old Bedine saying. "Now, tell me what you can about what is happening here."

Kadumi frowned at their secretive exchange, but the boy still seemed too confused by the sheikh's behavior to question his companions.

Ruha looked toward the other end of the tent and noticed the pale stranger watching her with his stony eyes. When she met his gaze, the man did not look away.

"Well?" Al'Aif prodded.

The widow studied her glassy-eyed father for a few moments. The sheikh was listening intently to the muted words of the seated stranger and was repeatedly nodding his head in agreement. Her father had always been a careful listener, but there was something in the steady rhythm of his bobbing head that made her think he was not so much listening as being mesmerized. She had no way of telling for sure, but it seemed to her that something had separated her father from his wits.

Ruha looked to the Mtair and nodded.

"As I thought!" Before the widow realized what was happening, Al'Aif drew his *jambiya* and started toward other side of the tent. "Out, dogs and sons of dogs!" he yelled. "Release the sheikh, or your brothers will lap your blood from the carpet!"

"Al'Aif!" roared Ruha's father. "You dare defile the hospitality of my *khreima*?"

The sheikh's protest did not slow the warrior. In four steps, he was at the back of the seated stranger, the blade of his weapon pressed against the man's throat. "Forgive me, Sheikh," he said, "but they have used magic. You're under their power."

"Don't be foolish," snapped the sheikh.

The pale stranger frowned in concentration, then began to fumble about in the pockets of his robe. Guessing that he was preparing to cast a spell, Ruha reached for her own dagger and started across the room. Before the widow had gone two steps, Kadumi dashed past her and pressed the tip of his *jambiya* against the belly of the purple-robed man.

"If your hand is not empty when it comes out," the youth said, "my knife will search for your heart."

The sheikh rose and started toward Al'Aif. "I will not allow this!"

Ruha intercepted the old man. "Listen to Al'Aif, Father."

The sheikh's eyes seemed to clear. "Ruha?"

"Yes."

Her father closed his eyes for a long moment. When he opened them, they seemed vacant once again. "What are you doing here, Daughter?" His voice was a bit too calm. "Why aren't you with your husband?"

"I am a widow," she replied, glaring at the purple-robed man Kadumi still held at bay.

The sheikh sighed deeply. "I am sorry to hear that, Daughter," he said. "But your place is still with the Qahtan. They are your tribe now."

"I *am* with the Qahtan," Ruha replied, motioning to Kadumi. "This is my husband's brother. He and I are all that remain."

Zarud scowled, but when he tried to speak Al'Aif pressed the knife more tightly against his throat.

"How can this be?" asked Ruha's father, his brow knotted in confusion.

"The Zhentarim massacred them," Al'Aif said. "Isn't that so, Zarud?"

The dark-robed man did not respond, but the question drew the sheikh's attention back to his guests. "How many times must I command you to release my guests, Al'Aif?" He acted as if he had not even heard the accusation made against the Zhentarim agents.

"A hundred times will not be enough, my sheikh," the warrior responded. "Not while they are using magic." He drew Zarud's head back, then scraped the blade along the captive's throat as if shaving him. "Tell Sheikh Sabkhat you've been using magic," he said. "Tell him or die."

It was the pale stranger who Kadumi guarded that answered. "Your man speaks the truth, Sheikh. We meant no harm. I cast a spell so we could speak your language. That was all." The stranger glanced at Ruha and frowned, then turned his attention back to her father. "Please accept my apologies if we offended you."

The old sheikh looked from his daughter to Al'Aif to the pale stranger, then dropped his gaze to the ground and shook his head in confusion. He remained that way for several moments, and they all waited for his response in silence.

Finally he turned toward Zarud. "No tribe has abided magic in all the generations since the Scattering," he said.

"The Scattering?" asked the pale man.

"My father told me that once there were three great tribes of Bedine," the sheikh said, beginning the explanation with the words traditionally used to denote a myth. "The sheikhs of these Three Ancient Tribes dreamed of ruling all the people, and so they had their sorcerers summon N'asr's denizens to make war upon each other. The war destroyed the land and gave birth to Anauroch. It took the gods themselves to set the world right again, and some of them died before the carnage could be stopped."

Al'Aif interrupted and bruskly finished the account. "The surviving gods scattered the Three Tribes to the corners of the world and forbade them to ever use magic again," he said, glaring at the purple-robed stranger. "That is why you must leave, Zhentarim."

The pale man ignored Al'Aif and looked to Ruha's father. "We are outsiders and did not know your customs, Sheikh Sabkhat. Surely we can be forgiven for this small mistake."

The sheikh nodded at the stranger's words, then began, "What you say is true. Perhaps we can overlook—"

"Father!" Ruha interrupted, locking gazes with him. "How can you make an exception for them?"

As the widow had hoped, her father found it difficult to reconcile making an exception for his guests when he had not made one for his daughter. He looked away, half-heartedly mumbling, "They don't know our customs."

"Were they unaware that it is not customary to attack a tribe with no cause?" Ruha pressed. "Will you ignore the oaths you swore with the Qahtan and make peace with those who slaughtered them?"

The sheikh looked to his daughter in horrified disbelief, then turned to Zarud. "Is this true?"

Zarud looked to the pale man.

"If you lie, my knife will open your stomach," Kadumi threatened, moving the blade toward the stranger's solar plexus.

Still speaking in an amiable, melodious voice, the pale Zhentarim said, "Lord Zarud made the same offer to the Qahtan that he presented to you. They refused."

"And you massacred them," Ruha finished spitefully.

The man shrugged, and an artificial smile crept across his lips. "You and the boy are alive. That is what's important, is it not?" He turned to Ruha's father and inclined his head respectfully. "Lord Zarud has extended the hand of the Zhentarim in friendship. You may ask the Qahtani about the consequences of refusing it." Even as he uttered the warning, his words remained as sweet as nectar.

The threat seemed to kindle a light in the old sheikh's eyes, but they grew confused and vacant again almost immediately. He turned toward Zarud, then said, "This is not a decision I can make alone. I will consult with the elders tomorrow, and then we will give you our decision. Until then, you may stay as a guest in my camp."

Zarud nodded. "I am confident you will make a wise decision."

Without looking away from Zarud, Ruha's father pointed at the pale man. "Your servant—if that is what he truly is—must go. He has used magic in my tent, and that I cannot abide."

Zarud looked panicked. "How will we talk?"

The pale man raised a hand to comfort his fellow. "Whatever the answer may be, I am sure Sheikh Sabkhat will make it known to you." He gave Ruha a long, thoughtful glance, then continued, "If my presence makes our host uneasy, then it would be better if I left. Perhaps you will walk me to my camel and tell me what I should relay to our masters—provided, of course, that the sheikh can secure our release."

Ruha's father scowled at Al'Aif. "The time has come to release our guests, unless you intend to kill them against my wishes."

The gaunt warrior reluctantly nodded to Kadumi, then they both stepped away from their captives. Neither one of them sheathed their weapons until the two Zhentarim had left the *khreima*.

Ruha's father returned to his seat, then held his head in his hands for several minutes. When the sheikh finally looked up, his face was ashen and his brow drooping with fatigue. The light had returned to his eyes, though, and the widow could tell that her father had regained control of his own will.

"Are you well, Sheikh?" asked Al'Aif.

"Who can say? I thought I was well before, but my judgment was apparently clouded," the old man answered. He turned to his daughter with genuine hurt in his eyes, then said, "Ruha, I cannot tell you how sad it makes me to see you here."

Ruha understood exactly what her father meant. As a man, he loved his daughter. At the same time, he was the tribe's sheikh and her presence would open a wide schism in the gathered families. Her return could only force him to make a decision as painful for him as it would be for her.

"Don't be sad for me, Father," the widow said. "I only returned to warn you of the danger that destroyed the Qahtan. I have no wish to burden the Mtair Dhafir."

Kadumi betrayed his bewilderment at this comment by furrowing his brow, but he politely waited for the sheikh to address him and did not say anything.

The sheikh pondered Ruha's answer for a moment, then wearily nodded his head. "You have always performed your duty well." He turned to Kadumi and raised an eyebrow.

"This is Kadumi," Ruha said, reacting to her father's signal of interest. "He is a son of the same mother as Ajaman."

The sheikh nodded grimly. "The Mtair Dhafir always have need of another blade. Al'Aif will make you welcome in his tent, I am sure."

Kadumi's eyes lit, and he could not restrain a proud smile, for the sheikh was treating him as a full warrior. Nevertheless, the youth glanced toward Ruha. "You are kind, but in my brother's absence, I must watch over his wife."

The young widow and Al'Aif grimaced simultaneously.

Reaching for her brother-in-law's arm, the widow said, "Kadumi, perhaps there is something I should say to you—"

The sheikh waved a weary hand to cut her off. "Say it later," he ordered. Turning to the boy, he said, "Ruha will be weicome in the *khreimas* of her father for as long as she cares to stay. Now, you will excuse us. I must hear exactly what happened to the Qahtan."

Five

Ruha spent the next two hours describing to her father what had happened to the Qahtan. Listening with growing concern, the old sheikh repeatedly interrupted her with questions, especially when she described the white bolt that had killed Ajaman and the lizardlike humanoids that had led the attack. When the widow at last finished the story, her father made her repeat the entire thing to be sure she hadn't missed anything.

Finally he shook his weary head. "The strangers speak with the honeyed tongues of bees, but it seems their bite carries the venom of a scorpion. I doubt we can trust them to keep their treaty, but I fear what they will do if we do not agree to it. This will be a difficult decision."

With that, he sent a messenger to summon the elders to council, then instructed his servant to take Ruha to her *khreima*. The boy led her to a small tent that had been erected a hundred yards outside the camp circle. Had she been a normal guest, one of her father's wives would have invited the young widow to stay in her tent. Instead, Ruha knew, this *khreima* had been erected especially for her.

The tent was large enough to hold ten or twelve people. It had been stocked with several carpets, a *kuerabiche* to use as a pillow, and an empty waterskin. Though exhausted from last night's long ride and the interrogation her father had given her, Ruha took the waterskin and went toward the spring. If she did not fill it before she went to sleep, she would have nothing to drink when she woke, hot and thirsty, in the afternoon heat.

As the widow approached the gully, she realized that something was wrong. Instead of the lyrical babble of the spring, she heard the raucous cries of alarmed birds. Ruha's first thought was that the Zhentarim were coming to attack, but she quickly realized that was impossible. She had heard no warning *amarat* horns, and it was inconceivable that an entire army had sneaked past the Mtair sentries in broad daylight.

Ruha crept along the edge of the ravine toward the alarmed birds. She moved slowly and cautiously, for she had long ago learned the value of prudence in the desert. It took fifteen minutes of crawling on hands and knees, carefully staying hidden behind the thin cover of *qassis* bushes, to reach the disturbance.

When she finally peered over the edge of the gulch, the widow gasped at what she saw lying ten yards below, in the bottom of the ravine. A dozen larks were perched in the twigs of the *ghaf* trees lining the small stream, screeching madly at a figure lying face-down in the stream. He wore a sand-colored *aba* and his *keffiyeh* was nowhere to be seen. Ruha immediately realized that he was no Bedine, for his head was topped by long golden hair.

The widow watched the motionless man for a moment, wondering how he had managed to sneak past her father's sentries. Ruha concluded that he must have come during the night. She started to back away, intending to summon her father's warriors.

The man lifted his head, cocking it as if to listen. It was then that Ruha realized she had seen him before. A black patch covered his left eye, and the pale skin of his face was red and blistered with sunburn. He was the man she had seen in her vision, who had appeared on the wake of the Zhentarim army.

A short, featherless arrow protruded from his right breast, and there was a dark stain below the wound. Ruha recognized the short shaft as being similar to the ones that had been used to slaughter the Qahtan. It appeared that the one-eyed *berrani* was no friend of the Zhentarim. That made the man her ally, for, as Al'Aif had whispered to her earlier that day, "the enemy of my enemy is my friend."

As Ruha contemplated what to do next, the stranger astonished her by looking in her direction. Ruha had not made the slightest sound while watching the man, and felt confident that she was well-concealed behind the lip of the gulch and the *qassis* bush. Yet the wounded man clearly knew she was there. Automatically she lifted a hand to make sure her veil was in place.

The *berrani* called to her. "Bedine, I have come to warn your people—the Zhentarim are coming."

Though his words were strained and weak, he spoke in unaccented Bedine. Ruha wondered whether he knew the same magic that Zarud and his purple-robed companion had been using to communicate, or if he had learned the language from some other tribe.

Without replying to the stranger, Ruha went down the slope, then rolled him onto his back. He had cracked, bleeding lips and a face haggard with the effects of dehydration. The wound was more serious than it had appeared from atop the ravine, for the *berrani* had torn both his *aba* and his flesh trying to pull the barbed shaft from his shoulder.

"Who are you?" she asked at last, filling her hands with water from the tiny stream.

The wounded man allowed her to pour the water into his mouth, then said, "I'm called Lander." The effort of talking drained his strength, but he continued to speak. "I've come to warn your tribe—"

"The Zhentarim are here. There is no need to warn us."

Looking alarmed, Lander summoned his strength and gasped, "They have already wiped out one tribe!"

"Save your strength," the widow said, holding her fingers over the stranger's mouth. "We know."

"But you don't—"

Ruha used her fingers to close his eyes. "I said to save your strength." With her free hand, she took a pinch of fine sand and sprinkled it over the man's face. "Sleep," she whispered, following her order with a spell that guaranteed he would obey.

After filling her waterskin, Ruha rolled Lander onto his side and whispered an incantation. The man's robe flapped as the breeze grew stronger and slipped beneath his body. Soon he hovered a foot off the ground, his weight buoyed by the wind beneath his back. The widow took the stranger's arm, then pulled him up the gulch in the general direction of camp. When she judged they were roughly even with her *khreima*, she left him floating in the bottom of the gulch and climbed to its edge to peer at the camp, a hundred and fifty yards away.

From what she could see, the women were busy with their weaving and the children were either with the camel herds or playing inside the main circle of tents. Neither Zarud nor any of the men were anywhere in sight, and everyone else was studiously ignoring her tent.

Breathing a sigh of relief, Ruha went back to Lander and

towed him out of the gulch. The last thing she wanted was to get caught using her magic, and she suspected it would also be better if Zarud remained ignorant of Lander's presence. Keeping a wary eye cast in the direction of camp, she pulled him to the back side of her tent, raised the camel-hair wall, and pushed him inside. Only then did she cancel the spell and let him drop to the ground.

Ruha entered the tent from the front, then dragged the stranger farther into the tent, where she could attend to his wound. Even in his magically induced sleep, Lander's face was drawn and contorted with pain. Ruha had the urge to look beneath his eye-patch, but resisted the temptation. If she were the one lying unconscious and wounded, she would not want him to lift her veil, so it only seemed fair to respect his privacy. Instead, she pulled the *berrani's* dagger from its sheath. Unlike her own *jambiya*, it had a straight blade that would be more useful for the tasks at hand.

Ruha cut the dirty robes away from the wound and removed a diamond-shaped amulet of gold from around his neck so she could inspect the wound. The featherless arrow had entered just below the collarbone. The flesh surrounding the black shaft was puffy and red. Lander had tried to work the arrow out by himself, and the edges of the wound were torn and raw. He had enlarged the puncture enough so that Ruha could almost see the head, buried deep within the sinews that held his shoulder and collarbone together. The flesh surrounding the head oozed pus and deep red blood.

The widow tugged gently on the shaft and saw why the *berrani* had not been able to extract it. The end of a barb poked its sharp tip through a muscle. Lander did not stir at all, and the young widow was glad his stupor would spare him the pain that would accompany what she had to do next.

Ruha had never before extracted an arrow from a man's flesh, but she did not feel queasy or hesitant. Like all Bedine, she had learned to clean game and butcher meat at a young age, and human flesh was not so different from that of a hare or a camel. Moreover, during her years with Qoha'dar, she and the old woman had had no one but each other to rely upon in the event of trouble. More than once, Ruha had set a bone or sewn up a gash for her mentor.

Grasping the shaft with her left hand, she used the other to tug gently at the arrow. When the barb appeared beneath a large sinew, she gently pushed the arrow back into the flesh and turned it a few degrees, then pulled up again. This time the tip showed through a mass of mangled red flesh. She guided the tip of the dagger down the arrow shaft until it reached the barb. With a quick flick, she severed the strands of meat holding the arrow in Lander's shoulder.

Ruha pulled the shaft free, and the *berrani* gasped in his sleep. She tossed the grisly arrow aside and pressed her palm against Lander's lips. He immediately returned to his stuporous sleep, and the young widow ripped a piece of cloth off the hem of his *aba*. She soaked it with water from the skin she had filled at the spring, then wiped the blood and grime out of the wound. The flesh she had cut to extract the dagger was still oozing blood, so she rolled the cloth into a small ball and pressed it into the puncture.

The widow ripped another piece of cloth from Lander's robe, soaked it, and cleaned the flesh surrounding the wound. Where it was not inflamed and red from the trauma of the injury, the *berrani*'s skin was as pale and milky as the moon. Had anyone told Ruha that a man could be so white, she would have imagined a grotesque, inhuman disfigurement. On Lander, however, the color seemed a creamy complement to his blue eye and golden hair. The young widow had to restrain herself from laying a hand on his chest to see if his skin felt as soft as it looked.

Disconcerted by her unexpected surge of curiosity, Ruha dressed the wound with the cloth she had used to clean it. When she removed Lander's cloth belt to use as a bandage, she heard something jingle in the pocket of his robe. She reached inside and found six glass vials. Five contained a thick golden liquid, but the sixth was empty. The widow had no idea what the fluid was, but she feared the unconscious man would roll over and shatter the containers, so she laid the vials aside.

After Ruha finished bandaging the dressing into place, she laid down in a corner, pulled a sleeping carpet over herself, and closed her eyes with her veil still covering her face. Later, when her father was not surrounded by the gossiping elders on the council, she would go to him and tell him of the *berrani*.

At dusk Ruha awoke. For a few minutes, she laid beneath her carpet, listening to the doves coo and the quail chatter as they watered in the gulch. From the camp came the roars of thirsty camels and the shrill voices of tired mothers ordering neglectful children to fetch the evening's water.

Lander lay just as the widow had left him, on his back, with his belt holding his blood spotted bandage in place. He remained so motionless that Ruha began to worry her surgery had killed him. Finally he drew a great deep breath, and Ruha knew that he was alive.

The widow rose and rubbed the sleep from her eyes, then took a long drink from the waterskin. When she finished, she placed it next to her patient in case he woke, straightened her *aba*, and left the tent.

Ruha went straight to her father's tent. As she passed through the camp, she could see that it was an unusual evening. The camel herds were tethered close to the tents, as if they were going to be loaded at any moment. The women were not quite packing, but they were arranging their possessions in neat bundles, as if they expected the order to leave at any moment. The eldest sons were sharpening their father's scimitars and testing bowstrings, casting anxious glances in the direction of the sheikh's *khreima*.

When she reached her father's tent, Ruha stopped outside the entrance. The elders were inside with the sheikh, as were several of the tribe's best warriors. All were arguing loudly. Loudest among the voices was Al'Aif's.

"The invaders will make drudges of our camels and slaves of our warriors," he declared. "I would rather die with my enemy's blood on my blade."

"And would you also leave your wife and daughters to the Zhentarim and their beasts?" countered an elder's shrill voice. "If we refuse the treaty, we perish like the Qahtan."

"But neither can we ignore our pact with the Qahtan. We swore that their enemies were ours," cried a sonorous voice that could only belong to the tribe's strongest man, Nata. "So let us scatter the women and children in the desert. With so many men and beasts, the invaders need a lot of water. We'll poison the wells within a hundred miles. The invaders will die within a week."

"What will we drink?" queried an elder. "And what will the other tribes think of us? Surely they will all swear a blood feud against us for such a sacrilege."

"The witch has brought this upon us," said a warrior. "Just as she brought it upon the Qahtan."

"Fool, do you think the Zhentarim will disappear when she leaves us?" demanded Al'Aif. "We must be concerned with the invaders, not her."

Ruha listened to the argument for several minutes and realized that it had long ago degenerated into angry shouting and the stubborn reiteration of contradictory positions. She was just about to turn and leave when she heard her father's weary voice rise above the rest. "Here is what we will tell the Zhentarim!"

The tent quieted immediately.

"You have argued for a full day without coming to any understanding," he said. "Therefore, it is my duty as sheikh to decide for us all."

Muffled murmurs of weary agreement came from inside the tent, and then Ruha's father continued. "Let any warrior who will not do as I ask leave the *khowwan* and call his family by some other name than that of the Mtair Dhafir."

A surprised mumble rustled from inside the tent, for Ruha's father was invoking the sheikh's ultimate threat to secure obedience to his will: that of banishment. It was a risky thing to do. If too many families took him at his word, the tribe would dissolve.

Whatever her father had decided, Ruha realized, he was determined that his decision would be the tribe's.

"We cannot fight the Zhentarim," the sheikh began. "They are too many and we are too few."

The tent rumbled with disgruntled murmuring.

"Neither can we become their slaves, for the children of the lion were born to roam free."

Again, discontent resounded throughout the tent.

The sheikh continued steadily. "Here is what we must do. We will agree to serve the Zhentarim as guides, biding our time and always keeping our camels ready for a long journey. Sooner or later, Kozah will send another storm, or the Zhentarim will grow unwatchful, or their army will dwindle as At'ar takes her due. When that happens, we will take our camels and disappear into the desert, leaving the Zhentarim and our troubles far behind."

A murmur of reluctant consensus whispered from the tent, but no one protested too loudly or threatened to force the sheikh to make good on his threat. Ruha realized that her father had developed the only compromise that would hold the tribe together.

Al'Aif was the only warrior to question the sheikh's plan. "Of course, I will do as you say, Sheikh," he said slowly. "But I do not like this plan. What if Kozah does not send another storm? What if the Zhentarim do not grow lax?"

Several warriors added their voices to Al'Aif's question, but the sheikh was ready with an answer. "If we cannot escape within six months, my friends, I promise that we will slit the throats of more invaders in one night than we could hope to kill by fighting now."

Save for Al'Aif, both the warriors and the elders greeted the sheikh's contingency plan with hearty approval, but Ruha could not help feeling they were fooling themselves. Remembering the shrewd, appraising eyes of the pale man that had accompanied Zarud, she suspected that the Zhentarim had already thought of this plan and developed a method to counter it.

"Now fetch Zarud, boy," the sheikh said. "The sooner we tell him what we have decided, the sooner we will be free again."

A moment later, the servant left the *khreima* and started for the far side of camp. Hoping to tell her father about Lander before the boy returned with the Zhentarim, Ruha entered the tent.

In the dim light cast by the flickering butter lamps, she saw that her father sat in his usual place at the head of the tent. To his left sat the five elders of the tribe, and across from them were seated Al'Aif, Nata, and four more warriors. As Ruha approached her father, they all turned toward her with disapproving frowns. In the Mtair Dhafir, decision-making was men's business and women were not welcome at the councils.

Ruha ignored their stern gazes and looked directly to her father. "I have heard your decision. Before—"

"Our decision does not concern you, witch," interrupted

Nata.

Ruha turned her stare on the burly warrior. Speaking in a calm, even voice, she said, "That is just as well, Nata. I would rather live a shunned life than share slave bonds with you."

The warrior's face darkened with anger, and he tried to stammer a reply, but Ruha turned back to her father before he could spout any words.

"Father, before you commit your tribe to this course of action, there is something I would like to show you."

The old man furrowed his brow. "Then show me quickly."

Ruha glanced at the curious eyes to either side of her. She still felt that revealing Lander's presence in front of all these men would be the same as telling Zarud herself. "It is for your eyes alone."

Angry mutters and grunts rustled throughout the tent. Her father looked from the warriors to the elders, then said, "Did you not tell me everything you knew earlier today?"

Ruha nodded. "There is something else."

"If it is important, then you can tell me here," the sheikh said. "Otherwise, it will have to wait."

"Then it will wait," Ruha sighed.

As she turned to depart, the servant boy returned with Zarud, Kadumi following on their heels.

"If it pleases you, Sheikh, I would like to hear what you have decided," Kadumi announced, pausing at the tent entrance.

Sighing, the sheikh waved the boy into the tent. "You deserve to know."

Glancing grimly at her brother-in-law, Ruha started to step past him and Zarud. As she passed, the Zhentarim caught her by the arm and shook his head, then said something in a language she did not understand and motioned for her to stay.

Ruha looked to her father, and he nodded.

Zarud took the widow's sleeve, then gently tugged her along as he stepped into the center of the semi-circle of the sheikh's council. When he stopped, both the warriors and elders frowned at his presumption in touching a Bedine woman. Ruha pulled free of his grasp.

Paying no attention to either the widow or the advisors, the Zhentarim asked a question. No one spoke his language, but there was no need to understand his words to know he requested the Mtair Dhafir's decision about the treaty. In the eyes of every Bedine present, however, there was an unspoken question: why had he wanted a woman, especially Ruha, to stay?

The sheikh glanced at his daughter, then looked back to Zarud, carefully masking whatever curiosity he felt behind a blank face. "The Mtair Dhafir accept your treaty," he said, nodding his head.

Wry grins crossed the lips of several elders and warriors. The sheikh had sworn no loyalty and pledged no friendship. In Bedine terms, at least, Sabkhat had not bound them to any alliance.

Smiling, Zarud inclined his head to the sheikh, then to the elders and the warriors. He spoke some more words that no one understood. The men of the Mtair looked from one to another with querying eyebrows and blank eyes.

Zarud spoke again, this time grasping Ruha's wrist and pointing toward the Bitter Well, where the Zhentarim were camped. He put his hand in front of his mouth and made speaking motions, then did the same for the widow.

"He wants to take her to teach them our language," concluded an elder.

Ruha jerked her wrist free. "Never!"

The Zhentarim grabbed her arm again, nodding and speaking sharply. He pointed to two elders, then to Al'Aif and Nata, and then toward the Bitter Well again.

"Why does he need with so many teachers?" demanded Nata. "This isn't right!"

Kadumi stepped toward Zarud, his hand drifting toward the hilt of his *jambiya*. He stopped when Al'Aif rose and motioned for him to stop. The scarred Mtair turned toward Ruha's father. "Already the Zhentarim tighten their reins, Sheikh. Is it still your wish to placate them?"

The sheikh locked gazes with Zarud, giving no sign that he had heard Al'Aif's question. Finally, without looking away from the Zhentarim, he said, "It is the only way, Al'Aif. You will all be ready to leave at dawn."

Kadumi stepped forward again. "No," he yelled. "Ruha is the wife of my brother. I cannot allow this!"

Al'Aif intercepted the young warrior. "The sheikh has decided, Kadumi," he said, pushing the boy toward the exit. "Don't worry about Ruha. I'll protect her."

After Al'Aif and the boy had gone, the sheikh looked at Nata and the two elders Zarud had selected, then rested his gaze on his daughter. "I'm sorry that it has to be this way," he said. "We must think of the welfare of the whole *khowwan*."

"*You* must think of the tribe," Ruha retorted, turning to leave the tent. "I have not been bound to do so since I was five summers old, when you banished me from the Mtair Dhafir."

Six

When Ruha returned to her tent,
Lander was gone. He had taken the
waterskin she had left for him,
abandoning the featherless arrow
and two empty glass vials in its
place. Nothing else was missing, and
there was no sign of a struggle, so
Ruha assumed the stranger had left of his own will.

The young widow could not understand how he had
managed to leave under his own power, though she
could certainly understand why he would want to leave.
With the Zhentarim in camp, almost any place would be
a safer haven than a Mtairi tent.

It is best that the *berrani* is gone, Ruha decided. It
would be difficult enough to sneak out of camp tonight
without taking an injured stranger along—or feeling
guilty about leaving him behind. The young widow took
a *kuerabiche* and stuffed her possessions into the carpet
shoulder bag. There was not much to pack: a ground
loom, Ajaman's *jambiya*, an extra *aba*, and three veils.
She did not pack her heavy cloak, for she would need it

later.

Ruha did not even consider becoming a Zhentarim captive on behalf of the Mtair Dhafir. Even if the sheikh rescued the hostages, she would never be welcome in the tribe. Besides, she knew her father well enough to doubt that he would even attempt such a rescue. Sheikh Sabkhat always thought of the welfare of the *khowwan* first, and trying to save the five prisoners would make the tribe's escape from the Zhentarim that much more difficult.

Still, the elders might force the old sheikh to try such a feat, for the Zhentarim had chosen their hostages well. The two elders were the heads of large families that would certainly never abandon their patriarchs. Al'Aif and Nata, the tribe's two best warriors, would also be sorely missed. Their absence would make the Mtair more reluctant to take up arms, and deprive the tribe of combat leadership if a revolt did occur.

Ruha felt that she was the only badly chosen hostage; the Mtair Dhafir would just as soon be rid of her anyway. The young widow could see why the Zhentarim had made their mistake, however. As the sheikh's daughter, the tribe leaders would normally hesitate to do anything to put her in danger. Ruha suspected there was more to the choice than that, however.

The pale, purple-robed man accompanying Zarud originally had struck her as being the real leader of the pair, and he had also used some sort of magic. From the way he had studied her during their original meeting, it would not surprise Ruha to learn that he had somehow sensed that she was a sorceress. No doubt, being magic-wielders themselves, the Zhentarim had concluded it would be better to have her where they could watch her.

When she finished packing, Ruha sat down to study the spells she had sewn inside her *aba*. She was certain she would need the wind shadow and sand whisper spells, and she also thought that a sand lion would be useful if she ran into any Zhentarim tonight. She did not know whether to memorize any sun spells, however, for it was difficult to decide what needs the light of day might bring with it.

Ruha was still contemplating her choice when someone cleared his throat noisily outside her *khreima*. The widow quickly rearranged her *aba*, then called, "Is there someone at my door?"

"Kadumi," came the response.

Before inviting the youth inside, Ruha thought about unpacking her bag, then decided that she could always claim it had been packed with tomorrow morning in mind. "Come inside, Kadumi."

The boy stepped inside, then sat very close to Ruha's side. "One of Nata's sons sits in the shadows twenty yards from your tent," he whispered.

Ruha nodded. "That does not surprise me. My father knows I have no wish to be a hostage."

"He is wrong to ask you," Kadumi said. "You are of the Qahtan now, not the Mtair Dhafir."

"Yes."

The boy nodded at the *kuerabiche*. "That is why you are leaving."

Ruha thought to deny it, then she realized that if Kadumi had not come as her friend, he would not have told her about the warrior watching her tent. "The Mtair have no right to ask anything of me."

"If it comes to you escaping this night, I will go with you."

"No. You should stay with my father's tribe." Ruha put a hand on the boy's arm. "We are a long way from your home sands, and it will be hard to find another of the Qahtan's allies for you to join."

Kadumi shrugged. "That doesn't matter. If you go, I must go as well. Yet that may not be necessary. Al'Aif thinks your father will change his mind."

Ruha frowned skeptically. "Al'Aif should know my father better than that."

"He seemed very sure of himself, and he thought you should know."

"Why?"

The boy shook his head. "He didn't say, but he is a man who can be trusted. Just wait until tomorrow. If your father has not changed his mind, then I will get you before you reach the Zhentarim."

The youth returned to his feet, saying, "I should leave before the guard thinks I am taking liberties with my brother's wife."

Beneath her veil, Ruha smiled at the boy's swagger. "We wouldn't want that."

"Until tomorrow, then," he said as he left.

Without unpacking her *kuerabiche*, Ruha returned to studying her spells. Whatever Al'Aif was doing, she didn't see how it affected her decision. Since her return, the warrior had treated her with a certain amount of respect, but she doubted that he or anyone else had changed their views on having a witch in the tribe.

Ruha continued studying her spells until an uncanny quiet crept over the camp and the night chill wafted into her tent on silent puffs of wind. Judging the time to be prime for sneaking away, Ruha went to the door of her *khreima* and peered outside. The moon cast a weak silvery light over the camp, but there were plenty of murky shadows to hide in beneath the *ghaf* trees and behind the tents. The sentry Kadumi had mentioned was nowhere in sight, but Ruha did not doubt that he was wrapped in a dark cloak and lying beneath one of the bushes or trees she watched.

Ruha backed away from the exit, then took her *kuerabiche* and went to the back side of the tent. She lifted a wall and pushed the bag outside, then started to squirm out herself.

A pair of dogs started barking on the far side of camp. Cursing the beasts, Ruha left the bag outside and crawled back into the tent. The dogs would awaken every other animal in camp, which would make it much more difficult for her to take a camel without causing a general tumult. Even with the animals alert, the widow could use her magic to move about undetected. Unfortunately, any camel she tried to take would be startled by her silent appearance from the shadows and bellow an alarm. It would be better to wait for the dogs to quiet down, then try again.

The dogs did not quiet. More joined the chorus, and then the camels began to bray. Soon the voices of sleepy men joined the uproar. Vexed by her bad luck, Ruha wrapped her cloak around her shoulders and waited for the men to put to rest whatever problem it was that had awakened the whole camp. When the tumult only grew worse, Ruha went outside to see the cause.

The first thing she saw was a stern-faced Nata striding purposefully toward her *khreima*. Behind him, in the center of the camp, her father and two dozen warriors stood gathered in a circle. They were all shouting at each other in puzzled, shocked voices.

As Nata approached, he said, "You'd better come with me, witch."

Ruha frowned in concern. "What's wrong? Is Kadumi hurt?"

The burly warrior shook his head, but before he could answer, a youthful warrior appeared from the other side of her tent. He was carrying the *kuerabiche* Ruha had packed earlier that night. "I found this behind the witch's tent, Father."

Nata took the shoulder bag from his son, then threw it back inside her *khreima*. "You won't be going anywhere tonight, Ruha. Come with me."

Frowning in confusion, Ruha followed the burly warrior back to the camp. Nata pushed through the jabbering men and moon-eyed children, keeping the widow close behind him. When they stopped moving, what Ruha saw made her gasp.

Al'Aif and her father stood in center of the crowd, holding torches. Al'Aif was watching her, but her father was staring at the lifeless and naked body of Zarud. The Zhentarim agent lay spread-eagled on the ground, as if someone had carried his corpse to the center of the camp and dropped him there to be inspected. The dead man had the sinewy build of a warrior, and his torso was blanketed with old scars. Ruha could scarcely believe a man could be wounded so many times and survive.

The most noticeable thing about the Zhentarim was the gaping gash below his jawline. Somebody had slit his throat from ear to ear, apparently with great relish. The wound was both deep and unnecessarily lengthy, and had left his body covered with blood from the shoulders to the hips. Ruha thought immediately of Lander, for he was clearly an enemy of the Black Robes.

She rejected the idea as quickly as it came to her. The last time she had seen the stranger, he had barely been able to walk, much less slit a healthy man's throat. She thought of Al'Aif next, wondering if he had believed murdering Zarud would convince the sheikh to change his mind about sending hostages to the Zhentarim.

Her thoughts were interrupted by a woman's curious voice. "How come he's not dressed?"

The Bedine removed their clothes for only one purpose. Since the Zhentarim had not brought any wives with him, his nakedness seemed peculiar to the tribesmen.

"Perhaps Ruha knows," suggested an aged warrior with a mouthful of rotten teeth. "What better way to catch a man off-guard?"

A flutter of murmurs rippled through the crowd.

"I can think of a dozen," she retorted, glaring at the old man. "Any one of which I might use to silence your lecherous tongue."

The crowd snickered openly at the widow's retort, and the old man flushed with embarrassment. He rudely brushed his nose at Ruha, then pushed his way out of the assembly.

As the man left, Al'Aif spoke. "If Ruha did this, she has performed us a great service."

Considering that she suspected Al'Aif of being the murderer, the accusation both astonished and angered Ruha. She stopped short of accusing the scarred warrior openly, however, for she knew it would work against her. Given a choice of believing her or Al'Aif, the crowd would place its faith in the warrior.

Nata spoke next. "When we went to fetch Ruha, my son found a packed *kuerabiche* behind her tent."

A wave of speculation rolled through the crowd. The widow realized that, aside from herself, the only one who did not believe she had killed Zarud was the real murderer.

The sheikh shifted his gaze to Ruha and stared at her in dismay for several seconds. Finally he said, "Do you know what you have done, Daughter?"

"She has saved us," Al'Aif interrupted. "Now there is no question of placating the Zhentarim. We must fight."

The sheikh whirled on Al'Aif. "We're out-manned thirty-to-one, you idiot!" he snarled. He looked back to Ruha, his ancient eyes welling with tears. "Our only hope is pay the blood price and hope the Zhentarim will accept it."

The pronouncement struck Ruha like a club. Her knees buckled, then she felt Nata's big hands beneath her arms. The burly warrior held her up while she spoke. "Father, you mustn't do this," she gasped. "I didn't murder your guest."

The old man dropped his gaze back to the corpse. "If you didn't kill the Zhentarim, who did?"

Ruha looked in Al'Aif's direction, but before she could speak, Kadumi stepped forward and threw his *jambiya* at the sheikh's feet. "There is the weapon that cut Zarud's throat," he declared.

"Kadumi's lying," Ruha said, pulling free of Nata's supporting hands. "He's just trying to protect me. The Zhentarim's blood is on neither of our *jambiyas*."

The old man picked up the youth's dagger. "The boy has admitted the crime. You were caught about to sneak from camp. What can you say to make me believe that one of you did not do this?"

It was Al'Aif who answered. "I say it doesn't matter who killed Zarud, because we owe the Zhentarim no blood price. They are our enemies, not our allies!"

"If you were sheikh, Al'Aif, we would be dead in two days," Ruha's father retorted. "Fighting is not always the best solution."

"Is paying the blood price with the life of your daughter or an innocent boy a braver solution?" demanded Al'Aif.

"What are you saying?" yelled the sheikh. When Al'Aif did not respond, the old man shoved the warrior, knocking him back into the crowd. "Do you call me a coward?"

As he regained his balance, the scarred Mtairi grabbed for his *jambiya*. In the same instant, Nata flashed past Ruha to stand before the sheikh, his hand on the hilt of his own weapon. As the two warriors glared at each other, the crowd backed away in tense silence, scarcely daring to breath lest they touch off a fight that would not stop short of death.

It was the sheikh who spoke next. Stepping between the two warriors, he said, "No matter what you said, that was wrong of me, Al'Aif. If we start fighting each other, the Zhentarim have taken us already. Nata, take Kadumi and

Ruha to her tent. We shall consider this matter again in the morning."

When neither Al'Aif or Nata moved to obey, Ruha's father snapped, "I have spoken!"

Reluctantly the warriors relaxed, and the sheikh turned to go. As the crowd parted to let him pass, a strange man moved from the edge of the gathering. He wore a yellow *aba* with a ragged hole in its breast, and a wide strip had been cut off the hem to make the sling in which the man now carried his right arm. In contrast to his dusty clothes, his face and hands were freshly washed, and he appeared remarkably alert for someone who had so recently suffered a serious wound.

When none of the astonished Bedine said anything, the man nodded to Ruha. "Aren't you going to introduce me?"

All the widow could reply was, "Where did you go? What are you doing here?"

"I thought it wiser to spend the night on the mountain," Lander replied, motioning at the craggy slope looming above the camp. "As for the second question, when I saw someone had done away with the Zhentarim, I thought it might be safe to speak with your sheikh."

"Who is this man?" asked Kadumi, the sheikh, and Al'Aif simultaneously.

Shaking her head, Ruha turned to her father. "He calls himself Lander, and he has come to warn us about the Zhentarim," she said. "He is their enemy."

The sheikh raised an eyebrow at her comment. "Is that so?"

Lander nodded. "As are all the Bedine, whether they know it or not."

"That shall be for us to decide," the sheikh responded curtly. He pointed at Lander's wound. "How did you come by that?"

"Zhentarim," Lander said, as if the word explained

everything.

"That Zhentarim?" he asked, pointing at Zarud.

Lander studied the dead man for an instant, then said, "If that will save Ruha and the boy, then yes."

Ruha's mouth dropped open at Lander's reply. She didn't know whether to thank him for saving her life or point out that she had dressed his wound before Zarud had been killed.

Her relief was short-lived. Pointing at the blood crusted around the stranger's bandage, Nata asked, "If you killed the Zhentarim, why is the blood on your wound so old?"

"A good question, but one that should not be answered tonight," the sheikh said. "Put the stranger with Kadumi and my daughter. We will sort this out in the morning, after our heads have cleared and our tempers have settled."

As the rest of the tribe returned to their beds, Nata supervised the internment of the prisoners. While his son fetched some rope, the burly warrior took the trio to Ruha's tent. There, he bound their hands in front of their bodies, then tied their feet and carried each one into the tent. Finally he stationed his son at the door as a guard.

To Ruha's amazement, the *berrani* laid down on the carpet, as if he were going to sleep. "Don't say anything you don't want overheard," Lander said, closing his eyes. Soon, resting on his uninjured shoulder, he was snoring in great deep roars that would have harried a lion.

"How can he fall asleep like that?" Kadumi asked, seated with his bound feet stretched straight out in front of him.

"The *berrani* is injured," Ruha answered. "He might sleep until morning. We might do well to join him."

Kadumi shook his head and silently mouthed something about Al'Aif, but Ruha could not make out what he was saying. Shrugging to indicate that she did not understand, she stretched out on her side. "Try to get some sleep,

Kadumi. You may not have a chance later."

The boy nodded, then rolled onto his own side and closed his eyes.

Through half-closed eyes, Ruha watched Nata's son. By the way he wearily shifted his weight from one foot to another, she could tell he was tired. That was good, for it would make him easier to catch off-guard.

The guard continued standing as the camp returned to normal. When, at last, the place fell completely quiet and he could be sure his father had gone to bed, the young man sat down at the tent entrance. Every so often, he glanced over his shoulder to check on his prisoners, but his main concern seemed to be watching the camp so he could be sure that his father would not catch him at less than full attention.

Eventually the glances grew less frequent. Nata's son began to doze fitfully. His head would sink slowly until his chin touched his chest, then bob up and stay upright for a few minutes before slowly descending again. The time soon came when the guard's head did not rise again.

On her elbows and knees, Ruha crawled to the *kuera-biche* that Nata's son had found earlier. Taking care not to make any noise, she pulled the contents from the sack and laid them on the floor beside her: her spare *aba*, her veils, and, finally, Ajaman's *jambiya*.

As Ruha unsheathed the dagger, Kadumi's eyes opened and she realized that the boy had not been able to sleep. An instant later, a great smile crossed his face and she feared he would cry out for joy. The widow looked meaningfully toward the door, and the youth nodded that he understood.

Ruha freed herself first, then crawled to her brother-in-law. As she cut his bonds, she leaned close to his ear and whispered, "Don't move yet."

Kadumi nodded, then looked toward Lander. "When you cut the *berrani* free, he may stop snoring."

Ruha saw the point of the youth's concern immediately. Though the guard had dozed off, it seemed unlikely that he had fallen into a deep sleep. If Lander's snoring suddenly changed rhythm or ceased altogether, the guard might wake suddenly. No doubt he would glance inside the tent and realize something was amiss.

The only way to keep him from sounding the alarm was for Kadumi to silence the guard before he could reach his *amarat*. Ruha did not doubt that Kadumi could catch the guard unawares and kill the young warrior, but she did not cherish the idea of Nata hunting her with a blood price in mind.

As she considered the problem, an alarm horn sounded on the far side of the camp. Several men began shouting. The guard woke immediately and jumped to his feet, crying, "What is it? What's wrong?" Fortunately he sensed the direction of the alarm, and his attention was turned toward the far side of camp.

Lander's eyes opened, but he continued to snore exactly as he had done since being interned in the tent. Ruha couldn't tell whether he had awakened instantly alert or had been pretending to sleep all the time.

Lander motioned toward his feet, still maintaining his snore. Taking the hint, Ruha cut the ropes with a quick slice. The *berrani* jumped to his feet and sprang toward the *khreima's* entrance as silently as a leopard stalking prey. In an instant, he slipped his bound hands over the guard's head. Pulling backward so that the rope caught the man across the throat, Lander dragged his victim back into the tent.

The *berrani* held his right arm pressed tightly against his side to avoid straining his injured shoulder, but the stranglehold still proved effective. Nata's son grasped at the arms looped around his neck and kicked at his attacker to no avail, and Lander controlled him easily.

Finally reacting to Lander's swift assault, Kadumi leaped to the *berrani's* side and pulled the man's *jambiya* from its scabbard.

"Don't kill him!" Ruha gasped.

"Never intended to," Lander replied, tightening the choke.

Kadumi also did as she asked, though he raised his brow at the request. Among the Bedine, ending a man's life was not considered much different than killing any other animal—save that a man's family might try to avenge the death. Ruha feared that Kadumi, as a youth, might not give enough consideration to what this would mean in the case of a son of Nata.

The guard soon stopped struggling, and his body went limp. Lander quickly tied the guard's hands and feet, then massaged the unconscious boy's chest. In instant later, the guard coughed and resumed breathing. Lander took the boy's *keffiyeh* and stuffed the scarf into the guard's mouth as a gag, then bound him to a tent pole.

Kadumi relieved him of his belt, scimitar, and scabbards, then asked, "What now?"

Before Ruha could answer, the sound of ripping fabric sounded from the rear of the *khreima*. The young widow spun around to see the blade of a scimitar slicing through the tent wall. Taking the guard's scimitar from Kadumi, Lander cautious stepped toward the gash, motioning to Kadumi and Ruha to do likewise.

An instant later, Al'Aif stepped through the hole he had just created. In one hand he held the scimitar that had opened the *khreima*, and in the other he held his *jambiya*. When he saw the trio standing unfettered and the unconscious guard bound to the tent pole, he raised an eyebrow and sheathed his dagger. "You were expecting me, I see."

Lander nodded, but Ruha and Kadumi stared at the scarred warrior with their mouths hanging agape.

"Come on," Al'Aif said. "Kadumi's camels are watered and packed."

Ruha refused to move. "You killed Zarud and were ready to let me pay the blood price," she said, fingering her dagger. "Why should I trust you now?"

"I do what I do for reasons of my own," he answered, meeting her gaze squarely. "I never intended to let Sheikh Sabkhat send you—or anyone else—to the Zhentarim. You can trust me." He turned to the back wall of the tent and spread open the gash he had created, then motioned for Ruha to step through.

When Ruha still did not move, Lander urged her toward the exit. "We can trust him. For his plan to work, he must help us escape. He killed the Zhentarim to prevent the tribe from allying with the invaders. If we're gone in the morning, the sheikh will have no choice except to flee."

"Or to fight," Al'Aif said.

"That would be very foolish," Lander said. "The Zhentarim have a large army and their commanders are sure to be capable."

The scarred Mtairi shrugged. "Fight or flee. It is the same to me—but never enslavement!" He reached toward Ruha to urge her through the slit, but the widow jerked her arm away and stepped outside before he could touch her.

Outside, the tasselled silhouettes of several *qassis* bushes perfumed the air with their stringent aromas. Fifty yards to the west, the bushy shadows of *ghaf* trees and the tinkle of the stream marked the gulch. On the other side of the tent, Rahalat's dark shape towered high over the moonlit sands, and a heavy sense of impending doom settled over Ruha.

The others stepped out of the tent, then Al'Aif silently motioned for them to follow him. The scarred warrior led the small group across the gulch, then around the shoulder of the mountain. After perhaps an hour of picking their way past thorny salt-bushes and scrub brush, the scar-faced warrior stopped at the edge of a small draw. In the bottom of the dry *wadi* were the milky silhouettes of Kadumi's camels and the darker outline of his brown gelding. The gelding and two of the white camels were fitted with saddles, while the remaining beasts were loaded with baggage.

Kadumi pointed at the third saddle. "That doesn't belong to me," he said. At El Ma'ra, he and Ruha had outfitted their beasts from the possessions of the dead tribesman, but they had only needed two saddles and had not thought to pick up an extra one.

Al'Aif laid a hand on the youth's shoulder. "Consider it a gift from one warrior to another."

Kadumi smiled at the older man. "Thank you, Al'Aif. Some day, I shall repay you a dozenfold."

"When you are the sheikh of the reborn Qahtan, no doubt," the scar-faced warrior said, giving Ruha a salacious glance. He turned to Lander. "Find someplace to hide until morning. The Zhentarim have sent spies to watch us, and they are lurking about in the sands. You will find it easier to find their trails and avoid their hiding places during the day."

The *berrani* nodded. "Sound advice."

"Go with the favor of Kozah, *berrani*," Al'Aif said, turning back toward camp. "You shall need it."

"My thanks for our rescue."

"No need to thank me." The scar-faced warrior did not look back. "If I had known you were doing so well on your own, I would not have bothered."

The trio descended into the *wadi* and inspected Kadumi's animals. Their humps were firm from a day of good grazing, and their bellies were bloated with a fresh watering. The baggage camels were loaded with full waterskins, a *khreima*, and *kuerabiches* filled with dried fruits, meats, and extra clothes. There were even two scimitars, a pair of bows with two fulls quivers, and an extra *jambiya*.

After he had finished his inspection, Lander said, "It appears Al'Aif is truly anxious to be rid of us. We have everything we need for a long journey."

"He is truly a generous man," Ruha commented cynically. "But where are we going?"

Taking the three heavy cloaks off a baggage camel, Lander said, "That depends upon what your tribe does and where the Zhentarim go, at least for me."

"Why?" Ruha asked. "What are the Zhentarim to you?"

Draping a cloak over her shoulders, the *berrani* said, "The Zhentarim are evil, rapacious, and they intend to enslave the peoples of the desert. I have come to help the Bedine defeat them."

"How?" Kadumi asked. "If an entire tribe cannot defeat them, what can you do?"

Lander regarded the boy with an even, honest expression. "I don't know yet."

Kadumi shrugged. "Well, they are our enemies also. We may as well ride together—for a time, at least."

The youth began to untether the camels. Lander joined him, leaving Ruha to wonder what the stranger really wanted from the Bedine.

Once they had checked the saddles and strung the baggage camels into a caravan line, Lander led the trio up the *wadi*. When the dry ravine ended, they dismounted and ascended onto the breezy shoulder of Rahalat.

Ruha envied the grace with which the *berrani* led the way over the broken ground, for she found the going hard on the steep terrain—especially since, as a woman, it was her duty to lead the baggage string. Several times she almost turned an ankle, and once she lost her balance as they topped a twenty-foot cliff.

As she crossed a rocky spine running between a pair of

thirty-foot precipices, Ruha decided that it might be best for Kadumi to lead the baggage camels. Before she could speak, the hollow knell of a goat bell sounded behind her. Her first thought was that the animal making the sound belonged to the Zhentarim, for the Mtair Dhafir kept no goats. Bringing the incantation for a wind wall to mind, she spun around ready to cast the spell and push her enemies off the mountain.

There was no one behind her. Without turning around, she asked, "Lander, Kadumi, did you hear anything?"

"Yes, down there," Lander replied.

"No, over here," Kadumi countered.

Ruha turned and saw Lander peering off of one side of the spine and Kadumi off of the other. The bell sounded again, and this time she realized it came from inside her head.

The widow's companions realized the same thing. Kadumi blanched and covered his ears with his hands, while Lander simply shook his head, vainly trying to clear it.

"Rahalat!" Kadumi gasped.

The youth began tugging on his camel reins, trying to turn his gelding around and start down. When the confused beast looked over the precipices to either side of it, it would not move. Lander grasped the boy's shoulder. "What's Rahalat?"

"The mountain spirit," Ruha explained.

"She does not want us here," Kadumi added, still trying to turn his camels around.

"A ghost?" inquired Lander.

Ruha shook her head. "A goddess."

"Rahalat was a shunned woman," Kadumi explained. "Her *khowwan* abandoned her here, and she claimed the oasis as her home. She was very bitter and used her magic to prevent any tribe from grazing here."

The bells sounded again, but this time they seemed to

come from all sides. Kadumi dropped the camel reins and started down the mountain, abandoning the confused beasts.

"During a drought, the Dakawa murdered her," Ruha continued, not attempting to stop her brother-in-law. "According to legend, the spring turned to blood. For the next ten years, anything that drank from it perished. Now, every tribe that camps at Rahalat must sacrifice a camel to the mountain goddess or the water goes bad."

Looking after Kadumi, Lander said, "We can't go back. When the sheikh hears we're missing, he'll search everywhere for us."

A terrible clatter sounded from above, and the air filled with the bleating of goats. A moment later, a herd of several dozen of the beasts materialized from the boulders on the slope above the rocky spine, then started moving down the mountain. The camels began backing away nervously, their footing coming precariously close to the cliffs to either side.

Kadumi called, "Come with me, you fools, or you will be driven off the cliffs with my camels!"

"We can't abandon the camels," Lander said to Ruha. "Without them, we're dead."

"And if we stay, we are also dead," Ruha answered, watching Kadumi descend the mountain. The widow did not blame him for leaving.

Lander was not intimidated, though. He started toward the goats, waving his arms and crying, "Go back to where you came from! Get out of here!"

Kadumi's brown gelding tried to turn and flee, then slipped and lost its footing. With a terrified bellow, it plunged off the cliff on the backside of the mountain, its body bouncing off the rocks with a series of muffled thuds.

Ruha realized that, whether or not he was a fool to challenge Rahalat, Lander was right about one thing: they could not afford to lose their camels. She waved her hand at the top of the rocky spine, at the same time whispering the incantation she had brought to mind earlier.

The breeze shifted, then whistled as it wove itself into an impenetrable wall in the spot she had chosen. The goats stumbled into the invisible barrier, then began to batter it with their horns or try to climb over.

Lander turned and stared at Ruha with an astonished expression. "Did you do that?"

"No," she said, speaking the lie automatically. It did not even cross her mind that Lander might not be offended by her use of magic. Ruha handed the reins to the baggage camel to the confused *berrani*. "Hold these. I'll go to the back of the line and see if I can coax them down backward."

As she worked her way past the apprehensive camels, the bleating of the goats and the knelling of their bells faded.

"Wait!" Lander called. "They're gone!"

Ruha turned around and saw that he was correct. The goats had disappeared, as had her wind wall. In their place stood the white, translucent figure of an unveiled woman. Her face was young and strong-featured, though there was a certain weariness to her countenance that gave her a lonely and heartbroken appearance. She was studying Ruha with an expression of sisterly sorrow.

"Kadumi! Come back! They're gone," called Lander. Without waiting to see if the youth heard him, the *berrani* turned and started back up the mountain. "We'd better get off this narrow ridge before something else happens."

"Wait," Ruha said, still looking past him to the translucent form of the goddess. "How do you know Rahalat has given us her permission?"

Lander looked directly at the place where the form of the goddess was standing. "There's nothing there," he said. "Just a moonlit rock."

Rahalat gave Ruha a sly smile, then suddenly looked in the direction of the Bitter Well. She scowled in displeasure, and then the goddess was gone.

Ruha led her camels across the rest of the spine, puzzling over the appearance of the goddess and the meaning of her final frown. From Lander's reaction, it was apparent that Rahalat had permitted only the widow to see her, and from that Ruha deduced that she was being shown some sort of special favor. She could not decide, however, whether the glance in the Bitter Well's direction had been a warning of some sort or whether the goddess had merely seen something in that direction that she did not like.

When Ruha reached Lander's side, he asked, "You didn't make that wall of force that saved us?"

"What's a wall of force?" Ruha asked, turning to look down the mountain. "Is Kadumi coming?"

The question was unnecessary, for the youth was already crossing the rock spine. He paused in the center long enough to cast a regretful glance down at his dead gelding. Then, a sheepish expression on his face, he rejoined them without saying anything.

Lander resumed his climb, finally calling a halt atop a section of steep crags and two-thousand foot cliffs that overlooked the oasis spring. Ruha could see the embers of the Mtairi campfires spread out in a semi-circle against the base of the mountain. In the darkness, she could not see individual silhouettes moving about the camp, but there was no sign of torches, so she assumed the trio's escape remained unnoticed.

Beyond the camp, the alabaster crests of the whaleback dunes and ebony ribbons of their dark troughs created an eerie sea of black and white that stretched clear to the eastern horizon. Somewhere to the northeast, Ruha knew, was the Bitter Well and the Zhentarim army.

"I thought we had walked farther," Kadumi commented.

"We did," Lander answered. "The only way to get here is around the back of the mountain. If anyone comes after us, we'll see them leave camp long before they reach us."

"Still," Ruha said, "it would be best not to let them see our silhouettes on this ridge."

The *berrani* nodded, then led the way a few paces down the other side of the shoulder. As Lander and Kadumi tethered the camels, Ruha heard the faint tones of an *amarat* horn. Her first thought was that their absence had been discovered, and she quickly scrambled back up the shoulder.

A moment later, Ruha knew she was wrong. She crested the ridge in time to see a bolt of light flash in the dunes outside the oasis, then a muffled peal of thunder rumbled up the mountainside. More *amarat* horns sounded.

"Zhentarim!" she gasped.

By the time Kadumi and Lander joined her, flickering pinpoints of torchlight were dancing between the *khreimas*. A solid line of the torches was forming at the edge of the camp.

"It appears Al'Aif got his wish after all," Lander commented. "The Zhentarim must know that Zarud was killed."

"How could they know so soon?" Kadumi asked. "That was only a few hours ago."

"Magic or spies," Ruha suggested. "Do they always attack so quickly after an insult?"

"The Zhentarim are careful planners," Lander said, his eyes fixed on the scene below. "As soon as Zarud presented their treaty, they probably started moving their army forward—just in case the sheikh did not accept their terms."

A familiar knot of cold dread formed in Ruha's stomach. "The Mtair will be slaughtered, just like the Qahtan."

Neither of her companions contradicted her.

Seven

"Where are the dead?"

The question was Kadumi's, but it troubled Lander and Ruha as well. The trio was perched on Rahalat's shoulder, at the top of a steep face of barren rock that dropped over two thousand feet to the campsite at the base of the mountain. The sun was just rising, and they were getting their first view of the devastated *khowwan* of the Mtair Dhafir.

From such a distance, the three survivors could make out only a few details of the scene below. Every *khreima* in the camp had been knocked down. The Zhentarim had tethered the Mtair's camels in a tight circle and were looting the possessions of the Mtair Dhafir. Hundreds of columns of gray smoke rose from campfires spread around the base of the mountain, and the camel drivers were taking their beasts to drink from the spring in small groups.

Missing from the scene were what Lander had most expected to see: the bodies of the Mtair Dhafir. At such a distance, it was impossible to tell a tribesman from an invader, for men looked like dark specks crawling across the pale sands. What troubled Lander and his companions was that all the dark specks were moving. If the Bedine were lying at the base of the mountain, at least two hundred of the dark specks would have been quite still.

"Perhaps the Mtair escaped," Kadumi whispered. "It was dark, and we could not see what was truly happening."

The trio had spent the night watching the battle, but they had not seen much. After the *amarats* had sounded a second time, the torches on the battleline went out, presumably extinguished by the warriors themselves in order to keep from drawing attention to their positions. A few minutes had passed, then muted cries had begun to drift up the mountainside.

In camp, the women, marked by the flickering lights of their torches, had scurried about, collecting children and supplies with renewed frenzy. As the Mtairi battle cries grew more desperate, the women had assembled on the far side of the camp, then fled the battlefield.

Before the line of yellow flames had traveled fifty yards, a muffled chorus of surprised screams had heralded an invader ambush. The refugees had scattered, but their torches had started to wink out immediately.

Recalling the agonized shriek that had accompanied each dying light, Lander knew that even if some of the women had escaped, there were many more who had not. The sand should have been carpeted with their bodies and with the bodies of the warriors who had died at the battleline.

Lander shook his head. "Everybody couldn't have escaped, Kadumi." The Sembian did not bother to speak in a hushed voice. With the Zhentarim nearly a half-mile away, there was no chance of being overheard. "There should be dozens of corpses at the very least. Do you see any?"

"No corpses," Ruha answered. She pointed at a knot of dark specks gathered at the tent in which the trio had been held last night. "But I don't like what is happening there."

As she spoke, the gathering began to break into groups of ten or twelve. As each group left, it moved in a different direction.

"Search parties!" Lander said.

Kadumi's brow furrowed. "Are they searching for—"

"Me," Lander said, assuming that his enemies learned of his presence from a captured Mtair. "Perhaps we should separate. If they find me, the Zhentarim might stop looking."

Ruha regarded him thoughtfully for a moment. Her dark eyes flashed with what Lander took to be irritation, then she said, "Either you have a very low opinion of Kadumi and I, or an exaggerated sense of your own importance, *berrani.*"

"That's not what I mean," Lander protested, feeling himself flush in embarrassment. "But if the Zhentarim know I am here, they won't stop searching until they find me."

"Why is that?" asked Kadumi suspiciously.

Lander considered the boy's question for a moment, then decided that he should reveal his identity to his companions so that they might understand the danger into which they were moving. He opened his robe and displayed the pin that he wore over his heart. "I belong to an organization called the Harpers," he said. "We work to protect the freedom of people everywhere, and that often places us into opposition against the Zhentarim."

"As in this case?" Ruha asked.

"Yes," the Harper answered. "If they catch you with me, it will mean a slow and agonizing death."

"If they catch us without you, it will mean a slow and agonizing death," Ruha countered. "The Zhentarim whom Al'Aif killed had a companion. That man knows that Kadumi and I came here to warn my father about the Black Robes, and he may even suspect that we had something to do with the murder. So we lose nothing by staying together, unless you feel you would be safer without a boy and a woman to defend. Of course, I don't know how long a *berrani* can expect to survive in Anauroch with no guides . . ."

The irony in Ruha's tone did not escape Lander. He raised his hand to quiet her. "Your point is well taken," he said. "Together, we all stand a better chance of surviving."

When Ruha nodded, the Sembian started to crawl back down the ridge toward the camels.

The widow caught his arm before he gone two steps. "Where are you going?"

"We'd better leave," he said. "If the Zhentarim find us up here, we'll be trapped."

Ruha shook her head. "Rahalat will not allow the Zhentarim on her slopes."

"How can you be sure?" Lander asked. The phantom goats had convinced him of Rahalat's existence, though he suspected she was a ghost and not a goddess. In either case, he saw no reason to believe she would protect them.

Ruha glanced toward the mountain's summit. "If Rahalat did not favor us, we would be dead. I doubt that she will favor the Zhentarim."

Lander glanced at Kadumi. "What do you think?"

The youth looked thoughtful for a moment, then nodded. "What my sister-in-law says makes sense," he said. "Besides, we would only draw attention to ourselves by moving. We should wait."

"I hope you're right," he said, crouching behind the ridge crest. "If I know the Zhentarim, they won't stop searching until they've scoured every inch of the oasis. Let's take care not to let them see us up here."

Lander motioned for the other two to conceal themselves in the rocks, and they did as asked. Their hiding places overlooked not only the camp, but the approach up the ridge as well. Even if Rahalat did not keep the Zhentarim off the mountain, the Sembian felt confident that they would see the enemy in plenty of time to flee.

The trio crouched on the ridge for most of the morning, watching the specks below scurry about their business. Soon, the Zhentarim began butchering the Mtair Dhafir's camels, and the breeze carried the smell of roasting meat up to them. Lander's mouth began to water, bringing back the memory of the special feasts he and his father had once shared.

As a merchant, Lander's father often ventured up the Arkhen River to purchase fruits, farm produce, and freshwater crabs. The people of the valley were haughty and arrogant, so Lander had often gone along on these trips to keep his father company. He and his father would sit in country taverns until late at night, eating roasted mutton and discussing the highest price they would pay for the next day's goods. Even then, Lander had never believed his advice was truly needed, but he had looked forward to the trips eagerly. For the son of a traveling merchant, any opportunity to spend time with his father had been precious.

Unfortunately, the meat making Lander's mouth water was camel instead of sheep, and Rahalat's barren shoulder was a poor substitute for the humid valley of ferns and lilies. Now Archendale's abundant orchards and sweet waters seemed a distant and fantastic mirage, much as Anauroch's empty wastes and scorched mountains would have seemed a bad dream to him then.

The Sembian opened his waterskin and took a long drink, trying to wash the recollection away before it became distressing. It didn't help. He was hungry and the smell of roasting meat automatically triggered memories of every feast he had ever eaten, especially memories he had thought long forgotten.

Trying to keep his mind focused on stopping the enemy's plans in Anauroch, Lander began to count the specks in the camp below. Sooner or later, he knew, the Bedine would fight the Zhentarim. When they did, it would be useful for them to know just what they were up against.

It was not an easy task, for invaders kept moving from fire to fire. Occasionally, one patrol returned to camp and scattered to a dozen different fires to eat, while another group left to take its place. Lander found that he had to keep track of the Zhentarim by scratching a grid in the ground and moving pebbles from one place to another to represent every ten specks that moved.

As Lander was finishing his count, Kadumi crawled to his side and peered over the Sembian's shoulder. "What are you doing?"

"Counting the Zhentarim," Lander replied.

"And how many are there?" asked Ruha, turning to face the pair.

Lander looked at the grid, then added the figures in his head. "I would guess about fifteen hundred."

"Impossible!" Kadumi objected.

"At least we know why they're so hungry," Ruha said, studying the cooking fires down in the camp. "The largest *khowwan* I've ever heard of numbers only three hundred. The invaders will never find enough grazing to keep all their camels in milk."

"Or enough game to fill their stewpots," Kadumi added.

"They don't need to," Lander replied. "The Zhentarim

don't intend to be in the desert long. They're carrying all
the food they need on their camels."

"You mean they'll go away in a few months?" Ruha
asked, her voice growing hopeful.

Lander shook his head. "No. A few months are all the
Zhentarim need to complete their task. They'll subdue a
dozen *khowwans*, then use hostages, bribery, and violence
to enslave the tribesmen. Once their powerbase is secure,
they'll take their army away and use the tribes they control
to overpower the others. Before the Bedine realize what's
happened, the entire desert will belong to the Black
Robes. The only way to stop them is to drive the Zhentarim from the desert."

"Then the Bedine are doomed," Kadumi said, pointing at
the specks in the camp. "No tribe can stand against so
many."

Lander frowned and pulled the boy's arm down. "Of
course not. Any tribe that fights the Zhentarim alone will
meet the same fate as the Mtair Dhafir and the Qahtan.
We'll need a hundred tribes."

Ruha and Kadumi looked skeptical. "That's impossible,"
Kadumi said. "No tribe has that many allies."

Lander shook his head. "Kadumi, this isn't a matter of
traditional alliances. Tribes that have never heard of each
other must ride and fight under the same banner. They're
all battling a common enemy."

"It will never—"

Ruha interrupted Kadumi's reply with an alarmed gasp.
Pointing over Lander's back, she cried, "Look out!"

Lander reached for the *jambiya* at his waist with one
hand and for his sword with the other. The effort made his
wounded shoulder burn with agony. He clenched his teeth,
then pulled the blades from their sheaths and spun around
on his knees to meet the unseen attacker.

There was no one there. Fearing his enemy to be

cloaked by invisibility, Lander jumped to his feet. He sliced through the air in front of him with the scimitar, then crossed the pattern with a slash from his dagger. Neither blade hit a target. Groaning with pain, Lander took one step backward and repeated the pattern first to his right and then to his left. Still nothing.

The Sembian backed away one more step. Kadumi moved next to him, scimitar drawn but held in a confused and tentative low guard.

"Where is it, Ruha?" Lander demanded.

There was no answer.

"Ruha, I can't see it," the Harper repeated.

When there was still no response, Lander hazarded a glance over his shoulder.

Ruha was staring at him as if he were ghost. Her eyes were glassy, and she had a confused, distant expression on her brow.

"Is something wrong?" the Harper asked, beginning to suspect that the cause for her alarm had not been an attacker. "Are you sick?"

The widow did not respond to the question. Instead, she looked him over from head to toe, then took the material of his filthy robe between her fingers. "Blessings to Rahalat," Ruha said. "You're alive."

"Of course he is," Kadumi said, scowling. "So am I. What made you think otherwise?"

Ruha shook her head, then said, "I saw a Black Robe behind Lander—or at least I thought I did. He had a dagger." She squinted toward the sun, then shook her head. "It must have been At'ar."

Kadumi sheathed his dagger and took his sister-in-law by the arm. "You're getting sun-sick again," he said. "Let's find some shade and get you a drink of water."

Ruha started to protest, then seemed to think better of it and allowed Kadumi to lead her off the ridge.

Lander crouched back down and peered over the rocky slope to the camp. To his relief, he saw no sign that the Zhentarim had not noticed their excitement. The flea-sized spots were still milling calmly about camp.

After assuring himself that they remained undetected, the Sembian found a hiding place on the shady side of a boulder. Gently rubbing his wounded shoulder, he drank down one of the healing potions Florin had given him, then followed it with a long swallow from his waterskin.

For the next few hours, Lander remained on watch while Kadumi tended Ruha. Nothing happened, save that a dozen vultures came to hover over the camp. With their red-rimmed eyes, nude heads, and snakelike necks, the birds normally appeared grotesque and repulsive to Lander. Watching them from above, as they circled a few yards below the ridge, was almost enough to change the Sembian's opinion. Their magnificent wingspan, gleaming black feathers, and keen ebony eyes gave a proud, almost noble streak to their character.

A vulture glanced up and fixed its dark stare on Lander's hiding place. A chill ran down his spine, for in the bird's look he saw the sable eyes of his mother. The expression seemed at once rapacious and dangerous, devoid of tenderness and demanding of veneration. The Harper's stomach knotted with an emotion somewhere between fear and anger. He felt his mother reaching out from Cyric's palace, imploring him to remember her face, to open his mind to her now as he had refused to open his spirit when she lived.

Lander forced himself to look away. The last thing he wished to do, now or ever, was contact his mother's spirit. She had chosen her new home, and to yield to her call would be to betray all that he had come to believe.

The Sembian kept his good eye closed, clearing his mind by concentrating on nothing but his breathing. His mother had reached out from her grave once before, after he had joined the Harpers, and he knew from that experience a bitter contest of wills would follow if he allowed her a hold in his thoughts.

At last Lander's stomach settled and his body relaxed. Sensing that his mother had retreated, the Sembian opened his eye. Once again the vulture was just a vulture, patiently circling the camp with its fellows. The Harper could not even tell which one had looked at him.

Lander kept a close eye on the approach to their ridge for the rest of the afternoon. If his mother had found him through a vulture, then Cyric might also know where he was. If what the Zhentarim were doing in Anauroch was important enough to the evil god, and if Lander posed a big enough threat to his plans, it did not seem unlikely that the Prince of Lies would try to communicate that information to his followers at the base of the mountain.

Twice Lander thought that a patrol was approaching the ridge, but each time the search party turned onto a different path. It appeared that either Cyric was not guiding the Zhentarim, or Rahalat had somehow turned them aside. Whatever the case, Lander was thankful. Fleeing during the heat of the day would have been hard on his wounded shoulder. If Ruha was sun-sick, he did not think it would do her any good either.

Periodically rotating search parties, the Zhentarim continued to feast and rest all day. Several times, Kadumi volunteered to change places, but Lander did not accept the offer. It made no difference to the Harper whether he spent the day watching the Zhentarim or sitting with Ruha, and he suspected that the youth knew more about preventing sun-sickness than he did.

When the sun dropped below the western horizon, both Kadumi and Ruha joined Lander. They all sat in silence for a few minutes, watching the birds of prey that nested on Rahalat's craggy slopes take wing with eerie silence. As the raptors spiraled down toward the spring, the cautious vultures widened their circle to give their ferocious cousins a wide berth.

"We should sneak away under cover of darkness," Kadumi said at last. "There is no telling how long the Zhentarim will rest at this oasis."

"Even in the dark, it is too dangerous to move until the invaders are gone," Ruha countered. "We would have to travel along the ridge all the way to the bottom of the mountain. Sooner or later, somebody would see our silhouettes."

Both the widow and her young brother-in-law looked to Lander for his opinion. Before giving it, he glanced at the camp. Already, dusk had cloaked the site in purple shadows and the dark-robed Zhentarim had disappeared. The hundreds of campfires they had kept burning all day twinkled in the night like orange stars.

"We have plenty of water and milk," Lander said. "Let's stay one more day. If the Zhentarim know we're still here, they'll be expecting us to leave in the dark."

Ruha nodded. "I've been resting all day, so I'll take the first watch."

After telling the widow to wake them if she felt weak before her watch ended, Lander and Kadumi agreed, then went down to sleep near the camels.

The Harper did not wake until shortly after dawn. Ruha sat atop the ridge, and Kadumi was still lodged between the two boulders that he had claimed as his bed last night. Lander stretched his sore muscles, then climbed up the hill and sat next to the widow.

"You should have wakened me," he said, taking a healing potion from his pocket.

Ruha shrugged. "You seemed tired, and I had slept all day." She regarded the glass vial in his hand. "What's that?"

"A potion for my shoulder," Lander explained. He opened the vial and drank the bitter contents in one swallow.

"Magic?" Ruha asked, one eyebrow raised.

Lander made a sour face and nodded. "Nothing else could taste that bad."

The widow studied him with a shocked expression. "Don't let Kadumi see you drinking those," she said. "The Bedine think ill of those who use magic."

Lander grimaced at his blunder, then slipped the empty vial back into his pocket. "You don't think magic is wrong, do you?"

Ruha shook her head. "I understand, but no one else." She studied him with an uncertain expression in her eyes, then nodded her head as if making up her mind about something. "There is something I must tell you, but only if you swear not to tell Kadumi or anyone else."

"Of course," Lander replied, wondering what the widow would tell him that she would not tell one of her own people.

"Sometimes I see mirages from the future," Ruha began. "That is what happened yesterday, when you and Kadumi thought I was sun-sick."

Lander nodded. "It did seem odd that you were affected and not me. What did you see?"

Ruha looked away. "I'm not sure. Someone is going to try kill you," she said. "He will attack from behind, with a dagger. You will be wounded."

Lander raised his eyebrow, unsure of how to take the news. "You're sure?"

The widow met his gaze evenly. "It is my curse that what I see always happens."

"Could you see what he looked like?" Lander asked.

Ruha shook her head. "All I saw was a dagger slicing

along your ribs. I don't know who was wielding it or what the outcome will be."

"Or when it will happen?"

The widow shook her head.

The warning did not frighten Lander, for he had long lived with the idea that the Zhentarim might try to assassinate him. Still, knowing that such a thing would occur—without knowing when or where—made him feel rather helpless. While sobering, the knowledge that such an attack would occur contained no hint as to what should be done about it—if, indeed, anything could.

"Thanks for the warning," Lander said. "I'll try to be careful about who I let behind me."

"It will do no good," Ruha said. "No matter what, you will be cut."

"At least you didn't see the dagger stuck in my heart," Lander said.

"I just thought you should know," Ruha replied. "I didn't say this to upset you."

"I know," the Harper replied, looking toward the base of the mountain and hoping to change the subject. In the growing dawn light, he saw a few wisps of smoke rising from a half-dozen dying fires, but otherwise the camp seemed empty and motionless. "Are they gone?"

Ruha nodded. "Their fires died last night, but I thought they had just fallen asleep. I didn't realize they were gone until nobody stirred with the dawn."

Lander studied the camp for a few minutes more. When he saw a vulture appear out of the east and drift straight into camp, he realized that there was no sign of the birds that had hovered below the ridge all day yesterday. The Zhentarim had, indeed, slipped away in the night.

"If the vultures are bold enough to land, then they're gone." The Harper called, "Kadumi, wake up! It's time to go."

As soon as the youth woke, the trio untethered the camels and led them down the mountain. By the time they reached the bottom, the sun had risen into the blue sky and the rosy morning light had faded to its usual white blaze. They paused at the spring to let the camels drink, then moved into the camp. Dozens of vultures took wing and hovered fifty feet overhead, watching the three companions with black, jealous eyes.

As at El Ma'ra, the invaders had razed all the *khreimas*, and the odor of singed camel-hair still hung thick in the air near the charred tents. There were Zhentarim fire rings everywhere, many of them still smoldering, and every combustible thing in camp had been burned. The entire area was littered with the hides and bones of half-eaten camels, and it appeared that even one or two dogs had been roasted.

The trio studied the ghastly scene in silence for several minutes before Ruha asked the question still troubling all three of them. "What happened to the bodies of the Mtair?"

Lander shook his head without speaking, then walked toward the edge of the camp. After picking up a waterskin to replace the one that had fallen off the mountainside with Kadumi's gelding, the widow and the youth followed with the camels. The companions soon found the spot where the Mtair warriors had made their stand. Crossbow quarrels, arrows, and broken-bladed weapons lay scattered along a quarter-mile battleline. Along the entire course, the sand was mottled with the brown stains of dried blood. Here and there lay camels or fleet-looking dogs unfortunate enough to have been caught in the crossfire, and Lander even found a golden jackal that had somehow gotten mixed up in the battle.

There were no human corpses. At El Ma'ra, the Zhentarim had taken care not to leave any of their dead behind, so Lander had not expected to discover any Black Robes or their reptilian mercenaries. On the other hand, he had expected to find the Mtair Dhafir's dead warriors. Instead, all he saw here were shredded *abas*, blood-stained *keffiyehs*, and discarded *jambiyas*.

"Look at this," Kadumi called, motioning for Lander to join him and Ruha.

The youth had discovered a trail of long, splayed-toed tracks. "Good work," Lander said, recognizing the footprints as those of the Zhentarim's mercenaries.

The trio followed the trail around to the north side of the mountain to a *wadi* they had not been able to see from their perch atop the ridge. As they approached the edge of the dry gulch, the thick odor of blood and entrails assaulted their nostrils, and all three of them nearly wretched. Lander motioned for the others to stand back, then stepped to the edge and peered down into the draw.

The bodies of the Mtair Dhafir lay scattered along the bed of the gulch, dozens of vultures feasting on their remains. If Lander was sickened by the desecrations of the scavenger birds, he was outraged by the mutilations that had been performed upon the bodies before the vultures began their grisly feast. The entire *khowwan* looked as though it had been attacked by man-eating beasts. The soft parts of their bodies had been ripped open and savaged as he had seen Sembian bears do to deer and other large game.

Kadumi and Ruha stepped to Lander's side.

"What happened?" asked the widow.

To Lander's surprise, his companions were not staggered by the sight. Their faces showed anger and outrage, but there was no sign of horror in either of their expressions.

"The men ate the camels," Lander said, wondering if all Bedine were made of such stern stuff. "The reptilian sell-swords ate the men."

"There must be over a thousand mercenaries with the Zhentarim," Kadumi said, studying the gruesome scene with a thoughtful air. "A few hundred could not have eaten so many."

"True, but this points out the Zhentarim's weakness," Ruha said. "The invaders must be running low on their food. Perhaps they will starve, after all."

"If that is going to happen," the Harper said. "We must reach the next tribe before the Zhentarim feed it to their mercenaries. Can we do it?"

Ruha nodded. "Colored Waters is a week away. With Kadumi's extra camels, we should easily overtake the Zhentarim."

The youth frowned at his sister-in-law. "Do you know who is camped at Colored Waters? Are they allies of the Mtair Dhafir?"

Ruha shook her head.

"Then perhaps it is not our place to go with the *berrani,*" he said. "Even if they let us into camp, those camped at Colored Waters may not believe us."

The widow shrugged. "I see no harm in helping Lander," she said. "Besides, it is our duty to avenge the slaughter of the Qahtan and the Mtair Dhafir, is it not?"

Kadumi regarded the corpse-filled wadi for several moments, then nodded. "It is."

"Good," Lander said. He glanced at the bodies uncomfortably. "Is there anything we should do?"

Ruha shook her head. "N'asr's children took their spirits away last night," she said. "There is nothing we can do but reach Colored Waters as fast as we can."

Lander did not understand what she meant, but he felt he should follow his own custom and warn the spirits about the dangers they faced in the Realm of the Dead. He stepped to the edge of the *wadi*, then called in a clear loud voice,

"Dead ones, Cyric—er, N'asr—has denizens everywhere. Remember your gods and keep their faith. If you doubt your gods, you will suffer as surely as the wicked."

When the Harper turned away from the gulch, Kadumi was openly smirking at him. Even Ruha's eyes were twinkling as she asked, "What did they answer?"

"It's sort of a prayer," Lander explained.

"It sounded like advice to me," Ruha countered. "Have you visited N'asr's camp?"

"No, of course not."

"Then how can you give advice to the dead?" demanded Kadumi, forcing his camel to kneel so he could mount it. "You don't know what they'll find."

Lander started to explain that he had learned about how the Realm of the Dead worked from his Cyric-worshiping mother, then thought better of explaining his family history. Instead, forcing his own camel to kneel, he simply said, "It can't hurt."

"That's right, Kadumi," Ruha said, also kneeling her camel. "After the vultures carry off the spirits of the dead, Lander can say whatever he likes to the corpses." She climbed into her camel's saddle, then added, "Now, if they start talking back, we'd better change our minds about riding with him."

Lander flushed, uncertain as to whether or not the widow was poking fun at him, and uncomfortable in either event. He mounted his camel and urged it to its feet. "I told you, they never talk back."

Kadumi laughed, then commanded his camel to rise and pointed the way into the desert.

On the western side of Rahalat, the sand dunes grew smaller and more yellowish in color. Within two miles, they assumed the parallel, ridgelike pattern of transverse dunes. To Lander, the sands resembled nothing so much as a lake of golden waters on a breezy day. In the wide troughs between the dunes, the sand was no more than a few inches deep and the camels found the going quite easy.

The dunes themselves rose no higher than thirty feet, with gentle slopes leading both up to and down from the crest. Where the Zhentarim had crossed them, the passage of so many thousands of feet had often pounded a small pass through the ridge. These passes made travel even easier, for they often reduced the height the Harper's small company had to climb by as much as ten feet.

As he reached the summit of one of these passes, Lander paused between its ten-foot walls and looked over his shoulder. He saw that the ground had slowly been rising as they rode away from the Shunned Mountain. The great whaleback dunes on the eastern side of Rahalat lay in an immense basin. From this distance, they looked like a stormy ocean of ice. Remembering the effort it had required to struggle over one of those monstrous dunes, the Harper was grateful for the easy travel through these golden sands.

When Kadumi and Ruha reached the summit of the little pass, Lander nodded toward the white sands. "It's like an ocean."

Kadumi looked confused. "We call it the Bowl of Loneliness. What do you mean, 'ocean'?"

Lander started to explain. "It's a pond of water so large—" A heap of sand sloughed off the northern wall of the pass, and the Harper stopped in midsentence.

"What's wrong?" Ruha asked.

Before Lander could answer, a black shroud burst out of the sand. At the same time, a swarthy voice called, "Show yourselves!"

The voice was speaking Common, so Lander assumed it belonged to a Zhentarim. Reaching for his sword with one hand and using the reins to whip his mount with the other, the Harper yelled in Bedine, "Ambush! Get out of here!"

Before the camel took two steps, a pair of crossbow quarrels sailed across Lander's path from the other side of the little pass. The Harper spun around to face the attack and found two men less then ten yards away. They held empty crossbows in their hands. Behind them, four more men were flinging the sand from their black burnooses and rising from their subsurface hiding places, crossbows cocked and ready to fire.

"Move and you die!" warned the figure that had first burst from the sand. "Stay still and perhaps you will live."

Lander reined his camel to a halt, then slipped his sword back into scabbard and turned to face the speaker. The invader wore the black burnoose the Zhentarim had adopted as their desert uniform. Narrow, steely eyes gazed out from beneath his furrowed brow. Behind him stood another five Zhentarim, sand running from their robes in yellow rivulets. That meant that there were a total of six men on each side of the pass.

The Harper did not answer the leader's question, for if he showed that he understood their words, the Zhentarim would realize that he was no Bedine. He suspected that the ambushers already knew his identity—or would deduce it from his light skin soon enough—but he saw no reason to make the enemy's job simpler. Perhaps he might even confuse them long enough to plot an escape.

"Dismount!" the Zhentarim demanded, still speaking Common. While his subordinates kept their weapons trained on the small party, the commander moved toward Lander and motioned for all three of his captives to kneel their camels.

Kadumi started to pull his scimitar from its scabbard, but Lander motioned for the youth to keep his blade sheathed. Ruha was the first to obey the Black Robe's command, slipping out of her saddle and kneeling at her mount's side. The widow held the reins drawn tightly to her body, forcing the beast to crane its neck around at an awkward angle. Her mount roared its indignation, but she ignored it.

Puzzled by Ruha's peculiar action, Lander also couched his own mount, then watched as Kadumi resentfully did likewise.

The Zhentarim walked straight to Lander. "Where are you going? Why are you following us?"

As he spoke, he reached for the Harper's *aba*, and Lander knew there was no use in trying to hide his identity. Beneath his *aba*, Lander still wore the harp and moon pin of the Harpers. After Bhadla had noticed its outline, he had taken care to keep that part of his outer clothing dirty enough to camouflage the pin beneath, but he had not removed the symbol. When Florin had fastened it on his breast, he had sworn to always wear the harp and moon over his heart.

The Zhentarim ripped Lander's *aba* open, then looked directly at the symbol. In Common, he called to his men, "This is the Harper. Let's take them all to Yhekal."

When the other Zhentarim started to step forward from the sides of the pass, Ruha yelled, "Ride, now!"

Kadumi obeyed immediately, commanding his camel to rise. The widow began chanting in the deep, mystic tones that Lander recognized as a spellcasting.

The Zhentarim commander's eyes widened in alarm and he pointed at Ruha. "Kill—"

That was all the commander said before Lander struck his shoulder with the edge of an open hand. Without pausing an instant, the Harper went into a well-rehearsed attack. He grabbed the back of the Zhentarim's neck and smashed the opposite elbow into the commander's face. When the astonished invader reached to cover his shattered nose, Lander kneed him in the groin, then slapped his open palms against the man's ears. The Harper finished the attack by slipping an arm around the back of the Zhentarim's neck, grabbing the chin, and pulling hard. The invader's neck popped, and the man collapsed into a lifeless heap.

Realizing he was now a target for the crossbowmen, Lander dove forward. The twang of crossbow strings filled the air before he hit the sand, half-a-dozen quarrels whistled past where he had been standing, and his camel roared in pain and terror.

Continuing his dive in one fluid motion, Lander rolled back to his feet, drew his weapon, then turned toward his companions. Most of the Zhentarim were cocking crossbows again. One had drawn his saber and was rushing Ruha, who had picked up two fistfuls of sand and was letting it sift through her fingers. Kadumi drew his scimitar and turned his camel to defend Ruha.

"No, Kadumi!" Lander called, rushing after the youth. "Take the camels and go!"

The youth paused long enough to glance over his shoulder and frown, then urged his mount forward. As he approached the Zhentarim, he screamed his battle cry and raised his sword to strike.

The invader hit the ground and ducked the boy's wild slash. As the Zhentarim returned to his feet, he lashed out with his saber and cleanly lopped off one of the camel's rear legs at the knee. The beast fell immediately, spilling Kadumi three feet from the attacker.

The Harper hazarded a glance at the men still fighting with crossbows. They were just securing their bowstrings into place and recocking their weapons. Realizing that he still had a moment or two before they loaded their quarrels, Lander rushed up behind Kadumi's attacker and brought a vicious slash down on the Zhentarim's collarbone. Screaming, the man dropped his sword and stumbled forward, falling onto the young warrior. Lander finished the invader with a thrust through the spine and pulled the dead man off of the boy.

Pointing at the string of white camels, Lander yelled, "Take the mounts and go! I'll protect Ruha!"

Without pausing to see if the wide-eyed youth would obey this time, he stepped past Kadumi. The surviving Zhentarim had reloaded their crossbows and were raising them to fire at Ruha.

Dropping his sword, Lander launched himself at the mage. He struck her full in the body just as the twang of crossbow-strings filled the air. As he hit the ground, the Harper heard more than four quarrels hiss over his head. A heavy groan escaped the throat of Ruha's mount, then it lay motionless in the sand.

The Harper leapt back to his feet and retrieved his sword. To his relief, he saw that Kadumi had obeyed him and was leading the string of surviving camels down the other side of the ridge. Lander stepped back toward Ruha, expecting to hear a chorus of Zhentarim battle cries. Instead, however, all he heard were screams as the sandy walls of the small pass avalanched down on top of them.

A small hand seized his free arm. "Come!" Ruha urged. "We must hurry!"

Pulling him by the arm, she led the way as they half-stumbled, half-ran after Kadumi and the camels. The pair was thirty yards from the dune's base before Ruha stopped. Panting and sweating heavily in the terrible heat, Lander turned to look at the ambush site.

All that remained of the small pass was a slight, barely noticeable dip in the ridge of the dune. The sand had rolled forward from both sides, completely burying the ambushers. There was no sign of any of the invaders.

"Do you think any survived?" Lander asked, noticing that the widow still held his hand.

Ruha shook her head. "No. It is one thing to hide in the

sand and another to be buried by it. If they are not dead already, they will soon suffocate."

Kadumi joined them, still leading the camels. Instead of thanking Lander for saving his life, as the Harper had expected, the youth studiously avoided meeting the older man's gaze. Instead, he turned to Ruha and spat at her feet.

"Witch!"

Eight

Ruha's mount suddenly slowed its jolting pace, jarring the widow out of the lethargic daze into which she had fallen. For the last five days, the three companions had been riding hard, hoping to overtake the Zhentarim. The effort had exhausted Ruha and, despite her best efforts to stay alert, she often felt as if her mind had left her body to fend for itself.

When Ruha looked up to see why her camel had halted, she saw Lander stopped twenty feet ahead. He was staring at the horizon, where a broad, black line of apparent nothingness separated the dun-colored ground from the cerulean sky. Ruha squinted at the dark line. When it did not disappear or become more distinct, she dismissed it as one of the desert's thousand and one visual illusions.

"What's he doing?" Lander demanded, pointing at a black fleck on horizon, where the blue sky met the black strip of illusion.

The speck was Kadumi. At his own insistence, the boy

was riding ahead to scout. Since learning that his sister-in-law was a sorceress, the boy had said no more than a dozen words to her, and all of them had been disparaging. Ruha was not surprised by his reaction, for she suspected that he blamed her magic for the bad fortune that had brought the Zhentarim down upon his tribe. Most Bedine would have done the same.

Whatever the cause for Kadumi's detachment, it set Lander's nerves on edge. The Harper preferred to do his own scouting and did not like trusting his safety to some-one else.

"Why's he dismounting?" Lander demanded.

Ruha squinted at the distant figure. "You can see that?"

"Of course," he responded gruffly. "You don't think I'd let him out of my sight!"

"But that far—and with only one eye?" Ruha immedi-ately regretted her question, fearing that she would touch a sore nerve. "Please forgive me. I didn't mean—"

The Harper chuckled and raised a hand. "No offense tak-en," he said. "It's a badge of my own damn stupidity."

"How so?" Ruha asked, anxious to appease the curiosity she had felt ever since meeting the stranger.

"When I was a boy, my mother gave me a pet hawk that didn't want to be a pet. I had to keep it on a tether." He paused, unconsciously rubbing a finger along the edge of his patch.

"And?" Ruha prompted.

"One day it made its feelings known."

Ruha grimaced, imagining the raptor tearing at Lander's boyish face. "What did your father do?"

Lander smiled. "Let it go, of course."

"A Bedine would have killed it," Ruha said. "I think I would have, too."

"Why?" Lander asked, meeting her gaze with his one good eye. "You can't blame an animal for wanting to be free. Your people should realize that more than anybody."

"The Bedine would have been more concerned with vengeance than with what is right."

Instead of commenting on Ruha's reply, the Harper turned his attention back to Kadumi's distant form. "Why is he stopped? Is it the Zhentarim?"

The faint whistle of a high-pitched *amarat* horn wafted across the barrens. "I don't think it's the invaders. Kadumi's signaling us to come."

Urging his camel forward, Lander asked, "Why?"

"We're there," Ruha replied. "He dismounted to meet a sentry."

The Harper scanned the horizon with a scowl. "That's unfortunate."

"Why?"

"I'd rather Kadumi didn't meet this new tribe without us being there," Lander replied. "I don't trust him to keep your secret, and there's too much at stake here to let superstition get in the way."

Ruha glanced back to make sure everything was in order with the string of Kadumi's camels she was leading. "We can only hope that he remembers his duty to protect his brother's wife."

"Will he?"

Ruha shrugged. "I think so. He's seemed very bitter since the fight, but that's only natural, considering what he's been through in the past weeks. The blood runs hot in boys that age, and any Bedine would be upset to discover that his brother had married a witch. Still, I don't think he will let his emotions overcome his honor. He impresses me as a boy who listened closely to his father and knows what is expected of a man."

"And what happens if you're wrong?"

"I don't think the sheikh will kill me," she said, avoiding the Harper's gaze. "But he won't listen to you, either. You and I will have to leave."

Lander frowned. "The Zhentarim—"

Ruha lifted her hand to quiet his objection. "If it comes to that, nothing you say will change the sheikh's mind. In that case, I'll help you find another tribe. You can repay the favor by letting me ride with you to your land."

The Harper raised an eyebrow and looked her over from head to toe. "I don't think you'd like Sembia," he said. "Still, if you really want to go, I'll take you there."

"Sembia," Ruha said, smiling to herself. "That is a nice name for home." Aside from its name, she knew only one thing about Lander's home, but it was the only thing she needed to know. In Sembia, at least if the Harper was any example, no one would care that she was a sorceress.

After a moment of silence, Lander scanned the horizon with a furrowed brow. "If we're getting close to Colored Waters," he asked, "why do I see no sign of an oasis?"

"You will," Ruha replied. Though she had never been to Colored Waters, she had heard descriptions of it. The black strip on the horizon was no illusion. It was the great basin where the oasis sat.

As they rode, the sable strip took on the distinct appearance of the abyss marking the site of the final battle before the Scattering. The Bedine believed this was where, centuries before, the gods had destroyed the denizens from the Camp of the Dead. When Ruha was close enough to see the far edge, the hollow assumed the shape of a great, ebony bowl. It was ten miles long, eight miles wide, and over a thousand feet deep.

Except for a few star-shaped dunes of golden silt, its steep walls were covered entirely with a fine, sable-colored soot. In the center of the basin floor, an amber cone, said to be made from the ashes of the denizens, rose nearly as high as the lips of the great bowl.

Five lakes, each the crescent shape of a scimitar's blade,

ringed the base of the cinder cone. Each lake was a different color: emerald-green, turquoise, silver as the hilt of a *jambiya*, sapphire blue, and red as a ruby. According to legend, the different colors resulted when the dried blood of the immortals was washed or blown into the water and dissolved.

Around each lake were clumped wild fig trees, tall golden grasses, and leafy green bushes. Over the entire floor of the basin, salt-brush and hardy lime-green *qassis* plants poked through the ebony ash, and the grayish yellow camel herds grazed in every part of the black bowl. The huge valley was as close to paradise as any place Ruha had ever seen.

"In the name of Mielikki," Lander gasped. "What hell has that boy led us to?"

Ruha ignored the Harper's question to ask one of her own. "Who is Mielikki?"

"You wouldn't worship her here," Lander answered, unable to rip his gaze away from the ancient caldera before him. "Mielikki is the goddess of the forest. She's my patron and protector, at least until I go down there. What is it?"

Amused by Lander's reaction, Ruha smiled. "Colored Waters, of course."

A few minutes later, they reached the edge of the basin. Ruha could feel heat rising in swells, and the air shimmered in liquid waves that made every distant line a serpent. Noting the caldera's shape and dark color, she could only guess that it acted like a giant funnel for collecting At'ar's radiance. It was a good thing there was plenty of water at the bottom, for any living being staying down there for even a few minutes would grow very thirsty.

Kadumi was waiting with a thin Bedine dressed in sooty black robes. As Ruha and Lander approached, the sentry came forward with a waterskin.

"Stop and drink, *berrani*." The sentry offered his skin to Lander, repeating a typical Bedine greeting. "You have had a long ride and must be thirsty. Are you hungry as well?"

Lander accepted the other waterskin. "Hungry, no," the Sembian said, taking a long gulp.

The sentry did not mind the rudeness. He grinned and turned to Kadumi. "At least he shows more courtesy than the Black Robe and his short guide."

Lander pulled the waterskin away from his mouth, spewing water all over his camel's neck.

"Black Robe?" he gasped.

Kadumi nodded. "The Zhentarim arrived this morning," he said. "We'll have to wait until he leaves to meet the sheikh."

"No!" Lander protested, thrusting the skin back at the sentry. "We must meet the sheikh before the Zhentarim poisons his thoughts. Perhaps if I had reached the Mtair Dhafir's sheikh earlier, they'd still be alive."

Kadumi grimaced, but turned to the sentry. "At which lake is your sheikh camped?"

The sentry pointed at the emerald pool. "Sheikh Sa'ar makes his camp at the green waters. I'll announce your arrival." The sentry lifted his *amarat* and blew three shrill notes, then lowered it again. "I'd take you into camp myself, but the Zhentarim are only five miles to the north. The sheikh has ordered the sentries to stay at their posts under all circumstances."

"Sheikh Sa'ar is a wise man," Kadumi responded, climbing onto his kneeling camel.

The first five hundred yards of descent were steep. The camels plunged down the slope, almost galloping to keep from tumbling head over heels, kicking up great billows of black ash that engulfed each rider in a tiny dust storm. With each jolting lunge, Ruha gritted her teeth and grasped her saddle more tightly, expecting to go sprawling through the ebony cinders in a whirlwind of waterskins, *kuerabiches*, and roaring camels.

A few moments later, the beasts slowed into a jolting canter. With the ash clouds billowing no higher than the camels' humps, the trio could carry on a quivering conversation.

"You didn't tell the guard about my magic, did you Kadumi?" Ruha asked.

"Perhaps I will tell the sheikh," the boy responded, avoiding the widow's gaze.

"A man must do what he thinks is right," Lander agreed.

The Harper's statement stunned Ruha. She began to wonder if she had misjudged Lander's character.

Before she could condemn him, the Harper continued, "Of course, a man's duty to his brother's wife counts for a lot."

The youth glowered at Ruha. "My brother would not have knowingly married a witch."

Lander nodded. "Probably not. Still, Ruha *was* his wife . . ." The Harper let the statement drift off without adding anything further, and they continued in silence.

A short time later, Kadumi asked, "What will you say to Sheikh Sa'ar, Harper?"

"I don't know," Lander responded, grasping his make-shift saddle with both hands. "What do you think I should say?"

"The Zhentarim will no doubt promise him many great gifts for becoming his ally," Kadumi began.

"And threaten him with swift destruction if he does not," Ruha added.

"I can promise neither."

"What about your Harpers?" Kadumi asked, motioning at the pin still hidden over Lander's heart. "What will they give Sa'ar for joining them?"

Lander shook his head. "They don't work that way," he

said. "Even if I were in contact with them, they would promise him little. We prefer more subtle methods."

"Subtlety will not drive the Zhentarim from Anauroch," Ruha said. "That will require warriors."

"Bedine warriors," Lander replied. "Not Harper warriors. If the Bedine will not fight for their freedom, the Harpers have no interest in doing it for them."

"Then why did they send you here?" Kadumi demanded, precariously twisting about on his camel's back. "I lost three good mounts getting you here, and you brought nothing to offer Sa'ar?"

"I can offer him liberty," Lander replied.

His voice was so calm that Ruha knew the Harper was missing the point. "We do not know Sheikh Sa'ar," she said. "And he does not know us. The destruction of the Qahtan and the Mtair Dhafir mean nothing to him. You cannot expect him to turn the Black Robes away just because they destroyed two *khowwans* to which he had no ties."

They reached the bottom of the basin. As the terrain leveled, their camels slowed to a jolting walk.

"The Zhentarim are strong," Kadumi said, still taking care to avoid speaking directly with Ruha. "Sa'ar will want to ally with them."

"I thought the Bedine loved freedom," Lander countered, relaxing his grip on his saddle harness.

Ruha guided her camel closer to the Harper's. "They do, but the desert has always been here. No Bedine can conceive of the chains that will stop him from escaping into it."

Lander shook his head sadly. "The Zhentarim don't hold their slaves with chains—"

"They hold them with hostages, blackmail, fear, and worse," Ruha responded. "But Sa'ar will not know this. He will think only of what the Zhentarim can give him, not what they can take away."

"If we cannot promise gifts from the Harpers," Kadumi

said, driving his mount to Lander's opposite side, "perhaps we should concentrate on what we could steal from the Zhentarim. With such a big army, they must have a lot of camels and a fortune in steel blades. Raiding is something Sa'ar will understand."

Kadumi's idea was the best they had come up with so far, but Ruha did not think it would work. "Why raid when you can simply ask? Will the Zhentarim not promise all these things in return for an alliance?"

"Being paid is not the same as taking," Kadumi countered hotly, finally addressing Ruha directly.

The widow was not listening. A sudden flash of insight had just occurred to her. "We can never promise more than the Zhentarim," she said. "So what we need to do is get rid of the Zhentarim agent before the sheikh makes an agreement."

Both Kadumi and Lander frowned.

"Correct me if I'm wrong," the Harper said, craning his neck to look at her, "but wouldn't the sheikh take a dim view of assassinating his guests?"

"We're not going to kill the Zhentarim," Ruha laughed, pointing at Lander. "He's going to try to kill you."

The Harper frowned, then leaned close to Ruha so Kadumi could not hear what he whispered, "I'm beginning to understand why your visions always come true."

"Don't worry," Ruha replied, speaking aloud to prevent Kadumi from thinking any secrets were being kept from him. "You'll just make the Zhentarim so mad that he'll *try* to kill you."

Kadumi smiled. "Honor will dictate that the sheikh save you and banish or execute the man who assaulted his guest. You'll have the sheikh's ear to yourself."

"Just in time to warn him about the Zhentarim's impending attack," Ruha finished. She leaned close to Lander and added, "Do not worry about the attack I saw on Rahalat's shoulder, for in the vision you had clearly been surprised by the assault from behind."

When Kadumi scowled at the widow, she straightened and said, "If the plan works, Lander, you will be expecting the Zhentarim to attack. Kadumi will be there to protect your back, so you will have nothing to fear." Her brother-in-law stiffened at the compliment.

After a moment's consideration, Lander nodded. "I can do it."

They rode the rest of the way to the camp in silence. When they reached the golden grass surrounding the emerald lake, urging the camels onward became more effort than it was worth. They tethered the beasts and walked the rest of the way on foot.

Sa'ar's camp was typical. Each family had pitched its *khreima* with the entrance facing the center of the circle. The women were spinning camel's wool, repairing carpets, and tending to the dozens of other tasks required to maintain a household. The older girls were helping their mothers or watching the youngest children, who were running about between the tents or wrestling in the circle.

As the trio passed through the tent circle, the women welcomed them by whistling from beneath their veils, and the young children paused long enough to stare in open-mouthed amazement at Lander's fair, sunburned skin. Ruha suddenly felt lonely and sad, for the scene reminded her of the life she had enjoyed for only three days, a life she knew she would never have again.

Her sudden melancholy was a stark contrast to the last few days. Since leaving the desolated camps of the Mtair Dhafir, she had been too busy trying to reach Colored Waters, daydreaming about Lander's homeland, and worrying about the Zhentarim to dwell on her own status. Even Kadumi's reaction when he discovered her to be a witch had not been very painful. Part of the reason, she knew, was that Lander's attitude gave her hope of finding someplace she would not be an outcast.

When the trio reached the sheikh's audience tent, they found a large pavilion made from blond camel's wool. It was open on all sides, and Ruha could see Sa'ar sitting beneath it next to two guests. The sheikh was a powerfully built man of forty or fifty, his face lined with furrows, his eyes hard with confidence and cunning.

Ruha recognized both of the sheikh's guests immediately. One of them had flashing blue eyes with skin and hair as pale as white sand. He wore a purple robe and silver bracers, and had been posing as Zarud's servant in the camp of the Mtair Dhafir. The widow was dismayed to see the pale stranger, for he did not strike her as the type of man who would be easy to provoke into an attack on Lander.

The other guest's presence surprised Ruha as much as the first one's presence dismayed her. He stood no more than four-feet tall, was swaddled head to toe in a white burnoose and turban, and looked like one of Lander's companions at El Ma'ra. If it was the same individual, she could not imagine what he was doing with the Zhentarim.

The trio paused outside the pavilion and waited several seconds. When no one inside seemed to notice their presence, Lander impatiently cleared his throat, bringing the quiet conversation inside to an abrupt halt.

"Has somebody come to my *khreima* in need of help?" called the sheikh. His voice was deep, confident, and held mild irritation.

"Not in need of help, but bringing it," the Harper said. "I have come to warn you of treachery."

Before the sheikh could respond, the short guest called, "And why should the sheikh believe a liar who works fraud upon those he contracts?" He spoke in stilted, accented Bedine.

To Ruha's surprise, the question drew a smile from
Lander. "Bhadla, you're alive!"

"Musalim did not fare so well," Bhadla responded, his
tone accusatory.

"That is the Zhentarim's fault, not mine."

"This business has no place in the tents of the Mahwa,"
the sheikh interrupted. "*Berrani*, won't you come into my
khreima and drink some hot tea?"

"Your hospitality is legendary, Sheikh Sa'ar," Lander replied, leading the way into the tent and motioning at his two
companions. "I am Lander. My friends are Kadumi and Ruha of the Qahtan."

"Apparently you know Bhadla," Sa'ar replied, indicating
that the trio should sit opposite Bhadla and the Zhentarim.
"The D'tarig's master is Yhekal, sheikh of the Zhentarim."

Sa'ar's servant brought a pair of tiny cups and a pot filled
with hot salted tea. Sa'ar filled each tiny cup with black,
rich-smelling liquid, then handed one to both Lander and
Kadumi.

When he saw that the sheikh had ignored Ruha, Lander
held his cup out to the young widow. Though the tea
smelled delicious, she quickly shook her head to indicate
that she did not want the drink. The Mahwa did not permit
men and women to eat together, or the sheikh would have
offered her a cup himself. Ruha suspected that allowing her
to sit in his tent was the extent of the courtesy the sheikh
would normally show a strange woman.

Realizing his mistake, Lander withdrew the cup and
sipped from it himself.

"Tell me about your journey," Sa'ar said, inviting Lander
into conversation. "Where did you come from? What
brings you into the Mother Desert?"

The Harper did not waste any time with pleasantries.
Staring at Yhekal with a sneer so offensive that it could only
be intentional, he said, "The treachery of the Zhentarim. I

have come to warn the Bedine of their plans."

Sa'ar lifted a brow. "Is that so?"

As Bhadla translated Lander's statement, Ruha realized that the Zhentarim had learned from his failure with the Mtair Dhafir and was apparently foregoing the use of magic with Sa'ar.

After listening to the translation of Lander's charge, Yhekal replied to Bhadla calmly, and the D'tarig gave the reply to the Bedine. "My master says he has presented the Zhentarim's offer to Sheikh Sa'ar. He suggests the Harper do the same for his people."

"That seems fair," Sa'ar agreed. "The Zhentarim have offered me steel and gems. What will the Harpers offer?"

"Freedom," Lander replied with quiet nonchalance. He sipped his tea and watched the Zhentarim as the D'tarig translated the response for his master.

The sheikh snorted. "That is all? We have our freedom."

"Not after you sell it to the Zhentarim," Lander replied. "Did Yhekal also tell you how his people treated the Qahtan and the Mtair Dhafir?"

The sheikh nodded, his face showing no other response. "What is that to me? They were not my allies."

As Sa'ar responded, Ruha noticed a certain satisfaction creeping into Yhekal's eyes, and she realized that he was secretly using magic to understand Bedine. Thinking of the spell that had influenced her father, Ruha wondered if the purple-robed Zhentarim had also tried it on Sa'ar and failed, or if he was saving it for later.

"Sheikh Sa'ar, the Qahtan and the Mtair Dhafir were your allies, as are all the other *khowwans* of the desert," Lander said. He glared at Yhekal, then turned back to Sa'ar and said, "Whether you realize it or not, you have a common enemy. The Zhentarim wish to seize the desert from the Bedine."

Yhekal started to respond, but caught himself and wait-

ed. After Bhadla had translated Lander's charge and the
Zhentarim made a reply in his own language, the D'tarig at
last rasped, "My master says that the Harper is not speaking the truth. The Zhentarim do not want anything from the
desert. They merely wish to open a trade route across it—
with the cooperation of the Bedine tribes, of course."

"The Zhentarim is a liar!" Kadumi snapped, pointing an
accusing finger at Yhekal. "If the Zhentarim wish to make
allies, why have they brought so many warriors?"

After patiently waiting for the translation he did not
need, Yhekal gave his reply to Bhadla and the D'tarig
passed it on. "The desert is a dangerous place," he said.
"One must be prepared."

"For what?" Kadumi demanded hotly, turning to the
sheikh. "They have at least three thousand warriors in
their army!"

The sheikh turned to Lander. "Is the boy speaking
truly?"

"We can't be sure of the exact number, Sheikh Sa'ar,"
the Harper replied. "It is only an approximate count."

As her companions spoke, Ruha watched the Zhentarim's concern. She decided to give him something else to
think about. "If I may speak, Sheikh Sa'ar?"

Sa'ar nodded to Ruha. "All who sit in my *khreima* may
speak."

Ruha inclined her head. "How do you think Yhekal feeds
so many in the desert?"

The sheikh frowned thoughtfully. "Now that you ask, I
can't imagine. How?"

Both Lander and Kadumi smiled, anticipating what she
would say. She settled her gaze on the Zhentarim, then
said, "After the Zhentarim finished with the Mtair Dhafir,
they cooked a hundred camels and gave the bodies of the
Mtair Dhafir to their reptile soldiers."

Upon hearing the last part of the report, the sheikh's

mouth turned downward in disgust. "Cannibals," he hissed. When Bhadla started to translate what had just passed, the sheikh cut him off. "Yhekal obviously understands our words," Sa'ar said, "and I am tired of playing his game."

The Zhentarim's brow furrowed, but he did not lose his temper. "They're lying, Sheikh," he said, now speaking Bedine.

The sheikh looked the Zhentarim over thoughtfully. "I don't think so, Yhekal. You are the one who has presented himself as something he is not."

"Am I to take that as your reply, then?" the purple-robed invader asked.

The sheikh looked toward the camp outside his tent. "I have not yet decided. Now that I have heard the words of both the Zhentarim and these Harpers," he said, mistakenly waving his hand at Ruha and Kadumi as well as Lander, "we will discuss the matter. I will send for you when we are ready."

"As a friend," Yhekal said, his voice as even and cold as ever, "I warn you not to choose the Harpers over the Zhentarim—"

"Listen to this warning carefully, Sheikh," Lander interrupted. "Threats are the only truthful words you will ever hear a Zhentarim speak."

Yhekal closed his mouth, and Ruha saw his hand drop toward his *jambiya*. For a moment, she thought that the invader might actually lose control of himself and draw his weapon, but Bhadla gently laid a hand on the man's arm.

"Perhaps we should go, Lord," the D'tarig said. "Sheikh Sa'ar needs time to consider your proposal."

The Zhentarim relaxed instantly. Without looking at his translator, Yhekal said, "Of course, Bhadla." He glared at Lander with a menacing look, then turned to Sheikh Sa'ar. "I hope to hear from you soon—shall we say . . . tonight?"

Nine

A bitter wind gusted over the hillside, sending dust devils of sulphurous grit scuttling across the volcano's pale slopes. Lander sat in a ravine about a quarter of the way up the cinder cone, staring at the campfires three hundred feet below. Though he wore a *jellaba* given to him by Sheikh Sa'ar, the heavy camel's wool robe did not prevent him from shivering.

Sa'ar lifted the battered pot off the steaming rock-fissure upon which it had been placed to keep the tea warm. He poured a generous helping of the black liquid into a wooden cup, then offered it to Lander. "Here, something to warm you," the sheikh said.

The Harper accepted the tea with heartfelt gratitude, then wrapped his hands around the warm cup and sipped the rich drink. Though the steam vent kept the tea far from scalding, it was still hot enough to warm his insides. "Thank you," Lander said, at last bringing his shivering to a halt.

Sa'ar put the pot back in the vent-hole, then shook his head in amusement and shrugged Lander's thanks off without comment. It was a Bedine peculiarity, the Harper had noticed, that they did not express gratitude for food or water. From what he could tell, they regarded these two essentials as the property of whomever needed them at the time. It seemed a strangely charitable custom for a people who thought it praiseworthy to kill a man in order to steal his camel.

"You had better be right about the Zhentarim," Sheikh Sa'ar commented, studying the black basin of emptiness lying beyond his tribes' campsite. "I would not like to think I made my people abandon their *khreimas* for nothing."

"I'm right."

Lander's answer was confident, but even he was beginning to doubt the Zhentarim would attack. Already, Mystra's Star Circle was touching the western horizon, and by the constellation's position, Lander knew dawn would come in less than three hours.

The Harper and the sheikh had been sitting in the ravine since nightfall, when the Mahwa had silently snuck out of their camps, leaving their *khreimas* standing behind them. Under the cover of the moonless night, the tribe had ridden for the far side of the caldera. Behind them, they had left only two sentries and a half-dozen warriors to tend the campfires so that it would appear that the camp remained occupied.

Tethering their camels two miles away, about a quarter of the way around the volcano's cone, Lander and Sa'ar had come to watch the Zhentarim overrun the empty camp. Sa'ar had justified the adventure by claiming he wanted to study his enemies, but Lander suspected that the sheikh was more interested in witnessing the Black Robes' reaction when they learned they had been duped.

Fortunately for Lander's nerves, they had to wait only

twenty minutes longer. A familiar, shrill note wafted across
the black emptiness, and then a tiny bolt of bright light
flared in the distance.

"What was that?" Sa'ar demanded, rising to his feet.

"Lightning bolt," Lander explained.

"Magic?"

"Yes," the Harper replied, also standing.

The sheikh groaned. "My warriors won't like that."

"The Zhentarim try to eliminate the sentries, then overrun the camps quickly," Lander explained. "They won't
tolerate survivors."

"With good reason," Sa'ar responded, pointing at Lander. "You, Ruha, and the boy have certainly caused them
enough trouble. If you hadn't told me of their atrocities to
the Mtair Dhafir, I might well have allied with them. From
what Kadumi told me, the Mtair Dhafir would have also
joined them—if you hadn't cut their envoy's throat."

"Kadumi told you that?" Lander asked, surprised.

The sheikh turned and watched the dark shapes of two
warriors ride their camels out of camp. "No," he replied.
"Kadumi claimed it was someone named Al'Aif, but I think
you had more reasons than this Al'Aif."

Lander did not bother to deny the conclusion. At the moment, who had killed Zarud did not matter, and he did not
wish to offend Sa'ar. Instead of arguing with the sheikh, the
Harper reached for the tea pot. "May I?"

"Why do you have to ask?"

Lander filled his cup, then sipped the warm drink while
they waited for the Zhentarim to reach the camp. The
Harper barely finished his tea before dark shapes began
skulking through the golden grass around the lakes.

"Weren't the sentries stationed at the edge of the basin?" Lander asked.

"They were supposed to be," the sheikh responded, already thinking along the same lines as Lander. "But that

seems impossible. It should have taken the Zhentarim twice this long to reach the camp."

The two men watched silently as a long line of dark silhouettes appeared outside the camp. Though Lander guessed the line to be less than four hundred yards away, the shapes remained indistinct and small. For several minutes, the army held its ground, awaiting the resistance that would not come. After a time it began to creep silently, cautiously forward.

"All right," Sa'ar said. "Let us see what they think of our little ruse."

As Lander had expected, the first ranks entered the fire-lit camp scurrying on all fours. Even from two hundred yards, the Harper could see their distinctive shapes, with four limbs protruding from sinewy bodies at right angles and a serpentine tail twitching behind. As they stopped and stood on their two rear legs, about half of the reptilian mercenaries drew sabers. The others pulled crossbows off their backs.

"It is as I feared," Sa'ar whispered. "Asabis."

"What?" Lander asked, turning to the sheikh.

"Come," the sheikh said, grasping the Harper's shoulder. "We must leave here at once."

Lander did not move. "You know what those things are?"

Sa'ar nodded. "I suspected it when you and Ruha described what had happened to the Mtair Dhafir. My tribe and I are in your debt."

The sheikh started to leave, but Lander did not follow. "Why are you so frightened of them?"

"There's no time," Sa'ar said. "I'll explain after we rejoin the tribe . . . if we live that long."

Because Sa'ar was not the type to be easily frightened, Lander found the man's fear more than a little contagious. Still, the Harper was not ready to leave. He wanted to

study the asabis for at least a few minutes. "I'll catch up to
you later." Lander turned back toward the campsite, where
the asabis had made torches and were setting *khreimas*
afire. "I want to watch awhile. Maybe I'll learn something
useful."

The sheikh sighed. "I cannot leave you here alone," he
said. "Can we go after I tell you about them?"

Lander nodded, then picked up the tea pot and poured
the last of the black drink into a *bakia*. "I suppose that
would be fine." He handed the cup to the sheikh. To his
embarrassment, he noticed that his hand was trembling.

The sheikh glanced at Lander's trembling hand, then
chuckled and took the tea. "Very well," he said, his voice
and manner now absolutely calm. "We'll stay until you are
ready to go."

Sa'ar turned toward the campsite and squatted down on
his haunches. "Once, after my brothers and cousins had
raided too many other *khowwans*, my tribe was driven into
the Quarter of Emptiness. Our enemies did not follow us,
for they expected that our camels would starve and we
would die of thirst."

The sheikh's eyes grew hard and his attention seemed
focused on a distant land and time. "We would have perished, save that we stumbled across an ancient city. It was
half-buried in a massive dune, but its walls were made of
gray stone as thick as a camel is tall. Inside the walls, the
buildings stood as they had stood a thousand years ago, and
in the center of the city lay an abandoned fort as large as a
mountain."

Sa'ar sipped his tea absently. "That fortress was both
our salvation and our damnation. In its courtyard, there
was an ancient well. When some of the warriors climbed
down to clean it out, they claimed that it descended five
hundred feet and that it opened into a great labyrinth of
underground grottos filled with rivers of cool water.

"Of course, we thought they were exaggerating—at least until we began drawing water. It was sweet as honey and cool as the night, and the well's capacity seemed endless. We pulled hundreds of buckets of water, and the flow never slowed. Before dusk fell that day, the sheikh and the elders were already making plans to turn the fort into a secret oasis, to make it a stronghold from which to build our *khowwan* into the strongest tribe of Anauroch."

"What happened?" Lander asked, intrigued by the story of the lost city.

Sa'ar nodded toward the burning campsites below. "The asabis," he said. "They climbed from the well in the dead of the night, falling upon our warriors and our mothers in the tents. A few of us children, afraid of sleeping inside a city, had stayed outside with the herds. When we heard the screams of our parents, we went to investigate."

The sheikh paused. "You saw what the asabis did to the Mtair Dhafir, so I hardly need to describe what we found."

Recalling the sight of the corpse-filled *wadi* below Rahalat, Lander shook his head. "No. I can imagine."

"We went back to our camels and fled," Sa'ar began. "And that was when the horror truly began. The asabis heard our beasts roaring and came to the chase. We were already mounted and riding, but they ran across the sands on all fours. Though our mounts were strong and freshly watered, the asabis followed close behind, and our camels had to gallop to stay ahead.

"By dawn, there were only six of us left. Every time a camel stumbled or someone fell from the saddle, the asabis got him. Soon our tired camels could barely keep their footing. Three of the others gave up hope and drew their *jambiyas*, then turned to meet the beasts. They might as well have stopped and let the fiends take them."

The sheikh paused, then pointed at the campsite. "They're about finished."

Lander looked toward the camp and saw that all of the *khreimas* were engulfed in flames. In the center of the camp stood Yhekal, dressed as always in his purple robe. A hundred asabis had gathered around him, and he was gesturing at them wildly, waving his sword at both sides of the volcano. Lander suspected he was ordering the reptiles to sweep around the cone and destroy any living thing they encountered.

On the far side of the camp stood a line of black-robed Zhentarim and their camels, the eerie orange light of the fires reflecting off them, making them appear ghostly. The camels were frantically ripping at the lush grass, but the drivers had made no move to remove the baggage from their backs.

Now that he was finally ahead of the Zhentarim, Lander realized, he would have to ride hard to stay there. Without taking his eyes from the camp, Lander asked, "What happened to the rest of you?"

"We kept riding," the sheikh said. "About two hours after dawn, the asabis stopped and burrowed into the sand. That was the last I ever saw of them—until tonight."

"So that's why they always attack at night!" Lander exclaimed, rising.

"What?" Sa'ar asked. He made no move to follow the Harper.

"All of the Zhentarim's attacks have come at night. Until now, I thought they were just trying to take their enemies by surprise."

Sa'ar smiled. "But it's really because the asabis are creatures of the night," he said. "During the day, they're worthless."

Lander nodded.

In the camp below, the asabis scattered, gesturing wildly at each other. The acrid smell of burning camel-hair began to waft up the slope. Realizing that he and the sheikh would be trapped on the cinder cone if they did not leave soon, the Harper climbed out of the ravine.

When Lander reached the lip of the gulch, he perceived a curious silence behind him. Alarmed that something had happened to Sa'ar, he turned and saw the sheikh still sitting in the ravine, sipping his tea.

"Are you coming?" Lander asked.

Sa'ar looked up with a roguish grin on his lined face. "You want to leave so soon?" he asked, rising to his feet and slowly stretching his arms. He sauntered to the steam vent and picked up his battered tea pot. "Mustn't forget this. I paid two camels for it."

Carefully working their way from one ravine to the next, they hurried across the cinder cone's gritty slope and returned to their camels. By the time they untethered the beasts and mounted, they could hear the asabis barking orders to each other in a sharp, chattery language.

The two men reached their rendezvous point with the Mahwa at dawn. Without dismounting, the sheikh gave the order to ride for the Well of the Chasm. It was, he explained, the next waterhole in the Zhentarim's path. The tribe camped there was allied with Mahwa, so he was obligated to warn them of the approaching hazard.

Sa'ar flattered Kadumi by asking him to scout ahead with the Mahwa's best warriors. Lander and Ruha were assigned to ride with the sheikh's party.

To Lander's amazement, after Sa'ar issued all of his riding orders and the tribe began to move, the sheikh closed his eyes and fell asleep in the saddle. As the sun rose higher in the sky, the Harper found it increasingly difficult to keep his own eyes open, but did not dare imitate the dozing sheikh. Unlike Sa'ar, Lander was not so accustomed to camels that he could ride them in his sleep, and he did not fancy the idea of falling onto the hard desert floor from the height of a camel's back.

Lander tried to keep alert by studying the Mahwa caravan. At first glance, it seemed a disorganized herd, but the
Harper quickly realized that there was an order to the jum-
ble. Riding far ahead and far behind the tribe, mounted on
the fastest camels and well beyond sight, were the youngest and most daring warriors. Like Kadumi, they were
scouts who would alert the *khowwan* to any dangers lurking ahead—or approaching from behind, Lander added silently, remembering the Zhentarim.

Ringing the tribe at a thousand yards were the rest of the
warriors, accompanied by their eldest sons, sleek saluki
hunting hounds, and falcons. As they traveled, they periodically unleashed a dog or bird, or broke into a spirited gallop
themselves. At first Lander thought they were pointlessly
wasting energy on high-spirited displays of riding and animal mastery, then he noticed that after these bursts of ac-
tivity the sons returned to the center of the caravan with a
hare, lizard, or some other meat for the evening's pot.
Once he even saw a proud boy riding with a small gazelle
slung over his camel's back.

The boys delivered the game to their mothers and sisters, who were riding in the security of the caravan center.
The women of the wealthiest warriors rode in elaborately
decorated *haouadjejs*, but most of the families could not afford the extra camel's wool needed to make one of the box-
shaped litters.

As Lander studied this part of the caravan, he realized
that the Mahwa were moving at what must have been an
extraordinary pace for the *khowwan*. Every camel was carrying at least one person, sometimes two. Even the baggage camels had small children perched atop their bundles,
their little hands tightly gripping the leather thongs that
held the cargo in place.

Lander turned to Ruha, who had been riding at his side
all morning. "Do Bedine children usually ride the baggage

camels?"

Ruha laughed. "No. The women and children usually walk to avoid tiring the camels. Sheikh Sa'ar is anxious to stay ahead of the Zhentarim, though, so everybody must ride. With luck, we will cover forty miles today."

Lander glanced back over his shoulder. The ebony basin holding Colored Waters had already disappeared. For dozens of miles, all he could see was dun-colored barrenness. In the far distance, perhaps a hundred miles or more away, a low range of mountains rose out of the glassy heat waves drifting off the desert floor.

"I hope it will be enough," he said.

"What makes you think it won't be?" Ruha asked.

"Have you ever heard of asabis?" Lander asked, turning his attention to his riding companion's sultry eyes.

She furrowed her brow. "No. The name means 'eaters-of-parents'."

"Maybe you haven't heard of them, but you've seen them," Lander replied. He repeated Sa'ar's story to her, then added, "I have no idea how the Zhentarim made contact with them, but it appears our enemies already have one group of allies here in the desert."

"That explains why they're so quick to destroy the tribes who won't cooperate," she concluded. "They're more concerned about eliminating potential enemies than about making allies."

Lander nodded, impressed by the young woman's grasp of the situation. "Their intentions are worse than I thought," he said. "With the asabis, they have the allies they need to take military control of Anauroch. They only need the Bedine to use as slaves—in the worst sense of the word."

"Did you ever doubt that?" Ruha asked.

The young widow rode unusually close to the Harper's side for the rest of the day. She remained quiet and thoughtful, but Lander had the vague sensation that she enjoyed being next to him. The feeling was pleasant enough, but it also gave the Harper a giddy sense of excitement that discomforted him.

Late in the afternoon, Lander looked down and noticed that the ground had changed from barren, dun-colored dirt to a flat, endless mosaic of coin-sized stones. The pebbles were mostly red in color, varying in hue from blond to dark brown. All had been polished glass smooth, which gave the desert floor a fiery, pebbled appearance that seemed more appropriate to the caldera they had left behind than the open flats through which they were passing.

Leaning over to study the burnished stones, Lander asked, "Was there a lake here once?"

Ruha laughed. "Don't be foolish. This is At'ar's Looking Glass," she said, glancing toward the sun. "Kozah hopes to win his wife's heart back by keeping it swept clean with his wind so that she can admire her reflection in the pebbles."

Lander looked at the heavens above. Though the sun was white and the earth red, he could see why the Bedine associated the fiery ground with their cruel sun goddess. "Yes, I see it now," he said, sitting upright again.

Ruha chuckled at his ignorance as they moved onward. They rode across At'ar's Looking Glass for the rest of the afternoon, and Lander was soon convinced that burnished sea of stones continued forever. At first, it had seemed eerily beautiful. Now it seemed infuriatingly uniform.

Two hours before dusk, the entire tribe turned ninety degrees north. Lander searched the horizon for some landmark he had missed, but there was nothing but the fiery rock flats. Shadowed closely by Ruha, he urged his camel forward until he rode abreast of Sa'ar.

The sheikh still appeared to be asleep, but when the Harper approached Sa'ar opened one eye. He glanced first at Lander, then at Ruha, and raised an eyebrow at the pair's close proximity. "Yes? Is there something I can do for you?"

"Why are we turning?" Lander asked. "Are we close to the Well of the Chasm?"

Sa'ar shook his head. "No. We are turning so we are not in the Zhentarim's path when they overtake us tonight."

"What?" Lander nearly shrieked the question. He could not help thinking of how hard he had been trying to get ahead of them for the last few weeks.

The sheikh shrugged. "We cannot move as fast as the invaders. The asabis, at least, could overtake us tonight. Our only choice is to be out of the way when they pass."

"What about your allies at the Well of the Chasm?" Lander asked.

Sa'ar smiled. "Don't worry about them. The Zhentarim will not arrive before the messenger I sent ahead," the sheikh replied. "The Raz'hadi will stall the invaders until we arrive."

"You'll still be outnumbered. What will you do then?"

Sa'ar only shrugged. "I can't speak for Utaiba and his people," he said. "We'll see what happens when we get there."

"Sheikh Sa'ar is correct, Lander," Ruha said. "The Bedine do not plan everything out in advance."

The sheikh nodded, then pointed at Ruha. "You would do well to listen to this woman, my friend." A moment later, he scowled thoughtfully, then eyed Ruha and added, "But from a discreet distance."

Ruha's eyes went wide, then she allowed her camel to fall behind. Confused by the exchange, Lander also allowed his mount to fall behind and brought it alongside the widow's. When he came too close, she tactfully guided her camel away and opened the space between them.

"What was that all about?" the Harper asked, once again guiding his mount close to hers.

Ruha carefully moved her mount away. "Sa'ar thinks I've been brazen," she replied.

"That's ridiculous!"

The widow's eyes sparkled with agreement, but she shook her head. "Not really. In his eyes, I'm still part of my husband's family. Please don't ride any closer."

Sa'ar's admonition irritated the Harper, for he saw nothing wrong with talking to a widow and did not think it was anyone's business to tell a woman how close she could ride to a man. For the next hour, he tried to draw Ruha back into conversation, but she avoided his questions. The Harper felt hurt by the sudden distance between Ruha and himself, and he could not help silently cursing Sheikh Sa'ar for upsetting his friend.

When less than an hour of light remained in the day, Sa'ar called a halt to the caravan. Immediately the women began to unpack supplies and arrange them on the flat, rocky ground in tentless semblances of their normal camp.

Lander attempted to help Ruha unpack the supplies for herself, him, and Kadumi, but she curtly instructed him to go and sit with the sheikh. More confused than ever, the Harper went over to the area of ground that Sa'ar's first wife had staked out as his tent, then sat on a *kuerabiche* and sipped the cold tea that a servant provided. Fortunately, the sheikh was occupied with the details of posting sentries and arranging the camp, so Lander felt no obligation to make small talk.

When Ruha had laid out the camp, he returned to the area that would serve as the trio's *khreima*. Someone had provided her with a hare for the cooking pot. As she skinned the hare, the widow did not acknowledge Lander's presence. That only made him want to talk with her that much more.

If he was going to succeed, Lander knew he would have to say something to overshadow the warning that had passed between Ruha and the sheikh. Remembering her inquiry about Sembia, the Harper decided to lure her into a discussion about his home.

"In Sembia, the rabbits are as juicy as sheep," he began, eyeing the stringy hare she was skinning.

His tactic worked immediately. "What are sheep?" Ruha asked, nervously glancing in the direction of the sheikh's family.

The question caught him by surprise, for he had never before had to describe one of the beasts. He held his hand two and a half feet off the ground. "They're about this tall, they come in herds, and they're covered with wool—"

"Like tiny camels?"

Lander shook his head. "Not even close. Their fleece is soft and white."

"How much milk do they give?"

"They don't give milk," Lander corrected. "At least not that Sembians drink."

"Then what good are these sheep?" Ruha demanded.

Lander laughed at her desert pragmatism. "They give wool. We make clothes from it."

"That's all?" The widow pulled the hide off the rabbit and threw it to a saluki lurking on the edge of their camp.

"They can be eaten, too," he said. "My father and I used to eat mutton—sheep—every year when we went to Archendale."

"Archendale? Tell me about that," the widow demanded.

"It's a beautiful place," Lander said, closing his eyes. "The River Arkhen flows through a rocky gorge. The whole valley is filled with lilies and moss."

"It sounds wonderful."

Ruha's eyes were fixed on the Harper's face, and he could tell from their dreamy expression that she was trying to imagine the paradise he described.

"Archendale is a wonderful place," Lander confirmed.

"But it was almost destroyed. The Zhentarim tried to take it over, too."

"How did you stop them?" Ruha asked.

"It wasn't me. My father did it," Lander replied, growing melancholy at this turn of the conversation.

"Was he a Harper, too?"

Lander shook his head. "No, he was a merchant, but he was a good man."

Ruha's eyes remained fixed on Lander's face, and he realized she expected him to continue the story.

"Archendale's farms were the best within riding distance of Sembia," Lander began. "Every summer, my father and I would go there together to buy produce. One year, my mother wanted to come along."

"Why should that bother you?" Ruha asked, studying him carefully.

Lander looked away, uneasy that the widow had read his feelings so easily. "My father married a beautiful, charming woman," the Harper said. "What he didn't know was that my mother was also a deceitful Cyric-worshiper. She had intentionally married a wealthy merchant in order to gather commercial information for the Zhentarim—information they used to fill their own pockets with gold at the expense of honest men like my father."

Lander paused, a lump of anger growing in his breast as he recalled how his mother had used him to dupe his father. When he turned ten, she had started taking him to the house of a famous mercenary three times a week, presumably for lessons in swordsmanship. What neither the Harper nor his father had realized, however, was that while Lander was learning to fight, his mother was meeting with her Zhentarim masters in the back of the house.

"Go on," Ruha urged.

"The time came when the Zhentarim decided to take over the rich farms and orchards of Archendale. They assigned my mother the task of gathering the names of all the farmers and landholders in the valley. That was when she insisted upon joining my father and me on our annual trip," Lander continued. "Fortunately, my father was an observant man, and my mother, as usual, underestimated his intelligence. When she insisted upon meeting all of his business contacts and asked about men he did not even deal with, he decided to find out what she was doing.

"When we returned to Archenbridge, my father hired someone to follow my mother while he was out of town. The man was able to stalk her to a secret meeting of Cyric's evil sect and to see her meeting with a known Zhentarim agent."

"What a shock for your father," Ruha said, absent-mindedly holding her bloody *jambiya* in her hand. "What did he do? Kill her?"

Lander grimaced. "In Sembia, men don't do that sort of thing to their wives," he said. "My father set out for Archendale to warn the farmers about the Zhentarim plot. He sent me to another city with a message for a trusted friend.

"My mother saw me leaving town and came after me with two men. When she caught me, she tried to convince me to join the Zhentarim, but I couldn't help remembering all the wonderful times my father and I had shared in Archendale. I told her to let me go and, when her guards tried to take me prisoner, I killed them."

"And your mother?"

Lander shook his head. "I made the worst mistake of my life," he said. "I let her go."

Ruha gave him a exonerating nod. "A man shouldn't—"

"My mother went straight to her Zhentarim masters," the Harper interrupted, an intentionally sharp tone in his voice. "They sent their agents into Archendale."

"What happened?" the widow asked, her concerned eyes showing that she had already guessed the answer.

"I don't really know," Lander replied, looking at the ground. "I passed my father's message to his friend, then waited for him as he had made me promise. I didn't hear anything until nearly a fortnight later, when a Harper came and told me that both my parents had died in Archendale."

Ruha's voice dropped to a shocked whisper. "How did it happen?"

Lander shook his head. "A Zhentarim assassin caught my father shortly after he entered the valley. The Harper wouldn't tell me how my mother died."

They sat in uneasy silence, both of them staring at the pebbled ground. After a time, Ruha cleaned her *jambiya* on a piece of cloth and sheathed it. She took some dried camel dung out of a *kuerabiche*, then reached into her *aba* and withdrew a flint and steel. She handed the dried dung and the flint and steel to Lander. "Will you please light a fire?"

Without speaking, the Harper pulled some shreds off the hem of his tattered *aba* to use for tinder.

Ruha withdrew a pot from another *kuerabiche* and half-filled it with water. "I see mirages from the future," she said, avoiding the Harper's eyes. "When I was a little girl, I was not wise enough to hide this."

Lander piled the tinder on a dung-patty. "So? Seeing the future is a gift."

"Not among the Bedine," Ruha replied. "I was shunned."

"As a child?" Lander exclaimed.

The widow nodded. "It was my father's decision, but he had no choice, of course. The elders demanded it."

"The elders were fools!"

When Ruha did not meet his gaze, Lander leaned over the dung patties and began striking sparks. The third one caught, and he gently blew on it until it produced a small flame in the tinder.

"Who are fools?" asked a youth's familiar voice.

Lander looked up and saw that Kadumi had returned from his duty as a scout. The boy was standing at the edge of their campsite, his bow and quiver in one hand and the reins of his camel in the other.

"Er—nobody," Lander said.

The color rose to the visible part of Ruha's cheeks, and Lander looked uncomfortably back to the flame.

Kadumi scowled, then turned to unsaddle his camel. After a moment of tense silence, he asked again, "Who are fools?"

"Nobody," Lander replied, looking up from his fire. "Ruha and I were just talking about the differences in our cultures."

Though he wasn't sure why he should be embarrassed, Lander could sense from the attitudes of both Kadumi and Ruha that he and the young widow had violated an unspoken rule.

The Harper's explanation did not satisfy the youth. Tossing his bow and quiver aside, Kadumi advanced angrily. "Ruha is my brother's wife," he said. "You may not have secrets with her!"

Lander stood. "We don't have any secrets—"

Kadumi reached for his *jambiya*.

"Kadumi, no!" Ruha cried.

The Harper was so shocked by the action that the boy actually had the blade halfway out of the scabbard before Lander caught his arm. Grasping Kadumi's wrist tightly, he helped him pull the dagger the rest of the way out of the sheath, then quickly used his free hand to press inward against the joint. Kadumi cried out in pain and dropped the dagger.

"Don't draw a weapon on a man you can't kill," Lander said. His heart was pounding hard, but he kept his voice even.

Kadumi's response was direct and heated. "Blood!" he

yelled.

The word resounded across the rocky plain, bringing the camp to sudden silence.

Ruha shook her head violently. "Kadumi, don't do this."

Lander released the youth and pushed him away. Before the Harper could kick the boy's *jambiya* back to him, Sa'ar and several warriors arrived.

"What's happening here?" the sheikh demanded.

Kadumi pointed at Lander. "He's courting Ruha," the boy accused. "I have challenged him."

Sa'ar looked from the boy to Lander, then back to the boy again. "You're sure?" he asked. "We could have misunderstood you."

"You did not misunderstand," Kadumi snapped. "It is my family's honor."

The sheikh sighed, then gave Ruha an accusatory glance. "We had better do this according to tradition," he said. "Give the boy his *jambiya*, Lander."

The Harper did not move to obey. "Why?"

Sa'ar frowned. "He challenged you," the sheikh responded. "Kill him, and Ruha is yours."

The Harper looked from the sheikh to Kadumi. The boy was trembling, though Lander could not be sure whether it was with fear or anger. Regardless, he was standing tall and staring at Lander with an unwavering gaze.

"He's just a boy!" Lander objected.

"He's a Bedine warrior," Sa'ar corrected. "Don't worry. We'll witness the fight. Nobody will doubt your honor if you win."

Lander snorted his disbelief, then shook his head. "I won't do it. I refuse the challenge."

The warriors gasped, and Sa'ar looked confused. "What?"

"Kadumi can try to kill me if he wishes," Lander explained. "But I won't kill him. I refuse his challenge."

"You can't do that!" the youth yelled.

"I can, and I have," Lander replied calmly.

The Bedine stood, looking confused. Several moments later, Ruha burst out laughing. "Kadumi, if you must, try to kill him. I doubt that any harm will come of it."

The warriors could not restrain a few chuckles, but Sa'ar did not seem amused. He pondered the situation for what seemed like an hour, then turned to Lander and pronounced his judgment.

"Very well. Since you are not a Bedine, it is your privilege to refuse Kadumi's challenge," he said. "But being a *berrani* does not entitle you to ignore all of our traditions. Ruha is still the widow of Kadumi's brother, and it is a matter of family honor that he defend her reputation, whether she wishes it or not."

The sheikh glanced at the Harper meaningfully, then continued, "Therefore, you will not speak to Ruha except in Kadumi's presence. In return, he will not challenge—or attack—you again. This is my decision, and be it known that any who ignore it violate my hospitality."

Ten

 Ruha's camel had begun to limp, but the widow did not bother to dismount. After four days of travel on At'ar's Looking Glass, half the Mahwa were riding lame beasts. With the merciless goddess blazing down on the wind-burnished stones, the searing heat blistered even the tough pads of the camels' feet.

In order to reach his allies as quickly as possible, Sa'ar was pushing his tribe through the worst part of the day. Heat rose off the desert floor in rippling waves that gave the Looking Glass the appearance of a huge lake of molten rock. On the horizon, a line of tiny spires danced in the shimmering air. Though still so distant they looked like billows of violet smoke rather than minarets of desert rock, the obelisks were a welcome sight to Ruha's aching eyes. The stony towers marked the edge of At'ar's Looking Glass, and not far beyond lay the Mahwa's destination.

Upon sighting the spires, Sheikh Sa'ar had declared

that the Mahwa would not sleep until they reached the Well of the Chasm. The declaration had delighted Lander, who was eager to reach the next tribe before the Zhentarim enslaved or destroyed it. Despite her weariness, Ruha shared the Harper's impatience, though for a different reason. The sooner he became convinced that the Bedine were responding to the Zhentarim threat, the sooner he would return to Sembia—taking her with him, of course.

The widow closed her eyes, hoping she could adjust to the new hitch in her camel's rolling gait. She tried to imagine the green valley of Archendale, where cold water filled the canyon and Mielikki's forest was so thick that At'ar could not penetrate its canopy. Try as she might, Ruha could not picture such a scene. She would simply have to go and see it with her own eyes.

"Don't fall asleep," warned a familiar voice. "It's a long way down and the landing is hard."

Ruha opened her eyes and saw that Lander had moved his camel closer to hers. She reacted by nudging her own mount away. "You mustn't!" she whispered, shaking her head. "If Kadumi sees us speaking, it may be his dagger that cuts you open."

"Surely he wouldn't violate the sheikh's orders," Lander returned. "You did say that he was an honorable boy."

"It is because he is an honorable boy that he would violate the sheikh's word," Ruha countered. "He would do anything to avenge a wrong against his dead brother."

The Harper seemed unimpressed. "Kadumi's blade is not one that I'm afraid of."

"Then you are a fool!" Ruha countered.

"Perhaps," Lander replied, shrugging. "But the sheikh's prohibition is against speaking to you without your brother-in-law present." He nodded toward the rear. "Kadumi's less than thirty yards away."

The widow did not need to look to know Lander spoke

the truth. After Sa'ar's judgment, the jealous youth had even relinquished his scouting duties to watch her. He had barely let her out of his sight since.

Disregarding the Harper's reassurances, Ruha again steered her mount away. "He's supposed to hear what we say."

"What we say to each other is none of his business," Lander replied, not urging his camel any closer to Ruha's.

"That is not the Bedine way. What passes between us is very much his business." The widow's protests were due more to the desire to avoid trouble between Lander and Kadumi than to any respect for her people's tradition.

The Harper scoffed. "You aren't his property."

"Kadumi must protect his brother's marriage. It's a matter of family honor."

"His brother is dead!" Lander objected. Again, he guided his camel closer to Ruha's.

"For less than a month!" the widow answered, giving up and not bothering to move away. "I must mourn Ajaman for two years."

"And then what?" Lander asked, casting a furtive glance over his shoulder.

"It doesn't matter," she whispered, daring to give the Harper a wry glance. "In two years, I will be in Sembia, will I not?"

Her response drew an uncertain nod from Lander. "Perhaps, if that is what you want."

"Of course it's what I want!" Ruha hissed. "There's nothing for me with the Bedine."

"I truly hope you're right, Ruha, but how do you know there's anything for you in Sembia?" Lander asked. "You cannot imagine how different it is from Anauroch. For instance, women wear no veils, not even in public."

The Harper's revelation caught the widow by surprise. She started to claim she would do the same, then felt herself blushing and could not utter the words. "Their husbands permit this?" she asked, looking away.

Before Lander could respond, Kadumi's white camel edged between Ruha and the Harper. "You may not speak to this woman, *berrani*." He stared at Lander with a belligerent scowl, his hand brushing the hilt of his *jambiya*.

Lander eyed the gesture with a forbearing sneer, then laughed at the boy's bravado. "As I recall, Kadumi, Sheikh Sa'ar said that I cannot speak to her except when you are with us. Well, you are with us now, so I speak to her." The Harper turned to Ruha. "Shall I tell you more about Sembia?"

Though she would have liked to hear more, the widow shook her head. Ruha did not want Kadumi to know of her interest in the distant land, for she suspected his reaction would be violent if he knew she intended to leave him with the Mahwa and go with Lander. "I have heard enough of Sembia," she lied.

The Harper gave her an amused smirk. "Then I won't trouble you with more descriptions of it." He lashed his mount with the tail of his reins and trotted a dozen yards ahead.

"I wish to know what passed between you and the *berrani*," Kadumi demanded, looking from Lander's back to the widow's eyes.

Ruha felt herself growing increasingly angry at the boy's protective suspicion and the coldness with which he had treated her since learning that she could use magic. She turned to Kadumi with a condescending glower. "I want you to remember two things," she hissed. "First, if that *berrani*, as you call him, did not have the patience of a sheikh, he would have killed you with your own *jambiya* twice by now. If I were you, I would stop acting the fool and keep my hand away from it, lest he grow tired of hearing hollow threats."

Kadumi bristled at her rough treatment. "I am a Bedine warrior," he snapped. "I have killed three men!"

The youth's comment summoned the memory of the assault on Lander's back in her vision. She wondered if the attacker was destined to be her own brother-in-law. Immediately she twisted in her saddle to face Kadumi.

"You shall not kill that man!" she snarled.

The intensity of her reaction took Kadumi entirely by surprise. Once again, he seemed more like a confused boy than the hot-headed young man he had been playing lately.

A moment later, Kadumi collected his wits. "Lander is protected by the sheikh's *difa*," he said, neatly dodging the issue. "What is the second thing you want me to remember?"

"When you want something from me, you are to ask, not demand," she lectured sharply. "Before you have the right to demand anything of me, you must earn my respect."

Kadumi's bluster evaporated like a morning mist. His furrowed brow rose into an astonished arch, his set jaw fell slack, and his fiery eyes suddenly seemed very hurt and young. Ruha was about to balance her harsh words with some compassion when Kadumi spoke, his voice rather timid and meek.

"Very well," he said, "would you please tell me what passed between you and Lander? You and I are supposed to be family, so I have the right to know."

Beneath her veil, Ruha could not help but smile at the way Kadumi had phrased his request. It seemed to her the boy had actually taken her words to heart, but she did not intend to tell him of her plan to leave the Bedine. Even if he sympathized with her, he might still feel honor-bound to prevent her departure.

Instead, she said, "I only knew Ajaman for three days before the Zhentarim came."

Kadumi nodded. "Not much time for a marriage."

Ruha took a deep breath. "Your brother was a wonderful man. If there had been more time for him and I, we might have grown to love each other."

"And had ten sons to watch your herds," the youth added, resting his apprehensive brown eyes on her veiled face.

"Perhaps," Ruha sighed, "but I would have always had to hide my magic, for fear that Ajaman would have reacted as you have. Probably, he would have found me out anyway, and that would have been the end to our marriage."

Kadumi frowned and looked away, unable to deny what she said. "What does that have to do with you and the *berrani?*"

"Nothing and everything," she said, fixing her eyes on Kadumi's face. "Lander knows of my magic, and it does not offend him. Can you understand how it feels for me to talk to someone who accepts me for what I am?"

For several moments the boy did not look at her. Instead, he stared at the burnished pebbles on the desert floor with a vacant stare, his face marked by his conflicting emotions.

At last he looked up. "I can understand how you feel, but what does it matter? When you chose to become a sorceress, you chose the path of loneliness. When you spoke the marriage vows with Ajaman, you promised to honor him and his family. Nothing has changed."

After riding a few more steps in silence, Kadumi suddenly looked away and whipped his mount into a gallop, then rode off toward the front of the caravan.

Ruha groaned inwardly at his terse departure, then closed her eyes and tried to think of nothing.

The bells of the sheikh's camel soon brought an end to Ruha's glum meditation. "A young woman should not ride alone," Sa'ar said, drawing up beside her.

Ruha opened her eyes. "This one should."

Sa'ar nodded. "Ah, yes—the curse of the flesh," he said. "For your husband's sake, you must be patient."

The young widow studied the sheikh with an appraising eye. "What do you mean by that?"

The sheikh looked at the sky and shrugged. "Nothing," he said. "Only that Lander strikes me as a handsome enough man, and you are a young widow. If you were a weaker woman, it might be natural to have certain feelings . . ."

Sa'ar let the sentence trail off, and Ruha simply shook her head at his not-so-subtle warning. When the sheikh did not take her hint and leave her to ride alone, she closed her eyes. Before long, the rhythmic jingle of the sheikh's bells and her limping camel's rocking gait lulled her into a restful slumber.

The young widow did not really sleep, for she remained awake enough to keep from falling off her camel. She was also aware of a hot breeze blowing against her face and of the periodic cries of warriors when they urged their hounds or birds after a lizard or snake for the evening's meal. The sun sank lower in the western sky, and At'ar's merciless rays struck Ruha's eyelids at increasingly horizontal angles. Kadumi's protectiveness and the sheikh's suspicions became distant worries, and the widow was resting as peacefully as she would have on a bed of soft carpets.

Some hours later, Ruha felt her mount shift from its pebble-sore stride to a softer tread more suitable for dust or sand. She opened her eyes and saw that the caravan now traveled in a more tightly knit formation.

Sa'ar still rode next to Ruha, but his attention was focused on a scout urgently whispering at his side. The sun had already touched the horizon, and night would soon fall. The dusk seemed unusually quiet and tense. Aside from the scout's murmuring voice and Sa'ar's jingling bells, the only sounds breaking the twilight were the soft footfalls of weary camels.

The caravan had left the burnished pebbles of At'ar's Looking Glass behind. It now rode over a carpet of dust, indigo colored in the failing light. To all sides, the purplish towers of rock that had seemed so distant earlier rose like minarets into the sky.

The Well of the Chasm lay less than a mile ahead, Ruha knew, through a labyrinth of stony spires that led to a deep canyon. Over a distance of several miles, the canyon descended to a depth of five hundred feet and ended in a boulder-strewn hollow. In the center of this small valley, a deep pit penetrated the bedrock to tap an underground stream of rust-colored water.

While Sa'ar conversed with the scout, a knot of concerned warriors slowly gathered around. They rode in silence, straining to hear what the scout was reporting to the sheikh. Even Lander and Kadumi had returned, riding side-by-side a few yards to the widow's right. Ruha began to feel swarmed by the silent throng and wished that Sa'ar had selected some other part of the caravan for his conference.

When the scout stopped whispering to him, Sa'ar wasted no time with deliberations or thought. He simply looked up and addressed his warriors. "Ready your bows and your scimitars," he ordered, signaling the caravan to stop. "Have the women wait here. If we do not return by dawn or if I send word for them to flee, they are to scatter into the desert. Should this happen, tell them not to wait for us, for we will not be joining them."

When the warriors did not relay his orders quickly enough, Sa'ar barked, "Do it now!"

As the throng dispersed, Lander urged his mount close to Ruha and Sa'ar. "What is happening, Sheikh?"

"The Zhentarim are camped outside the canyon leading

to the Well of the Chasm," Sa'ar replied. "They are just sending their asabis to destroy the Raz'hadi. We assume that our allies will meet the attackers in the narrowest part of the canyon. We are going to try to drive the Zhentarim away from their campsite, then attack the asabis from behind and free the Raz'hadi."

Lander shook his head. "There are too many Zhentarim. You'll never drive them away. They'll just wipe you out while the asabis destroy your allies."

"Perhaps," the sheikh replied. "But we must fight. It is a matter of honor for the entire *khowwan*."

"Though it means dying in vain?"

"Even so," Sa'ar acknowledged, nodding. "This is not your fight, *berrani*. You and Kadumi should wait with the women. Flee if we do not return."

"I choose to fight," Kadumi called, drawing his scimitar. "The Zhentarim killed my father and my brothers in combat, and they slaughtered my mother and sisters without cause. It is my right to seek their blood."

The sheikh regarded the boy with a sad expression. "As you say, it is your right. You may ride with my warriors."

Lander spoke next. "This is not my fight, Sheikh, but I know more about the Zhentarim than any of your warriors. If you allow me to accompany you, I may be able to offer some advice."

Sa'ar nodded. "I was hoping you would volunteer to do this, for those who know their enemies will prevail more often. I will keep you safe."

"Then I'll stay with Lander," Ruha said, intruding on the conversation that had been going on all around her.

Both the sheikh and Kadumi scowled at the widow, and Lander studied her with an expression of surprise and puzzlement.

"Out of the question!" Sa'ar roared.

"Why?" Ruha countered. "You have promised to keep

Lander safe. Surely it will cause no trouble to extend that protection to me."

"Lander rides with me because he may prove of use during the battle," the sheikh said. "Aside from being an unnecessary source of worry, what can you contribute to the warriors' cause?"

Lander's good eye flashed with inspiration. He turned from Ruha to the sheikh. "Perhaps Ruha is concerned about what will happen to her if we do not return," the Harper said. "After all, she is a stranger to the Mahwa and has only Kadumi and me to watch after her."

Sa'ar looked irritated. "She can't think she will be safer at the battlefield!"

The widow said, "But I do. With Kadumi riding into the middle of the fight, I would feel much safer in Lander's company." Ruha glanced at her brother-in-law meaningfully. "Unless, of course, Kadumi prefers to stay with me and the other women during the battle."

The youth clenched his teeth, and the widow saw that her threat was not lost on him. After giving Ruha a quick scowl, Kadumi addressed Sa'ar. "If it pleases the sheikh, I would entrust my sister-in-law to Lander's care. I have seen him fight and believe that even in the thick of battle, she will be safe with him."

"If that's what you want, then I approve," the sheikh said, impatiently turning his attention away from the trio. "Now I must go and prepare my sons for battle."

The three hundred warriors of the Mahwa said good-bye to their loved ones over the next quarter-hour, then gathered with their camels and weapons. Along with Kadumi and Lander, Ruha waited at the edge of the gathering, wondering what the night would bring. Several times, Lander started to ask a question of her, but Kadumi, who was straying no more than twenty feet from her side, always came over to smother the conversation.

By the time the last radiance of At'ar had vanished from the western sky, the sheikh was satisfied with his tribe's battle preparations. He drew his scimitar and waved his warriors forward. The small force mounted their camels and formed themselves into a column, then slipped between the hulking rock spires without a sound.

As Sa'ar's advisor, Lander rode at the sheikh's side. Ruha and Kadumi were a few yards behind the Harper. Like the rest of the column, they proceeded in tense silence, their thoughts occupied with images of what the night would bring.

Within a half-mile of travel, the sheikh sent Kadumi forward to join the rest of the warriors. When the boy was gone, Lander allowed his camel to fall back, then turned to Ruha and whispered, "What do you have in mind?"

The widow frowned, confused. "I don't understand."

"What's your plan?" he asked. "Why did you ask to join the battle?"

"To watch your back," she replied honestly.

The Harper's jaw drooped. "What about your—?" He finished the question by gesturing as if he were casting a spell.

Ruha raised her brow. "That's not why I came," she whispered, glancing at Sa'ar's back to make sure he wasn't eavesdropping on them. "What do you think I can do that will give three hundred men victory over three thousand?"

"You did okay at the ambush," Lander countered. "I thought you had an idea."

"No," Ruha said. "I just didn't want to be left alone."

The Harper rubbed his chin, then looked toward the front of the column. "Just the same, it can't hurt having you here."

They rode for another ten minutes before the column rounded a wishbone-shaped spire familiar to the widow. This had been the first oasis that Ruha had visited after

Qoha'dar's death, so she recognized the terrain ahead. Less than two hundred yards away, a flat outcropping of rock rose from the desert floor, its walls draped in darkness. At the small plateau's southern end there was a narrow gap, barely visible in the pale light of the crescent moon. That gap was the beginning of the narrow, winding canyon that descended to the Well of the Chasm.

The scouts stopped in the shadow of the wishbone spire, awaiting the sheikh's command. Gathered in front of the canyon was the unsuspecting army of the Zhentarim. Their camels were unladen, and the men were gathered in small clusters, laughing and joking without regard to danger. From the dark gap leading into the chasm came a sporadic stream of shouting, *amarat* sirens, and guttural yells—the only sign that there was a battle nearby.

As Sa'ar paused to study the scene ahead, Lander turned to Ruha, an unspoken question in his eye.

"What do you think I can do?" she hissed.

The Harper shrugged. "It would be nice if the enemy couldn't tell how many of us there are," he answered. Without waiting for a response, he moved forward to take his place next to the sheikh.

Realizing that she might be able to accomplish what the Harper wanted, Ruha stopped behind the sheikh and forced her camel to kneel. She paused to make sure that everyone's attention was fixed on the Zhentarim camp. When she felt satisfied that she was last thing on anyone's mind, the widow picked up a handful of dust.

The sheikh raised his scimitar and signaled his warriors to charge.

Ruha whispered her wind incantation, then blew the dust from her hand. As the warriors galloped toward the unsuspecting Zhentarim, a gale rose at their backs, catching the dust raised by their camels and lifting it high into sky. Within moments, the cloud stretched across the entire valley and was billowing a hundred feet into the air.

"What's happening?" Sa'ar cried.

"Who can say?" Lander replied. Over his shoulder, he cast an approving glance at Ruha, then turned back to the sheikh. "But from the Zhentarim camp, it must look like you've sent ten thousand warriors into battle!"

Eleven

As the dust cloud descended on the Zhentarim, Lander's sword hand went to his weapon's hilt and fitfully rested there. He was still sitting at Sa'ar's side, below the wishbone-shaped minaret, and he found himself wishing he were riding into battle instead.

Two hundred yards ahead, the wall of dust was sweeping toward the canyon that led down to the Well of the Chasm. Inside that dark curtain were the sheikh's three hundred charging warriors. Lander hoped their surprise assault, combined with the dust cloud Ruha had arranged, would convince the Zhentarim that they were under attack by a much larger force. With a little luck, the Black Robes would panic and flee their camp, leaving a clear route into and—more importantly—out of the Well of the Chasm.

After that, rescuing Sa'ar's allies would be a simple matter of defeating the asabis, then collecting the other tribe and fleeing before the enemy regrouped and counterattacked. Even if the warriors drove away the Zhentarim camped outside the canyon, Lander had no idea how the Mahwa would accomplish the second half of the plan, but he saw little sense in worrying about it until the first part was achieved.

When muffled screams and roars began rolling out of the dust cloud, Lander knew the Mahwa had reached the enemy's camp. A warrior's blade sang out as it clanged against a defender's saber, then there was another chime, and another. It was not a sound the Harper was happy to hear. Ringing steel meant the Zhentarim were fighting, and the Mahwa could not win a battle outnumbered as badly as they were.

Wondering if there was anything else that Ruha could do, Lander glanced over his shoulder. She stood next to her kneeling camel, her eyes still fixed on the dust cloud, her robes flapping in the wind. The Harper realized she was still concentrating on her first spell and could do nothing else unless he wanted her to let the dust curtain die away.

When Lander turned back around, he saw Sa'ar scowl and reach into a *djebira*. When the sheikh pulled his hand from the saddlebag, it contained a huge *amarat*. "In case I need to call a retreat," Sa'ar explained, resting the horn in his lap.

The sheikh had no need to sound his *amarat*. During the next minute, another dozen blades clanged, then, save for the wail of the wind, the dust cloud fell ominously silent. A moment later, there were a few shouts and the murmur of Bedine voices, both muffled by Ruha's wind magic, but the voices quickly fell silent again. The sheikh scowled, concerned.

"Is this Zhentarim magic?" he asked Lander.

The Harper shook his head. "Their sorcerers prefer more spectacular displays."

A single warrior came galloping out of the dust cloud.

Sa'ar leaned forward in his saddle, looking for more men behind the rider. When the Mahwai reached the pair, Lander saw that his *aba* was spattered with dark stains, and the Harper could smell the coppery odor of blood. The warrior's camel was so charged that the young man could barely keep his mount under control.

As the rider reined his camel to a halt, the sheikh asked, "What happened?"

The warrior smiled. "With Kozah's wind, we drove the Zhentarim before us like gazelles before the lion," he said. "They have fled into the desert."

Sa'ar shouted for joy. "I shall ride the Zhentarim into the sands of death."

After sending the warrior galloping back with orders to assemble the elders, Sa'ar slowly started forward. Lander followed, but Ruha remained standing next to her camel.

The sheikh twisted about in his saddle and called, "You wanted to see the battle. Aren't you coming?"

When Ruha showed no sign of responding, Lander quickly covered for her. "There may still be Zhentarim hiding in the dust storm. It would be safer for her to wait here."

Sa'ar shrugged, then turned back toward the invaders' camp. As Lander and the sheikh approached it, Ruha thoughtfully allowed the dust cloud to drift to the other side of the battlefield, and the gale quieted to a gentle wind.

It was wrong to think of the site as a battlefield. Several hundred campfires, flaring and flickering in the breeze, were strewn over two acres of barren, dusty ground. Near each fire lay two or three corpses wrapped in black robes. Sa'ar's warriors were bustling from fire to fire, slitting the throats of those who moved or groaned.

The casualness with which the Bedine dispatched the wounded shocked Lander, who was not accustomed to murdering captives in cold blood. Nevertheless, the Harper realized that taking prisoners was a practical impossibility for the Bedine, and he certainly had no wish to let the evil men go free. Instead, he motioned in the direction of a Zhentarim who was about to be dispatched, then said, "Perhaps you should save one for interrogation. It would also be wise to have someone count the enemy dead."

Sa'ar nodded. "I see you are a practical man. That is good."

The sheikh called a warrior over, then relayed Lander's request. The man returned a few moments later, dragging along a Zhentarim with a bloody leg. The warrior dumped the prisoner at a nearby campfire without ceremony, then trudged off to tally the dead.

Sa'ar went to meet with his elder warriors, and Lander dismounted to interrogate the prisoner. The Zhentarim was chubby and slovenly, with a thick double chin and a face that had not been shaved in a week. His eyes were glazed with terror, and the Harper had little trouble seeing that the prisoner hoped to make a bargain that would save his life.

"You look more like a merchant than a mercenary," Lander began, speaking in Common and taking a seat next to the corpulent man.

"A bit of both," the wounded man grunted. "Yhekal promised me a caravan concession."

"And you believed him?" Lander asked incredulously.

The prisoner shrugged. "Somebody will have to run the caravans. I thought it might as well be me."

A Bedine warrior stopped near their campfire to cut the throats of two unconscious Zhentarim. The prisoner watched the death of his comrades, and a cold sweat broke out on his forehead. He looked to Lander with an unspoken question.

"I'm not going to lie to you," the Harper replied. "The Bedine don't take prisoners. If they don't kill you tonight, you'll die a worse death tomorrow. Perhaps if you help us . . ."

The fat man's eyes grew angry. "Why should I tell you anything?"

"That's up to you," Lander shrugged. The best way to make a prisoner talk, he knew, was to make him think you did not need the information he was giving you. "I already know you number about fifteen hundred, you're all hungry, you have fifteen hundred asabis—"

"Asabis?" the prisoner asked, grimacing at a wave of pain from his injured leg.

Lander pointed toward the canyon mouth. "The reptile mercenaries clearing the canyon."

The merchant nodded. "They call themselves 'laertis.' "

"Gruesome creatures," Lander commented. "I thought they only lived in the middle of the desert."

The Zhentarim moaned, then held his leg with his hands. "The laertis have tunnels everywhere. We picked those up a hundred miles outside Addas Babar. They crawled out of a deep well."

Lander nodded, noting the similarity between the prisoner's report and what Sa'ar had told him.

The prisoner licked his lips. "Do you have any water?"

"Of course," Lander answered. He went to his camel and returned with a waterskin, then offered it to the portly man. "I don't blame you for not wanting to die thirsty."

The prisoner nodded his thanks, then opened the waterskin and began pouring the contents down his throat. The fat man drank so greedily that water spilled out of his mouth and ran down his grimy cheeks in waves.

Lander grimaced at the thought of wasting so much precious liquid on a dead man, then felt ashamed for being so hard-hearted.

When the man lowered the waterskin from his lips, he wiped his mouth with his sleeve and said, "I shall die a happy man. What do you want to know?"

Twenty minutes later, the Harper knew everything that the prisoner did about Yhekal's plan. Lander had correctly guessed the Zhentarim's intent to enslave the Bedine and even the size of their army. He also confirmed that the invaders were traveling at night because of their mercenaries.

The Harper learned two new things, as well. First, the asabis had to spend the day burrowed underground, either a few feet beneath the sand, in a cave, or sometimes huddled in a rock crevice. Second, when the Mahwa attacked, Yhekal had been in the camp and presumably fled with the rest of the Zhentarim. Unfortunately, he had sent a wizard, along with fifty human officers, into the canyon to lead the reptiles in the attack on the Raz'hadi.

After the prisoner had drunk the last of Lander's water, his wounded leg sent a violent shudder of pain through his body and he cried out. The fat man waited for the wave to pass, then turned to Lander. "I've told you all I know of the Zhentarim," he said, handing the empty skin back to the Harper. "If you are going to kill me, do it now. This leg is beginning to throb."

Lander accepted the skin, saying, "I suppose that's fair."

The Harper took the waterskin back to his mount and hung it on the saddle, then drew his dagger and crept up behind the prisoner. Lander tried to move as quietly as possible, but he saw the Zhentarim flinch. The doomed man had sensed his presence. Nevertheless, the fat man continued to stare into the desert night.

Lander killed the Zhentarim merchant as quickly and painlessly as he could, plunging the straight blade of his dagger into the man's heart from behind. Afterward he knelt beside the body until the desert night began to chill him.

At last, the Harper cleaned his dagger on the dead prisoner's robe, scoured the blood off his *aba* with a handful of sandy earth, then took his *jellaba* off his camel and put it on. When he felt ready to join Sa'ar, Lander urged his camel to its feet and led it to the campfire where the sheikh and his elder warriors had gathered.

As the Harper approached, Sa'ar turned with a broad smile. Lander saw that Kadumi stood in the middle of the sheikh's entourage.

"Kadumi killed three men!" the sheikh announced.

"Good for him," Lander replied, forcing a smile. "Let us hope he lives to kill many more."

"My warriors counted just over five hundred dead," Sa'ar reported proudly. "We lost only fifteen."

"That means nearly a thousand Zhentarim escaped," Lander said, turning his thoughts to the task at hand. "We'll have to be careful that they don't rally and return unexpectedly."

Sa'ar frowned. "Do all your people look only at the bad side, Lander?"

"Five hundred dead is five hundred dead," he said without emotion. "We'll have to kill many more before we chase the Zhentarim from the desert. Now, how are we going to get your allies out of the canyon? There are fifteen hundred asabis and a powerful wizard in that canyon." He pointed at a narrow crack leading to the Well of the Chasm.

Sa'ar turned his attention to the canyon. "If we could wait until morning, our task would be simple."

"That, we cannot do," said a gray-haired warrior with rotten teeth. "I sent my sons to scout along the rim of the canyon. From what they report, our allies are meeting the asabis in the canyon as we expected. My sons think the Raz'hadi will not last more than a few hours."

"And in the morning light, the surviving Zhentarim will see our true number," added another warrior. "If they returned, we would not survive long."

Everyone nodded and muttered their agreement.

"Then we must attack tonight," Sa'ar responded. "Gather your sons."

"Wait," Lander interrupted. "The canyon is too narrow for everyone to fight in at once, is it not?"

The old man with rotten teeth nodded. "That is so, *berrani*."

"Then we lose nothing by leaving half of our warriors behind to defend our rear in case the Zhentarim return," the Harper said. "It will do the Raz'hadi no good if we allow ourselves to be trapped in the canyon with them."

The old man nodded. "This is a good plan."

"Perhaps we can send some of them up to the canyon rim to fire arrows down at the asabis," suggested another warrior.

Sa'ar paused and considered this plan, but it was Lander who said, "The canyon is very deep, and it will be very dark. How will your warriors tell their friends from the Zhentarim?"

"*Amarats*," responded Kadumi, smiling. "When we blow our horns, the Raz'hadi will certainly respond. The warriors on the rim can fire between the horns."

"And my horn will be the signal to stop," Sa'ar said, grinning at the boy. "It is a good thing you are so young, my friend. When you are old enough, my warriors will want to make you sheikh."

There was no mockery to the laughter that followed.

Sa'ar issued the necessary orders to his elder warriors, and they scattered to make their preparations. Realizing that Ruha's magic might prove as useful in the battle to come as it already had tonight, Lander mounted his camel and returned to where he had left her. The widow was still staring at the dust cloud.

"How long can you keep that dust cloud going?" he asked. When Ruha did not respond, the Harper waved his hand at her face. "The battle's over. You can let it down."

Ruha looked away from the dark curtain, and the breeze died immediately. "To answer your question, the dust wall lasts as long as I can concentrate on it," she said, rubbing her temples. "Which would not have been much longer."

"You're not feeling weak, are you?" Lander asked.

The widow shook her head. "My head aches, that's all."

"Thanks to Mielikki," the Harper sighed. "Mount up and come with me."

Ruha obeyed, asking, "Where are we going?"

"Into the canyon," Lander replied. "We may have need of more magic."

The widow was so shocked that she nearly fell from her camel's back as it returned to its feet. "What if somebody sees me?"

"We'll try to avoid that," the Harper replied, urging his camel back to the camp. "But there's too much at stake to let that worry us."

"That's easy for you to say. I'm the one they'll banish!"

Lander stopped his camel and twisted in his saddle to face the widow. "There are fifteen hundred asabis in that canyon. A wizard, as well. Sa'ar is about to attack with a tenth that number and not even the faintest idea of what magic can do to him. Whether they know it or not, you're probably all that stands between the Mahwa and annihilation. Ruha, there is only one thing you can do."

Without waiting to see if the widow would follow, Lander started riding. When he reached the fire, he found a hundred and fifty of the Mahwa's best warriors mounted and awaiting their sheikh.

As Lander and Ruha approached, Sa'ar turned to them. "This time, I have no need of your advice, *berrani*. I know asabis better than you."

"True," Lander said. "There is also a wizard or two in the canyon, and I know magic better than you."

"I cannot argue," the sheikh replied. He looked beyond

Lander. "Will you take Ruha into the canyon?"

The Harper looked over his shoulder and saw the widow stopping her camel just behind him. She spoke before Lander could respond to Sa'ar's question. "My thoughts have not changed, Sheikh. I will be safest in Lander's company."

"No!" Kadumi cried. He was mounted on one of his white camels and sat in the company of the sheikh's warriors. "It is too dangerous!"

Ruha turned her gaze on the youth. "This will not be the first time my *jambiya* has tasted the invaders' blood," she said, her voice stern and steady. "Or have you forgotten who was the rescuer when the Zhentarim ambushed us outside of Rahalat?"

The boy quickly looked away. Lander could not tell whether he was embarrassed at recalling the mistake that had almost gotten him killed or upset at the memory of Ruha's magic. In either case, the widow's tactic worked well. Without turning his gaze back to Ruha's face, Kadumi nodded to Sa'ar. "If it pleases you, Sheikh, allow my brother's wife to ride with the *berrani*. As she claims, she will not cause us any trouble."

Sa'ar raised an eyebrow, then nodded to Lander. "See that she stays out of the way." The sheikh went to his camel. As he mounted, he pointed at Kadumi. "Why don't you lead the way, fearless one?"

"Isn't he a little young?" Lander objected.

The sheikh frowned at the Harper. "Did you not hear me earlier? This boy killed three men tonight."

Kadumi paused to cast a self-righteous glance at the Harper, then turned to lead the way toward the canyon. Lander and Ruha waited for the end of the column with the sheikh before they fell into line. A few minutes later, the line switched to single file and rode into a narrow, dark ravine. The Harper rode behind the sheikh, and behind

Lander came only Ruha.

Three feet to either side of the riders, the canyon walls rose high into the starry sky. On the ledges and shelves of the cliffs, heaps of yellow sand reflected the pale light of the crescent moon, making the rock itself seem all the more dark and foreboding. The floor of the canyon, too, was covered with a thick layer of sand.

Lander felt the footing grow softer beneath his mount's feet, and the camel began to lunge as if going downhill. Ahead, the dark silhouettes of the war party were descending down the narrow chute two abreast, the shoulders of their mounts almost brushing the rock walls. Already, Kadumi had disappeared around a dark corner.

Though the tight quarters made Lander nervous, he knew that they worked to the Bedine's advantage in this instance. It would be impossible to attack more than four abreast. Under such circumstances, the Zhentarim's numerical superiority would do them little good. On the other hand, the Bedine could hardly mount a charge, and it would be an easy matter for the asabis to defend themselves. The Harper found himself searching the canyon rim, hoping to glimpse the warriors Sa'ar had assigned to attack from above. He saw nothing but the jagged silhouettes of rocks and, directly overhead, thousands of brightly twinkling stars.

Less than ten minutes into the canyon, a shrill *amarat* trilled from up ahead.

"That was Kadumi!" Ruha gasped.

"Don't worry," Sa'ar reassured her. "He's as good a scout as I've seen in many a year. He'll be fine."

A murmur of excitement ran up the length of the column. The sheikh's warriors pressed forward, nocking arrows in their bows. Lander could not see what was happening at the front of the line, for it was out of sight around a sharp bend.

An *amarat* with deep, rich tones called from the canyon, its sound muffled and softened by distance and the snake-like rift.

"Utaiba!" Sa'ar exclaimed, smiling. He fished his own massive *amarat* out of his *djebira* and hung it around his neck, ready to call off the attack from above when the time came.

A moment later, Lander and his companions rounded the corner. Because of the path's steep slope, Lander could see over Sa'ar's men for quite a distance. Fifty yards ahead the ravine, still descending at a steep angle, bulged out to a width of eighty feet. The bulge continued for a distance of a hundred yards, then the canyon once again narrowed to a width through which only two men could ride abreast.

Sa'ar's warriors were crammed into the canyon in twos and threes. The front ranks, still led by Kadumi's youthful form, had stopped and were firing their bows. The rear ranks had also stopped and drawn their bows. By slightly elevating their aim, many of these riders were using the advantage of the steep slope to lob arrows over the heads of their fellows.

The target of both groups was a throng of asabis, crowded into the bulge so thickly that they could hardly move. Under the direction of a Zhentarim officer, two dozen of the mercenaries had turned around to meet the attack from the rear, but most of the reptiles remained unaware of the peril. Their attention was directed at the far end of the bulge, where Lander could just see the silhouettes of a second group of Bedine warriors blocking the way deeper into the canyon.

The sheikh pointed at the Bedine obstructing the far end of the bulge. "My allies, the Raz'hadi," he explained. "The asabis and their masters are trapped between us."

As Sa'ar suggested, the Bedine were in excellent tactical position, but Lander felt far from confident. "I don't like this," he said. "The enemy is smart enough to have a rear-guard."

The sheikh chuckled and pointed back up the canyon. "It is gone. We chased it away!"

"Perhaps," Lander allowed. Even if they had realized the Mahwa were coming to attack, the Zhentarim would never have believed that the force protecting the canyon mouth could be driven away. Still, he suspected that the enemy would spring a surprise or two of its own before the battle ended. "I hope we can take advantage of our good fortune."

No sooner had he spoken than a flight of arrows whooshed down from the canyon rim. The Harper looked up and, two hundred feet above, he saw the dark forms of seventy-five men loosing another round into the bulge. Pained moans and confused growls rolled from the crowded ranks of the asabis. The Mahwa in the canyon gave a boastful cheer and added a volley of their own to the attack.

"The invaders are caught between the lions and the leopards," Sa'ar bragged. "Not one shall escape!"

As the sheikh spoke, a hooded silhouette in the rear ranks of the asabi turned toward them. It pointed a finger at the forward ranks of the Mahwa.

"The wizard!" Lander yelled, pointing at the hooded figure. "Shoot him before—"

A tremendous clap filled the canyon, and Lander closed his eyes just before everything went white. The battle fell momentarily silent. By the time Lander opened his eyes again, the air already smelled of scorched camel hair and seared human flesh. The first eighty feet of the Mahwa ranks had been decimated. Dozens of camels and men lay on the canyon floor, some with tiny fires smoldering where the lightning bolt had hit them. Those who had not fallen, including the warriors in the rear ranks, were frantically rubbing their eyes, trying to recover their night vision.

At the edge of the bulge, Lander saw the stunned silhouette of a boy struggle to his feet, scimitar in hand. His knees looked weak and he seemed confused. Yet the boy—who could only be Kadumi—managed to stand, which was more than many of the men around him could do.

Beyond Kadumi, the hooded figure that had cast the spell was yelling at the asabis and waving them back toward the ranks of the Mahwa. Lander turned to Ruha and, to his relief, saw that she had also had the sense to shield her eyes. Pointing at the enemy wizard, he said, "That man must die!"

Ruha hesitated, glancing at Sa'ar and the other Bedine. In the same instant, the asabis began showering the Mahwa with crossbow bolts. Sa'ar's men screamed in panic and confusion. The few who had begun to recover their sight returned the fire, and another volley of arrows hissed down into the bulge from the canyon rim.

"Do something or the Mahwa are lost!" Lander snapped.

"Give me sand," the widow said, holding out her hand.

The Harper moved his camel a step closer to the canyon wall, then scraped a handful off a ledge and passed it to Ruha. When he looked back to the battle, the enemy sorcerer seemed to be facing the Mahwa again, though it was difficult to tell in the darkness. Lander feared he was preparing to cast another spell.

"Now, Ruha!"

Even as he spoke, he heard the widow whisper her incantation. The silhouette of a great cat appeared behind the enemy wizard, leaping in the Zhentarim's direction. As it enclosed the man in its front paws, a terrified scream pierced the din of the battle. The cat dragged the man to the ground, and they disappeared into the mass of shadows cluttering the bulge. A moment later, there was a flurry of waving swords, and the cat's defiant yowls implied that it was taking a few more Zhentarim with it.

Unfortunately the wizard's death did not take the fight out of the asabis. Dropping their crossbows and drawing short swords, several hundred turned and charged the Mahwa. Lander saw Kadumi and a handful of other warriors brace to meet the charge, each carrying a scimitar in one hand and a *jambiya* in another.

"Fill the gap!" Sa'ar shouted, waving his rear ranks forward.

The column started down the canyon, moving too slowly for Lander's tastes, but there was little he could do to urge it on. He pressed his camel as hard as he could, but in the tight quarters his mount could work its way past no more than the sheikh's camel and a handful of other beasts.

At the edge of the bulge, the asabis rolled over Kadumi and the others. Lander saw the youth fall and disappear into the press. Drawing his scimitar and dagger, the Harper slipped off his camel.

"What are you doing?" Ruha called.

Surprised that the widow had managed to stay with him, Lander paused to say, "Kadumi's in trouble."

Ruha shocked him by drawing her own dagger and slipping from her mount's back. "Given the way he's been treating you, I'm surprised you care."

On foot, the pair found it much easier to work their way forward. Although they could no longer see what was happening ahead, they slipped past the camels without trouble. As they moved, Lander could tell by the rhythm of volleys that the warriors on the canyon rim were keeping up a steady stream of fire, but the Mahwa in the canyon had put away their bows and drawn their scimitars.

Ahead of him, steel began to ring on steel, and the Harper knew the battle had turned desperate for both sides. If the sheikh's men could prevent the invaders from breaking out of the bulge, the archers on the canyon rim would deci-

mate them. If not, the asabis would cut them off and both
the Mahwa and the Raz'hadi would be lost.

Twenty yards from where Kadumi had fallen, Lander
found himself in the thick of the melee. As he stepped past
a camel, a short blade came whistling toward his head. His
body reacted automatically, pivoting at the waist to avoid
the blow. Lander brought his scimitar down on the scaly
arm wielding the short sword, then turned and thrust his
dagger into the attacker's abdomen. Only then did he have
an opportunity to look at the reptile, which was staring at
him with astonished, slit-pupiled eyes.

After that, the battle became a maelstrom of whirling
blades and chiming swords. Lander advanced steadily, using the sword to block and the *jambiya* to kill, sometimes
reversing his pattern and parrying with the dagger then
slicing off an arm or leg with the curved blade of his scimitar. He dimly realized that a knot of Mahwa warriors had
dismounted and were following his lead, pressing forward
in a bloody hand-to-hand combat.

The Harper was also aware that Ruha trailed close behind him, for every now and then her dagger flashed into
view. They made a good team, for her quick hand and alert
eye were always ready to parry a thrust from his blind side
or force an unseen attacker to hesitate long enough for the
Harper to finish him off.

At last they reached the place where Kadumi had fallen.
No more asabis stepped in to attack and, instead, began
retreating into the bulge. A chorus of throaty cheers went
up from the warriors behind Lander, and arrows began to
sail over their heads as the Mahwa in the rear ranks resumed their attack.

"We forced them back!" Ruha said, her breath coming in
labored gasps after the exertion of the battle.

"So it seems," Lander said.

On the far side of the bulge, a series of *amarat* horns

sounded, which the Harper hoped meant that the battle was also going well there. Without giving the matter any more thought, he sheathed his sword and, keeping his dagger handy, started to turn bodies over.

Lander found Kadumi not far from where he remembered seeing the boy fall. From what he could see in the dim light, the youth had suffered a nasty blow to the head and several minor gashes, but all of his limbs were still attached and he was breathing.

"Is he going to live?" Ruha asked.

"Maybe," Lander answered. He sheathed his dagger, then picked the boy up. "But only if we get him out of here before the asabis charge again."

The deep tones of Sa'ar's *amarat* sounded from the rear of the Mahwa column. Instantly an eerie silence fell over the battlefield as the warriors on the canyon rim ceased their rain of arrows. A great cheer sounded from the far side of the bulge. Lander turned just in time to see a column of trotting camels come into sight, moving as fast as they could up the steep sands. The asabis were scattering toward the walls, leaving an open path up the center of the canyon.

"The Raz'hadi have broken through!" Ruha cried.

As the column of camels approached, the Harper did not know what to say. He could not imagine that the asabis, still nearly a thousand strong, had given up the battle and decided to let the Raz'hadi flee. Yet, that was exactly what it appeared had happened.

Lander watched for a few moments more before he realized what the mercenaries were doing. As the Raz'hadi approached the middle of the bulge, the asabis began climbing the canyon walls, scurrying up the cliffs just as if they had been running along the ground. Within seconds, they were streaming along the rock walls toward the mouth of the canyon.

"They're going to cut us off!" the Harper said.

A concerned murmur rustled through the knot of warriors near Lander. The asabis were moving fast enough to overtake the camels, and trying to shoot so many before they passed would be hopeless.

Sheathing her weapons, Ruha said, "I can stop them."

Without another word, the widow picked up two handfuls of sand and raised them high over her head. The warriors who had joined Lander in repulsing the asabi charge regarded her with suspicious expressions, but Ruha ignored them. She closed her eyes and recited her incantation, then began to hum in a steady, mournful note.

A soft hiss filled the canyon. By the light of the silver-white moon, Lander could see the sand piled on the ledges and shelves of the cliffs running down the rocks like the waterfalls of Archendale. Cursing and crying out in their guttural language, the asabis began dropping from the cliffsides in tens and twenties.

The warriors began backing up the canyon, their eyes wide with disbelief and trepidation. Only one dared to say anything, and then a single word: "Witch!"

Twelve

In At'ar's early radiance, the rocky minarets outside the Mouth of the Abyss showed the hue of dried blood. The spires cast long, midnight-colored stripes over the tawny hollow, plunging the first battlefield of the previous night into an eerie contrast of murky shadow and fervid color. A pall of silvery smoke hung over the campfires Sa'ar's rearguard had kept burning all night, and the ghostly silhouettes of men and camels were just now taking on a more earthly form.

The Zhentarim had not returned during the night, and the asabis were still in the canyon. After Ruha's spell had knocked the reptilian mercenaries from the cliff walls, the Raz'hadi and Mahwa had fled the chasm together. Only a handful of warriors from each tribe had been required to stay behind to keep the enemy from escaping.

With her brother-in-law and the Harper, Ruha sat in the middle of a circle formed by the sheikhs of the two victorious tribes and twenty of their blood-spattered

warriors. Kadumi wore a bandage around his head, and the
minor gashes on his arms and legs were still oozing a little
blood. If Lander had not poured one of his healing potions
down the boy's throat earlier, Ruha doubted that the youth
would even be conscious.

Despite last night's triumph, a somber mood hung over
the gathering. Sa'ar was conversing solemnly with his
Raz'hadi counterpart, Sheikh Utaiba, regarding what
should be done about Ruha and her companions. The warriors of both tribes sat without speaking, their eyes cast on
the ground to avoid looking at the trio under discussion.

Ruha knew as well as the warriors did that when the
sheikhs' finished their discussion, she would be banished
from the Raz'hadi and the Mahwa. Last night, dozens of
warriors had witnessed her use a spell to knock the asabis
from the canyon walls. Though her action had saved the
two tribes, when it came to magic, Bedine tradition was
universally clear. Witches and sorcerers were to be out-
casts.

The only question in Ruha's mind was whether or not
Lander and Kadumi would be exiled with her. After all, her
brother-in-law had been at the head of the column when it
rode into the canyon, and the Harper had spearheaded the
countercharge against the asabis. The widow thought that
simple gratitude would dictate that their association with
her be overlooked. For Kadumi's sake, she hoped the
sheikhs would agree—though it might mean that she would
be separated from the Harper, at least until he was ready to
return to Sembia.

Sa'ar cleared his throat, indicating that he and Utaiba
were ready to announce their decision. "Last night, our
warriors killed five hundred Zhentarim and five hundred of
their asabis," the sheikh began, wisely preceding what everyone knew would be a difficult decision with a positive
statement.

Utaiba, a wiry man with a graying beard and piercing black eyes, nodded. "It was a great victory for our tribes, Sa'ar. Your warriors fought splendidly, and we Raz'hadi have reason to be glad they did."

The warriors remained silent, a formality Lander did not observe. "The Mahwa and the Raz'hadi fought like lions," he said, pausing to smile at the assembly of warriors. After allowing the warriors an opportunity to accept his praise, he continued, "Yet the Zhentarim still outnumber your warriors by ten-to-one."

"This is true," agreed Sa'ar, frowning at being drawn into a conversation when he had intended only to announce his decision. "But we lost less than two hundred warriors between both our tribes. It shall not be long before the odds are more to our liking."

Lander shook his head. "Sheikh, you know that I wish it were so, but I must speak my heart in this matter. Last night you caught the Zhentarim unprepared. They will be ready for you the next time, and they will have magic."

"What are you saying?" demanded Utaiba, squinting at Lander from beneath his coarse eyebrows. "Should we give them the run of the desert and stay out of the way? Is that what you would have us do?"

"No," Lander answered calmly, turning his one good eye to meet the sheikh's hard gaze. "I want you to drive them out of Anauroch. If you do not, more Zhentarim will follow these. Soon the sands will be crawling with black burnooses, and there will be no place left to graze your camels or fill your waterskins."

"We intend to fight," Sa'ar said, clenching his fist and holding it proudly in front of him. "If that is what you want from us, you can go home, *berrani*."

From the sheikh's sharp tone, Ruha guessed that home was exactly where he and Utaiba had intended to send Lander. She was impressed by the Harper's diplomacy, for he had neatly turned what was to be a pronouncement of doom into a discussion of strategy. The widow did not think that his plan would work, of course, but she admired him for trying.

"I want the desert tribes to fight," Lander said, pausing to gaze into the eyes of several nearby warriors. "But more than that, I want the Bedine to win!"

Several of the men murmured their agreement. As a man who had carried himself well in battle, Lander was entitled to a certain amount of respect, and he was making the most of it.

The warrior's support was not lost on the sheikhs, who gave each other concerned glances before turning back to the Harper. Sa'ar said, "We have no intention of losing—"

"You may lose no matter what your intentions are," Lander interrupted, laying a hand on Ruha's shoulder, "unless you accept the magic that this woman can provide."

Ruha saw the Harper's influence slipping away as the jaw of warrior after warrior went slack in shock.

"You can't win this argument," she hissed. "Don't even try."

Lander ignored her and continued to address the assembly. "With their magic, the Zhentarim have an overpowering advantage."

Ruha angrily shrugged his hand off her shoulder, then angrily shook her head. "What makes you think I want to help these tribes?" Her words were sharp, for she did not like being ignored—especially when it was her life that being discussed.

Lander faced her, not fazed. "Your people need magic, all they can get."

"They are not my people," Ruha retorted, glaring at Sa'ar and Utaiba. "They wouldn't have me and I wouldn't have them!"

"That is unfortunate—" the Harper began.

"And it is irrelevant," interrupted Sa'ar, trying to retake control of the conversation. "Utaiba and I have a plan for defeating the Zhentarim that will not offend the gods. You may take Ruha and leave." The sheikh glanced at Kadumi, then added, "This fine young warrior will be welcome in either of our tribes."

"I go with Ruha," Kadumi declared, starting to rise.

Without looking away from Sa'ar, Lander caught the youth's wrist and gently restrained him. "As you know, I have come far and risked my life to warn the Bedine of their danger," he said in a reasonable tone. "Would it be too much to ask in return to know the nature of your plan?"

Sa'ar looked uncomfortable, but Utaiba nodded. When the wiry sheikh spoke, however, he looked at his warriors instead of the Harper. "We have seen that the Raz'hadi and the Mahwa are stronger together than they are alone, have we not?"

Several warriors voiced their agreement.

"Then does it not stand to reason that ten tribes will have ten times the strength of one?"

"It does," affirmed a burly warrior. "But even between our two tribes, do we have ten allies?"

Sa'ar shook his head. "Not yet, Kabina. Remember, though, that the enemy of our enemy is our friend."

Before Kabina could respond, Utaiba continued Sa'ar's explanation. "The Zhentarim are enemies of all our people. So, at least where the Black Robes are concerned, all Bedine are friends."

"We have sent messengers to all the tribes within riding distance," Sa'ar concluded, waving his hand at the horizon. "We will tell their sheikhs what the Zhentarim have done and ask them to meet us at Elah'zad. There, we will shape a grand alliance to drive the invaders from Anauroch."

"A worthy plan," Lander said, nodding eagerly.

The warriors looked pleased by the Harper's approval,

but Sa'ar and Utaiba each raised suspicious brows.

"Yet, in the time it takes you to assemble, the Zhentarim will not be idle. They will discover what you are doing and move to prevent it."

Utaiba smirked, then said, "I doubt they can stop us in ten days. Even if they knew our intentions, they would have to find Elah'zad—and travel to it."

Ruha approved of this portion of the sheikhs' plan, at least. Located one hundred and fifty miles to the north, Elah'zad was an out-of-the-way oasis protected by a formidable mix of salt flats and rocky hills. It would not be an easy place for the Zhentarim to reach or attack.

Lander conceded the point by inclining his head, then turned the subject back to his earlier argument. "Even with ten tribes, you will still need Ruha to counter the magic of the Zhentarim. What would have happened had she not been in the canyon last night?"

The sheikhs and their men all frowned, but they knew the answer to Lander's question. Still, being correct did not mean the Harper had won the argument. The warriors scowled at him stubbornly for several moments.

Finally Kabina spoke again. "We did not know about the witch last night, so the gods will not blame us for what she did." The burly warrior fixed an icy glare on Ruha. "If we ride with her now, they will surely deliver us into defeat and slavery."

"It is not the gods who will deliver you into slavery," Lander countered patiently, still speaking in a reasonable but unyielding voice. "It is the Zhentarim, and your only hope of victory lies with Ruha's magic. Instead of banishing her, you should be begging her to help you."

"You do not understand the gods of the Bedine," Sa'ar declared.

"Perhaps I don't," the Harper responded, fixing his one-eyed gaze on the sheikh. "But *you* don't understand the

Zhentarim. They won't hesitate to use their magic. Unless you fight back with magic, you are doomed."

A grisled, gray-eyed warrior said, "If we need magic, our gods will provide it for us, as Kozah provided the dust storm last night."

Lander turned toward the warrior and shook his head. "Kozah had nothing to do with that storm."

Ruha grabbed the Harper's arm. In his muscles, she felt a tension that did not show in his face, though she could not say whether it was caused by anger or fear. "Lander, talk no more," she whispered. "Nothing you say can change their minds." The widow did not add that his argument was also hardening their hearts.

The Harper did not heed her warning. "The dust storm was Ruha's doing."

A burst of astounded cries ran round the circle, and warriors glanced at one another with disheartened and angry expressions. They had taken the dust curtain to be a sign that Kozah favored them and were not happy to hear that a sorceress had caused the storm instead of their god.

Sa'ar studied Ruha for several moments, then asked, "Is this true, witch?"

The widow hesitated before replying. If Lander was arguing just because he was stubborn, it might be wiser to deny casting the spell and avoid upsetting the warriors any further. On the other hand, if the Harper actually believed he could convince the Bedine to accept her magic, she did not want him to think she was unsupportive.

"Speak the truth," the Harper urged.

Ruha swallowed once, then made her decision. "I created the dust storm," she said. "Not Kozah."

A few stubborn warriors muttered half-hearted denials, but most of the Bedine received the news in dumfounded silence.

Lander seized the opportunity to continue his argument.

"In my land, N'asr is called Cyric, and Kozah is known as Talos," the Harper began. "But by whatever name they are called, the gods watch over all of Toril, not just Anauroch."

The Bedine greeted his statement with a mixture of blank stares and suspicious curiosity, but they did not interrupt. Ruha began to suspect that there was, indeed, a method to Lander's argument.

"In my land, magic is common," the Harper continued. "So my question is this: if magic is so terrible, why do the gods permit it in one part of the world and not in the other? Could it be possible that in all the centuries since the Scattering, they have entrusted it to mankind again? Is it possible that Kozah did not help us last night because Ruha was there to work his will instead?"

Utaiba raised his brow thoughtfully, and Sa'ar pursed his lips and rubbed his chin. Even the warriors appeared to be considering the matter, and a flutter developed in the widow's stomach as she realized the Harper actually had a chance to win over the Bedine. Ruha found herself wondering how it would feel to be a fully accepted member of a tribe.

Her contemplation was short-lived. A few moments later, Sa'ar found a weakness in the Harper's argument. "Your people did not make a desert of their home, *berrani*, so the gods have no reason to punish them. You and the Zhentarim may use magic, but that does mean it is permitted for a Bedine. It may even be that the Zhentarim have been sent into Anauroch to test our resolve."

Lander's face reddened, and a vein began throbbing in his temple. "In the name of Mielikki, why are you so determined to be Zhentarim slaves?" he yelled. "Are you fools? Isn't living in this desolate waste punishment enough for you?"

"Quiet!" Sa'ar roared, glowering at Lander. "We have

decided. You and the witch must leave!"

"As you wish," the Harper spat. "Other tribes may have wiser sheikhs. I will take Ruha to Elah'zad and see."

"Then you will die," Sa'ar threatened.

Lander sneered. "Someday, but not by your blade."

The sturdy sheikh reached for his *jambiya* and Ruha realized that the matter was about to come to blood. The widow knew that this was not a battle she and the Harper could hope to win, so she rose and positioned herself between the two angry men.

"Hold your tongues and your blades," she said. "We will let the gods themselves resolve this argument."

"That was what I intended," Sa'ar snarled. His hand remained on his dagger hilt, but he made no move to finish standing.

"Let us consider the widow's suggestion," Utaiba said, laying a restraining hand on Sa'ar's arm. "What do you have in mind, Ruha?"

The widow inclined her head to the sheikh. "I was raised at the Sister of Rains oasis with the witch Qoha'dar," she said. "When my mistress died, I buried her book of magic spells in the ruins of the ancient fort that stands there."

"What does this have to do with gods?" demanded Sa'ar.

Ruha smiled and turned her attention to the stout sheikh. "With that book, my magic would be much improved," she said. "Lander and I will go to the Sister of Rains to recover it, then meet you at Elah'zad in ten days."

"But, from here, that means crossing the Shoal of Thirst—twice!" Kadumi objected. "It can't be done!"

"That's right," the widow said, fixing her gaze on Sa'ar. "If we reach Elah'zad with the spellbook, it will surely be a sign that the gods favor my magic. If we don't, then . . . well, everyone knows what that will mean."

Lander rose and smiled at Sa'ar. "Is that acceptable?"

"You have no idea what you're riding into."

"Nevertheless, do you agree?"

Sa'ar looked to his counterpart, who nodded. "It is their bones At'ar will bleach," Utaiba said. "And if they should survive, it will truly be a sign from the gods."

"Then it is decided," Sa'ar said, standing.

Utaiba also rose, indicating the meeting had come to an end. As the circle of warriors followed the lead of their sheikhs and began to break up, Kabina yelled in astonishment, then fell headfirst to the ground. The other warriors laughed at his clumsiness.

"Quiet, you fools!" snarled the Mahwai, scowling. "There's something here."

Kabina reached out and clutched at the empty air. A familiar voice uttered a shriek, then the sand near Kabina erupted as something hit the ground. A noise followed, as of something tearing, and the burly warrior was left holding the tattered hood of a white burnoose in his hand. "A djinn!" he cried.

"That's no djinn, it's Bhadla!" Lander corrected. He reached for his sword and stepped toward Kabina. "I recognize the man's yelp. He must be spying on us for the Zhentarim!"

Utaiba intercepted the Harper. "The spy was intruding on our council," the sheikh said. "You must leave this to us." He turned to the warriors. "You men, find the intruder!"

The warriors drew their scimitars and began waving them through the air in tentative, uncertain slashes. Their brows were arched in skeptical, worried expressions.

"If this is a D'tarig and not a djinn, why can't we see him?" Sa'ar asked, echoing the concerns in the hearts of all his men.

Lander looked into the sheikh's eyes and said one word, "Magic."

Within a few moments, it became apparent that the warriors were not going to locate the invisible spy by slashing randomly through the air. Lander turned to Ruha. "Bhadla's probably gone by now, but do you have any spells that will reveal his location?"

Utaiba did not allow the widow to reply. "No magic," he ordered. "You have not crossed the Shoal of Thirst yet."

The search continued for a few minutes more before Kabina located the spy's tracks and led the warriors off to stalk him. Ruha did not think they had much chance for success, for the D'tarig had a good headstart and it would be difficult to trail him when he reached a patch of rocky ground.

"Do you think he heard our plans?" she asked Lander.

The Harper nodded. "We have to assume he did."

"I would not worry," Sa'ar said. "The Zhentarim will find it no easier to cross the Shoal of Thirst than you. If they try to follow, they will meet a slow and terrible death." He paused and gave Ruha a mocking grin. "Unless, of course, it is the gods' will that they catch you."

"And what of your council?" Lander asked. "If Bhadla heard where it is to be held, the Zhentarim will be sure to go there."

"I doubt anyone who is not Bedine knows of Elah'zad," Utaiba answered. "The oasis is well hidden, and that is why we picked it. Even if the spy knows Elah'zad, there is little we can do. The messengers have already been sent. Trying to change the site would only result in hopeless confusion."

Sa'ar nodded his agreement. "The best thing that we can do is leave this place quickly. Once the spy reports to his masters, they will realize how few we are and may try to attack." The stout sheikh turned to Kadumi and placed a hand on the boy's shoulder. "You may ride with my tribe. We always have use for a sharp sword."

The youth shook his head, saying, "I will go with my

sister-in-law and the *berrani*."

Ruha turned to the boy. "You have been wounded, and I am not what your brother thought I was when he married me," she said. "Under the circumstances, I do not think that family honor dictates you protect me any longer."

"This has nothing to do with family honor," Kadumi answered. "You and Lander saved my life last night, and you will need me and my camels in the shoal."

"I'm sure we'll manage," the widow said. "An extra person will only—"

"Let the boy come if he likes. It's his choice," Lander said, grinning at the young warrior. "Besides, he's right. Somebody's going to have to take care of me."

Kadumi smiled at the Harper's joke, then turned to Ruha and asked, "Do you really think we can cross the Shoal of Thirst?"

"I've already crossed it," Ruha said. "After leaving the Sister of Rains two years ago, this is the first oasis I came to."

The widow did not add that her camels had been freshly watered and grazed before she had ventured into the Shoal of Thirst the first time, or that they had all died, leaving her to walk the last ten miles on foot.

Thirteen

Ruha could not stop thinking about the extra waterskins. Perhaps the mouths weren't tied properly, she worried. Perhaps one has developed a friction hole. Despite her anxiety, the witch resisted the temptation to stop the small caravan and inspect the skins. She had already done so twice that day and knew her fears to be unwarranted. Her preoccupation was caused more by her thirst than by valid concerns.

Though five days had passed since parting from the Mahwa and Raz'hadi, it had only been four days since she and her companions had descended into the Shoal of Thirst. The great basin stretched for miles in all directions, as flat as a pan and as endless as the sky. Gleaming salts covered the entire valley, making it seem as though the trio was riding across a cloud. Ruha's eyes ached from the constant sting of salt, and her throat was clogged with mordant-tasting grit.

Ruha tried not to think about the two days of travel

remaining before she and her companions reached the Sister of Rains. She also tried to forget that as soon as they arrived, they would have to turn around and spend another three days in the northern tip of the Shoal of Thirst in order to reach Elah'zad in time to help the tribes gathered there.

Instead Ruha focused her thoughts a few hours ahead. At'ar hung only three spans above the horizon, an orange disc without heat or brilliance. Dusk was slowly approaching, and after it fell, the trio would ride for perhaps two more hours. When the camels began to snort and groan with exhaustion, the trio would stop and wash the salt from their parched throats with warm milk. No one would drink any water, for they were saving it for their mounts. During the crossing, the camel's milk would serve as both food and water.

Lander suddenly stopped and turned around, inspecting the salt-crusted ground behind him with one bloodshot, red-rimmed eye. Although the day was still hot, he wore his *jellaba* over his shoulders. The heavy cloak trapped a layer of clammy air next to the body, keeping the wearer from dehydrating so quickly. Unlike Ruha and Kadumi, though, Lander did not wear his *jellaba* wrapped tightly around himself. It hung loose and open at the throat, allowing precious body moisture to escape.

Ruha dutifully stopped the haggard string of camels. Although there had been no sign of Zhentarim pursuers for two days, the Harper continued to search the horizon at irregular intervals.

"There! Look!" Lander said, pointing. His lips were so dry and chapped that they cracked and bled when he spoke.

The witch obediently turned her mount around and stared to the east. She saw nothing but the darkening horizon. "What?"

"Something's following us," he insisted.

Kadumi joined the pair, stopping on the other side of Lander. The youth's eyes were bloodshot, but rimmed with far less red than the Harper's. "Where?" the boy asked.

Lander adjusted the direction in which his finger was pointing. "Right there. It's just a shadow."

Kadumi peered at the horizon for a minute, then glanced at Ruha and shook his head.

The young widow took a few moments to search the horizon herself. "There's nothing there, Lander," she said at last.

He nodded. "It's gone now, but we'll have to be careful."

The widow shook her head sadly. Lander had been saying the same thing all day, apparently fearing the Zhentarim were still following. Ruha and Kadumi did not discount the possibility entirely, but they both thought it more likely that the invaders had turned back two days ago. The Shoal of Thirst was so scorching that most Bedine could not survive a journey across it, so it seemed impossible that the water-loving Zhentarim could endure such a punishing journey.

To Ruha it appeared more likely that Lander was suffering from a delirium. The combination of heat and thirst were making him imagine things. The widow forced her camel to kneel, then removed a waterskin from one of the milk-camels. She opened the skin's mouth and walked to Lander's side.

"Drink," she said. "You're seeing phantoms."

"I'm not seeing things. Somebody is following us," the Harper insisted. Nevertheless he accepted the waterskin, then looked from Ruha to Kadumi. "Are you and Ruha drinking?"

The youth shook his head. "We're not thirsty," he said. Despite what he told Lander, he could not take his eyes off the waterskin. "There is plenty of water, though. Drink."

"If we have plenty of water, there's no harm in you and

Ruha drinking with me," Lander countered, holding the
waterskin toward the boy.

"We'll have milk tonight," Kadumi said. "Bedine prefer
camel's milk to water."

The Harper snorted. "Nobody prefers camel's milk to
water." He turned to Ruha and leaned down to offer her the
water. A spoonful of the contents spilled out of the mouth
and trickled down the side.

"Be careful!" Ruha said.

The Harper smiled. "I think Kadumi is not telling the
truth." He tied the waterskin's mouth, then held it toward
Ruha.

"You must drink," she said, not accepting the skin.
"You're growing delirious."

The Harper shook his head, then licked the blood from
his chapped lips. "I may be thirsty," he said, "but I'm not
imagining things." When she did not take the water, Lander
said, "This skin is heavy. I'm about to drop it."

"You are a stubborn fool," Ruha said, accepting the waterskin. Nodding at the open throat of Lander's cloak, she
added, "Are you *trying* to kill yourself? Close your *jellaba*."

The widow returned the waterskin to the back of the
haggard milk-camel, then mounted her beast again. The
trio turned their camels into the setting sun and resumed
their trek. This time, they rode three abreast, Lander between Ruha and Kadumi, where they could keep a watchful
eye on him.

As they rode, the Harper periodically twisted around in
his saddle and stared at their backtrail. Ruha did likewise,
just in case Lander was not imagining things and they really
were being followed. She did not see any Zhentarim, but
the widow did notice that the milk-camels were beginning
to stumble, a sure sign that they were dehydrated. This
came as no surprise to her. Under good summer conditions, a camel could go for two weeks without drinking.

Crossing the Shoal of Thirst could hardly be considered good conditions, and the trio was pressing their beasts hard. The white glare of the endless flat made At'ar's heat even more unbearable. To make matters worse, the salt prevented plants from growing in the basin, and when camels could not eat, they had to drink.

Finally Kadumi could stand the twisting and squirming no longer. As Lander pivoted to stare at the backtrail for perhaps the twentieth time, the youth asked, "Have you seen anything yet?"

The Harper shook his head. "Not since we stopped."

Kadumi sighed in relief. "At least your delirium is not constant."

"I'm not delirious," the Harper responded patiently.

"And how would you know?" Ruha asked. "An incoherent man cannot tell a mirage from an oasis until he tries to drink from it."

"This is no mirage."

Kadumi groaned and shook his head, then the riders continued in silence. Ruha was glad that the youth had insisted upon coming along. After being rescued by her and the Harper during the Battle of the Chasm, the boy had matured a great deal, and he was proving a real asset on this journey. He was an excellent desert traveler, but more than that, his competence and steadfast attitude were a comfort to Ruha whenever Lander's delirium began to worry her.

At'ar fell to within a span of the horizon, and her disc vanished into the yellow, cloudless sky. Air currents began to eddy around the riders, whipping their faces with invisible salt grains borne on warm, withering winds. Ruha's eyes started watering, and she envied Lander the patch that protected his bad eye.

"I hope your spellbook is worth this," Kadumi said. He pulled his *keffiyeh* off his head and wrapped it around his face like a woman's veil.

It was Lander who responded. "Any magic is worth—"

The roar of a camel interrupted the Harper. Immediately Ruha stopped the string and spun around in her saddle. The second camel in line was collapsing to its front knees, its eyes rolled back in their sockets.

"Kadumi!" she called, leaping from her camel.

"What's wrong?" Lander asked, staring at the dying camel.

Ruha did not answer as she ran.

The widow could not move fast enough. The haggard beast rolled over onto its side, bursting one of the waterskins it carried.

"No!" Ruha grabbed the halter and tried to pull the camel back to its knees, but its sinewy neck had already fallen limp. The widow gave up on the dead beast and stepped around to its back. There was a slight depression where the water had dissolved some salt, and a dark stain was spreading out from beneath the beast as the ground absorbed the spill. Otherwise, not a sign remained of the four gallons of water they had lost.

Ruha grabbed the collapsed skin and tried to pull it from beneath the camel, hoping it still contained a few cups of water. Kadumi moved to her side and lifted the dead camel's back enough for the widow to withdraw the skin. There was perhaps two quarts of water remaining in the bottom.

Lander joined them a moment later. "What happened?" he asked, eyeing the dead camel.

"Exhaustion," Ruha explained. She handed him the waterskin. "Drink." It was a command, not a suggestion.

The Harper accepted the skin and carefully lifted it to his lips.

"It's time," Kadumi said, removing the waterskins from the side of the camel that had not fallen to the ground.

"We'll stop here for the night."

Ruha ran an appraising eye over the other four haggard beasts. They all stood on wobbling knees, their flank and shoulder muscles quivering.

"We can go no farther," the witch agreed.

Lander took the waterskin away from his lips and passed it to Ruha. "Time for what?" he asked.

"You'll see," Kadumi explained, moving to the head of the line. "Help me unload the camels."

While Kadumi and Lander unloaded the first camel, Ruha allowed herself a few swallows from the skin. The water was awful stuff, hot and stinking of its container, but it refreshed her regardless of the taste. When she judged she had drunk about a quarter of its contents, she passed the skin to Kadumi and helped Lander unload the other camels.

After they had stacked their nine remaining waterskins together, Kadumi milked each of the live camels. He extracted less than a gallon, but Ruha was grateful to have that much. Exhausted camels did not produce much milk.

As Ruha laid out their beds, Lander eyed the meager bucket of milk. "You and Kadumi have the milk tonight," he said. "I'm not hungry."

"You're a terrible liar," Ruha observed. "But don't worry. There will be more."

Lander raised an eyebrow. "There will?"

"Of course," Kadumi answered, picking up the waterskin they had salvaged from the collapsed camel. "Tonight, we shall have a feast."

The Harper grimaced.

"What's wrong?" Ruha asked.

"I'm not sure that I'd call any meal in this desert a feast."

"Perhaps we shouldn't call it a feast," Kadumi admitted. "Still, our bellies will be full."

He went to the string of milk camels, then selected the three weakest and led them away.

"Where's he going?" Lander asked.

"Those camels are too weak to continue," Ruha answered.

"So what's he going to do?"

"Kill them," Ruha answered, surprised at the Harper's foolish question. "Help me water the others."

She went to Kadumi's mount and removed a large skin bucket, then was surprised to see that the Harper had not followed her. Instead, Lander was staring after Kadumi with a dismayed expression. Leading Kadumi's camel toward the stack of waterskins, she said, "Lander, hold the other camels. I don't want to get trampled when I start watering."

Ruha allowed each beast to drink two full skins, a total of about eight gallons per animal. For a camel, it wasn't much water, but she hoped it would be enough to get them to the Sister of Rains. The last skin of water she saved for herself and her companions. Without milk, they would need plenty of water over the next two days.

Kadumi returned just as dusk fell. The rich odor of blood clung to him, and he carried a full waterskin over his shoulder. Ruha poured the milk into the same bucket from which she had watered the camels, then took the warm waterskin from Kadumi and also poured its dark contents into the bucket.

Lander regarded the whole operation with an expression of disgust on his face. "Is that what I think it is?"

"Blood and milk," Ruha confirmed.

She scraped a handful of salt off the ground and crumbled it into the concoction, then used her *jambiya* to mix it all together. When she was satisfied with its consistency, she dipped Kadumi's *bakia* into the bucket and handed the wooden cup to him, then did the same for Lander.

Kadumi drained the cup in a single swallow, then smacked his lips. "Still warm."

"You must be mad," Lander said, pouring his back into the bucket. "What's wrong with a little camel meat?"

Ruha snatched his cup from his hand and refilled it. "Eating meat makes you thirsty for days," she snapped. "Drink this—you won't get much else."

When she thrust the cup back at him, the Harper stared at it in disgust.

"What's wrong?" Kadumi demanded, passing his cup back to the widow. "This is good."

Lander glared at the boy for several moments, then lifted the cup to his lips and drank it down in one long gulp. When he finished, he wiped his mouth with his sleeve and pushed the cup back at Ruha. "Another," he said, struggling to keep from retching.

"That's more like a Harper," the widow said, smiling beneath her veil.

Lander and Kadumi managed to drink four more cups before the Harper began to look as though he would be ill. When they gave their *bakias* to Ruha for a fifth refill, she said, "I think you've had enough. If you vomit, it'll take half a skin of water to replace the fluids you lose."

"Bless you, Ruha," Lander gasped, turning toward his bed. "I'll take the second watch—I hope." He collapsed onto his side and lay there in a fetal position.

The following morning, there were clouds in the sky. They were high, ashen things that hid At'ar's face, but did little to lessen her fervor. If anything, the heat seemed thicker and more acute.

The trio broke camp quickly then resumed their journey, Lander still pausing at odd intervals to search their back trail. The trio passed the morning in weary silence, the overcast day providing relief from At'ar's glare but not from her heat. The scenery never changed. The basin stretched on endlessly, its tablelike surface shimmering pearl-gray in the overcast light. The flat, gray-white terrain did not vary even a foot in elevation, and Ruha felt as though she were riding across an immense cooking pan. The sky remained drab and ashen, the bands of silvery light streaking the clouds the only variation in the monotonous panorama.

In late morning, purple veils began to drift down from the clouds. At first, the sight of the distant rain lifted the trio's spirits, but as the shower moved toward them, it became apparent that the rain was not reaching the ground. The hot air rising from the salt flats was changing the water into vapor long before it reached the desert floor. Ruha cast one forlorn glance at the shower, then shook her head and kept her attention fixed on the crusty ground beneath her camel's feet.

Both the clouds and the shower vanished with the arrival of afternoon. Once again the basin was a glistening sea of salt and the sky a blue canopy. A shimmering lake appeared on the horizon. Ruha knew the distant water to be nothing but a reflection of the sapphire sky, but the mirage was unbearable. Most of the time, she was conscious of her thirst only as a constant discomfort that kept her from swallowing. With the blue lake on the horizon, she could think of nothing but the half-full waterskin. Her thirst became a raging fire, and she had to fight every moment to keep from opening the waterskin and drinking until she burst.

By evening a line of indigo mounds floated on the waters of the mirage, and Ruha realized they were closing on the edge of the salt flat. She told Kadumi to steer their path toward the largest of the dark-colored pyramids.

Encouraged by the sight of the mountains, they rode well past dark, not stopping until the ground began to rise and the footing became unsteady. The trio finally made camp in the bottom of a dry gulch and even found enough dried brush to make a fire—although they had nothing to cook on it.

The next morning, they rose with the dawn and saw that they were camped in the foothills at the base of a small mountain range. To the west, the mountains themselves rose five thousand feet into the sky, forming a jagged wall of gray rock. Their dun-colored slopes were dotted with dark spots that could only be plants.

Ruha pointed at the large peak she had told Kadumi to use as a landmark yesterday. "The Sister of Rains lies at the base of that mountain," she said. "If we ride hard, we shall eat wild figs and drink spring water tonight."

"Then why are we standing around?" Lander asked, untethering his camel.

The trio rode along the base of the mountains, fighting a constant struggle to keep their hungry camels from stopping to devour every stray saltbush the small company came across. Throughout the morning, Lander checked their backtrail for the Zhentarim, but by afternoon he no longer bothered. Ruha guessed that the Harper's reason had more to do with the difficulty of spotting pursuers in the rolling terrain than with feeling sure they hadn't been followed, but she did not care. Without Lander twisting about in his saddle or stopping the caravan to search the horizon, they made better time.

When they reached a large *wadi* leading down from the mountains, Ruha directed the small company to turn up the sandy gulch. Their camels, sensing that the journey was near an end, moved with renewed vigor. Once, a hare bolted across the ravine. Kadumi leaped off his camel to follow the animal and pull it from its sandy burrow, but that was the only time they stopped.

Just before dusk, the tinkle of running water began to echo down the *wadi*. The camels started snorting and roaring in excitement, and it was all the three riders could do to keep their mounts from galloping. The walls of the gulch grew steeper and became cliffs, and a carpet of lush grass soon blanketed the sandy floor.

The trio came to a stone wall stretching clear across the canyon and standing fifteen feet high. There was an ancient gate of rusty iron in the center of the rampart, but it would do little to keep anyone from crossing the barrier now. Several huge breaches gapped the wall, apparently caused by the sporadic floods that flashed down the canyon. On the southern wall of the *wadi*, a dozen tiny springs spilled out of the rocks, then cascaded down the cliff.

"The Sister of Rains," Ruha said, pointing at the tiny waterfalls.

The widow led the way through the closest breach. Behind the wall, the springs collected in several small pools at the base of the cliffs, giving life to dozens of fig trees and a grove of other fruit-bearing plants. Ruha was surprised at how wild the thicket had grown since she had left, for she and Qoha'dar had worked hard to tend the garden and keep it orderly.

On the other side of the *wadi*, thirty feet above the floor of the gulch, lay a wide ledge where an ancient tower had once stood. Most of its stones were scattered and half-buried in sands below the ledge, but the foundation was still intact.

The widow could not stop a tear from coming to her eye. As a young girl, the oasis had been a cage to her, a cage into which she had been cast because of the shame and trouble her visions had brought down on her father's head. Now, her mind was flooded with memories of tending the fruit trees with Qoha'dar, of ignoring her guardian's stern warnings and exploring the tower ruins, of sneaking down to spy upon the rare *khowwan* that had worked its way along the edge of the Shoal of Thirst to graze at the Sister of Rains. With the Zhentarim invading Anauroch and slaughtering whole tribes, even the hot, dreary work of herding goats and making cheese seemed a peaceful and cherished memory.

"Is something wrong?" asked Kadumi, jarring Ruha out of her reverie.

She shook her head. "No. I was just thinking that this is one oasis I hope the Zhentarim never visit."

"The only way to ensure that is to help the Bedine drive them from the desert," Lander said. "For that, we need the spellbook. Where is it?"

"The spellbook has been safe for years," Kadumi said, guiding his mount toward the ponds. "First, we must drink!"

Both Ruha and Lander laughed, then let their camels follow Kadumi's. The thirsty beasts pushed their way through the hedge of vegetation surrounding the closest pond and lowered their heads to drink, ignoring their riders completely. The trio had to slip from the backs of standing mounts.

Ruha and her companions went to the next pool to quench their own thirst. Lander and Kadumi simply stuck their faces in the cool pond and sucked water into their mouths, imitating their eager camels. Despite a burning wish to do the same, modesty forced Ruha to fill an empty waterskin and drink from it.

Once the trio had finished drinking, Kadumi assigned himself the task of setting up the night's camp. Ruha and Lander went to the collapsed tower, then climbed down into its foundation and spent an hour digging sand out of one corner. By the time they reached the floor, night had fallen.

Lander went to the camp and started a torch from the fire Kadumi had built. When he returned, Ruha took the torch and pointed to a trap door of carefully fitted stone. "Pull that up."

Lander did as asked, then Ruha used the torch to peer down into a dark pit. It was filled with spider webs and looked as though it hadn't been disturbed in years.

"I'll go," the Harper volunteered.

Using the torch to clean the spider webs away from the entrance, Ruha said, "Fine with me. You'll find a short corridor. If you turn left, it runs down the gulch. If you turn right, it ends in at an old vault. Inside the vault, you'll find a sealed box of sun-fired clay. That's what we want."

The Harper nodded, lowering himself into the cramped pit. Ruha passed him the torch, and he disappeared down the tunnel. She heard him curse once, then everything was quiet for several minutes.

Ruha began to worry that something had happened to the Harper, but, just as she was about to call to Kadumi from camp to bring her another torch, Lander returned. In one hand he carried the torch and in the other the spellbook.

"What took so long?" she asked.

"Bats." He passed her the box, then threw the torch back down the corridor. "They were all over."

As Lander climbed out of the pit, Ruha smashed the clay box. The spellbook remained inside. They returned to the camp, and the widow immediately inspected it in the firelight. Her old teacher's words rang in her memory as she turned each page. Ruha almost felt as though she were holding Qoha'dar herself in her hands.

At last, Lander asked, "Any damage?"

Ruha closed the book and hugged it to her chest. "No. Every page is the same as the day I sealed it away."

"Let's hope that's for the best," Kadumi said, casting an uneasy glance at the thick tome. "Right now, though, we should eat." He set a plate of figs and roasted hare in front of Ruha, then another before Lander.

"A banquet!" the widow exclaimed. She took the plate and turned her back toward her companions so she could remove her veil and eat.

The trio ate in appreciative silence, then cleaned their

hands with sand, rinsed in the oasis pools, and tethered the camels for the night. They drank their fill of cool spring water and, making his usual cautionary statement about Zhentarim pursuers, Lander assigned watches, taking the first for himself. Ruha pulled her *jellaba* over her shoulders, laid down with her back to the fire, and closed her eyes.

Sometime much later, Ruha woke, still groggy and confused. The night was quite chilly and still, but something poked her repeatedly in the back. She rolled over, asking, "Is it my turn already?"

"Shhhh!" Kadumi warned.

He was kneeling next to her with his *jambiya* drawn and staring in Lander's direction. The youth's jaw was set in grim determination and his eyes were narrowed menacingly.

"What are you doing?" she demanded.

"I heard something near Lander!"

Ruha rubbed her eyes and looked toward the Harper, who was still sleeping with his back to the fire. The light of the moon was shining over the entire camp, and Ruha could not see even a shadow within fifty feet. The image of the attack on Lander's back flashed through her sleepy mind, and she found herself wondering if Kadumi had crossed the Shoal of Thirst to murder the Harper and avenge some imagined trespass against his family's honor.

She grabbed the boy's arm. "You're lying."

Kadumi looked away from Lander and frowned. "Why would I do that?"

Before she could respond, the boy tore his arm free of her grasp and sprang toward the Harper.

"Lander!" she screamed, reaching for her own *jambiya*.

The youth reached the Harper an instant later, then slashed wildly over his prone form. A saber flashed out of midair, slicing into Kadumi's collarbone at the neckline.

The boy did not even scream. His hand went slack, and his *jambiya* tumbled to the ground. A dark silhouette appeared on Lander's far side, lifting its foot to kick Kadumi's lifeless body off the blade.

In the same moment, apparently waking from a sound sleep, Lander twisted onto his back and slammed his fist into the figure's lower abdomen. The man doubled up, then stumbled backward, groaning in pain.

Ruha leaped over Lander and was on the assassin in an instant. He lifted his blade to defend himself, but the witch slashed at the hand holding the saber. The man screamed again and dropped his weapon. With her free hand, she grabbed the wounded arm and used it to pull the man toward her, at the same time kneeing him in the midsection. He merely gurgled in pain and threw himself at Ruha.

The widow lifted her *jambiya* to meet his lunge. As the assassin fell on top of her, she turned the cutting edge up. As if gutting a gazelle, she ran the blade the length of the man's belly. He went limp, then Ruha hit the ground, and he landed on top of her.

The widow slipped from beneath the eviscerated man. Leaving him to die in agony, she turned to where Kadumi had fallen. Lander was already there, cradling the boy in his lap. Kadumi's eyes were closed and there was a terrible gash across his sternum. Ruha did not need to ask to know the boy was dead, and she felt sick that the last thing he had heard from her lips was a false accusation.

"Where did he come from?" she asked, motioning at the assassin.

"Magic," Lander replied. "Probably the same ring that made Bhadla invisible when he was spying on Sa'ar and Utaiba's council."

Ruha then glanced around their little camp. "What if there are more of them?"

Lander shook his head. "No. He was the only one to

make it across the Shoal of Thirst. If there were any more, they would have attacked with him."

The widow stared at the boy for a long time, then dropped her dagger and fell to her knees at the Harper's side. Lander laid Kadumi's body gently aside and touched Ruha's shoulders. "I'm sorry—"

Ruha spun and buried her face on Lander's chest, then began weeping in uncontrollable waves. "Before he died, I called him a liar," she sobbed.

Lander held her more tightly, but said nothing.

"When Kadumi drew his *jambiya*, I couldn't see the assassin. I thought my vision was coming true," she said. "I thought he was attacking you."

"You were sleepy. It was a natural mistake."

The widow pushed away from Lander and looked at the ground shamefully. "No. I was wrong to think that. Kadumi intended you no harm."

Lander reached out and gathered her back into his arms. "Don't blame yourself," he whispered. "The boy shouldn't be dead at all. I knew we were being followed, and I should have foreseen that the Zhentarim would use magic."

"But we didn't believe you," Ruha objected, looking up at the Harper's face.

"Which is why I should have been even more careful." A cloud of self-reproach fell over Lander's face, and he remained silent for several moments. Finally he shook his head sadly and returned Ruha's gaze. "We can't bring Kadumi back. The only thing we can do now is make sure he did not die in vain."

Ruha nodded, realizing that the youth's death had affected her in a way that the slaughter of the Qahtan and the Mtair Dhafir had not. Suddenly nothing seemed more important to her than stopping the Zhentarim. "Tomorrow, we'll wash and bury Kadumi," she said. "Then we'll take Qoha'dar's spellbook to Elah'zad. Yhekal will pay for what he's done."

"Yes, but tonight you must rest," Lander said, gently urging Ruha to lie down. "If we're to succeed, we have a hard ride ahead."

"Yes, we must save our strength," Ruha agreed. She stretched out on the ground with her shoulder pressed against Lander's strong thigh. "Tonight, there is no need to keep a watch," she said, pulling the Harper down next to her. "We may as well rest comfortably."

Fourteen

Lander and Ruha crested the last of a seemingly endless chain of thousand-foot knolls. The Harper did not need to ask to know they had reached Elah'zad. The hill sloped down to a small basin encircled by grayish ridges similar to the one upon which they sat. Over a hundred small springs opened on the hillsides and trickled down the gentle slopes. Crimson-leafed shrubs with blue stems and twiggy trees with copper and silver sprigs bordered each stream. From the ridge, the vividly colored shrubs resembled magic fires and the metallic-hued trees looked like billows of enchanted smoke.

The colorful bands of vegetation were spread over the basin like an immense spider web. Each strand followed a life-giving stream down the hill to a sapphire nucleus of water, a lake covering fully a square mile of the bottom of the basin. In the center of the lake sat a small, grassy island. On the island stood an alabaster palace built in the shape of a three-quarters moon.

Along a band of lush grass girding the lake, fifteen *khowwans* had pitched their tents in tribal clusters. Men were gathered in small groups in the areas between the tribes, but the women and children remained steadfastly within their own camps. Lander saw no sign of any camels.

"It's magnificent!" Lander gasped.

"Elah'zad was the home of the moon goddess," Ruha explained, forcing her camel to kneel. "But At'ar drove her away and made it a prison for the Mother of the Waters."

"Why?" the Harper asked.

Ruha gave Lander an alluring, mocking glance. "The usual reason women quarrel. At'ar was jealous of Eldath's beauty."

Lander was surprised to hear Ruha use a familiar name for the goddess of the singing waters. "Eldath is free," he objected. "She is worshiped all over Faerun."

The widow looked over her shoulder. In the distance, just beyond the farthest set of hills, the white salts of the Shoals of Thirst still gleamed in the sun. "Perhaps Eldath is free in Sembia," she said, "but in Anauroch, she is At'ar's prisoner."

The young widow slipped off her camel, then motioned for Lander to do the same.

They led their mounts down the hill as far as the first spring. Ruha carefully tethered the beasts to a smoke-twigged tree, well out of reach of the water. "Camels are not allowed to drink of the sacred waters," she explained. "Some boys are coming to take them to the camel well."

Lander raised an eyebrow. "How do you know that?"

"By now the sentries have relayed word of our arrival to Sa'ar and Utaiba. One of them will send some boys from his tribe to tend our camels."

"That makes sense," the Sembian replied. He had given no thought to the sentries surely posted around the oasis, for he had not heard them sound any alarm. "Why didn't we hear any *amarats*?"

"I don't know, and it worries me. But rest assured that we have been seen."

"Should we take their silence as a warning?" he asked. "Could Sa'ar and Utaiba have changed their minds and be planning some sort of an ambush?"

The widow shook her head. "Most Bedine keep their word," she said, pulling the *djebiras* containing Qoha'dar's spellbook off her mount's back. "Still, there are many other sheikhs down there, and they were not a party to our agreement."

Lander scowled, his stomach already growing knotted at the prospect of being turned away after his difficult journey.

When the Harper did not move toward the camps, Ruha said, "Let's go. We are not going to stop the Zhentarim and kill Yhekal by standing around up here."

She started down the hill, leaving the camels roaring in protest at not being allowed to drink. As she passed Lander's mount, it even tried to nip at her. The Harper could sympathize with the beasts' fury. The animals had not had any water since leaving the Sister of Rains three days ago.

On the morning following the assassin's attack, Lander had taken the camels to drink from the springs while Ruha washed Kadumi's body. After the corpse was prepared for its journey, the pair had buried it near the wall, covering the grave with rocks to prevent scavengers from digging it up. They had bothered with no such courtesy for the Zhentarim. Instead, Lander had taken the man's magic ring, then dragged his body away from the oasis and left it in the open for the vultures.

After that, they had picked the last of the wild figs, then dashed across the northern edge of the Shoal of Thirst. Though the journey had seemed hotter than the first crossing, it had been alleviated by a surplus of drinking water and the fact that the milk camel had started providing again.

Now Lander was looking forward to a meal of solid food. Other than the figs and the rabbit Kadumi had caught at the Sister of Rains, he and Ruha had eaten nothing but camel's milk and blood since the Battle of the Chasm. The Harper was surprised at how well it had sustained him, but the effects of his liquid diet were beginning to tell. His scabbard belt was now wrapped three times around his waist instead of the customary two, and he had taken to chewing scrub twigs just to exercise his teeth.

As the pair descended toward the lake, a handful of boys rushed up the slope to meet them. When the group arrived, Ruha told them where to find the camels, then the youths rushed off to fulfill their responsibility. A few moments later, another group of older boys, about ten or twelve, approached.

"You are to come with us to Sheikh Sa'ar's tent," said the tallest. He studied them carefully, then looked past them up the trail. "We were told there would be three of you."

"Kadumi isn't with us," Lander answered, not bothering to explain what had happened.

The boys glanced from the Harper to Ruha, exchanging knowing looks and regarding Lander with suspicious expressions.

"Lead the way," the Harper ordered, upset by the iniquitous assumptions that he guessed were running through the youths' minds.

The boys surrounded the pair and eventually led them into one of the camps at the edge of the lake. As the escort brought Lander and Ruha through the circle of tents, the women and the children stared at the small procession. The children's eyes were round with curiosity, and they were plainly wondering why the pair of strangers was receiving so much attention. The expressions of the women, mostly hidden behind their veils, were harder to read.

Their eyes betrayed both interest and fear, but Lander could not guess why the women were frightened.

The Harper noticed that everything in the camp seemed new and fresh. The *khreimas* had been recently colored with henna juice and other dyes. They were in such excellent repair that Lander guessed all the tents were newly made, which would only make sense if this was Sa'ar's tribe. The Mahwa had lost all of their *khreimas* when they fled the Zhentarim at Colored Waters. He was surprised that they had recovered so quickly, however, and wondered if the other tribes had helped them. If so, that was a good sign, for it indicated that the Bedine were already working together.

The procession stopped in front of a large closed tent, around which were gathered dozens of mature warriors. Lander recognized Kabina and a few others from the Mahwa and Raz'hadi, but most of the faces were new to him. Their *keffiyehs* were decorated in the varying patterns popular in different tribes: red and white checks, solid browns or blacks, green stripes, and many more. Some even wore turbans.

Kabina waved the boys away, then regarded Lander and Ruha with a surly frown. No one said a word, and the gathering remained as silent as the Shoal of Thirst. From inside the tent came the scent of roasted meat and the quiet murmur of polite conversation. Lander's mouth started watering, and he felt his knees grow weak. He took an absent-minded step toward the open *khreima*, but Kabina held up a restraining hand. "No," he said. "The sheikhs are feasting."

"Tell them we are here," Ruha demanded. "We have had a long journey." Her gaze was fixed on the tent, and the Harper could tell that the smell was having the same effect on her.

Kabina did not lower his hand. "They know," he said.

They waited for several more minutes, straining in vain to hear the muffled words of the sheikhs. Lander had not expected Sa'ar to be overjoyed at seeing him and Ruha, but he had expected a more civil reception. He began to worry that the other sheikhs were resisting the agreement that Sa'ar and Utaiba had made regarding Ruha's magic.

At last, Sa'ar stepped out of the tent, Utaiba and thirteen more sheikhs behind. "So, *berrani*, you dare set eyes on Elah'zad, the secret paradise of the Bedine?" He addressed Lander alone, ignoring the widow.

"I do," Lander replied. He motioned to Ruha, who was still holding the *djebiras* containing the spellbook. "We have crossed the Shoal of Thirst and recovered the spellbook of Ruha's mentor, and we have crossed it again to meet you here. Surely, the gods look well upon us."

Sa'ar grunted an acknowledgement.

Ruha interrupted the conversation by sniffing loudly at the air. "What's that peculiar odor?"

Utaiba frowned and stepped to Sa'ar's side. "What odor?"

The widow stepped toward the *khreima's* entrance. "It's coming from in there," she said, pointing at Sa'ar's tent. "It smells like cooked meat. Perhaps we should go and eat it before something happens to it—though after ten days on the trail, I'd rather drink a bowl of warm camel's blood."

A chorus of laughter rustled through the warriors, and Lander could tell that every one of them had endured similar experiences.

Utaiba grinned sheepishly and laid a hand on Sa'ar's shoulder. "We've forgotten your manners, my friend. Our guests must be fed."

Sa'ar scowled in embarrassment. "Accept my apologies," he said. "All I have is a big buck that my arrow downed yesterday. My wives have spent the morning basting it with honey and spices, but I'm sure it cannot compare to camel's blood."

Lander smiled, relieved that Ruha's joke had lightened the atmosphere. He hoped the change of mood indicated that the cold reception did not mean the other sheikhs were opposing the agreement.

Sa'ar stepped aside, waving Lander and Ruha toward his tent. "Save some for Kadumi. I'm sure his palate is less demanding than yours."

Lander stopped in his tracks, his hopeful mood deflated. "Kadumi won't be coming."

Sa'ar's face fell. "I was hoping you had decided to leave him with the camels for some reason."

"No," Ruha said, stepping to Lander's side. "He's dead."

"What happened?" demanded Utaiba.

"A Zhentarim assassin killed him," Lander explained. "He died defending me."

Sa'ar frowned, as did Utaiba and several other sheikhs. "An assassin?" he demanded. "How could he follow you across the Shoal of Thirst?"

"The Zhentarim can go wherever we can go," Lander answered. "Don't underestimate them."

"You would have seen him from miles away," Sa'ar protested.

"A party followed us for two days, then disappeared," Ruha supplied. "Kadumi and I thought they had all turned back, but Lander kept glimpsing one who hadn't. We didn't believe him, and the assassin caught us at the Sister of Rains."

"Surely you posted a watch?" asked a sheikh Lander did not know. The man had a heavy brow line and a sour expression.

"He used magic to make himself invisible," Ruha replied.

The sour-faced sheikh rolled his eyes. "Invisible," he scoffed. "Were you attacked by an assassin or a djinn?"

"The Zhentarim can do this, Sheikh Haushi," Utaiba said. "Both Sa'ar and myself have seen it."

Haushi shook his head. "I don't believe it."

Lander took the assassin's ring from his pocket and slipped it on. When he disappeared before their very eyes, both the warriors and the sheikhs gasped and stepped away, automatically reaching for their weapons.

The Harper removed the ring and held it up for the sheikhs to see. "Magic. With it, the Zhentarim can do many things you would think impossible." The Harper turned to Sa'ar. "Kadumi's death grieves us all," he said, hoping to change the subject. "But Ruha and I have survived to bring magic to the Bedine. You conceded that we could only do this with the favor of the gods. Here we are. Will you honor your agreement?"

Sa'ar avoided Lander's gaze, looking toward Utaiba. "We didn't think you'd make it."

"That does not change our agreement," Ruha said.

Lander was surprised at how hard the widow was pressing the issue. Before Kadumi's death, she had seemed more interested in joining him in Sembia than in working to save her people. Now, she appeared positively determined to drive the Zhentarim out of Anauroch.

It was Utaiba who finally answered Ruha. "As far as the Raz'hadi and the Mahwa are concerned, you have proven that the gods favor your magic," the wiry sheikh said. "The other sheikhs are not yet convinced."

"No doubt because you did not bother to tell them of our agreement," Ruha observed.

"True," Utaiba admitted.

"We have convinced all the sheikhs to take the matter before the Mother of the Waters," Sa'ar added defensively. "We will take you and your spellbook to the House of the Moon."

"We agreed to take Ruha's magic only," Haushi interrupted, pointing at the ring in Lander's hand. "We said nothing of Zhentarim magic."

"The ring is not important. Do with it what you will," Lander said, holding it out to Haushi.

The sour-faced sheikh backed away as if the Harper were offering him the head of an asp. "I don't want that thing!" he snapped, pointing at the lake. "Magic is for the gods!"

"As you wish," Lander said, spinning toward the lake and throwing the ring as hard as he could. It landed two hundred yards from shore with a barely perceptible splash. "Now let us go to the House of the Moon!"

"You should eat first," suggested Utaiba. "This could take some time."

"We will eat later," Ruha said, casting a hungry look in the direction of the roasted gazelle.

Lander also cast a longing glance at Sa'ar's tent. As hungry as he was, it seemed more important to resolve the issue of whether or not Ruha's magic would be accepted by the Bedine. "My stomach will wait," he said. "The Zhentarim will not."

"Then, by all means, let's go to the House of the Moon," Sa'ar said, motioning toward the lakeshore.

The sheikh led the way down to the lake. Two round boats, made by stretching camel hides over a wooden frame, lay beached on the shore. Sa'ar, Utaiba, Lander, Ruha, and two more sheikhs piled into one of the boats, and six sheikhs climbed into the other.

Paddling toward the small island in the middle of the lake, Lander realized that the tribesmen were not very good boat-makers. Water poured through the stitches, and the awkward craft rode low and clumsy. The Bedine showed no sign of anxiety, but the Harper was glad when they reached the grassy shore of the small island. Had either of the boats foundered, he was sure he would have been the only one who could swim.

The island was a small, grass-covered hill no more than a hundred yards across. The alabaster palace stood on top of the hill. Its three-quarter circle trapped At'ar's light and cast it back with a silvery radiance that immediately struck Lander as unimaginably soft and peaceful. He could easily see why the Bedine had concluded Eldath inhabited the structure. If they were right, Lander hoped the goddess would favor them with a sign.

While two sheikhs returned across the lake to fetch the five who had been left behind, Lander and Ruha followed the others to the palace. When they reached it, a warm shiver of exhilaration ran down the Harper's spine. The building was made of a chalky, translucent desert rock cut so thin that he could see the shapes of a throne and chairs through it.

The small company waited for a few others to cross the lake and join them, then entered the palace through a gracefully curved foyer. The short corridor had been carved from a single stone and shaped without any visible joints. It opened into a circular room, on the far side of which sat a huge throne gilded with hammered copper.

To each side, the throne was flanked by a row of stout chairs of darkly colored wood. The marble floor was so black that, if the chairs and throne had not been sitting upon it, Lander would have sworn it was a bottomless pit. The ceiling was a single slab of translucent rock. Through it filtered a light that bathed the room in warm radiance.

A tangible feeling of tranquility came over Lander, and he found himself bowing his head to Eldath. Simply entering the palace, it seemed to him, was worth missing the feast now languishing back in Sa'ar's tent.

"I've never seen anything so magnificent," the Harper said. "Who built it?"

The sheikhs shrugged.

"The House of Moon is as old as the gods. It was here before the Scattering."

The words came from Ruha's mouth, but the voice that spoke them did not belong to the widow. The sounds were almost a song, with a peaceful, soothing quality to them that Lander had never heard in any woman's speech. The voice, which could only be described as higher than soprano, seemed to enter his head without passing through his ears.

"Eldath?" Lander gasped. He did not know whether he was hearing the goddess's voice or the effects of one of Ruha's spells.

"What magic is this?" demanded Haushi.

The widow glared at the astonished sheikh. "This is no magic," she answered in the strange voice. She waved to the dark chairs, then sat in the copper-gilded throne herself. "There are sixteen chairs—fifteen for the sheikhs of the fifteen tribes that will fight the Zhentarim, one for the Harper who has risked his life to help you."

When the stunned sheikhs did not move, Ruha-Eldath said, "You do not have much time, Sheikhs. The Zhentarim have made an alliance with the Ju'ur Dai, and even now the traitors are leading the Zhentarim into the hills guarding Elah'zad. Do you intend to make a battle plan or to let the invaders defile the Sacred Grove?"

The sharp words stunned the sheikhs and Lander into taking their seats, then Haushi asked, "What of Ruha's magic?"

As the sheikh spoke, Ruha's chin sank to her chest and she slumped down in the chair. Lander stood and rushed to the widow's side and found her breathing in quick, shallow gasps. He tried to wake her, but she had fallen into a deep slumber that could not be disturbed.

"She seems to be sleeping," Lander reported, though he could not say whether the sleep had been caused by the strain of serving as a goddess's mouthpiece or by the effort required to cast some peculiar kind of magic he had never seen before.

Sa'ar said, "We have seen a sign from Eldath. Now we must do as the goddess asks and turn our thoughts to defeating our enemies."

"How do we know the witch wasn't using her magic to fool us?" demanded Haushi.

"Ruha couldn't have known about the Ju'ur Dai and the Zhentarim's location," Utaiba replied. "Then, too, there is the furniture in which we sit—sixteen chairs for sixteen men. I, for one, believe it was Eldath who spoke to us."

There was a general murmur of agreement, then Sa'ar said, "Lander, you know the Zhentarim best. What strategy do you suggest?"

Returning to his chair, the Harper asked, "How many warriors do we have?"

Utaiba was the first to answer. "The Raz'hadi have two hundred and fifty men who will die to drive the Zhentarim from our desert," he said, proudly thumping himself on the chest.

Sa'ar spoke next. "Over one hundred Bait Mahwa have already died fighting the Zhentarim, and two hundred more are ready to join their brothers."

A toothless sheikh wearing a black turban said, "We have one hundred and fifty warriors, all thirsting for the blood of the invaders."

Lander held up a hand. "I meant to ask, how many warriors do we have all together?"

Utaiba and Sa'ar frowned, then Sa'ar said, "We are telling you. I have two hundred men."

"I have two hundred and fifty," Utaiba added.

"And we have one hundred and fifty," repeated the toothless sheikh.

"Go on," Lander said, nodding to the next sheikh and

starting to add figures in his head. Before they could hope to match the coordination of the Zhentarim army, the Harper realized, the Bedine would have to adjust their way of thinking.

When the fifteen sheikhs had each listed the number of warriors in his tribe, Lander said, "We have a little less than three thousand warriors, about a thousand more than the Zhentarim. Is there any place we can get more?"

Utaiba answered. "We have sent riders to all the *khowwans* within a fortnight's journey," he said, waving his hand in all directions. "Their allies have not been attacked, so they can see no good in fighting the Zhentarim. The only tribes we can count on are those gathered at this oasis."

"The others will change their minds when the asabis eat their sons and the Black Robes enslave their daughters," Sa'ar growled.

"No doubt," Utaiba agreed. "But for now, these tribes are all we have. Perhaps more will join us later."

"Then I suggest you send your women and children to a safe place, along with a third of your warriors to protect them," the Harper said. "If the Zhentarim realize that your families are unprotected, they will try to destroy them."

"We will send our tribes north together," Sa'ar said. "If we perish, or if the Zhentarim follow them, they will scatter. At most, the invaders will capture only a few hostages."

The other sheikhs nodded their agreement, then Utaiba said, "We have made provisions for our families, but we still have not discussed the most important thing. What is the best way to attack the Zhentarim?" He looked to Lander, deferring to the Harper's knowledge of the enemy.

Lander considered the question for a moment, then said, "We'll have about the same number of men as the Zhentarim, counting their asabis. We should attack during the day, when the reptile mercenaries are burrowed beneath the sand. That way, we'll have a numerical advantage. With luck, we'll destroy the enemy in a single battle."

Sa'ar smiled at the Harper. "We?" he said. "Are we to take it that you do not intend to be an observer in this battle?"

Resting his eyes on the widow's sleeping form, Lander shook his head. "Where Ruha goes, I go," he said. "If I hadn't talked her into staying, she'd probably be in Sembia by now."

To the Harper's surprise, both Sa'ar and Utaiba greeted his comment with frowns, and the other sheikhs muttered in displeasure. It was Haushi, however, who voiced their concern. "What about the witch?"

From the murmur that rustled through the room, the Harper knew he had spoken the question on the mind of many of the other sheikhs.

"She'll be coming with us, of course," Lander said, glancing at Ruha's inert form. "Providing she wakes up in time."

"Of course, we've all agreed to that now," said a wizened little man with a scraggly beard. "But where will she sleep? In your *khreima*?"

The question caught Lander off guard, and he had to pause for a moment to consider it. After reflecting on the interrogation the sheikhs' had given him when he reported the news of Kadumi's death, as well as the suspicious looks of the boys who had come to take care of their camels, Lander thought he understood the source of the trouble.

Deciding to get right to the heart of the matter, he said, "If you think I had something to do with Kadumi's death, I don't see that I can do anything—"

Sa'ar interrupted, saying, "What passed between you and Kadumi is not our affair. If you killed him, I'm sure that he deserved it."

"I didn't kill him!" Lander said. "It was a Zhentarim

assassin!"

"Whatever," Utaiba answered. "It doesn't matter. No-body here is related to the boy, so there'll be no blood price."

Lander could only shake his head. He did not know whether he should be upset at having been accused of kill-ing the boy—if that was what the sheikhs were implying—or at the casualness with which they were willing to dismiss the murder. To make matters worse, he realized that he did not have any idea of what was upsetting the sheikhs. "If nobody cares about Kadumi, what's the matter?"

Sa'ar pointed at Ruha, then at Lander. "Her," the sheikh said, "and you."

"It's wrong to bed a widow while her husband's spirit is still restless," said the toothless sheikh. "You'll bring N'asr's plague down on us."

Lander studied Ruha's sleeping form. The sheikhs' as-sumptions regarding what had passed between him and the widow upset him more than they should have—in part, he knew, because they had read so well what he felt in his heart. "How long does it take to calm a husband's spirit?"

"Two years," answered Haushi. "If you sleep with her before then, you will curse us all."

The Harper rose and walked over to the copper-gilded throne. Standing opposite Ruha, he said, "Then I'll wait."

"Have you bedded her yet?" Utaiba asked.

Lander did not look away from the widow. "No."

"Then it is decided!" Sa'ar exclaimed, rising. He pulled his *jambiya* and stepped to the middle of the room. "Let us swear an *akeud*! Victory or defeat, let us find it together!"

The burly sheikh drew the blade across his palm, then held up his hand so the others could inspect the dripping wound. As the blood touched the floor, it vanished into the black marble.

Fifteen

When Ruha woke, all the *khowwans* had broken camp. The tents were gone, the fires out, and the waterskins filled. Guarded by a thousand warriors and clustered into fifteen tribal groups, the women and children were already riding northward along Elah'zad's western ridge. In the dawn's tawny light, their gray figures were mere shadows, but the widow could see by their slow pace and lethargic movements that they were not leaving cheerfully.

On the eastern ridge, the scene was different. Two thousand warriors sat anxiously on their camels, their *keffiyehs* flapping in the cool morning breeze and their jocular voices echoing across the valley. The silhouettes of lances and spears danced against the yellow orb of the rising sun, and Ruha could tell that the prospect of battle had put the warriors in high spirits.

Lander came and kneeled next to Ruha. "You're awake," he said, offering her some water. "Good. I thought I'd have to lash you to a camel."

Ruha declined the water, then looked around and saw that she lay on the grass next to the lake, covered by a sleeping carpet. Behind her, a half-dozen men were folding the *khreima* that, she assumed, had covered her until a few moments ago.

"What happened?" Ruha asked. Her hand automatically rose to see if her veil needed adjustment. "The last thing I remember is walking into the House of the Moon."

"Let's just say you and Eldath have a lot more in common than you realize," Lander said, slipping a hand under her arm. "I'll explain later. Right now, we'd better hurry. The sheikhs are riding on the Zhentarim, and if we don't want to be left behind, we'd better hurry."

The Harper helped the bewildered widow to her feet, then led her up the hill to where a young warrior was holding their camels. They joined Sa'ar and Utaiba on the ridge, and within minutes the Bedine army was riding into the sun.

As they rode, Lander explained all that had passed in the House of the Moon. At first Ruha refused to accept that Eldath had spoken through her, but she gradually grew accustomed to the idea. Soon the notion gave her a giddy sense of excitement. Even after she and Lander had entered Elah'zad with Qoha'dar's spellbook, she had not truly believed that the gods favored her magic. After Eldath's manifestation, however, she could not doubt that fact. At least temporarily, she was no longer an outcast.

Yet the widow was far from happy about all Lander told her. The sheikhs' concerns over her relationship with the Harper angered Ruha, for she abhorred having her emotions and private life scrutinized by any man. The widow realized that her resentment was due largely to the strong feelings she did have for Lander, but she did not think that what passed between her and the Harper was the concern of the sheikhs. Neither did she believe that her dead husband's spirit would be offended by her actions; Ruha was certain that there were many things Ajaman had held more dear than her in his life.

Neither the sheikhs nor Ajaman's spirit seemed concerned over the fact that Lander and Ruha were riding at each other's side. The pair traveled behind the sheikhs most of the time, periodically joining them when the leaders felt the need of Lander's advice or wanted to ask Ruha some question regarding magic.

At the end of the second day of riding, the scouts reported that the Zhentarim were camped just ten miles away, at the Well of the Cloven Rock. The sheikhs called a halt and told their men to prepare for an attack the next day. Because they had stopped in a region of small knolls, it was impossible to find a defensible campsite for the entire army. The sheikhs finally decided to let each tribe set up its own camp atop a separate hill, though Lander objected to this plan because the hills they selected were separated by as much as three hundred yards.

The Bedine ignored their advisor and built their camps as they pleased, posting their sentries in a wide perimeter around the entire area. The Harper and the widow went with Sa'ar's tribe and laid out their sleeping carpets in separate *khreimas*. While the men eagerly debated battleplans, Ruha and Lander sat together at the edge of the group, the widow studying Qoha'dar's spellbook and the Harper quietly sharpening his sword. Occasionally Ruha would catch a curious warrior watching her study. In such instances, she took great pleasure in the fact that she no longer had anything to hide.

When dusk fell and it grew too dark to read or sharpen swords, the widow and Harper put away their preparations. Rather self-consciously, for Sa'ar's sharp eyes were turned in their direction, they said good night and went to their separate *khreimas*. Ruha would have liked to go with

Lander to discuss the coming battle, but that would not have escaped the warriors' attentions, and she suspected that they would take it as a bad omen.

Most of the Bedine stayed up late into the night, discussing the camels they would ride into battle and arguing over whether it was better to kill a man with a down or side slash. Judging from their swaggering tones and their easy manner, they were as confident of victory tomorrow as they were of At'ar's rising.

By morning the tone was different. An alarmed messenger rushed up the hill, calling for Sheikh Sa'ar and waking everyone in the camp. Ruha quickly covered her face and pulled her *jellaba* over her shoulders, then stuck her head out the door of her *khreima*.

The gray hues of first light were just creeping over the knoll. Groggy warriors were climbing out of their *khreimas*, scimitars and bows in hand. Sa'ar himself, as well as Lander, were already standing outside their tents, strapping their scabbard belts onto their waists.

"What is it?" Sa'ar demanded. "Are the Zhentarim on the move?"

The messenger shook his head and pointed eastward, toward the hill upon which Haushi's tribe was camped. More than a quarter-mile away, the knoll was one of the most distant that the Bedine had selected for a campsite. Still, it was close enough for Ruha to see that a half-dozen vultures were circling its summit, their ravenous heads gazing at some grisly scene below.

"Sheikh Utaiba asks that you join him there," the messenger explained. "And he asks that you bring the Harper and the witch along."

Before Sa'ar could turn to summon her, Ruha climbed out of her tent. "I'm ready," she said.

Ruha, Lander, and Sa'ar walked to the knoll. As they climbed to its summit, they were joined by the sheikhs of the other tribes.

The hill was capped by tangle-branched frankincense trees with gnarled trunks and spiny leaves. A few scrub bushes, stripped bare by hungry camels, also dotted the stony ground, but it was otherwise barren of vegetation.

It was not the Ruwaldi custom to arrange their *khreimas* in a circle, as was the case with most other tribes. Instead, they pitched their tents in a series of parallel rows, the mouths facing each other across narrow corridors of open ground. The Ruwald claimed that, because their arrangement was more orderly, it was more secure.

What Ruha saw now suggested otherwise. Before each Ruwaldi tent, six heads were set out in neat rows. Though N'asr's children had already plucked out the eyes and tore the ends of the noses away, enough of each man's face remained for the young witch to see they had died in their sleep. Their jaws were not set in determination. Neither were their mouths agape in horror. Sometimes the heads' lips were turned down in drowsy frowns, sometimes they were smirking at some dream, but their expressions remained uniformly sedate.

Ruha was not the only one to notice this disconcerting serenity. "In the name of Eldath!" Sa'ar gasped, slowing running his eyes up the row of tents. "How could the Zhentarim kill them *all* in their sleep? Wouldn't at least one man wake and scream before the steel was drawn across his throat?"

Utaiba glanced accusingly at Ruha, then scowled at Lander. "Have you slept with the widow, Lander?" he asked. "Only N'asr's curse could cause this."

The Harper, staring at the heads in anger and shock, did not seem to hear the question.

Ruha answered for him. "Our sleeping arrangements are not your concern, Sheikh, but you may rest assured that this is not N'asr's curse."

When Utaiba frowned at Ruha's reply, Sa'ar said, "The widow and the Harper slept in my camp last night, and I swear they did nothing to anger her husband's spirit."

"I would not doubt the word of a brother sheikh," said Didaji. He was a tall, gaunt man swathed in a brown turban, and a crimson scarf was pulled across his face. In his tribe, it was the men who covered their mouths and the women who went without veils. "But if this is not N'asr's doing, how did it happen?"

"Zhentarim magic," Lander answered, his attention still fixed on the heads.

Utaiba walked to one of the heads and picked it up by the hair. Pointing at the stump of the neck, he said, "This was cut by a sword, not by a magic charm."

"A dozen asabis could have killed every man here," Lander said, waving his hand at the camp.

"I don't see how," objected Sa'ar. "Even if a dozen men could sneak past our sentries, someone would have seen or heard the attack."

"Not if you didn't know what to look for," Ruha said. When the sheikhs looked at her with curious expressions, she continued, "I can show you how they did it."

"Please do," requested Didaji.

Ruha pointed at the *khreima* closest to the group. "Sheikh Sa'ar, would you take your sword and begin striking a tent pole?"

The burly sheikh raised an eyebrow, but went to the entrance and did as asked. As his blade began to bite into the wood, hollow thuds throbbed across the hilltop.

"That is something like the sound a beheading would make, is it not?" Ruha asked.

"Close," Utaiba replied, tossing the head in his hand aside and rejoining the others.

The widow removed a pinch of clay from her pocket and cast it into the breeze, at the same time speaking her incantation. The sound of Sa'ar's blade striking the tent pole faded to silence, but everyone could see the sheikh swing several more times.

The Mahwai stopped and frowned at Ruha, angrily asking a question that no one could hear. Several of the sheikhs chuckled.

"This is all very funny," said Didaji, "and I can see why no one was awakened by sounds of struggle. But there is still the matter of sight. Even in the night, the asabis would not be invisible."

"They might be," Lander said. "Remember the ring I brought to Elah'zad."

Utaiba brow rose in alarm. "How many of those could they have?"

"Not many," the Harper replied. "But there are spells that do the same thing for a short time."

Utaiba looked at Ruha with renewed respect. "Can you do that?" he asked.

"I cannot make people invisible," she replied, "but I can conceal them in the darkness."

The sheikh nodded thoughtfully. "Then I am glad the gods have blessed you with their favor," he said. "We shall have to make a list of your other talents."

The comment sent a wave of contentment through Ruha's veins, and she was surprised at how good it felt to be needed.

Sa'ar interrupted her satisfaction by stepping to her side. "What did you do to—?" The burly sheikh stopped speaking in midsentence, astounded to hear his own voice again.

Ruha chuckled at his astonishment. "I didn't do anything to you," she said. "I did it to the pole you were hitting. It was a spell that absorbs sound from everything within a few feet of its target."

Flushing with embarrassment, Sa'ar sheathed his scimitar and turned to his companions. "What are we waiting for?" he asked, waving at the campsite. "This changes nothing. Let us go to battle."

"No," Lander replied, walking toward one of the Ruwaldi tents. "That's what the Zhentarim want, so we'd better come up with another plan."

"What do you mean?" asked Yatagan, a toothless man with a wizened face. In contrast to the *abas* of the other Bedine, he wore billowing, brightly colored trousers and a loose shirt covered by a green vest.

"The Zhentarim's leader is trying to be sure that we attack, otherwise he wouldn't have sent his mercenaries to commit this atrocity," the Harper explained. "To me, that suggests that he's picked his ground carefully and prepared a few surprises. I think we'd be wiser to change our plans." He peered into a tent and made a disgusted face, then withdrew his head and looked toward the sheikhs. "That's only a suggestion, of course."

Utaiba nodded, then said, "There is truth to the Harper's words. Let us discuss them in my camp."

"After we send someone to wash and bury the dead," Yatagan added.

Sa'ar and several others grumbled at the delay, but they were outnumbered and had no choice but to agree to the council. They descended the hill without inviting either Lander or Ruha to join them. It was, the widow realized, a diplomatic omission. With the warriors anxious for battle, it would be better if it appeared that neither she nor Lander were responsible for delaying the fight.

Once the sheikhs were gone, Lander began moving from tent to tent, repeating the peculiar warning that Ruha heard him speak to any dead he encountered. "Dead ones, you will meet N'asr's denizens everywhere. Remember your gods and keep their faith, or you will suffer as surely as the wicked."

Ruha followed a few steps behind, peering into the *khreimas* as Lander spoke to the corpses. The scene was always similar. In the back of the tent was a large gash, apparently cut by the attackers. Six sleeping carpets lay in a rough circle in the center of the tent. At the head of each carpet lay the *kuerabiche* that had been serving as the warrior's pillow when he was decapitated. In some of the tents, the six headless corpses had each been dragged into a corner, as if by a greedy dog, and the soft parts of the body had been devoured.

When she could stand looking at the grisly scenes no longer, Ruha took the Harper's arm and stopped him. "I have seen enough of Yhekal's work," she said. "Why don't you tell me what it is that you're doing?"

"The camp of the dead is filled with N'asr's evil servants. They hunt the spirits of those who lose their faith or those who never had any," he explained. "So I'm warning the dead to remember their gods. As long as they don't lose conviction in their gods, they'll be safe."

"How do you know all this?"

The Harper flushed, but he did not look away. "My mother worshiped Cyric, who is N'asr to the Bedine," the Harper explained. "This is what she learned from her priests."

"And you really think the dead will remember what you say?" Ruha asked.

Lander shrugged. "I'm not even sure they can hear me," he said. "The warning can't do any harm, though."

Ruha nodded. "That's true," she said. "Go ahead and finish."

As the Harper returned to his task, the first of the burial detail arrived. The widow allowed them a few minutes of disgust and outrage, then directed them toward the dead to whom Lander had already spoken.

By the time the Harper had finished his task, At'ar was

two spans above the horizon and the day was already beginning to grow warm. Realizing that neither she nor Lander had eaten anything since last night, Ruha suggested they return to her *khreima* for breakfast.

As they walked toward Sa'ar's camp, Lander's face seemed vacant and weary. Recalling the effect that viewing even a few of the tents had had upon her, the widow decided that the Harper might not want to eat. Her own emotions were torn between elation at the feeling of acceptance she had experienced that morning and revulsion at what the Zhentarim had done to the Ruwald.

"Perhaps you're not hungry," she suggested. "Maybe you would prefer to find someplace to graze our camels."

Lander smiled gratefully, but he said, "I'm not very hungry, but we should try to eat anyway. If the sheikhs decide to attack after all, it could be a long time before our next meal."

"You seem to know a lot about fighting battles," she observed.

Lander shook his head. "Not any more than any other Harper," he said. "I think we have more of them in the rest of the world than here in Anauroch."

"That wouldn't be hard," the widow replied. "This is the first true war the Bedine have had since the Scattering."

Lander's gaze dropped to the ground. "I'm afraid it won't be the last. Even if we defeat Yhekal's army, the Zhentarim will send another."

The pair reached a gnarled frankincense tree at the base of Sa'ar's knoll. Before starting up the hill, Lander paused and looked into Ruha's eyes. "When the next army comes, the Bedine will need your magic as much as they need it now, perhaps even more. Are you sure you want to go to Sembia?"

The widow's heart sank, and she felt as though the Harper had struck her. "You don't want me to go to Sembia, do

you?" Before he could answer, she turned away and
climbed the hill.

Lander scrambled after her. "Wait!"

Ruha ignored him and rushed past a group of astonished
warriors, then went into her tent. The Harper's question
had hurt her more than she cared to admit, for she *did* want
to go to Sembia—though now she had a different reason
than at first.

Lander rushed into the tent two steps behind her. "Let
me finish—"

"Leave me!" the widow snapped, turning away to hide
the tears welling in her eyes.

The Harper kneeled at her side and grabbed her shoulders. The touch of his firm grip sent Ruha's blood racing.
She could not stop herself from throwing her arms around
his neck and burying her head in his shoulder.

"I didn't mean that I want you to stay," he whispered,
"only that now there is a place for you with the Bedine.
After the war, surely Utaiba or Sa'ar—"

Ruha touched her hand to his lips. "After the war, my
place is with you."

Lander gently pried her arms from his neck, then held
her a few inches from his body and stared directly into her
eyes. His touch sent waves of passion through her body.
Ruha knew then that she had never wanted anything as
much as she wanted to fold herself into his embrace.

"And what of your vision? What if I die?"

As he asked his question, a feeling of horror crept over
the widow. The vision flashed through her memory again,
and she closed her arms around the Harper. Placing her
face next to his ear, Ruha reached up and removed her veil.
"We cannot know what my vision means, so there is nothing to be gained by thinking of it," the widow whispered. "I
want to share whatever the future brings you."

The Harper grabbed her shoulders and held them tightly,

drinking in the nakedness of her face. His hands were trembling, and he seemed on the brink of yielding to the desire burning in his blue eye.

Lander leaned down to kiss her, then someone shuffled into the entrance of the *khreima*. "Pack your things!" commanded a warrior's voice. "The sheikhs have decided that it is a bad time to fight."

Sixteen

The young witch sat in her saddle, impatiently squinting at the cracked ground beneath her camel's feet. The sun reflected off the white clay, as blinding and as hot as the merciless goddess herself, and Ruha felt as though she were sitting in a kiln.

Along with rest of the Bedine, she was in the bottom of a tiny *mamlahah* no more than two miles across. The small, flat-bottomed valley was surrounded by a cluster of low mountains. The canyons running out of the peaks were steep and short, with walls as sheer as ramparts. Within the last century, Kozah had raged mightily in the mountains, and the gorges had poured torrents of water into the *mamlahah* and created a shallow lake. Over the decades, At'ar had undone her husband's work, drying up the lake, baking the moisture from the clay-rich soil, and leaving in its place a plain of irregular, alabaster pentagons fired to ceramic hardness. In the middle of the plain sat all that remained of the lake, a muddy pond surrounded by a copse of acacia trees.

The area around the pond was dotted with black scars from Zhentarim cooking fires. Hundreds of shallow pits had been scratched into the hard ground where asabis had dug the holes in which they hid from the punishing heat of the day. In a circle around the pond, at distances ranging from two hundred to three hundred yards, lay the bodies of thirty Zhentarim sentries.

The guards had been killed yesterday by small parties of Bedine warriors using hit-and-run tactics. Twenty or thirty would ride into bow range and launch a volley at a few of the guards, then flee before the Zhentarim could counterattack. Sometimes two or three groups assaulted from different directions at the same time, but they always fled before the enemy could respond in force.

It was the same tactic the Bedine had been using since the destruction of Haushi's tribe. In daylight hours, the Zhentarim had to camp so their asabis could burrow into the ground and hide from At'ar. During this time, Bedine war parties lurked in a circle around the Zhentarim camp, firing their arrows whenever the opportunity to hit a target arose.

The invaders, handicapped by the necessity to protect their asabis, could not chase the war parties without leaving the sleeping mercenaries vulnerable to an attack by the main body of warriors. If the Zhentarim sent out a smaller patrol to attack a war party, the Bedine simply gathered enough force to wipe it out. The enemy had no choice but to accept the casualties and counterattack at night.

Even that had proven difficult for the invaders. When dusk came, the Bedine mounted and scattered into the desert, camping in small, widely dispersed groups. The Zhentarim could occasionally hunt down and destroy two or three war parties, but then they had to spend all night fighting instead of traveling—which could cause them even more trouble. The invaders had to find fresh pasturage al-

most daily, for the thousands of camels in their army decimated the foliage around their small campsites within a
matter of minutes. In the end, the Zhentarim were left with
only two choices: take the casualties inflicted by the war
parties, or starve their camels and counterattack. So far,
they had chosen to accept the casualties.

Unfortunately, it appeared to Ruha that they were trying
a new tactic. Scattered around the muddy oasis were the
contorted bodies of dozens of hares, a pack of jackals, and
even a pair of ostriches that had come to drink after the
Zhentarim departed last night. All of the animals had died
within fifty yards of the pond. For the past few minutes,
the Bedine army, which had gathered in a large crowd
around the pond, had been staring at the scene with a mixture of outrage and disbelief.

As of yet, Lander was the only one who had dismounted.
He was kneeling next to a jackal, using his dagger to pry
the animal's mouth open. "This one bit its own tongue in
two," the Harper said. "I'd say they all died of some sort of
seizure."

"Poison," Sa'ar hissed, staring at the bodies of the other
dead animals.

For several moments, no one said anything else. The
warriors and the sheikhs just stared at the poisoned water,
unable to comprehend the malevolence of men who would
commit such a profane act.

At last Utaiba said, "It would have been bitter water anyway. Standing ponds always are."

"Bitter or not, it was an oasis, and it is a blasphemy to
foul it," said Kabina, Sa'ar's burly warrior. He pointed toward the mountains. "They shall pay for this atrocity with
their blood."

"Especially the Ju'ur Dai," said Sa'ar. "For a Bedine
tribe to do this . . ." The burly sheikh shook his head, unable to find the words to express his outrage. "No punish-

ment can be too terrible. Let us find them today!"

A chorus of agreement rose from the throats of hundreds of thirsty warriors, but Lander shook his head.

Sheathing his dagger, he approached Utaiba and the other sheikhs, saying, "That's what the Zhentarim want. In the past three weeks, you've killed more than five hundred of them without losing even a hundred Bedine. Yhekal poisoned the well because you're winning this war. He's trying to force you into making a mistake. Don't fall for his ruse."

Utaiba regarded the Harper thoughtfully, then nodded. "What you say is true—"

"Truth doesn't put water in our skins," Sa'ar interrupted. "If Yhekal is trying to push us into action, he has succeeded. Our camels are thirsty and our waterskins are nearly empty. The only oasis within five days of here is on the other side of those mountains." The stout sheikh thrust his finger in the same direction that Kabina had pointed earlier. "We cannot reach it without going through the same pass that the Zhentarim are in now. Our only choices are to attack or to return to the last oasis and let the invaders escape."

"Or to let thirst swell our tongues until we choke on them," added Kabina, glancing at the other warriors. "I prefer to fight."

Utaiba nodded, then addressed his fellow sheikhs. "Sa'ar and Lander are both correct. As Sa'ar says, we must attack, but Lander is also right. In that canyon, the advantage of terrain will go to the Zhentarim. I am afraid that our only choice is to return to the last oasis for water. Only then should we try to catch the invaders again."

"Giving them time to poison another oasis?" Sa'ar demanded. "If we do that, Anauroch is lost."

"As it is if the Zhentarim destroy this army," Utaiba said.

"Perhaps there is another way," Ruha suggested.

The sheikhs looked to her with arched brows, unaccustomed to having women intrude during such debates. Their surprise lasted only a moment, however, for they were growing used to the idea that Ruha was no ordinary Bedine woman. "Can your magic cleanse the water of its poison?" Utaiba asked hopefully.

The widow shook her head. "Unfortunately, I have no spells that can restore the oasis," she said. "But I do have one that might deceive the Zhentarim into thinking a small attack was a large one."

"What good would that do?" Sa'ar asked, frowning.

"Given the opportunity, the Zhentarim would surely destroy us, would they not?" Ruha asked.

All of the sheikhs nodded their heads in agreement, but it was Lander who picked up on the widow's plan. "Are you suggesting that we turn Yhekal's trap against him?"

Ruha nodded. "We will take two *khowwans* and attack as the Zhentarim want us to," she said, smiling beneath her veil. "My spell will make it look like all of our tribes are assaulting. The battle will go against us, and we will have to flee. Yhekal will no doubt send his men to pursue, anxious to destroy us while we are vulnerable."

"And the routed *khowwans* will lead the Zhentarim into an ambush manned by the other twelve tribes," Lander added. "A brilliant plan!"

"And after we finish with the Zhentarim, we will destroy the asabis in their burrows," Sa'ar added enthusiastically. He gave the widow a conniving smile. "You think like a camel thief, Ruha."

The other sheikhs gave their approval to the plan. As they worked out the details, Ruha forced her camel to kneel, then dismounted and removed Qoha'dar's spellbook from her *djebiras*. Each night the young widow memorized the spells she thought might be useful the next day, but she wanted to look over the spell with which she intended to fool the Zhentarim.

"Do you have everything you need?" Lander asked, stepping to her side.

Ruha nodded, then said, "And a few things I don't need."

Lander frowned in concern. "Like what?"

"Trembling knees, uneasy stomach, shaky hands."

The Harper took her hand in his. "Relax. You survived the Battle of the Chasm. This one won't be any worse."

"I'm not worried about dying," the widow said, squeezing Lander's fingers. "I just hope my plan works."

Utaiba rode his camel to the pair, scowling at their clasped hands. "You will come with Sa'ar and me, Ruha. The Mahwa and the Raz'hadi will serve as the decoys," the wiry sheikh said. Looking to Lander, he added, "We thought it would be best if you stayed with the others."

The Harper frowned. "I'll go with Ruha. She'll need protection if the Zhentarim see her casting spells."

"There are others who can protect her," Utaiba said, his expression firm and stubborn. "But you are the only one who knows the Zhentarim well, so you should be safe. The other sheikhs have agreed to respect your advice in preparing the ambush. More importantly, if something goes wrong, your knowledge may make the difference between victory and disaster."

Realizing that the sheikhs had made up their minds on this matter, Ruha mounted her camel and prodded it back to its feet. "I'll be fine," she said, smiling down at Lander. "You make sure the ambush works."

The Harper nodded, but Ruha could see that he was far from happy about being left behind. "It'll work. You make sure you come back alive."

"I'll make sure of that," Utaiba said, urging his camel toward the place where the Mahwa and Raz'hadi had gathered.

After Ruha and Utaiba joined the two tribes, Sa'ar gave

the order to ride. The war party crossed the dried lake bed quickly, moving toward a point well south of their final destination to prevent anyone watching from the mountains from getting a good look at them. The rest of the tribes would not follow for another two hours, when the Mahwa and the Raz'hadi had had ample time to drive enemy observers away from the edge of the mountains.

Once they reached the base of the mountains, Sa'ar stopped the column and looked to Ruha. "After you cast your spell, how long will it disguise our true number?"

"An hour or so," the widow replied. "Not much longer."

"We'd better send some scouts ahead to chase away the enemy sentries right away," Sa'ar said. "We don't want them to get a good look at us before you create your mirage."

The sheikh sent two dozen men forward to act as a vanguard, then waited fifteen minutes before allowing the column to continue. The two tribes moved along the base of the mountains for an hour, then turned up a winding, rocky canyon. Craggy brown cliffs immediately flanked the riders and rose more than a hundred feet to either side. They were laced with wide fissures.

Sa'ar sent some men forward to check random crevices for hidden sentries, but the gesture did little to make Ruha feel more secure. The column was moving too fast to check every crevice, and the widow did not put it past the Zhentarim to hide assassins there. Uncomfortably aware of the conspicuousness of her veiled presence among the long line of *keffiyehs* proceeding up the canyon, Ruha did her best to ride between Utaiba and Sa'ar. From her previous encounters with Yhekal, it seemed likely to her that he had deduced she was a magic-user. In that case, the lone woman among a column of warriors would no doubt be a prime target for enemy arrows.

The sheikhs allowed themselves to fall back to the middle of the column and tried to stay in the center of the canyon, as aware of Ruha's prominence as she was. Unfortunately, it was not an easy task, for the gulch was no more than fifty yards wide in many places, and a good man's arrow was accurate at twice that range.

Thirty minutes of careful riding passed, and no one had fired at Ruha or anybody else. The scouts returned to the main body of the column, reporting that they had approached to within a hundred yards of the enemy camp without encountering a single sentry. It appeared that all the Zhentarim were asleep, for there was no other sign of the invaders in the canyon other than their sealed tents.

Utaiba furrowed his brow, "I do not like this. The Zhentarim are not fools. They would not leave themselves so exposed."

"Perhaps not," Sa'ar agreed, drawing his sword. "But what choice do we have? Even if they have prepared an ambush for us, we must attack in order to lure them into our own trap."

Utaiba considered this for a moment, then said, "You are right. Let us hope that Eldath, not N'asr, is with us today." He also drew his scimitar, then looked toward Ruha. "Now is the time for your spell."

The young witch took a deep breath, then nodded and said, "We'll need to be at the head of the column."

The two sheikhs glanced at each other with concern, but Sa'ar nodded. "Whatever you say."

They urged their camels closer to hers and moved to the head of the long line of warriors. Ahead of them, the canyon climbed through a stretch of steep boulder-strewn ground, then turned sharply to the left and disappeared into a maze of brown rock laced by deep, man-sized fissures. After that, the scouts had reported, it twisted back to the right and opened into a sandy dale that must have been a pool when there was water in the canyon. It was there that the tents of the Zhentarim were pitched.

Ruha took a small quartz crystal from her pocket. As it caught At'ar's rays, she faced the long column of warriors and manipulated the crystal in her hand until she could see their wavy image in the clear quartz. She selected a brawny warrior at the head of the column and focused on the *jambiya* in his belt.

When she uttered her spell, Sa'ar gasped. "Incredible!"

Ruha opened her eyes and saw that the spell had worked. Beyond the brawny warrior whose dagger she had selected as a focus, a sheet of wavering heat filled the canyon from wall to wall, obscuring the Bedine behind it. It was impossible to see anything beyond that single warrior clearly, for the images were all distorted. However, it did appear that there were about eight times as many men in the canyon than were really there.

Ruha pointed at the warrior. "Everything behind that man's dagger is distorted by the spell," she said. "If he falls, the spell will stop moving until someone else takes his dagger and continues with it."

"Magic is not without its shortcomings, I see," Utaiba noted wryly.

"Neither are we," Sa'ar answered. "But we shall do our best anyway. Now, let us return to our place in line. If we only have an hour, we must hurry."

"Be careful when you pass through the sunwarp," Ruha said, urging her camel toward the column. "Don't tarry inside, or you will have reason to regret it."

As the widow spoke, she urged her mount into the distortion, ferociously lashing at its neck with her reigns. The camel sprang forward into a wave of blistering heat. The beast roared in surprise and terror, but under Ruha's prodding it continued forward, and, an instant later, they were on the other side of the sunwarp.

On the downhill side of the distortion, a stiff breeze ran

along the ground as the spell sucked the fire from the desert and sent it climbing toward the sky in a great wavering sheet. Sa'ar and Utaiba sat on the other side of the wall, staring in Ruha's direction with awe and fear.

"What do you see?" asked Sa'ar's burly warrior, Kabina. "You look as though you are facing an army of djinns."

"We see nothing but wavering forms, and many times the number we know are there," Sa'ar answered, still staring at the wall. "It is as if At'ar has blinded us!"

"She has," Ruha replied. "Now, come back here."

Setting their jaws as if riding into a wall of flame, the sheikhs urged their mounts forward and galloped through the sunwarp in two swift strides. When they reached the other side, their faces were as chalky as a white camel and they stared at the witch with expressions of awe and respect. Their mounts were so excited that it was all they could do to control them.

Sa'ar pointed at a dozen warriors, then directed them toward the Bedine upon whom Ruha had centered the spell. "You men, ring Dahalzel. If he falls, one of you must take his *jambiya* and continue forward. If that man falls, someone else must take the dagger."

"I will need my dagger in N'asr's camp!" objected the confused warrior.

"Don't argue," Utaiba answered, drawing his scimitar. "Your *jambiya* is the center of the witch's spell."

The man's swarthy complexion paled to a sickly shade of yellow. "My dagger?"

A roar of laughter went up from the twelve men assigned to escort Dahalzel. "We will protect you from the enemy's arrows, my friend," said one of them. "But you must look to the gods to save you from the witch's magic."

"Enough!" Sa'ar roared, guiding his camel into place at Ruha's left side. "Let us attack!"

With a queasy look, Dahalzel turned his attention up the

canyon. He nocked an arrow, then urged his camel forward and led the way toward the Zhentarim camp.

A few minutes later, the column of nervous warriors emerged from the maze of fissure-laced rock. It stopped at the edge of the sandy hollow where the sheikhs had expected to fight the Zhentarim. As the scouts had claimed, several hundred tents stood in the dale, but there was still no sign of the enemy.

Sa'ar looked immediately to Ruha. "Is your spell hiding the enemy?"

Ruha shook her head. "No."

"It isn't the witch," Utaiba said, motioning six men forward. "I fear we are too late. The Zhentarim are gone." The wiry sheikh sent the men to track the invaders up the canyon.

"It cannot be!" Sa'ar objected. "What of the asabis? They cannot move during the day."

"Perhaps they are still in their burrows," Ruha suggested.

"Perhaps," Sa'ar nodded. He sent a rider back to report the deserted camp to the tribes waiting in ambush, and five dozen men ventured into the dale to probe the sand with their spears.

The probers spread out across the width of the dale and began searching for sleeping asabis. While one man pushed his spear deep into the sand, a comrade stood by with a drawn scimitar, ready to defend him if the prober got lucky and struck a sleeping reptile. When they found nothing, they moved a yard farther up the canyon and tried again. Occasionally a man fell excitedly to his knees and scooped the sand away, only to uncover a submerged rock or the half-petrified trunk of an acacia tree.

The rest of the column waited in the sun, fighting the urge to open their waterskins and quench the thirst that always seemed worse when doing nothing. Now and then, the camels belched or roared, as irritated by the wait as their riders were. In hushed whispers, a few men suggested to their fellows what Ruha and the sheikhs had already guessed: the Zhentarim had escaped.

Ruha's spell fell long before the probers reached the other side of the dale, but it did not matter. The spearmen returned with nothing to report. Though their spears had often sunk clear to the bedrock, they had not found so much as a single asabi burrowed into the sand.

A few minutes later, one of the scouts Utaiba had sent to track the Zhentarim returned. He reported that the canyon was full of camel tracks, but there was no sign of the asabis.

"The Zhentarim are running for Orofin!" Utaiba concluded.

"And they must have left the asabis behind," Sa'ar added, scowling. "But where?"

Utaiba shrugged. "Let's find out."

Sa'ar nodded, then ordered the entire column forward. As Ruha and the sheikhs moved into the dale, a muffled clack echoed from a crevice on the north side of the canyon. Ruha heard a hiss, then felt her mount's withers flinch. The beast roared in astonishment and rolled to its left. As the camel's legs buckled, the young witch leaped free. She landed a foot behind the Sa'ar's huge mount, already summoning a spell to mind. She spun around and pointed her hand toward the fissure, raising the other toward At'ar.

A bolt of white fire burst from her fingers and streaked into the fissure, then a tremendous boom echoed from the canyon walls. A limp asabi flew out of the crevice amid a hail of stones and dropped to the canyon floor.

"Ambush!" cried Sa'ar, waving the column back down the canyon.

No sooner had he spoke than dozens of muffled clacks sounded from the canyon walls. A flurry of black streaks crossed in both directions. As the crossbow bolts found their targets, men cried out in pain and camels bellowed in astonishment. The canyon erupted into a cacophony of alarmed shouts and cries of warning.

Sa'ar's big camel swung around in front of Ruha, and she saw the sheikh's brawny hand reaching down for her. She jumped up and grabbed at the arm, then felt her feet leave the ground as the burly man pulled her onto his mount's back. They sprang a few yards down the canyon, then ran into a confused mass of riders that had been at the end of the column when the asabis opened fire.

Realizing that those at the back of the column still did not realize that the front of the column had been ambushed, Ruha tugged at Sa'ar's *amarat* and yelled, "Blow the retreat!"

As the sheikh raised his horn, another round of bolts tore out of the crevices. More men screamed and more camels bellowed, then the rumbling tones of Sa'ar's *amarat* echoed off the cliffs. The back of the column immediately reversed direction and rode back down the canyon, clearing the way for their trapped fellows. Within moments, the entire line was trotting away from the ambush.

On the other side of the winding narrows, the procession met Lander and the sheikhs galloping up the steep valley. Behind them, in a long line that stretched all the way down to the *mamlahah*, were the rest of the Bedine warriors.

The warriors of the Raz'hadi and the Mahwa neatly parted ways to allow the Lander and the sheikhs to pass through unhindered. As they approached Sa'ar, the thirteen men stopped whipping their camels. The drained beasts ceased their running immediately.

"What happened?" demanded Didaji. His brown turban was half-unwrapped, and he was self-consciously holding its tail over his lower face.

"Ruha found the asabis for us," Sa'ar said, hitching his thumb over his shoulder at his passenger.

"They ambushed us when we started into the dale," Utaiba added. "But not very well. They're hiding deep in the fissures to keep away from At'ar, so their field of fire is not very wide."

Lander moved past the other sheikhs and stopped his mount alongside Ruha. "What happened to your camel?"

"Shot from beneath her," Sa'ar explained.

The widow was pleased to see the Harper's brow furrow in concern. He started to reach for her hand, but quickly withdrew it when Sa'ar moved to intercept it. "I'm glad you are well."

"Of course she's well," Utaiba responded. "I promised you that Sa'ar and I would take care of her, did I not?"

"Your messenger told us the Zhentarim were gone," Didaji interrupted. "Was he wrong? Is our plan spoiled?"

"The plan is spoiled," Utaiba responded. "But only because the Zhentarim abandoned their asabis. They're heading toward Orofin."

Didaji cursed.

"Why are you upset?" Lander asked. "Yhekal has made his first big mistake. Now that he's split his force, it will be a simple matter to wipe them out separately."

"It's not going to be as easy as you think," Utaiba responded. "An ancient fort guards the well at Orofin. The Zhentarim can hold out inside for weeks. As short as our water supply is, we cannot last nearly that long."

Sa'ar pointed toward the dale. "There is no way to ride around the ambush, but if we ride through it at a gallop, we won't suffer too many casualties. With luck, we'll catch the Zhentarim by tomorrow afternoon—a half-day before they reach Orofin."

"No," Lander said, shaking his head in disappointment. "That's what they want. If we bypass the asabis, we'll be caught between the hammer and the anvil."

"What do you mean?" asked Sa'ar.

Lander held one hand out flat. "Here are the Zhentarim," he said. "Whether we catch them before Orofin or at it, we'll have to stop and fight." He formed a fist with the other hand, then brought it down into his open palm with a loud pop. "When that happens, the asabis will smash us from behind, just as a hammer smashes against the anvil."

Utaiba frowned. "I see what you mean." He turned to the other sheikhs, then said, "I agree with the Harper. If we don't pause now, we'll regret it later."

"What of Orofin?" countered Didaji. "Surely they will poison all water that lies outside the fort. Our tribes will die of thirst."

"The asabis must have water with them," Sa'ar said. "It will be enough to get us to Orofin so that we can attack. After the battle, we'll have all the water we want, or we won't have need of any."

"Before the Zhentarim started poisoning oases, I would never have agreed to such a plan," Utaiba said, addressing the other sheikhs as well as Didaji. "Now that I know how corrupt they are, it is clear that we must drive them from our home, even if it means risking everything."

Didaji reluctantly nodded, then turned to the closest warriors. "Pass the word to dismount and come forward with lance and sword. We must pry these lizards from their dens."

The fourteen tribes spent the rest of the day in the canyon, working carefully and methodically. Starting at the near end of the dale, four or five warriors approached each fissure and tried to draw the asabi's fire by throwing rocks into the crevice. Usually, that did not work, so they drew lots and the loser had to jump past the front of the crevice, at the same time throwing his lance into it. Most of the reptiles fired their crossbows as the decoy flashed past and, more often than not, deftly avoided the lance.

Several other warriors then leaped in front of the crevice. One of them threw a torch into the crack to illuminate the target, and the others pierced the creature with their long spears. Once it died, they pulled the lifeless asabi from the crack, took its waterskin, and moved on to the next fissure.

When the mercenary refused to fire its crossbow even at the decoy, the warriors resorted to smoke. They pulled a withered bush and lit it with their torch, then reached around the edge of the fissure and stuffed the burning brush inside. If the resulting smoke flushed the asabi out, they sliced it to pieces with their scimitars as it rushed out of the crevice. Otherwise, three or four of them leaped in front of the fissure and probed into the smoking crack with their lances until they heard the reptile's death hiss. They tried to avoid this last option whenever possible, however, for one of them usually took a crossbow bolt before the asabi died.

Sometimes, after the decoy threw his lance and drew a crossbow bolt from the crack, the warriors discovered that there were two or three mercenaries in a single fissure. As the Bedine leaped in front of the fissure to attack, several unexpected bolts flashed out and took them square in the chest. A short pause followed while a dozen men fetched their bows, then they positioned themselves twenty yards from the fissure and fired into it until the crossbow bolts stopped coming back at them.

Once in a while, the warriors ran into a problem they could not solve, such as an asabi crouching behind cover or hiding in an unusually deep crevice. On these occasions, Utaiba or Sa'ar would call upon Ruha to flush out the mercenaries. With Lander standing close by to defend her, she would cast a spell and fill the crack with poisonous smoke, send in a sand lion to maul the reptile, or funnel so much of At'ar's heat into the fissure that the asabi literally fried to death. Her spells were so much faster and more effective

than the warriors' attacks that Ruha wished she could have
used them on every fissure in the canyon. Unfortunately,
that was impossible. She had a limited number of spells
compared to the hundreds of crevices around the dale.

By the time dusk fell, the Bedine had worked their way
to the far end of the dale and the warriors were no longer
finding asabis in the fissures. The Bedine were so exhausted by the hot, tedious work that Ruha was the only one
who bothered to pitch a tent. Unfortunately for her, as
soon as she finished, it became the center of camp. The
sheikhs gathered a few yards away to discuss the day's
events before retiring to their own sleeping carpets.

"All in all, I would say this was not a bad day. I had a man
count the asabi bodies," Sa'ar boasted, his voice carrying
through the tent walls as if he were standing inside.
"There are almost a thousand."

Ruha lit a candle and took Qoha'dar's spellbook from her
djebiras. In order to replenish all the spells she had used
during the day, she had several long hours of study ahead of
her.

Outside her tent, Utaiba said, "We lost only a hundred
and nine warriors ourselves. I think we can call this battle a
Bedine victory."

Yawning, the widow turned to the first spell she had used
that day, the sunwarp.

"It wasn't much of a battle. It was more like digging mice
from their dens," Didaji objected.

Ruha found herself hearing the gaunt man's words instead of concentrating upon the runes in the book. Sighing
in frustration, she set the book aside and started toward
the door of her tent. That was when Lander's voice said,
"If it's a battle you want, Didaji, wait until Orofin."

"You too, Lander?" Ruha muttered under her breath. "I
thought you'd have better sense than to disturb a witch's
study time."

Oblivious to Ruha's whispered admonishment, the Harper continued, "When we storm that fort, I promise there'll be plenty of fighting."

Ruha shook her head, then slammed her spellbook shut and blew out her candle. "I might as well sleep," she hissed to herself, half-amused and half-angered by her girlish reluctance to speak crossly to Lander. "When I'm upset, I can never concentrate anyway!"

Seventeen

After the Battle of the Fissures, the Bedine army rode straight to Orofin. The warriors did not tarry to let their camels graze upon the heaths of salt brush they passed, and, though they traveled through the finest gazelle country in Anauroch, they wasted no time hunting. Even with the skins they had recovered from the asabis, the fourteen tribes were short of water, and that meant they were short of time. They had to reach Orofin, and then they had to storm it.

It took the army four days of hard travel, stopping only a few hours each night to sleep, before they crested a ridge and Sa'ar pointed into the broad valley below. In the center of the dell, a stand of swarthy foliage stained the tawny ground, its lush color muted by the graying light of dusk.

"Orofin," Sa'ar said. "If we hurry, I know a good place from which to inspect its battlements."

The sheikhs ordered their tribes to encircle the fortress with their camps and eat the best meal they could manage. After the orders had been given, Sa'ar led the sheikhs down into the valley, into several acres of ruins, then finally stopped at a two-story bridge that spanned a canal of stagnant water.

Like Anauroch itself, the bridge was at once stark and beautiful. The square pediments were made of granite blocks, now entirely covered with a lush growth of thick green moss. Above the pediments stood two tiers of roadway, consisting of three arcades each. The arches were shaped like horseshoes and crowned by a shallow point, reminding Lander of Sembia's cottonwood leaves. A colored-stone mosaic of different geometric patterns faced each arcade, save that the central arch on both tiers was decorated with a diamond motif.

Lander forced his camel to kneel. He cast a longing eye at the waterway, but didn't even consider drinking from the obviously poisoned streams. Twilight was almost upon Anauroch, but the valley was quiet. No raptors welcomed the lengthening shadows with their eerie screeches, no lions roared a challenge to the newcomers, no hyenas betrayed their presence with cowardly yelps. The silent animals all lay within a few yards of the water, their bodies bloated and rank from exposure to the sun. Even the vultures that had come to prey on their carcasses lay dead.

The scene in the water itself was more gruesome. The gentle current had carried dozens of human corpses down the canal and heaped them against the east side of the bridge. They were floating in the murky dark water, bloated and inert and reeking of decay.

Utaiba pointed a finger at the terrible scene. "The Ju'ur Dai," he said.

"I thought they were the Zhentarim's allies," commented Didaji.

"Perhaps they were," Lander answered, fighting the urge to wretch. "They outlived their usefulness. Yhekal would not want to risk having them change sides in the middle of the battle."

"They got what they deserved," Sa'ar grunted, spitting into the canal. "Without the Ju'ur Dai to guide them, the Zhentarim might not have realized the importance of Orofin."

The stout sheikh led the way up to the second tier of the ancient bridge. As the others followed, the Harper could see why the sheikh had selected this vantage point. From the added height, he could see that Orofin had once been a mighty city, with four canals radiating outward from a fortress guarding the deep well at its heart. Not much remained of the metropolis now. Wind-blown silt covered the foundations of long-fallen buildings, crisscrossed here and there by crooked lines that had once served as avenues and alleys. Thick hedges of green briars, interspersed with acacia and wild apricot trees, lined the four canals that still divided the city into quarters. A grand avenue, connecting this bridge to three others that spanned the other canals, formed a great circle around the entire oasis.

Lander and the sheikhs were more interested in the fortress than in the city. It still stood in the center of the oasis, its crumbling ramparts breached in nine or ten places by man-sized gaps. Dark shadows skulked among the ancient crenelations topping the walls, reminding Lander more of underworld spirits than distant Zhentarim soldiers.

"How should we attack?"

It was Sa'ar who asked the question. The burly sheikh rested an elbow against the arcade wall and did not take his eyes off the fortress when he spoke.

"Under the cover of darkness, tonight," said Didaji, his face swathed in his red scarf.

"Our men are too tired," countered Utaiba, kicking a stone off the bridge into the stinking canal. "Besides, the Zhentarim well be alert for an assault tonight."

"We cannot wait for tomorrow night," objected Yatagan, the wizened old sheikh of the Shremala. "My men have only swallows of water remaining. If they do not drink from Orofin's wells by noon tomorrow, they will never fight again."

"You would rather they died tonight?" retorted Utaiba. "Who among them has the strength left to draw a bow more than a dozen times?"

As they were wont to do, the sheikhs fell to bickering. Lander simply shook his head, then stepped to the next arcade and stared at the fortress in frustrated silence. Apparently Ruha was the only one who noticed his disgust, for she came to his side while the sheikhs continued to argue.

"Now is not the time to quarrel," the Harper said, looking in the direction of the cacophony.

Ruha shrugged. "They are sheikhs of different tribes," she said. "They must argue before they reach a decision."

"There isn't time for debate," the Harper said.

"If you have a plan, tell it to them," Ruha said. "You have earned their respect. They will listen."

"I don't have a plan," Lander sighed, turning back to the fort. The admission made him realize that he was as frustrated with his own dearth of ideas as he was with the bickering of the sheikhs. "Utaiba is right; we're too tired to attack tonight. But Yatagan is also right. If we wait until tomorrow night, half our men will be dead."

"We can't attack in the morning?" Ruha asked.

"It looks like that's our only choice," Lander said. "But the Zhentarim arrows will have a much easier time finding our men."

"Perhaps that is where I will be of help," Ruha replied, stepping closer to his side.

The sweet odor of frankincense, the Bedine equivalent of perfume, wafted up from her *aba*, and a familiar longing washed over the Harper. The vision of the young witch's beautiful face flashed through his mind again, and his thoughts were quickly wandering away from the battle at hand. Lander's desire for her had become as hot and engulfing as the sands. He often found himself unable to think of anything but the time when the Zhentarim would be destroyed, when he would be free to take Ruha and leave this blistering land.

A muffled hiss drew Lander's thoughts back to the present. The sound was followed immediately by a quiet splash in the canal, then by another muted hiss and the ping of steel striking rock.

"What was—?"

Lander did not let Ruha finish her question. He pulled her into the shelter of an arcade column. "They're trying to hit us with arrows fired from longbows," he explained, peering around the corner toward the fortress. Though the archers were hidden in shadowy crenelations of the wall, the Harper did not doubt that he and Ruha had been good targets, framed as they were by the arch.

For a moment, Lander lingered in the shadow of the column, savoring the closeness of Ruha's body. To kiss her, all he needed to do was lean toward her. Even with the sheikhs so close, she would willingly slip her veil aside. The young witch had made it clear that she would be his— whenever and wherever he wanted.

Lander wanted her, but, even if the sheikhs would leave them alone for more than a few minutes, he was reluctant to violate the taboo against sleeping with a widow. The Harper was not so much afraid of offending the dead husband's spirit as he was concerned about upsetting the living Bedine. As superstitious as they were about all things magical, he feared that if they discovered that he and Ruha had made love, they would throw down their weapons and leave the Zhentarim free to roam the desert.

Somewhat belatedly, Sa'ar called a warning. "Lander,

Ruha! They are shooting arrows at us! Are you all right?"

Another arrow splashed into the water at the base of the bridge.

"We're fine," Lander responded. "Perhaps we should return to camp."

"An excellent suggestion," said Utaiba. "We have seen enough to make our plans."

Lander waited for the next arrow to bounce off the stone bridge, then scurried from the protection of one arcade pillar to another. Ruha followed a few steps behind. After leaving the bridge, they returned to their camels and rode out of arrow range.

"Perhaps we should assemble at my camp to discuss our strategy," Utaiba suggested to the other sheikhs. "I haven't much water, but I can offer dried figs and a few drops of camel's milk."

The other sheikhs accepted the Raz'hadi's offer, but Ruha shook her head. "If I am to be of much use tomorrow," she said, "it would be better for me to return to Sa'ar's camp and study my spells."

Utaiba and Sa'ar nodded, but Didaji said, "The gods gave your magic to us for a reason, Ruha. I am certain that whatever plan we develop, it will rely heavily on your spells."

"Then I will tell you the spells I can use," the widow countered. "But if I don't study them before I rest, I will not have them when you are ready to attack."

"What she says makes sense, Didaji," Sa'ar noted. "The witch does not sleep in your camp, so you may not have noticed that she spends every evening poring over her book. If Ruha is to be of use to us, we must do our planning without her."

Didaji nodded, then Ruha spent the next half-hour describing her spells to the sheikhs. They asked her several questions about each one, then assigned one of their num-

ber to repeat its capabilities. When they had discussed
every spell the widow knew, she listed the ones she intended to memorize and told them to send word to her as
soon as possible if they wanted her to learn a different one.

By the time they were done, it was well after dark. The
sheikhs went toward Utaiba's camp to make their plans,
leaving it to Lander to escort Ruha back to her tent. In the
Mahwa camp, the slow rasp of sharpening stones upon
steel was punctuated by an occasional heavy twang as a
warrior tested the strength of his bowstring. Some of the
men were chanting an eerie, mournful song of war:

> *Be gone, strangers, be gone!*
> *Leave the grass of our meadows*
> *For the camels of our tribes.*
> *Be gone, strangers, be gone!*
> *We ask Kozah for one of those bloody battles*
> *Where brave men die in pride and glory*
> *And not from some wasting illness.*
> *Ride, young men, ride!*
> *Arrows do not kill*
> *It is only fear that slays.*
> *Ride, young men, ride!*

Lander paused to take a burning twig from a campfire,
then followed Ruha to the tent that Sa'ar's men had pitched
for her. Inside, it was mostly empty, save for a single sleeping carpet and the widow's *kuerabiches*.

Ruha opened one of her bags and set out a simple meal
for them to share. It consisted of nothing but water and a
plateful of raw tubers that looked like fat, white asparagus
stems.

"How soon will we leave for Sembia after capturing Orofin?" Ruha asked.

The Harper thought he detected a melancholy note in

her question. "Are you sure you want to go with me?" Lander's stomach tightened with apprehension even as he voiced the question, but it was one that he had to ask. "The Bedine are growing accustomed to having a sorceress around, and you may not find Sembia to your liking."

Ruha offered him the plate. "If you are there, I will find it to my liking."

The Harper smiled. "Then we'll leave as soon as the battle is won." Lander took one of the roots and bit into it. It had the powerful taste of an onion, but did not make his eyes water. "Now that you're safe in your own tent, I should leave you to your studies."

Ruha shook her head. "I already know most of the spells I'll use tomorrow—unless they send word to learn new ones."

"But you said—"

"That I need my rest," the widow interrupted. "And it's true. Whether or not I need to learn a lot of new spells, I will need my rest. But there's no hurry, and for once the sheikhs have too much on their minds to worry about what we're doing."

Ruha locked gazes with Lander, leaving him with no doubt about what she meant.

"I should join the sheikhs in their planning," he said, feeling the heat rise to his face.

"They will argue for another two hours. Join them later."

"Tonight, of all nights, we should not give the sheikhs anything to worry about," Lander objected.

"Tonight, of all nights, we should not care," she countered. Ruha's dark gaze remained fixed on his face, her unspoken demand unmistakably clear. "Tomorrow, what the sheikhs think will not matter. The Zhentarim will be gone or we will be dead."

"Then wait a little longer," Lander said. He could not bring himself to look away, though Ruha's eyes were doing more to win her argument than her words ever could. "We will not die. I promise that."

"That promise is not yours to make. Only N'asr knows when we shall die, and he will not tell even an emir." The young widow uncovered her face, revealing her tattooed cheeks and full lips. "Have you not sacrificed enough for the Bedine?"

"But your husband's spirit—"

"I knew my husband for three days," she said. "Certainly his spirit is concerned about a great many things, but I am not one of them."

The young widow kneeled in front of Lander, then took his face in her hands and drew his lips to hers. When she kissed him, a wave of fire coursed through his body. The Bedine's superstition, tomorrow's battle, even the Zhentarim, no longer seemed important. All that mattered was the burning thirst that racked his body. Nothing could quench it except Ruha.

Lander felt the young widow slip the *keffiyeh* from his head, and then his own hands were clutching at her *aba*. In an instant, he had pulled it over her head and tossed it aside. Ruha let him run his callused hands over her soft sienna skin, then she unclasped his dagger belt and dropped it at his side. Her hands slipped beneath his robes, soft and caressing and igniting him with desire wherever they touched.

The widow moved closer, and the frankincense odor of her body filled his breath. Lander found her lips, and they kissed again, their desire raging hotter than the rocks of At'ar's Looking Glass. Ruha tugged the Harper's *aba* over his head, plunging him into darkness.

As they drank from each other's lips, the scorched world outside the tent faded to a mirage, and Ruha became Lander's cool well. He quenched his thirst with the sweetness of her love, and she took from him the comfort of his strength. Together, they made an oasis in the parched sea and, if only for a time, they held at bay the troubled sands of Anauroch.

*   *   *   *   *

Later, Lander lay with Ruha pressed against his side, one of her arms and one of her legs thrown protectively across his body. Like a leopard on the stalk, tomorrow's battle was creeping back into his thoughts. Instead of being anxious or worried, though, he felt strangely at peace.

Tomorrow there would be a battle, and his task would be completed. If the Bedine won, he and Ruha would depart Anauroch together. They would return to his father's house in Archenbridge, probably with Ruha still insisting upon wearing her veil in the streets. Behind them they would leave all of the witch's years of loneliness and, Lander hoped, the shame of his mother's secret life and the anger caused by her betrayal of his father. He and Ruha would start a new life together.

Unfortunately, there was still one more battle between them and their newfound serenity. If the Bedine were going to win, it was time for him to join the sheikhs and to leave Ruha to study the few spells she needed to learn before morning.

When Lander stirred, Ruha opened her eyes. "What's wrong? You're not sorry—"

The Harper put his fingers to the young witch's lips. "I'm not sorry at all," he said. "I'm looking forward to spending my life making love to you." He gently moved her arm off his chest and sat up. "But we both have things to do before morning."

Lander reached for his *aba* and slipped it over his head.

"Yes, and I'm still enough of a Bedine that winning this battle is important to me," Ruha said, reaching for her own aba. "I just pray to Eldath that the sheikhs have made a good plan."

Lander smiled, then leaned down to kiss Ruha. "I'll make sure of it."

Ruha pulled away. "You are very confident of yourself," she laughed, slipping her robe over her head. "How can you—"

The widow suddenly gasped. "Lander!" she cried, pointing toward the entrance of the tent.

The Harper spun around, expecting the angry face of Sa'ar or Utaiba. Instead, he saw a slight figure wrapped head-to-foot in the black burnoose of a Zhentarim. The yellow eyes of a D'tarig gleamed out from the folds of the black cloth swaddling his head, and he held a gleaming *jambiya* in his hand.

"Bhadla?" Lander gasped. "How'd you get here?"

"The Zhentarim have ways of bypassing your sentries," he said. "And the rest of your warriors are either sleeping or staring into their campfires and singing their death songs. Perhaps you have one you would like to sing?"

The Harper laughed, instinctively reaching for his dagger. When he did not find it, he remembered that he had not yet put his belt back on.

"I don't have much of a voice," Lander said, unconcerned. If Bhadla was foolish enough to attack, he did not think being weaponless would cause him much trouble. "Surely, you didn't come here to listen to me sing. Have you come to beg for your—"

Behind him, Lander heard the sound of fabric being cut, and he knew the D'tarig had not come to beg for anything. Realizing that Bhadla was a distraction, the Harper spun around, stooping to reach for his dagger belt.

A black-robed figure, his sabre drawn, was just stepping through a slit in the *khreima*. Behind the first man, Lander could see another blade gleaming in the moonlight. The

Harper did not pause to wonder how the invaders had managed to sneak past the sentries and into the camp. From what he had seen of Yhekal, the Zhentarim leader was a powerful spellcaster. There was little doubt that he could call upon his powers for the necessary spells to help a small band of assassins sneak into the Bedine camp.

Lander pulled his dagger from its scabbard, then started to move toward his scimitar.

"Step back, Lander!" Ruha ordered.

The Harper heard her chant the words to an incantation and did as instructed, realizing that the beautiful witch was better equipped than he to deal with a group of assassins. No sooner had he stepped aside than a fiery blast of air crackled past him, engulfing the intruders in a white blaze.

The Harper took an involuntary step backward, raising his arm to shield his face.

"Now you die!" Bhadla rasped, already directly behind him.

Lander sidestepped quickly, then felt the D'tarig's blade run along his ribs. The cut began to sting immediately. Groaning, the Harper dropped his raised arm down to clamp the D'tarig's knife hand.

With his free hand, the Harper grasped Bhadla's leathery wrist, then brought his knee up against the D'tarig's forearm and broke it with a loud snap. Bhadla screamed and dropped the dagger. Without setting his leg back down, Lander swept the would-be assassin's feet from beneath him, at the same time pulling forward on the broken arm. The D'tarig landed flat on his back directly in front of Lander.

Before the Harper could do anything else, Ruha stepped around him. Her *jambiya* flashed once, opening a six-inch gash across Bhadla's throat. Blood began pouring onto the same carpet that the Harper and the witch had been lying upon moments before.

"Are there any more?" Lander asked, scanning the sides of the tent.

"Wasn't that enough?" Ruha responded. "How badly are you hurt?"

Lander felt warm blood running over his fingers and realized that he was holding his wound. He pulled his hand away and looked at the cut. "Not bad," he said. "It's not—"

His rib cage erupted into agony, sending fiery fingers of pain shooting through his torso. He let out an involuntary groan, then stumbled backward and dropped into a seated position. The blaze was spreading through his body like a wildfire, and he could feel himself beginning to sweat.

Ruha rushed to his side. "What's wrong?" she asked.

"Poison," the Harper croaked. Already, his mind seemed lost in hot vapors, and the roar of an immense blaze filled his ears. He could think well enough, though, to remember something Florin Falconhand had once told him: Zhentarim assassins often carried counteragents to their own toxins, for they were afraid of accidentally poisoning themselves.

Lander rolled onto his side and pulled himself toward the D'tarig. Ruha's hands were on his back, and she screamed something at him, but the firestorm in his head muffled her words.

"Antidote!" he gasped, finally latching onto Bhadla's lifeless arm. His vision had narrowed to a tunnel, and he could see nothing but the D'tarig's body at the end of his own long arm. He ran his fingers through Bhadla's robes, searching for a vial or a tin of powder.

"There is no antidote," said a woman.

Lander felt Ruha's hands brush his fingers aside, and he knew she was taking over the search. He sank back on his haunches and looked in the direction of the voice. "Who's there?"

"You know me." The voice was as sweet as the song of a morning dove.

The tunnel of Lander's vision closed altogether and became a white light. The light wavered for a moment, then took the shape of a ghostly, unveiled woman. "Mielikki?"

The Lady of the Forest nodded, coming closer. She kneeled at Lander's side, then wrapped her arms around his body and pulled him into her lap.

"Save me," he whispered.

"No."

"But the Zhentarim—we're not finished."

"*You* are," the goddess answered, stroking his brow.

The agony in Lander's body began to subside, and he realized that the fire was dying because it was running out of fuel. "I violated the taboo," he cried. "I slept with Ruha, and now the Bedine will pay."

The ghostly woman kissed Lander's forehead. He felt the last of his pain gather in his brow and flow out where her lips had touched his skin. "No, you helped a woman find her place," she whispered. "Now her people will have a chance at freedom."

Eighteen

 Ruha heard two warriors rush through the entrance of the *khreima*. The young witch did not wait for them to ask what had happened. "Leave!" she ordered, hoping to hide the tears streaking down her bare face.

They did not obey. "What of the assassins?"

"All the Zhentarim are dead," Ruha answered, barely able to keep the grief out of her voice. "We have no need of help."

There was a silence as the two sentries studied the scene in the *khreima*.

"Go!" Ruha ordered. "Or must I use magic to ensure my privacy?"

The warriors withdrew, and Ruha finally felt free to cry. Her tears fell on Lander's brow, for she was kneeling on the bloody carpet where he had fallen. His lifeless head was cradled in her lap.

The fatal attack had come so suddenly that Lander was cut and Bhadla lying on the ground before the widow realized she had seen it happen once before. She had reached for her *jambiya* with a disjointed feeling of being a helpless spectator, and when she had cut the D'tarig open it had seemed as if she were watching someone else kill him. There had been an eerie quality to the whole fight that made it seem like a recurring dream, but, just as in a bad dream, she had not been able to change the outcome.

Looking toward the roof of the tent, Ruha let out an agonized sob. "If I can do nothing to change them, why do you torture me with mirages from tomorrow?" she cried. "If I knew where this loathsome sight came from, I would tear out the organ and fling it to the vultures!"

The gods did not answer, though Ruha had no doubt that they were watching her with cruel amusement. She sat staring at the *khreima's* roof for a thousand pained heartbeats, looking past it in her mind's eye to the starry sky above. "How much longer must I endure your curse?"

Again the gods remained silent, and the young widow dropped her eyes from the impassive roof. Her gaze fell on Bhadla's *jambiya* and then rested on the glistening blade. She remembered that Lander's death had been quick. No matter how painful the poison, it could not hurt any more than the grief she now felt. The widow reached for the dagger, still talking to the gods, "You always destroy those beloved to me and leave me with nothing. Why?"

As Ruha's fingers closed around the hilt of the venomous *jambiya*, she thought of the man who had sent the treacherous weapon here with Bhadla. She was wrong, she realized, for at least one very important thing remained to her. Yhekal was still alive, the Zhentarim were still in Anauroch, and the Bedine needed her magic to win the victory.

Ruha removed Ajaman's *jambiya* from the sheath on her belt and replaced it with the poisoned blade Bhadla had carried into her tent. "I know what you would want, my love," she whispered. "I will not fail you."

Sa'ar's concerned voice sounded at her tent entrance. "Ruha, Lander!" he cried, bustling into the tent. "The warriors say there was a stream of fire and—"

The burly sheikh stopped next to Ruha and stared at Lander's lifeless face. Utaiba entered a few steps behind him, but Sa'ar quickly turned to him. "Something terrible has happened."

Utaiba reactions were quick. He turned to the men following him. "Post a guard. Nobody is to enter this *khreima*," he said. "Not even another sheikh. If anybody asks why—"

"Tell them I am preparing my magic and it is very dangerous," Ruha called.

The warriors turned to obey, then Utaiba stepped to Sa'ar's side. The two sheikhs stood next to each other, staring at Lander's body with rueful expressions on their faces. Ruha could not tell whether they were angry or despondent, but she had no doubt that they were shocked. Neither of them said a word or looked at Ruha, nor did they show any sign of grief.

Finally Sa'ar reached down and pulled Ruha's veil across her face, tucking it into her headwrap. "I suspect that the Zhentarim did not uncover your face, any more than they removed Lander's sword belt from his waist," the sheikh said.

Ruha did not bother to deny his charge. Though she held it in her hands, she had not yet wrapped her own belt around her *aba*, and it was obvious that neither she nor Lander had been fully dressed when the assassins entered her *khreima*.

Utaiba said, "You have cursed us all!"

"It was not my love that poisoned Lander," Ruha snapped, wrapping her belt around her waist. "It was the laziness of your sentries!" She pointed at the assassins she had killed with her fire stream. "How did so many Zhentarim escape Orofin?"

"When you and Lander broke the widow's taboo, your husband's spirit made them invisible," Sa'ar answered confidently.

"As you can see, they were not invisible when they reached us," Ruha countered. "Do not ascribe your men's ineptitude to spirits!"

Sa'ar's face clouded over with anger, and his jaw slackened in astonishment. "How dare you blame us!" he snapped. "The Bedine will pay the price for your lust! You and Lander caused this tragedy, no one else."

"We caused nothing," Ruha cried, still kneeling next to Lander's body. "We loved each other, and not even Ajaman's spirit would begrudge us that. But you are ready to forsake the man who risked his life to warn you of the Zhentarim in the first place! I wish I were a djinn! I would lay a curse on all of you!"

"Perhaps you are a *djinn*," Sa'ar retorted, reaching for his *jambiya*.

In an instant, Ruha pointed a hand at the sheikh and summoned an incantation. "If you draw your weapon against me before Lander is washed and buried, I will burn even your bones to ashes."

Sa'ar stopped, then glanced at the Zhentarim whom Ruha had charred earlier. At the same time, he did not push his dagger back into its scabbard, for he was not the kind of man to back down from any confrontation.

"What shall it be?" Ruha asked, her fingers already rehearsing the spell gestures.

"It makes no difference," Sa'ar replied, growling. "I can die of fire tonight or thirst tomorrow."

Utaiba stepped between the angry pair. "Do not violate your host duty by threatening the beloved of your guest," the sheikh said, gently laying a hand on Sa'ar's and pushing the *jambiya* back into its scabbard. Next he turned to Ruha.

"And you should not make the mistake of thinking that because we are not overcome with anguish, we do not grieve the loss of the Harper. As a warrior, he would recognize the need for clear thinking and decisive action at a time like this."

"What is there to think about?" Ruha asked.

"What is there to do?" added Sa'ar. "We are doomed."

"That may be," agreed Utaiba. "Certainly the violation of the widow's taboo is a bad omen. If the warriors hear of it, they will lose their spirit." He cast a melancholy look on Lander's lifeless face, then continued. "Still, we must attack. We have nothing to lose. As you have pointed out, Sa'ar, if we do not die in the morning, thirst will kill us by evening."

Sa'ar looked thoughtful, then took his hand away from his scabbard and met Ruha's gaze. "Utaiba speaks wisely, as always," he said. "If your husband's spirit has cursed us, there is nothing we can do about it now. We have no choice except to fight. Let us do it together."

Realizing that the gesture was as close to an apology as she would get from the proud sheikh, Ruha dismissed the spell from her mind. "Ajaman was only my husband for three days," the widow said, "But I knew him well enough to say that, even if his spirit were angry with me, he would do nothing to prevent us from destroying the Zhentarim and avenging the death of his tribe."

"Then you will help us tomorrow?" Utaiba asked.

"I have more deaths than any Bedine to avenge," Ruha replied, running her hands over Lander's brow and closing his eyes. As she slipped his head off her lap and stood, she said, "I am hurt that you must ask."

"Good, that is something," Utaiba said. "We must think of something to tell the warriors so that they will not take Lander's death as a bad omen."

Ruha took a sleeping carpet from one of her *kuerabiches*

and spread it over the Harper's body. "They will not hear of Lander's death."

"How can you hope to keep such a thing secret? Every camp already knows that the Zhentarim attacked you and Lander," objected Sa'ar. "When they do not see him in the morning, they will know he died. They will assume your husband's spirit arranged it."

"Tell your men that Lander and I killed the assassins," Ruha said. "Tomorrow, he will join them in battle."

The two sheikhs looked at each other with mixed expressions of nervousness and skepticism.

Ruha did not give them time to argue. "Tell the sheikhs that Lander was not hurt by the attack, but that I was terrorized. That will keep anyone from wanting to see him tonight and give me time to prepare."

The sheikhs nodded. "We can do that much," Utaiba confirmed.

Ruha pointed at the dead Zhentarim. "Those men had to come from somewhere," she said. "And I don't believe they sneaked past our sentry's noses. We must find out how they left Orofin. Perhaps we can use their route to our advantage."

"A good thought," Sa'ar confirmed.

Ruha considered the two sheikhs for few more moments, then said, "Utaiba, would you bring me Lander's *djebiras*?" When a scowl flashed across the wiry sheikh's face, Ruha quickly added, "I'd ask you to send a guard, but he would gossip, and that's the last thing we need right now."

The frown disappeared from the man's face, and he nodded. "Of course, you are right. I will be back soon."

While Utaiba fetched Lander's belongings, Sa'ar pushed the scorched remains of the Zhentarim assassins out the gap they had sliced in the *khreima*, then returned and carried away Bhadla's spindly body. The young widow spent the time stitching the gap closed. By now, Ruha knew, word of the assassination attempt had spread to all of the tribal camps, and she did not want any curious warriors peeking through the hole.

Utaiba returned just as she finished, bearing the single *djebira* containing Lander's belongings. Ruha went through the bag and extracted Lander's extra clothes, then put the bag aside.

"I shall see you an hour before dawn," the young widow said.

Utaiba said, "I'll send some guards to stand watch tonight."

Ruha shook her head. "Guards will only draw comment," she said. "Better to let the warriors think that Lander is confident of his ability to defeat more assassins."

Sa'ar objected, "But if the Zhentarim try something else—"

"I will deal with them," Ruha interrupted.

"If you are awake, yes. But what happens if you fall asleep?" This time, the questioner was Utaiba.

Ruha pointed at Qoha'dar's spellbook. "I'll be too busy to sleep," she said, ushering the sheikhs toward the exit. "Find out how the Zhentarim escaped their hole. I'll see you before dawn."

"As you wish," Sa'ar answered, stepping outside.

After the sheikhs left, the widow pored over Qoha'dar's spellbook, searching for a way to keep her promise. Finally she found an enchantment that would fulfill her need. Ruha spent the next few hours memorizing the new spell, as well as two others that she thought might prove useful supplements.

When she heard the warriors beginning to stir in Sa'ar's camp, Ruha sensed that the hour of battle was upon them. The widow put Qoha'dar's spellbook away, then took Ajaman's *jambiya* and slit a hole in the roof of the tent. She enlarged it until the moon cast a silvery light on the carpet covering her lover's corpse.

Ruha kneeled next to the body and pulled the carpet from Lander's head. She looked upon his sallow face for a full minute, fighting to hold back her grief, swearing vengeance on those who had taken his life. Finally she removed her veil and kissed him on the mouth.

Still holding her lips close to those of the dead man, she recited the incantation she had learned earlier that night. As she spoke, Lander's dead features softened, becoming darker and more feminine. The yellow stubble of his beard faded, his skin darkened to a deep sienna, his eyes assumed the almond shape of Ruha's, and his cheekbones grew high and prominent. Within seconds, the witch was looking at her own face. It looked so lifelike it almost seemed she had breathed life back into Lander's body.

A moment later, the vision in her right eye became milky and blurred, then faded to blackness. When she could see only out of her left eye, she knew the transformation was complete. Lander had her face, and she had his.

Ruha removed the Harper's eyepatch and put it over her now-useless eye, then took Lander's spare *keffiyeh* from his *djebira* and slipped it onto her head. Within a few minutes, she was dressed head-to-toe in his robes.

Before she could cover Lander's body again, Sa'ar and Utaiba approached, stopping outside the *khreima* and politely clearing their throats.

"Enter!" Ruha called. The voice issuing from her throat was Lander's, not her own.

Frowning in wary confusion, the two sheikhs obeyed, both stopping a step inside the entrance with their jaws hanging slack.

"Lander?" gasped Sa'ar.

"You look terrible!" added Utaiba. "Your eye is sunken and your skin is the color of a camel's water. Wait, where is—"

"I am Ruha," she announced softly. "I told you that Lander would join the attack." She waved the astonished sheikhs the rest of the way into the tent. "I did not say he would look well."

The sheikhs dropped their eyes from Ruha's face to Lander's body, which still lay in the center of the tent. The corpse now had the young widow's face, which was immodestly exposed. Flushing, Ruha kneeled down and quickly pulled the carpet over Lander.

"What have you done?" gasped Utaiba, still staring at the covered body.

"I don't think you want to know," Ruha answered. Lander's loose robes made her feel awkward, and the fact that she was not wearing a veil gave her the uncomfortable sensation of being naked.

"Not in my worst nightmares," Sa'ar agreed. He forced himself to look back to Ruha.

After a slight shudder, the sheikh began describing the plan he and Utaiba had developed with the other leaders. "We followed the assassins' tracks back to a tunnel that opens in the desert outside the old city," he began. "Apparently, it was an old escape tunnel, in case the *ksur* was sieged."

"Without doubt, the Zhentarim are guarding it," Utaiba added. "But if we can lull them into thinking we don't know about it, perhaps we can use it to gain entrance to the fortress."

Ruha nodded. "What do you have in mind?" she asked.

Sa'ar smiled enthusiastically. "We will attack the breaches in the wall with a dozen tribes," he said. "Even without the tunnel, this tactic could succeed, for the Zhentarim will be hard pressed to defend all their weak points at once."

"When we make no effort to utilize the tunnel and our attacks on the breaches begin to threaten the fortress, the

Zhentarim will have to decide whether to use the men guarding the tunnel to reinforce the walls, or to leave them in place to guard against an attack that might or might not come," Utaiba expounded, speaking as eagerly as Sa'ar. "If they leave the tunnel guards in place, then there will be fewer men fighting at the walls, and that is good. But if they move the guards to the wall—"

"Then it will be better. We will send the last two tribes down the tunnel to attack from inside Orofin," Sa'ar declared. "They will be caught between the anvil and the hammer, as you—er, Lander—would say."

Ruha considered the plan for several moments, then nodded. "I like it," she said. "But everything depends on how well we can press the attack against the breaches. I assume that is where you plan to use my magic?"

"It is the most dangerous place—"

"I have faced danger before, Utaiba," Ruha replied curtly. "Or have you forgotten?"

"We haven't forgotten," Sa'ar said. "But with your magic, we thought you might be more useful attacking from inside Orofin."

"If the attack on the breaches goes poorly, then nobody will attack from inside the fortress," Ruha countered. "There is a more important consideration, though. If the warriors are to fight with all their spirit and not worry about bad omens, they must see Lander in the vanguard."

Utaiba nodded thoughtfully. "And so must the Zhentarim," he agreed. "Otherwise, they'll worry about where the Harper is, and then they won't abandon the tunnel."

Sa'ar regarded the pair for several moments, then finally nodded his accord. "If that is what you think best, then it is decided. Let us go outside and prepare the warriors."

Nineteen

The Bedine were ready to attack. At'ar had just shown her flaxen orb above the horizon, and the goddess's amber light was creeping across the saffron desert. Orofin was surrounded by a dozen tribes, each clustered tightly about its sheikh and waiting two hundred and fifty yards from the fortress's dark walls. Most of the warriors were mounted on their camels, waiting directly in front of the breach they had been assigned to attack.

Two of the tribes were not mounted, however. The *khowwans* of Utaiba and Didaji waited behind the other tribes on opposite sides of the fortress, their warriors standing next to their camels with impatient expressions on their faces. These two tribes were being held in reserve. They would not join the battle until the Zhentarim began to crumble. Only then would they charge the weak spot. The invaders would either have to respond by drawing their own reserves away from the secret tunnel, or risk having the Bedine punch a hole in their defenses. It was a nuance of the plan that the sheikhs had not originally explained to Ruha, but one of which she thoroughly approved.

Sa'ar and his tribe, along with the Bai Kabor and their sheikh, were hiding near the tunnel mouth where the Zhentarim could not see them. They would not move from their hiding places until Sa'ar's observers reported that both Utaiba and Didaji had lead their tribes into battle.

Atop a small hill overlooking Orofin's fortifications, Ruha sat on her camel next to Yatagan, the toothless sheikh of the Shremala. With them was Utaiba, for his Raz'hadi were standing in reserve behind the Shremala. When the fighting started, Ruha would stay with Utaiba and the Raz'hadi. In their final pre-battle conference, the sheikhs had all agreed that it would be wiser to see what surprises the Zhentarim had for them before committing their witch to battle.

Ruha was shivering, for she was dressed only in Lander's *aba* and *keffiyeh*. Fearing that there would be no chance to remove a *jellaba* after the battle began, the widow had elected to endure the early morning chill in dress that would be appropriate for later in the day. Utaiba, however, sat huddled deep within his heavy *jellaba*, and Yatagan wore one of the heavy night furs of his tribe over both shoulders. The toothless sheikh was holding his camel's reins taut to keep the spirited beast from capering.

In contrast to those around her, Ruha felt eerily calm. She had no idea whether she or any of the Bedine would live to see dusk. Still, she was not afraid and felt no apprehension about what lay ahead. It seemed as if someone else were riding the Harper's mount, preparing to join the charge that would result in a thousand deaths.

Yatagan leaned toward Ruha, then motioned at an empty camel behind her. "Unless the witch sees some reason to wait, I will signal the others to start the attack."

Yatagan did not really believe that Ruha was sitting invisible on the empty mount. Like the other sheikhs, he knew that the witch had taken Lander's face in order to keep the men from learning of the Harper's death. He was simply playing out his part of a little charade Utaiba had proposed.

Realizing that the warriors would wonder where the witch was, the wiry sheikh had suggested that Ruha lead an empty camel behind hers. Yatagan would pretend that the widow was invisible, and Ruha-Lander would explain that the witch's beast had to be led so she could have both hands free to work her magic during the battle. Once Ruha began using her magic, Utaiba also hoped that the warriors would assume that it was the invisible witch who was casting spells, instead of "Lander."

It was a complicated scheme, but so far it was working. The warriors knew nothing about magic, so they were perfectly willing to believe that the witch had turned herself invisible. Ruha had suggested it might simplify things for her to assume her own identity and claim that Lander was invisible, but the sheikhs had all feared that the men would find it much easier to believe that a witch had turned herself invisible rather than someone else.

Realizing that Yatagan was still waiting for her response, Ruha nodded and said, "We're both ready, Yatagan. Victory or death!" The sound of Lander's voice issuing from her throat made the young widow feel even more distant from the events that were about to occur.

The wizened sheikh lifted his *amarat* and sounded a long, piercing tone. An apprehensive flurry rustled the Shremala warriors as they stretched their cold-stiffened arms and shifted their quivers into more accessible positions. Nine distant *amarats* trumpeted an answer to Yatagan, and Ruha knew the other *khowwans* were ready.

Yatagan raised his horn to his lips again and blasted a long, trilling note. The sheikh's mount danced in anticipation, then Yatagan lowered his horn and led his *khowwan* down the hill into battle.

A short time later, black slivers began to fly back and forth between the Shremala and the defenders lurking behind the fortifications on the wall. The other tribes were too distant for Ruha to tell if they were also coming under fire, but she assumed that they were. Fortunately, though a man fell from his camel every now and then, the Zhentarim arrows were having little effect on the charge.

The Shremala continued forward beneath the black rain, driving strait for a ten-foot breach in Orofin's fortifications. When the tribe closed to within fifty yards of the wall, silver gleams began to flash from the front of the charge, and Ruha knew the first ranks had drawn their scimitars in anticipation of hand-to-hand fighting.

As the Shremala approached the breach, a half-dozen tiny, black-robed figures rose from behind the wall's crenelations. At first Ruha could not tell what they were doing, but then they heaved several bundles onto the top of the wall and emptied the contents over the side. Just as the first Bedine warriors reached the breach, dozens of melon-sized rocks poured out of the bundles and clattered down on them. A muffled crash rolled across the empty ground between Orofin and the hill upon which Ruha and Utaiba waited.

The hail of rubble stopped the attack, knocking more than two dozen warriors from their saddles and littering the ground in front of the breach with bodies. The rear ranks of the charge pulled up short, spraying the top of the fortifications with arrows while a half-dozen of their unmounted companions rushed back to their ranks.

One of the figures stopped a few paces in front of the others, then waved his scimitar toward the gap. Two dozen men immediately slipped off their camel's backs and followed him toward the breach, drawing their own blades. The rest of the tribe remained in place, firing arrows at the top of the wall or into the fortress itself.

When the running figures began to pick their way through the rubble in front of the breach, a flurry of arrows streaked from the gap. The men on foot fell in their tracks, then a handful of Zhentarim filled the breach and began firing arrows at the warriors who were still mounted. Soon, more Black Robes appeared along the top of the wall, and the Shremala had to fall back and trade arrows with the Zhentarim from longer range.

Ruha scanned the other breaches at which Bedine were attacking and saw a similar situation at each of them. "Idiots!" the widow cursed, slapping her thigh.

"Not at all," Utaiba objected, scowling. "Our warriors are dying bravely."

"Not them!" the witch snapped, looking toward the sheikh. "Us. We should have expected this! If La—" She stopped herself from saying the Harper's name in midsentence and finished instead by saying, "I should have known they'd have more than one way to defend the walls."

Utaiba nodded sadly, his eyes betraying his own regret. "We can't blame ourselves," he whispered. "When have any of us ever stormed a fort? The important thing to do now is deal with this tactic."

Ruha nodded, but did not answer. She was trying to think of a way to protect the warriors from the rubble showers. An overhead shelter would protect the Bedine warriors, allowing them to mass in front of the breaches and match the Zhentarim's firepower. Unfortunately, they had neither the materials nor the time to build such shelters. Yet, she knew that if the sheikh's plan was to succeed, the Bedine had to maintain the attacks on the breaches.

After a few moments of studying Orofin's walls, Ruha's good eye settled on a three hundred-foot section of unbroken wall. Apparently the Zhentarim were not concerned about defending that section, for there were only four men along the entire stretch. The thing the widow liked best about this particular length of wall, however, was that there was a small sand dune standing ten yards in front of it.

Ruha turned to Utaiba. "Our warriors must stop wasting their arrows by firing blindly into the fortress. Instead, each tribe should put its twenty best archers in front of the breach. Everybody else must give their quivers to the archers, who are to fire at anybody moving along the rampart, but only if they have a good target."

"That is madness," Utaiba answered, shaking his head. "With so few archers, the enemy will mass his own bowmen on the walls and pick us off like gazelles."

"No they won't," Ruha countered. "Not if they're too busy defending the breaches against the others. The rest of the warriors are to draw their scimitars and rush the breaches, but they mustn't mass together. Tell them to spread out along the base of the wall, at least three feet apart. They should slip into the gaps one at a time, and they must die rather than retreat."

Utaiba frowned. "What will this accomplish?"

"By not massing together, the warriors will prevent the Zhentarim from dumping rubble on them—or at least keep that tactic from being very effective when they use it. Our archers will keep some of the Zhentarim occupied and pinned behind their fortifications, preventing them from leaning over the top of the wall to shoot at our men along the base."

"And the attacks against the breaches? Do you think this will prove more successful than what we're already doing?"

Ruha shrugged. "I don't think it will be any less successful, but the main purpose of those attacks is to keep the Zhentarim inside the fort busy. When you and I lead the Raz'hadi into Orofin, we'll want to have as many of the

Black Robes as possible thinking about other things."

Utaiba raised his eyebrow, interested but still puzzled. "And how is my tribe going to get through a breach when no one else can do it?"

The widow turned Lander's manly lips into a confident smile, then gestured toward the empty camel at her side. "Ruha is going to make a new breach for us—one the Zhentarim won't be able to defend."

Utaiba looked doubtful. "I don't remember Ruha describing any spell that could knock a hole in Orofin's walls."

"She has thought of a new way to use her magic," Ruha replied, pointing to the stretch of unbroken wall she had selected for her plan. "That part of the fort is manned by only four sentries. Ruha can use her magic to punch a hole through it. If the Raz'hadi move quickly, they will be into Orofin before the Zhentarim realize what has happened."

A careful smile creased the wiry sheikh's lips. "The witch is sure she can open a gap in that wall?"

"There is some risk, but she thinks her spell will have the power. It's certainly worth a try. If it doesn't work, all we have to do is turn around and ride away."

Utaiba nodded. "If I understood magic better, I would ask for more of an explanation. For now, however, I will have to trust that the gods knew what they were doing when they sent the witch to us."

The sheikh summoned ten messengers, then sent them to the other sheikhs with Ruha's suggestion. After the riders were gone, Utaiba turned his camel toward his men, calling, "It is time for the Raz'hadi to mount!" he commanded. "We ride to glory!"

The warriors cheered in enthusiasm, then did as their sheikh ordered. Ruha led Utaiba and his warriors a quarter-mile to the west, stopping in front of the unbroken stretch of wall. They were still over two hundred yards from Orofin, so the widow could not see if the Raz'hadi's shift of position concerned the four Zhentarim guards. It was a good sign, however, that no additional Black Robes were appearing atop the wall. Apparently the enemy still believed this section of the fort was secure.

"Now what?" asked Utaiba. "Do we fly over the wall?"

"No," Ruha answered, laying her reins across her lap. "We ride through it."

"Ride through it?" he said.

Ruha nodded, then pointed at the dune standing between them and the wall. "There."

"Over the dune?" Utaiba asked.

"The dune will be gone when we get there," Ruha answered. "Tell your men that the witch is casting a spell. They are to follow us—no matter what."

As Utaiba passed on the order, the witch prepared her spell. Keeping her back to the warriors, she took a small pouch from her robes, then withdrew a pinch of glittering white sand and packed it between her lower lip and teeth. It had a bitter, acrid taste that made her want to spit.

When the sheikh finished his orders and looked back to Ruha, she asked, "Are you ready?"

He drew his scimitar. "Through the wall?"

Ruha nodded. "Like the wind," she mumbled.

After whispering her incantation, the witch spit out the sand. Instead of falling to the ground, it streaked toward the wall with gathering momentum. As it picked up speed, the small torrent of sand gathered more particles. After flying twenty yards, the stream had become a raging river of tiny granules.

"What are you waiting for?" Ruha cried, pointing at the spell. "Follow it!"

His mouth hanging agape, Utaiba turned his mount toward the wall and urged it into a full gallop. Ruha did likewise, and then she heard the Raz'hadi voicing their war cries as the rest of the tribe joined the charge.

As they raced forward, Ruha watched the four sentries
scurry back and forth along the wall, trying to summon
help. They were too late. By the time the Zhentarim could
organize a response, the Raz'hadi would be inside Orofin.

The stream of sand crossed the dune in front of the unbroken stretch of wall. The mound exploded with a ferocity
that surprised even Ruha, causing a howl that echoed
across the desert like the cry of Kozah himself. In an instant, the spell sucked up the entire dune and hurled it
against the fortress, blasting a hole ten feet in diameter
through the wall's glazed mudbricks. The four sentries
abandoned their posts and fled along the ramparts.

As Utaiba passed the place where the sand dune had
been, he looked over his shoulder with a triumphant grin,
screaming wildly as a cloud of brick dust and sand billowed
out of the newly opened breach to engulf him. The witch
rode into the gray boil an instant after Utaiba. It was only
then that she realized there had been a flaw in her plan.

The silt filled her nose and throat so thickly that she felt
like she had ridded into a bed of quicksand. The sand grains
stung her eyes and forced her to close them, not that it
mattered. Even if she had possessed the long thick eye-
lashes that enabled camels to see in sandstorms, she could
not have seen past her mount's head, much less guided it
through the breach. Instead, the widow simply folded herself flat against her mount's back and trusted the beast to
find its own way, hoping that the riderless camel still tethered behind her would follow.

Despite the certainty of facing combat if she made it suc-
cessfully into Orofin, Ruha did not bother drawing Lander's
saber. She wore the Harper's face, but that did not mean
she possessed his skill with the sword. The long blade
would only get her into trouble. Instead she placed a hand
on the hilt of her *jambiya*, ready to draw it if need be, but
equally prepared to cast a spell.

The sand stopped stinging Ruha's face, and muffled shouts of alarm drifted to her from directly ahead. Realizing that her camel had found the breach, she opened her eyes. Utaiba's mount was directly in front of her, charging out of the other end of the hole, a full fifteen feet ahead. As she watched, the beast bowled over a Zhentarim and bolted into the courtyard beyond.

The widow reached the end of the little tunnel a second later. A pair of Zhentarim lay directly in front of the breach, the skin stripped off their bodies by the final blast of her magical sand stream. Ruha's mount and the riderless beast behind it jumped the corpses, then the witch guided them a few paces to the right and reined them to a halt out of the way of the warriors that she hoped would soon be pouring into the fort.

The interior of Orofin was anything but the mass of confusion Ruha had expected. The fortress was about fifty yards across, with the ruins of buildings hugging the walls. Orofin's artesian well sat in the center of the courtyard, it's bubbling waters filling a square basin. On each of the basin's four sides, a small spout emptied into a water duct. Protected by a rusty steel grating, these ducts ran to the edges of the fort, each emptying into a shallow pool that fed the canals outside the fort.

Next to each pool rose a staircase that led to the ramparts. At the top of these staircases, the Zhentarim had made huge stacks of rubble, and a steady stream of black-robed men were carrying the deadly packages to locations above the breaches that the Bedine were attacking. There they passed the bundles to men standing over the breach, who would in turn drop them onto the warriors below. To both sides of these men stood archers, who were returning the fire of the Bedine bowmen. Ruha guessed that about half of the Zhentarim force, between four and five hundred men, were engaged along the walls.

At the bottom of the wall, in each of the ten breaches that the sheikhs had selected for the attack, half-a-dozen Zhentarim armed with swords, daggers, and spears were fighting Bedine warriors. Behind them stood two dozen reinforcements, ready to take the place of any black-robed fighter who fell. Another ten to fifteen men waited in the ruins to either side of the various melees just in case any Bedine did manage to break through.

Utaiba had already ridden his camel into the midst of one of these Zhentarim companies and dropped his reins. The sheikh was slashing at crossbowmen while his mount kicked and bit at the astonished reinforcements. Ruha caught a glimpse of the animal's eyes, and it seemed to her the beast was enjoying the fight as much as his rider. She searched her mind briefly for a way to aid the sheikh, then realized that any spell she cast into the melee stood as much chance of killing Utaiba as the enemy. Besides, from the looks of things, it appeared the wiry sheikh and his camel were a fine match for the shocked Black Robes.

The widow continued her survey without seeing any sign of the Zhentarim she wanted to find most: Yhekal. As the invaders' leader, Ruha felt certain that the white-haired man had sent Bhadla to kill Lander, as well as the assassin that had tracked them to the Sister of Rains and killed Kadumi. If the Bedine accomplished nothing else by storming Orofin, she was determined to see him die.

Vengeance was not her only reason for looking for Yhekal. Ruha knew that the Zhentarim leader had used magic to enthrall her father, and she had no doubt that he could use it for other purposes as well. The sooner she eliminated him, the more likely a final Bedine victory became.

As her one uncovered eye searched for Yhekal, Ruha was surprised at how quiet the interior of Orofin seemed. Upon breaking through the fortifications, she had expected to meet a wall of arrows and a host of flashing blades. Instead, with the Zhentarim busy at the breaches the Bedine had originally attacked, the courtyard was empty, and no one came to defend the newly opened breach.

The widow doubted that the calm would last for long. Even now, the sentries who had been guarding this section of wall were probably alerting their superiors to the breakthrough. Regardless of where Yhekal was hiding, Ruha had to take advantage of the Zhentarim's temporary shock and open the way for more Bedine to enter Orofin.

She pulled a yellow ball of gum from her pocket and summoned an incantation to mind. She was no longer concerned about being observed using magic. In the heat of the battle, she did not think any warriors would see her casting a spell. Even if a few of them did, they would be too busy fighting to gossip with their fellows or wonder why Lander was acting so strangely.

The witch threw the sticky glob at the nearest company of Zhentarim. A sphere of orange flame erupted in the ruins and spewed into the breach the Black Robes had been defending. A few agonized cries rang from the hole, but most of the men simply turned to ash without a sound.

Ruha watched the smoking gap for what seemed like ages. A few charred Zhentarim staggered out of the ruins, moaning in agony and stumbling a few steps into the courtyard before they died. No Bedine warriors followed them from the blackened hole.

"What now, Lander?"

The voice startled Ruha. Drawing her *jambiya*, she whirled around to see a Raz'hadi warrior at her side. Behind him were two dozen more.

"Where is the rest of your tribe?" Ruha asked, frowning at the small number warriors with the man.

The warrior shrugged. "The dust was very thick. I heard many men scream as their camels hit the wall instead of running into the breach. I am sure that those who can will follow soon."

"Let's hope so." Ruha pointed at Utaiba, who was still waging his solo battle—and beginning to lose. Several Zhentarim swordsmen had finally surrounded him and his ferocious camel. "Your sheikh could use some help opening that gap."

Ruha had no sooner pointed out Utaiba's position than the alarmed warriors gave a war cry and rode off to aid their leader. The witch looked back toward the charred ruins she had just cleared with her fireball. There was still no sign of any Bedine coming through, so she rode to the breach. When she looked into the narrow crack, she saw a nervous Bedine peering through it from the other side.

The warrior dropped his jaw in shock. "Lander?"

"Come on!" Ruha snapped. "The way will never be more clear."

A look of chagrin crossed the man's face, then he turned and waved to the men behind him, screaming, "Follow me, Binwabi warriors!" A moment later, nearly a hundred Binwabi were pouring through the breach.

The witch heard the clacking of crossbows behind her. A dozen black bolts flashed past her, and Ruha lashed her camel with its reins, urging the beast to move quickly. She expected to feel the sharp pain of a steel shank any moment. Instead, the camel tethered behind hers roared in agony. Its knees buckled and it collapsed, causing the widow's mount to stumble as it tried to obey her command.

The beast fell, and Ruha jumped clear, landing in the charred remains of the Zhentarim who had fallen prey to her fireball. Out of the corner of her eye, she saw several Binwabi warriors also take shelter in the ruins. The one who had led the way through the gap yelled, "Send a runner to fetch our bowmen!"

Keeping her head low, Ruha spun around to face the attack. A few yards away, two dozen Zhentarim armed with crossbows were taking positions behind the fountain in the middle of the square. Behind them, a steady stream of Black Robes armed with sabers were charging out of a cellar to meet the Bedine breakthrough. With this second group came a man wearing a deep purple robe and silver wrist bracers. His hair and skin were as pale as salt, and his eyes were as blue as the sky.

"Yhekal!" Ruha whispered. Instantly she realized that he and the men with him were the reinforcements Sa'ar and Utaiba had predicted would be guarding the tunnel.

The pale-skinned invader stepped over to the crossbowmen and pointed at the camel Ruha had been leading behind her mount. "The witch is under the protection of the gold-haired *berrani*," he said. "She may even be invisible. Keep the Harper pinned down, and I will flush her out!"

While his men fired blindly in the general direction of the fallen camel Ruha-Lander had been riding, Yhekal stood at the edge of the fountain and began to chant. Several Binwabi warriors, fearful of the enemy's magic, rose from behind their cover and started to run, but their flight was cut short by the enemy's crossbows.

Ruha crouched in the ruins and collected a handful of small stones. A couple of stray quarrels passed over her head, then the Zhentarim leader completed his spell.

The blackness in Ruha's left eye changed to a milky blur, then light began to seep in around the edges of the patch. The widow ran a hand over her face, and when it touched smooth skin instead of Lander's rough beard stubble, she realized that Yhekal had dispelled her magical disguise. Ripping the patch off her eye with her free hand, Ruha muttered her own incantation and held the stones she had collected up toward the sun. As she completed the spell, they started to glow with a fiery red.

Peering over the top of the ruin, Ruha saw that the Zhentarim crossbowmen were busy reloading their weapons.

Yhekal's blue eyes were fixed on the rubble, and his brow was furrowed in an angry frown. Behind the mage, the last of the Zhentarim reinforcements had finally left the cellar and were rushing to meet a steady flow of Raz'hadi pouring through the breach Ruha had created.

The witch stood, raising her hand to throw the glowing stones. Yhekal's gaze shifted to her face, and the crossbowmen stared at her with slack jaws.

"You!" snarled the Zhentarim leader. "Where is the Harper?"

Ruha did not give him the satisfaction of an answer. She threw the glowing stones in his direction, then dropped back into the rubble before a crossbowman could bring his weapon to bear on her.

The stones streaked straight at Yhekal, picking up speed and trailing flame. The Zhentarim leader's eyes widened in fear, then he dived for the well at his side.

The mage was far too slow. As he stretched out over the pool, the stones struck him square in side. He screamed in searing pain and splashed into the water head first. There was a loud hiss, then a column of vapor began billowing out of the basin.

When one of the Zhentarim warriors pulled his commander out of the pool and laid him out next to the basin, Ruha smiled. Yhekal did not move or even groan, and she could still see the sun stones glowing in the charred wound. Even if the assault on Orofin failed now, she would count it at least a partial victory. With that single spell, she had avenged the deaths of her husband, her father, her brother-in-law, and her lover.

The Binwabi warrior who had called for the archers leaped into the ruin at Ruha's side. Studying the woman's unveiled visage, he asked, "What magic is this, witch? What did you do with Lander?"

The invaders' crossbows clacked again. Both Ruha and

the warrior ducked as bolts streaked over their heads, then the widow instinctively tried to cover her face. When her hand found no veil, Ruha blushed, then she reminded herself that the women in Sembia never covered their faces.

"Where Lander is at the moment is not important," she said, meeting the warrior's gaze directly. "What is important is destroying the Zhentarim. Tell your men to prepare for a charge."

The Binwabi would not be sidetracked so easily. "Have you hidden the *berrani* from the Black Robes?"

Before Ruha had to answer, an *amarat* sounded from the other side of the courtyard and a Bedine voice cried, "Death to the invaders!"

Ruha's heart leaped for joy. She peered over the edge of the ruins and saw a mass of warriors charging out of the same cellar from which Yhekal had entered the courtyard. It could only be the two tribes that had been assigned to come through the tunnel. The sheikhs' plan had worked. Soon there would be three hundred Bedine warriors inside Orofin, and the invaders would be caught between the hammer and the anvil.

The Zhentarim who had been pinning Ruha and the Binwabi in the ruins turned to meet the charge. They fired their crossbows once, then threw them aside to draw their sabers. Ruha drew her *jambiya* and stood. Ignoring the warrior at her side, she looked to the other Bedine lurking in the ruins and pouring through the breach.

"Death to the Black Robes!" she cried, turning toward the fight.

"Death to the invaders!" cried dozens of voices.

Ruha led the Binwabi rush. The courtyard began to ring with the chime of steel-on-steel, and the shrill cries of the wounded and the dying echoed off the ancient bricks. The Zhentarim at the walls joined the desperate battle in the courtyard. When they left their posts, more Bedine tribes broke through the breaches and poured into the fort. Some entered the fight in the courtyard. Others rushed to the gaps that the Black Robes still controlled. Soon, there was not a corner of the ancient fort that did not resound with the clang of clashing swords and not a square yard of ground that was not stained by blood.

For Ruha, the battle became a hazy maelstrom of confused violence. She stabbed anyone wearing a black robe and sliced at any throat swaddled by a black turban. Twice, she was nearly slain. The first time, as she sidestepped a clumsy lunge, the Zhentarim grabbed her throat with his free hand and nearly crushed her larynx. She escaped only by driving her *jambiya* deep into the man's midsection and slicing his belly open with sharp curve of her blade. The second time, the invader took her by surprise, and his saber flashed toward her head almost before she realized he was there. She threw herself to the ground and slashed his legs as she rolled away. Screaming, the man dropped his sword and fell. Ruha finished him by opening a vein in his throat, then returned to her feet.

Everywhere the witch looked, steel blades were ringing against each other, men were lying on the ground clutching their wounds, Bedine and Zhentarim were cursing, slashing, stabbing, even kicking and wrestling. Ruha helped when she could, but most often she was too busy dodging wild swings or parrying blades herself to do much for anyone else.

At last the fighting began to grow less desperate. The angry screams of the Zhentarim changed to cries of panic and appeals for mercy. The maelstrom in the square thinned as the Bedine warriors trapped the Black Robes in the crumbling corners of collapsed buildings or followed them out of the gaps in the wall.

When their were no more Zhentarim to kill, the widow

stood in a daze, barely hearing the moans of the wounded and only half-aware of Lander's blood-soaked *aba* hanging so heavily on her shoulders. The heat of battle slowly drained from her body, leaving her legs numb and weak, her hands trembling with nervous exhaustion. So many corpses littered the square that a camel could not have picked its way from one side to the other without stumbling, and the dusty ground had been turned to mud by all the blood spilled upon it.

"Here you are," said a familiar voice. "I was afraid something had happened to you."

Ruha looked up and saw Sa'ar's burly form approaching from the direction of the fountain. In one hand he held a full waterskin and in the other a scimitar dripping red.

He gestured at Ruha's bloody robe. "I hope none of that is yours."

The widow shook her head. "I am unhurt."

"Good. I fear the gods would not forgive me if I had allowed anything to happen to their gift."

Ruha felt the heat rise to her cheeks. Coming from Sa'ar, the comment almost seemed like flattery. She wondered if he meant it that way, or if the exhilaration of victory was loosening his tongue.

Sa'ar passed the waterskin to the witch, paying no regard to her uncovered face. "Drink."

Ruha accepted the skin. She had not realized how thirsty the battle had left her, and the water tasted as sweet as honey and as cool as a night rain. She swallowed a few long gulps, then said, "That's the best water I've ever tasted."

"You don't realize how precious something is until you fight for it," Sa'ar agreed. He studied the ground for several moments, then lifted his gaze and looked into Ruha's eyes. "If the Black Robes come back to the desert, I'd like to think you'll be with my tribe to show them that this place is not for their kind."

Ruha returned the sheikh's waterskin. "I will," she answered, giving him a melancholy but sincere smile. The dreamlike images of lush, green Sembia that haunted the back of her mind faded like a mirage under At'ar's burning brilliance. "Where else do I have to go?"

DragonLance® Saga

The sweeping saga of honor, courage, and companions begins with . . .

The Chronicles Trilogy

By *The New York Times* best-selling authors
Margaret Weis & Tracy Hickman

Dragons of Autumn Twilight
Volume One
Dragons have returned to Krynn with a vengeance.
An unlikely band of heroes embarks on a perilous
quest for the legendary *Dragonlance!*
TSR #8300
ISBN 0-88038-173-6

Dragons of Winter Night
Volume Two
The adventure continues . . . Treachery,
intrigue, and despair threaten to overcome
the Heroes of the Lance in their epic quest!
TSR #8301
ISBN 0-88038-174-4

Dragons of Spring Dawning
Volume Three
Hope dawns with the coming of spring, but then
the heroes find themselves in a titanic battle
against Takhisis, Queen of Darkness!
TSR #8302
ISBN 0-88038-175-2

Sug. Retail Each $4.95; CAN $5.95; £4.99 U.K.

COMING FALL/WINTER '94

The Ogre's Pact

Book One in the new Twilight Giants Trilogy by Troy Denning, *New York Times* best-selling author

When ogres kidnap Brianna of Hartwick, her father forbids his knights to rescue her. Only a brash peasant, who covets Brianna's hand, has the courage to ignore the duke's orders. To Tavis's surprise, slaying the ogres is the easiest part . . . the challenge has only begun!

TSR #8546
ISBN 1-56076-891-6

Realms of Infamy

The incredible companion volume to the *Realms of Valor* anthology

From the secret annals of Realms history come never-before-published tales of villains – Artemis Entreri, Manshoon of Zhentil Keep, Elaith Craulnober, and many others – told by your favorite authors: R. A. Salvatore, Ed Greenwood, Troy Denning, Elaine Cunningham, and others.

TSR #8547
ISBN 1-56076-911-4

Sug. Retail Each $4.95; CAN $5.95; £4.99 U.K.